HER PERMANENT RECORD

SEE WHAT PEOPLE ARE SAYING ABOUT Jimmy Gownley's AMELIA RULES!

"Haven't read comics before? This is where you'll want to start."
—*Girls' Life*

"Perfectly captures the heartbreak, humor, and high drama of the middle school experience."
—Gene Yang, author of *American Born Chinese*

"Comic genius."
—GraphicNovelReporter.com

"I wish I could go back to middle school and make a friend like Amelia. I wish I could go back and *be* a friend like Amelia."
—the-trades.com

"So clever, smart, funny, and true. . . . This is one of the best graphic novel series out there for kids—and for adults with vivid, funny memories of childhood."
—Elizabeth Bluemle, the Flying Pig Bookstore

"One of the best cartoonists I know of, [Gownley] has never written a story that hasn't left me grinning madly."
—The Geeky Librarian

"Amelia Rules! remains my favorite graphic novel series for kids!"
—Tweendom.blogspot.com

"A Peanuts for the twenty-first century."
—*Comics Buyer's Guide*

"Simply one of the best all-ages comics I've ever seen."
—Mark Crilley, author/illustrator of the Akiko books

"Delightfully drawn and cleverly written."
—Orson Scott Card

"Side-splittingly hilarious. . . . Highly recommended for all ages and all libraries."
—*Library Journal*

"Full of wise-cracking jokes and quips, ingenious gags, screamingly funny dialogue, and the best of classic comic book antics."
—Megan McDonald, author of the Judy Moody series

"Amelia Rules! is . . . absolutely essential. Not only is it one of the finest comics of all time, it is one of the best examples of children's literature I have ever read."
—Kidz Corner Comic Reviews

"Smart and genuine."
—David Fury, writer/producer for *Lost* and *Buffy the Vampire Slayer*

"Inspiring and uplifting in ways that will make you want to stand up and cheer. . . . Here's hoping the series continues for a good long time."
—the-trades.com

"Amelia's family and friends will take up permanent residence in your heart."
—Bob Schooley and Mark McCorkle, creators of *The Penguins of Madagascar*

"Wonderful all-ages comic."
—*New York* magazine

"Gownley excels at putting a powerful message inside of a kid-friendly story."
—BSCKids.com

"Amelia Rules! . . . is a delightful entry for lovers of comics and realistic fiction. . . . She is a character to rival Ramona and Judy Moody."
—*School Library Journal*

"These kids are real . . . Gownley is a genius at capturing their perspective."
—ComicsWorthReading.com

MEET THE GANG!

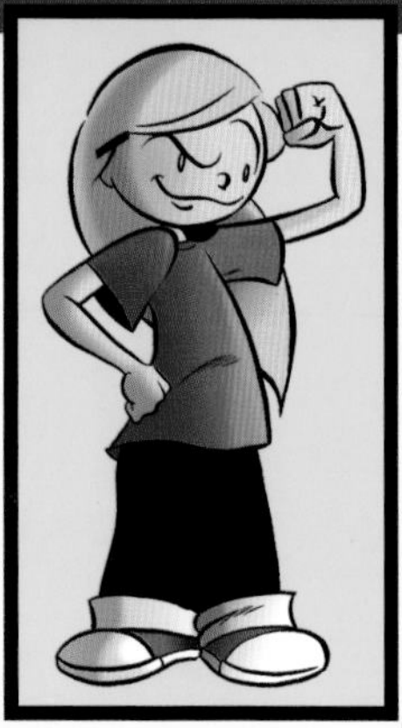

Amelia Louise McBride:
Our heroine. Wise cracking, yet sweet. She spends her time hanging out with friends and her aunt Tanner.

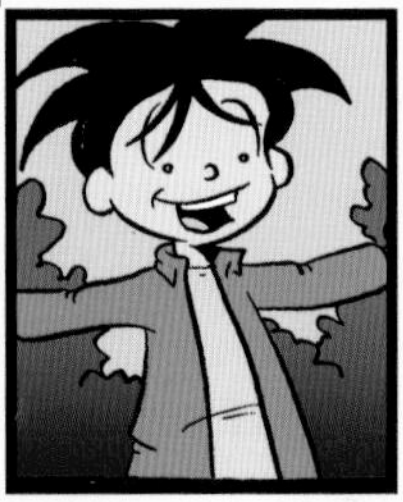

Reggie Grabinsky:
A.k.a. Captain Amazing. Founder of G.A.S.P., which he forces . . . er, encourages, his friends to join.

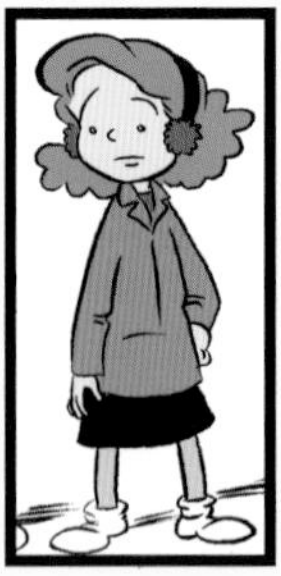

Rhonda Bleenie:
Smart, stubborn, and loud. She wears her heart on her sleeve and it's filled with love for Reggie.

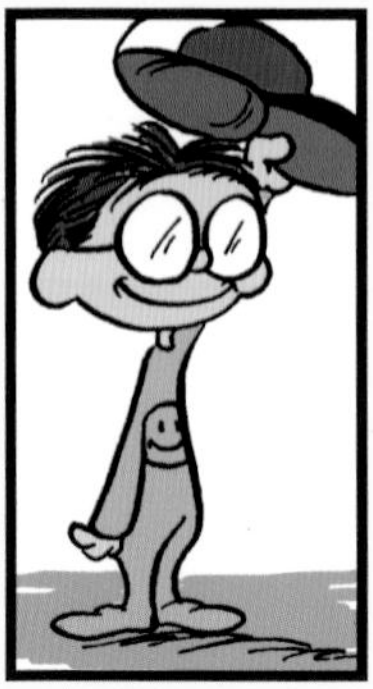

Pajamaman:
Never speaks. Always cool. His feetie jammies tell you what's on his mind.

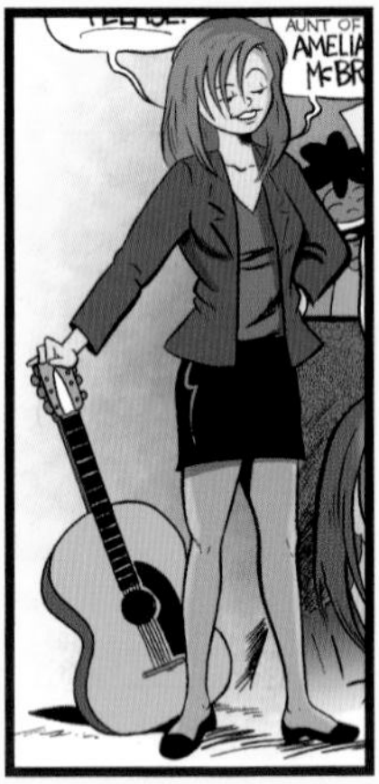
AUNT OF
AMELIA

Tanner:
Amelia's aunt and a former rock 'n' roll superstar.

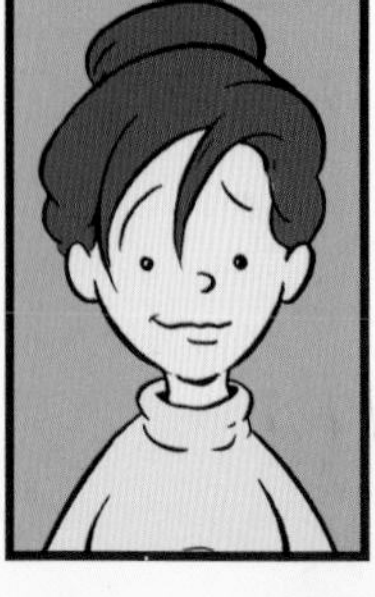

Amelia's Mom (Mary):
Starting a new life in Pennsylvania with Amelia after the divorce.

Amelia's Dad:
Still lives in New York, and misses Amelia terribly.

G.A.S.P.
Gathering Of Awesome Super Pals. The superhero club Reggie founded.

Park View Terrace Ninjas:
Club across town and nemesis to G.A.S.P.

Kyle:
The main ninja. Kind of a jerk but not without charm.

Joan:
Former Park View Terrace Ninja (nemesis of G.A.S.P.), now friends with Amelia and company.

Tweenie Zeenie:
A local kid-run magazine and Web site.

Jimmy Gownley's

AMELIA RULES!™

HER PERMANENT RECORD

A
atheneum   **Atheneum Books for Young Readers**
New York   London   Toronto   Sydney   New Delhi

ATHENEUM BOOKS FOR YOUNG READERS

An imprint of Simon & Schuster Children's Publishing Division

1230 Avenue of the Americas, New York, New York 10020

For information about special discounts for bulk purchases, please contact Simon & Schuster Special Sales at 1-866-506-1949 or business@simonandschuster.com.

The Simon & Schuster Speakers Bureau can bring authors to your live event. For more information or to book an event, contact the Simon & Schuster Speakers Bureau at 1-866-248-3049 or visit our website at www.simonspeakers.com.

Also available in an Atheneum Books for Young Readers paperback edition.

Book design by Sonia Chaghatzbanian

The text for this book is hand-lettered.

The illustrations for this book are digitally rendered.

Manufactured in China

1217 SCP

2 4 6 8 10 9 7 5 3

Library of Congress Cataloging-in-Publication Data

Gownley, Jimmy.

Her permanent record / Jimmy Gownley ; [Illustrated by] Jimmy Gownley. — 1st ed.

p. cm. — (Jimmy Gownley's Amelia rules ; [8])

ISBN 978-1-4169-8615-7 (hardcover)

ISBN 978-1-4169-8614-0 (paperback)

1. Graphic novels. [1. Graphic novels. 2. Voyages and travels—Fiction. 3. Aunts—Fiction.

4. Friendship—Fiction. 5. Schools—Fiction.] I. Title.

PZ7.7.G69Her 2012

741.5'973—dc23   2011053039

This book is dedicated with love
to Karen, Anna, and Stella.

HER PERMANENT RECORD

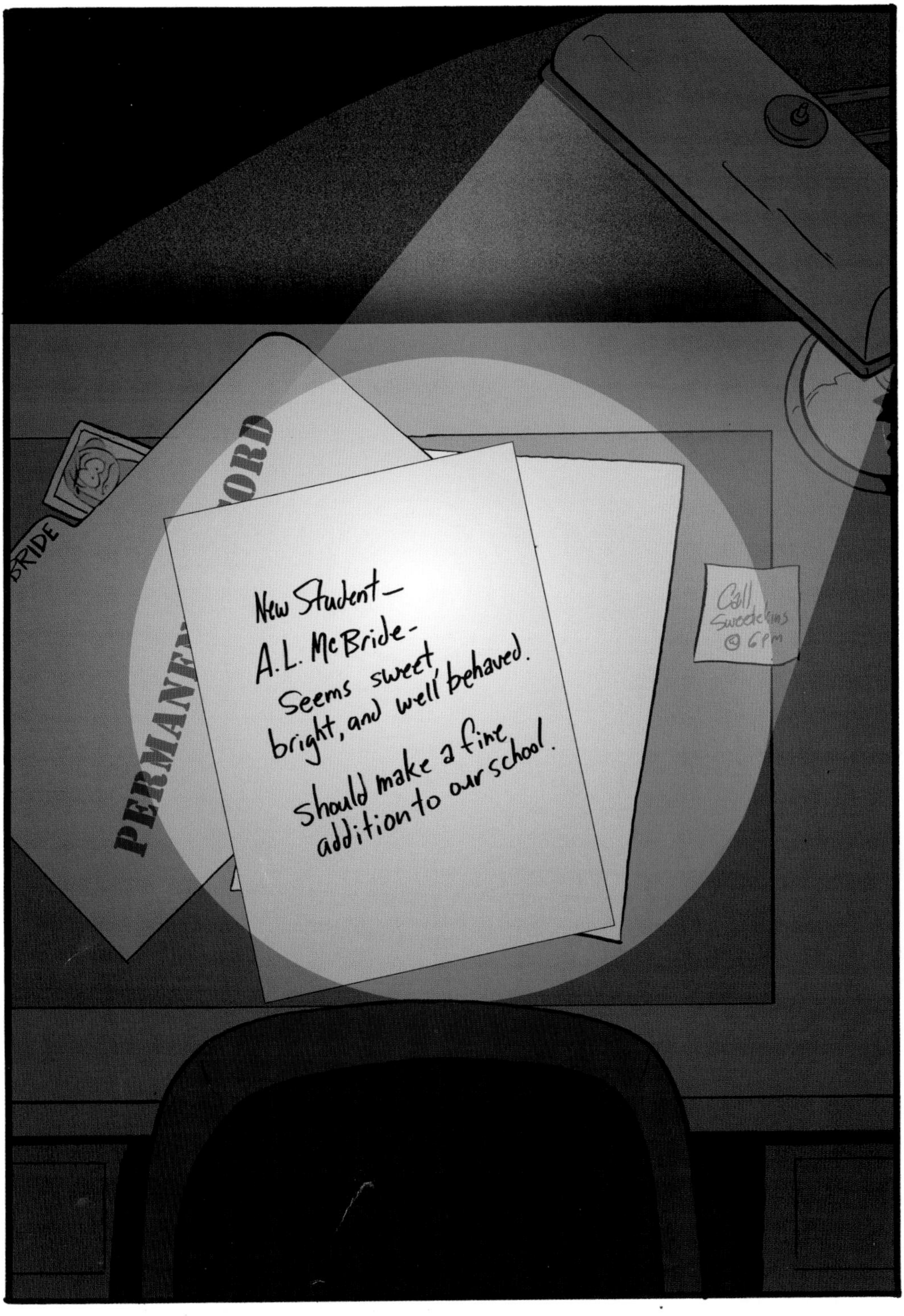
New Student—
A.L. McBride-
Seems sweet, bright, and well behaved.
should make a fine addition to our school.
PERMANENT RECORD
Call Sweetcheeks @ 6PM

SO...

...WHO IS AMELIA LOUISE McBRIDE, ANYWAY?

AND WHAT, *EXACTLY*, IS GOING TO END UP ON HER PERMANENT RECORD?

WELL...

...THAT'S A *GOOD QUESTION.*

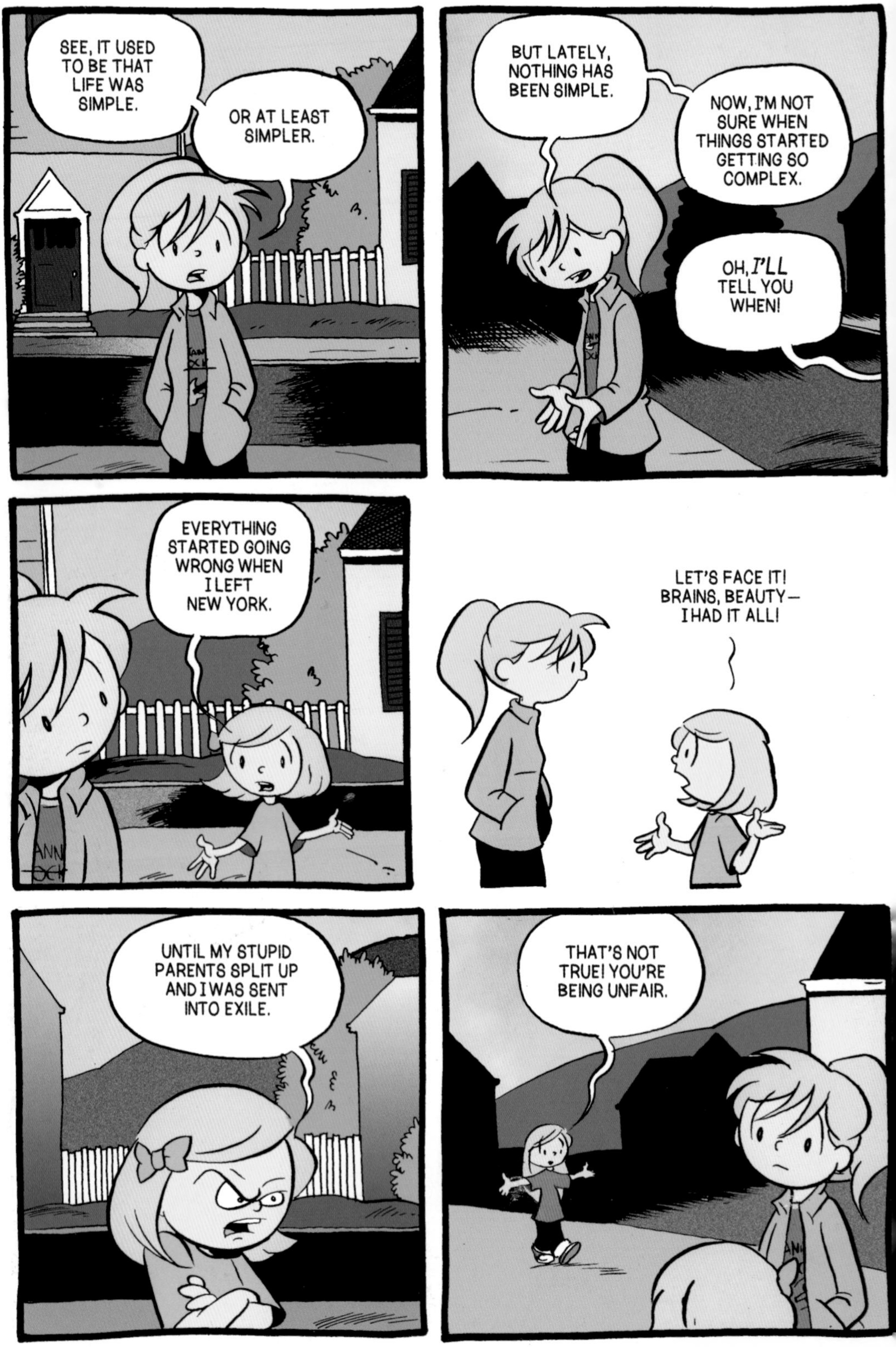
SEE, IT USED TO BE THAT LIFE WAS SIMPLE.
OR AT LEAST SIMPLER.
BUT LATELY, NOTHING HAS BEEN SIMPLE.
NOW, I'M NOT SURE WHEN THINGS STARTED GETTING SO COMPLEX.
OH, *I'LL* TELL YOU WHEN!
EVERYTHING STARTED GOING WRONG WHEN I LEFT NEW YORK.
LET'S FACE IT! BRAINS, BEAUTY— I HAD IT ALL!
UNTIL MY STUPID PARENTS SPLIT UP AND I WAS SENT INTO EXILE.
THAT'S NOT TRUE! YOU'RE BEING UNFAIR.

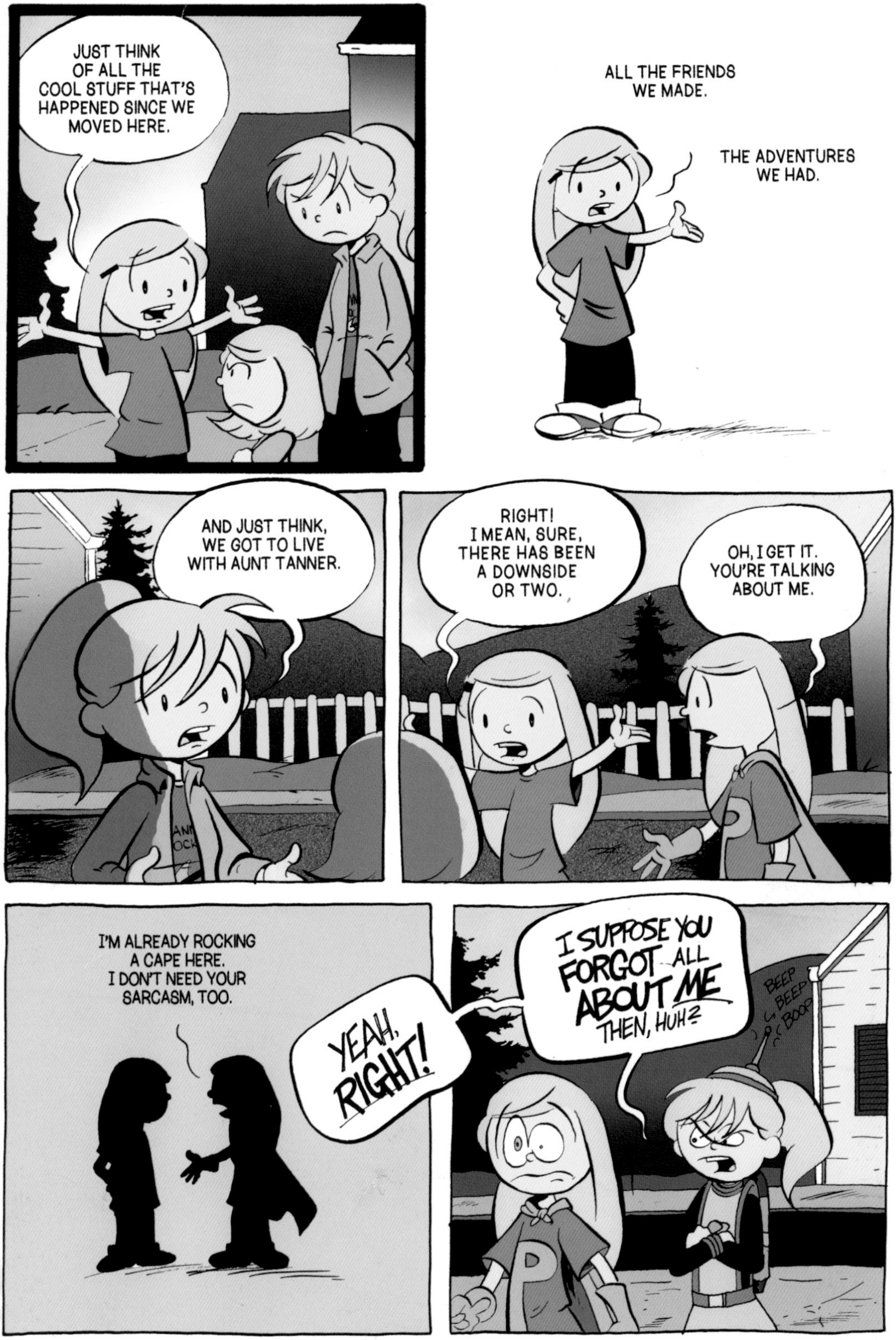
JUST THINK OF ALL THE COOL STUFF THAT'S HAPPENED SINCE WE MOVED HERE.
ALL THE FRIENDS WE MADE.
THE ADVENTURES WE HAD.
AND JUST THINK, WE GOT TO LIVE WITH AUNT TANNER.
RIGHT! I MEAN, SURE, THERE HAS BEEN A DOWNSIDE OR TWO.
OH, I GET IT. YOU'RE TALKING ABOUT ME.
I'M ALREADY ROCKING A CAPE HERE. I DON'T NEED YOUR SARCASM, TOO.
YEAH, RIGHT!
I SUPPOSE YOU FORGOT ALL ABOUT ME THEN, HUH?
BEEP BEEP BOOP

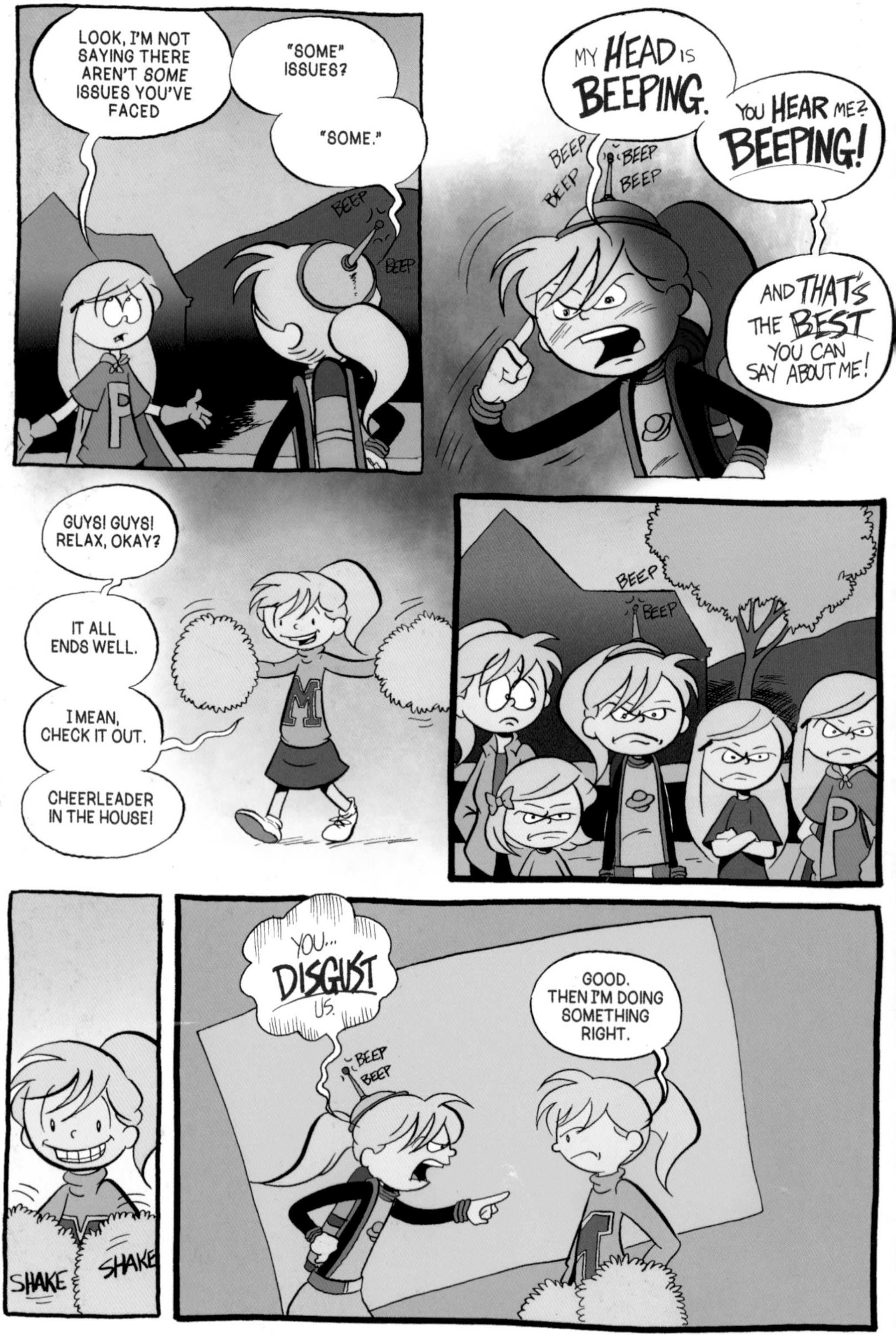
LOOK, I'M NOT SAYING THERE AREN'T *SOME* ISSUES YOU'VE FACED
"SOME" ISSUES?
"SOME."
BEEP
BEEP
MY HEAD IS BEEPING.
YOU HEAR ME? BEEPING!
BEEP BEEP BEEP BEEP
AND THAT'S THE BEST YOU CAN SAY ABOUT ME!
GUYS! GUYS! RELAX, OKAY?
IT ALL ENDS WELL.
I MEAN, CHECK IT OUT.
CHEERLEADER IN THE HOUSE!
BEEP
BEEP
SHAKE
SHAKE
YOU... DISGUST US.
BEEP BEEP
GOOD. THEN I'M DOING SOMETHING RIGHT.

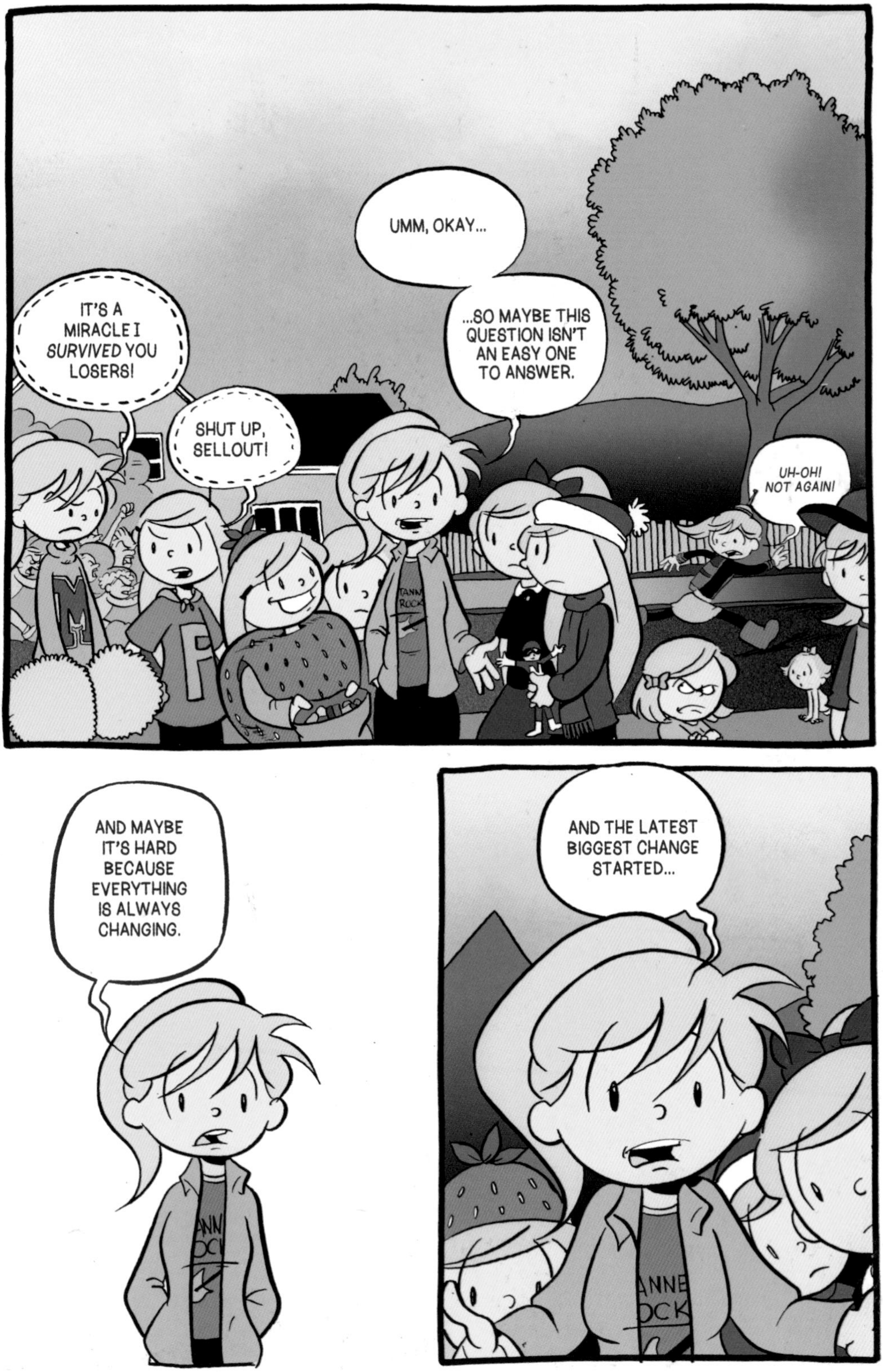
UMM, OKAY...
...SO MAYBE THIS QUESTION ISN'T AN EASY ONE TO ANSWER.
IT'S A MIRACLE I *SURVIVED* YOU LOSERS!
SHUT UP, SELLOUT!
UH-OH! NOT AGAIN!
AND MAYBE IT'S HARD BECAUSE EVERYTHING IS ALWAYS CHANGING.
AND THE LATEST BIGGEST CHANGE STARTED...

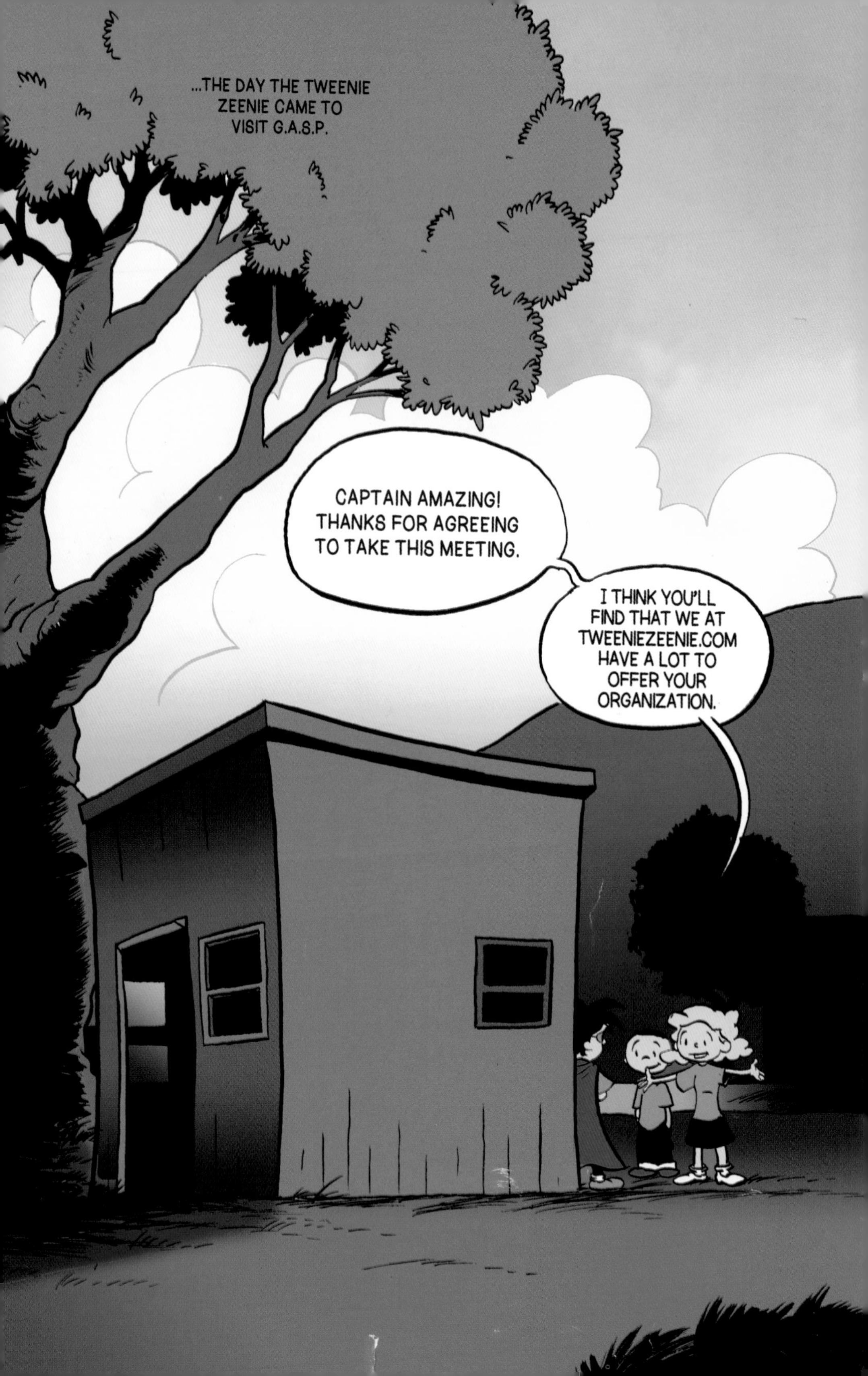
...THE DAY THE TWEENIE ZEENIE CAME TO VISIT G.A.S.P.
CAPTAIN AMAZING! THANKS FOR AGREEING TO TAKE THIS MEETING.
I THINK YOU'LL FIND THAT WE AT TWEENIEZEENIE.COM HAVE A LOT TO OFFER YOUR ORGANIZATION.

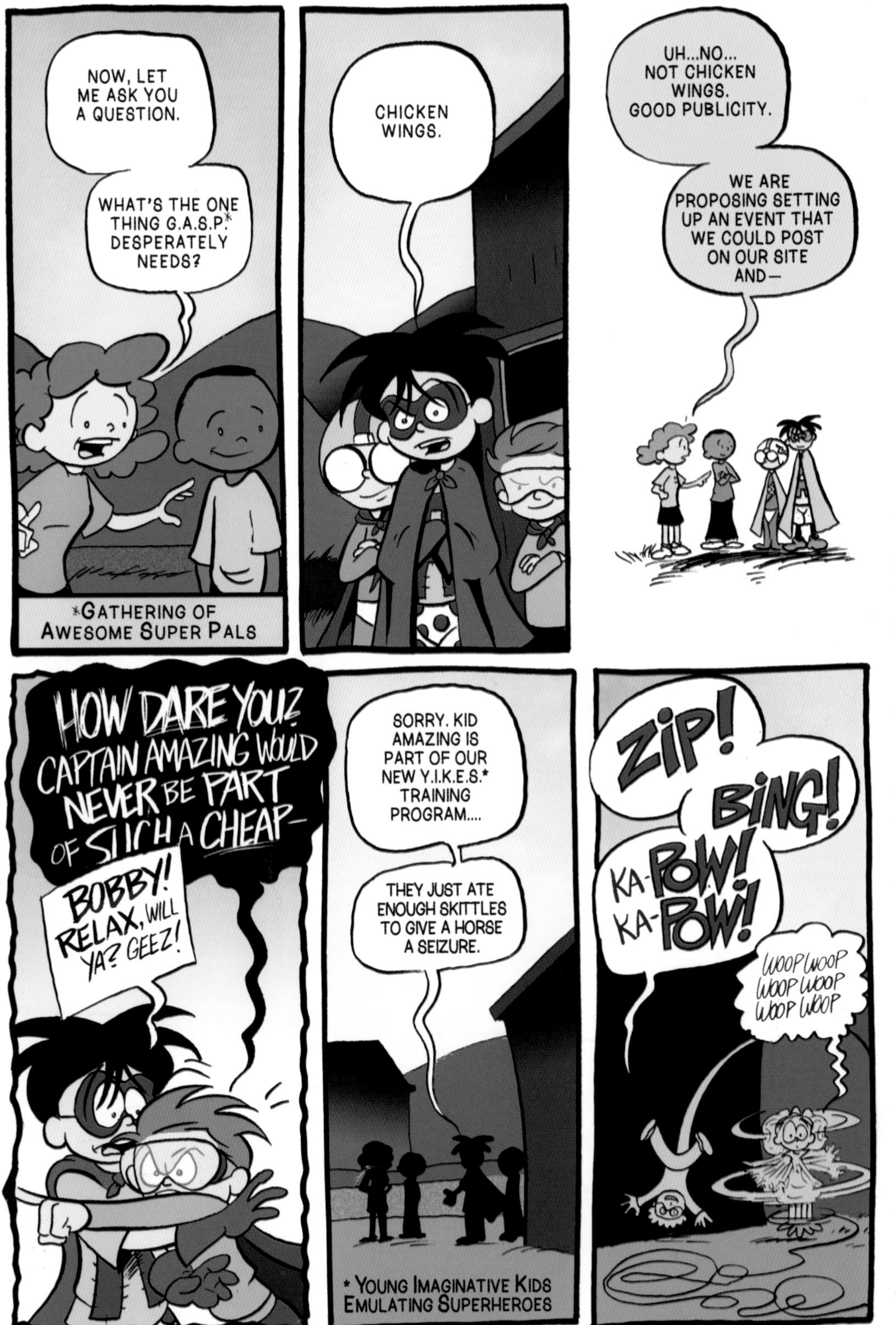
NOW, LET ME ASK YOU A QUESTION.
WHAT'S THE ONE THING G.A.S.P.* DESPERATELY NEEDS?
*GATHERING OF AWESOME SUPER PALS
CHICKEN WINGS.
UH...NO... NOT CHICKEN WINGS. GOOD PUBLICITY.
WE ARE PROPOSING SETTING UP AN EVENT THAT WE COULD POST ON OUR SITE AND—
HOW DARE YOU? CAPTAIN AMAZING WOULD NEVER BE PART OF SUCH A CHEAP—
BOBBY! RELAX, WILL YA? GEEZ!
SORRY. KID AMAZING IS PART OF OUR NEW Y.I.K.E.S.* TRAINING PROGRAM....
THEY JUST ATE ENOUGH SKITTLES TO GIVE A HORSE A SEIZURE.
* YOUNG IMAGINATIVE KIDS EMULATING SUPERHEROES
ZIP!
BING!
KA-POW! KA-POW!
WOOP WOOP WOOP WOOP WOOP WOOP

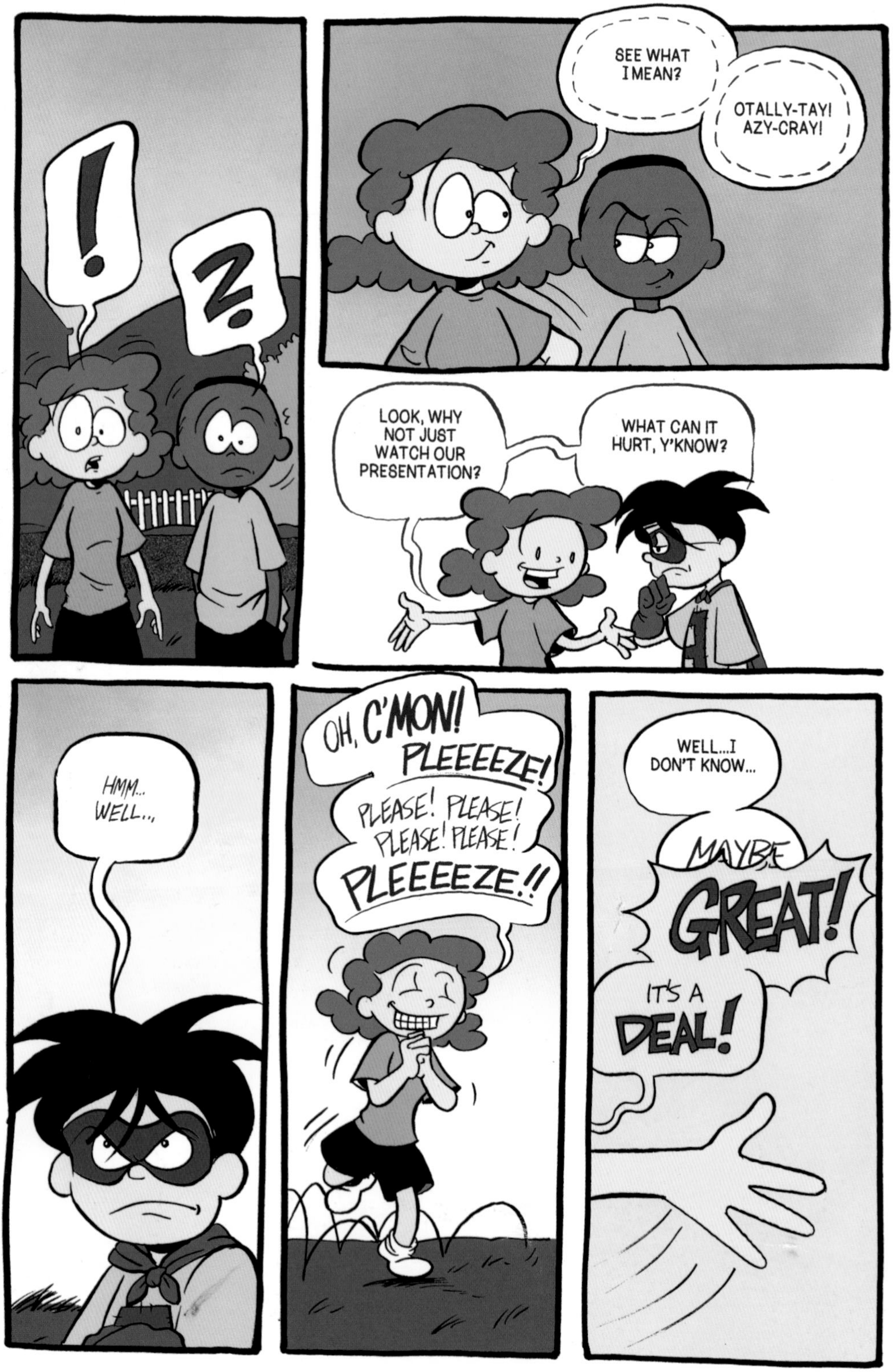
!
?
SEE WHAT I MEAN?
OTALLY-TAY! AZY-CRAY!
LOOK, WHY NOT JUST WATCH OUR PRESENTATION?
WHAT CAN IT HURT, Y'KNOW?
HMM... WELL...
OH, C'MON! PLEEEEZE!
PLEASE! PLEASE! PLEASE! PLEASE! PLEEEEZE!!
WELL...I DON'T KNOW...
MAYBE
GREAT!
IT'S A DEAL!

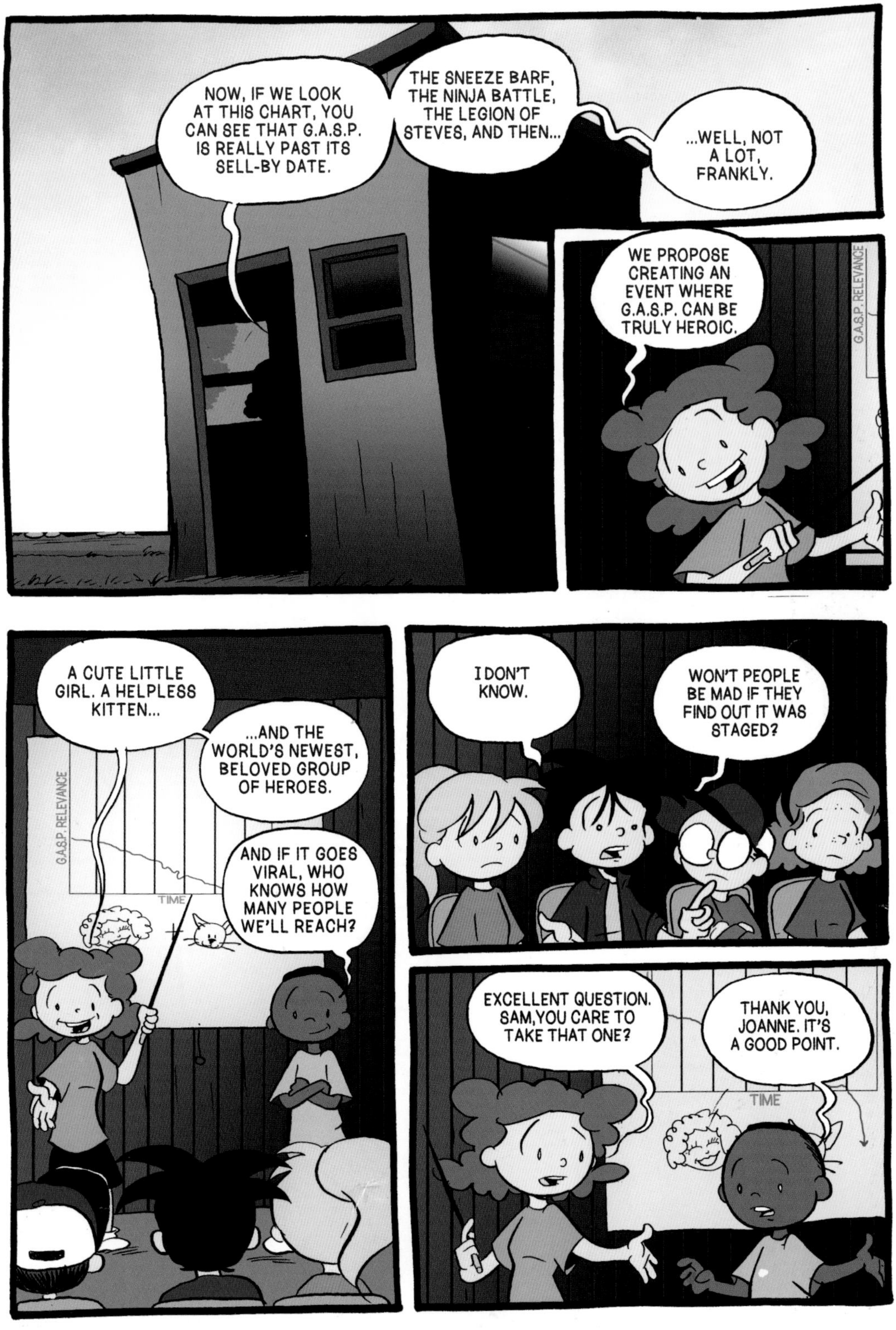
NOW, IF WE LOOK AT THIS CHART, YOU CAN SEE THAT G.A.S.P. IS REALLY PAST ITS SELL-BY DATE.
THE SNEEZE BARF, THE NINJA BATTLE, THE LEGION OF STEVES, AND THEN...
...WELL, NOT A LOT, FRANKLY.
WE PROPOSE CREATING AN EVENT WHERE G.A.S.P. CAN BE TRULY HEROIC.
G.A.S.P. RELEVANCE
A CUTE LITTLE GIRL. A HELPLESS KITTEN...
...AND THE WORLD'S NEWEST, BELOVED GROUP OF HEROES.
G.A.S.P. RELEVANCE
TIME
AND IF IT GOES VIRAL, WHO KNOWS HOW MANY PEOPLE WE'LL REACH?
I DON'T KNOW.
WON'T PEOPLE BE MAD IF THEY FIND OUT IT WAS STAGED?
EXCELLENT QUESTION. SAM,YOU CARE TO TAKE THAT ONE?
THANK YOU, JOANNE. IT'S A GOOD POINT.
TIME

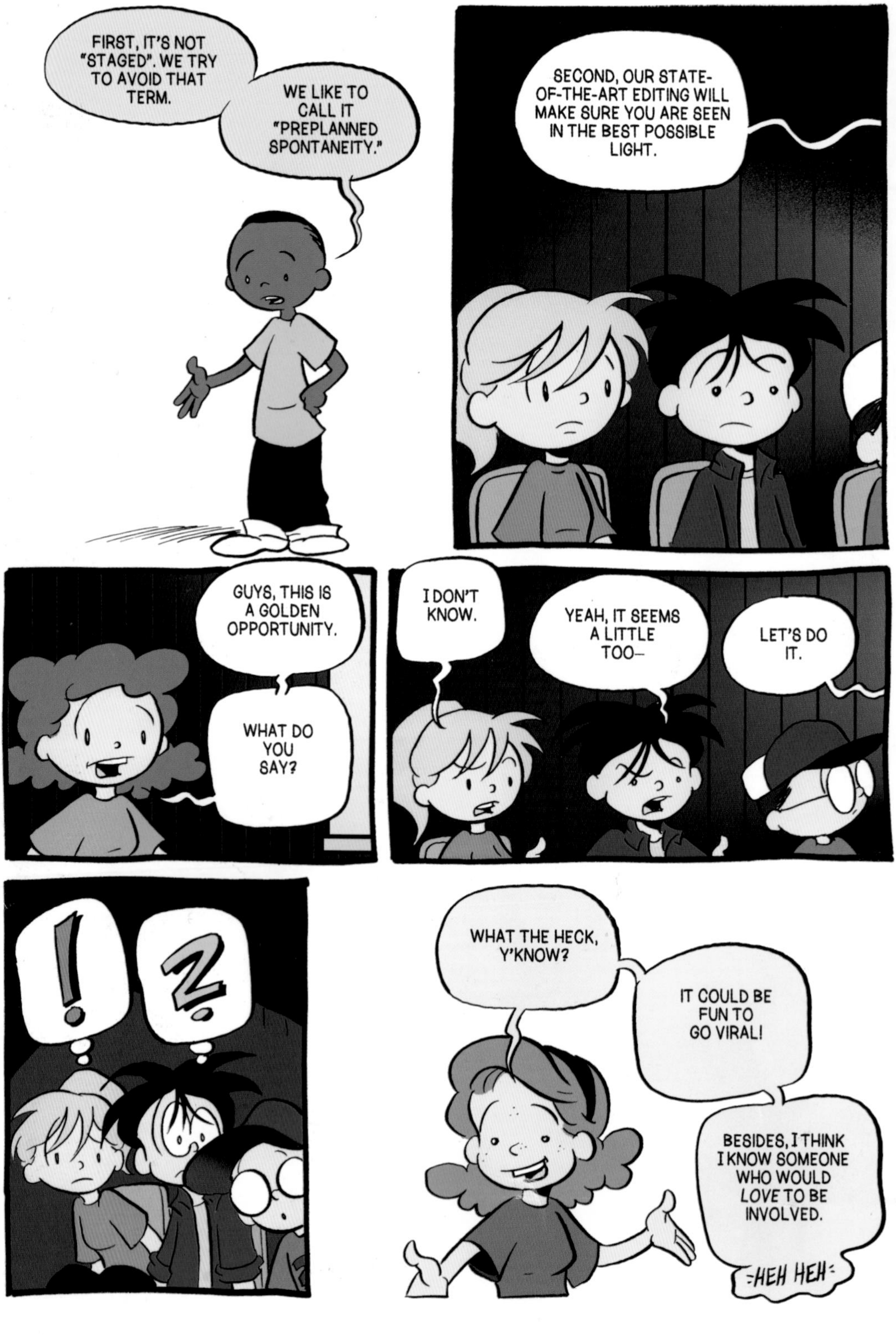
FIRST, IT'S NOT "STAGED". WE TRY TO AVOID THAT TERM.
WE LIKE TO CALL IT "PREPLANNED SPONTANEITY."
SECOND, OUR STATE-OF-THE-ART EDITING WILL MAKE SURE YOU ARE SEEN IN THE BEST POSSIBLE LIGHT.
GUYS, THIS IS A GOLDEN OPPORTUNITY.
WHAT DO YOU SAY?
I DON'T KNOW.
YEAH, IT SEEMS A LITTLE TOO–
LET'S DO IT.
!
?
WHAT THE HECK, Y'KNOW?
IT COULD BE FUN TO GO VIRAL!
BESIDES, I THINK I KNOW SOMEONE WHO WOULD *LOVE* TO BE INVOLVED.
HEH HEH

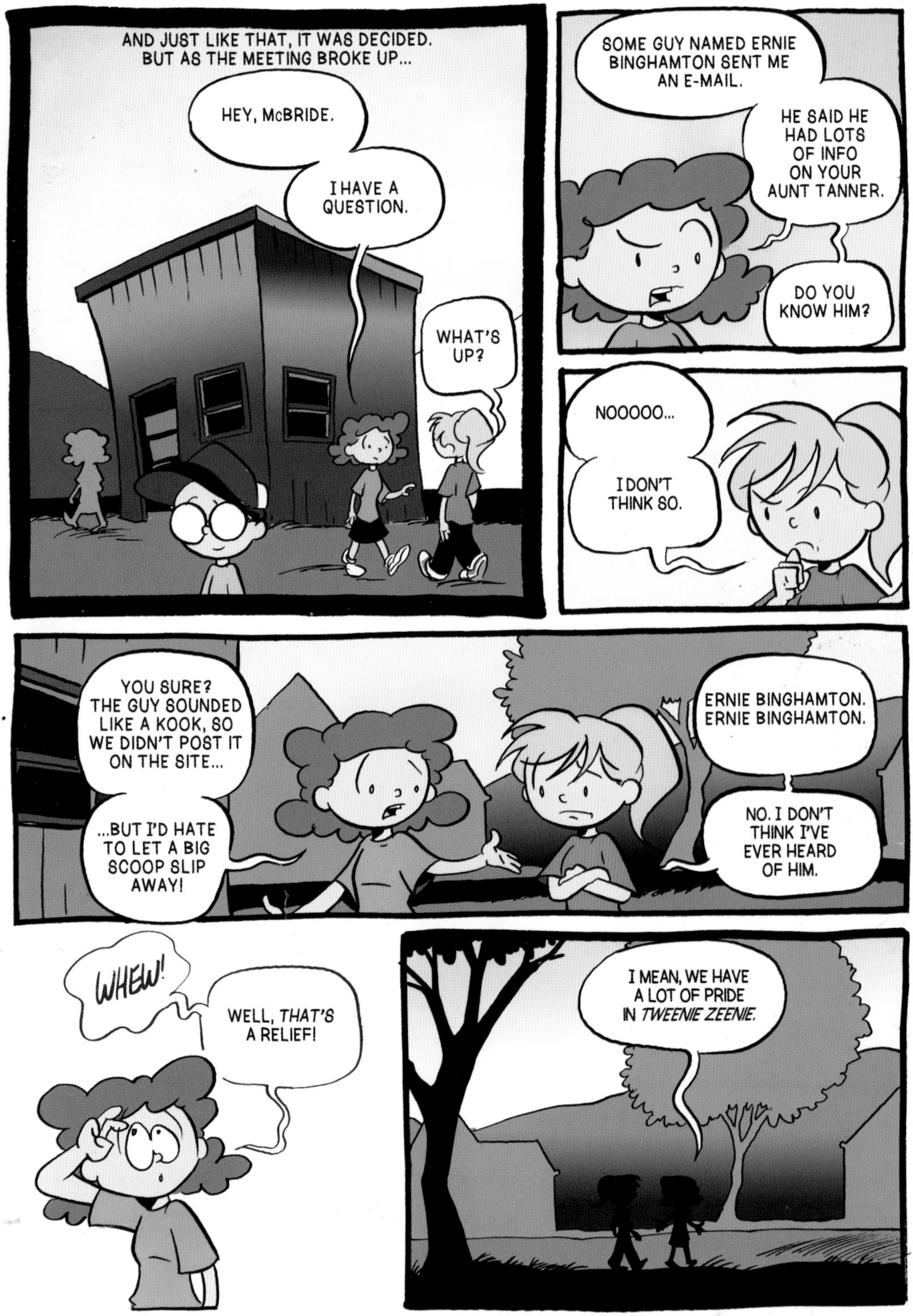
AND JUST LIKE THAT, IT WAS DECIDED. BUT AS THE MEETING BROKE UP...
HEY, McBRIDE.
I HAVE A QUESTION.
WHAT'S UP?
SOME GUY NAMED ERNIE BINGHAMTON SENT ME AN E-MAIL.
HE SAID HE HAD LOTS OF INFO ON YOUR AUNT TANNER.
DO YOU KNOW HIM?
NOOOOO...
I DON'T THINK SO.
YOU SURE? THE GUY SOUNDED LIKE A KOOK, SO WE DIDN'T POST IT ON THE SITE...
...BUT I'D HATE TO LET A BIG SCOOP SLIP AWAY!
ERNIE BINGHAMTON. ERNIE BINGHAMTON.
NO. I DON'T THINK I'VE EVER HEARD OF HIM.
WHEW!
WELL, *THAT'S* A RELIEF!
I MEAN, WE HAVE A LOT OF PRIDE IN *TWEENIE ZEENIE.*

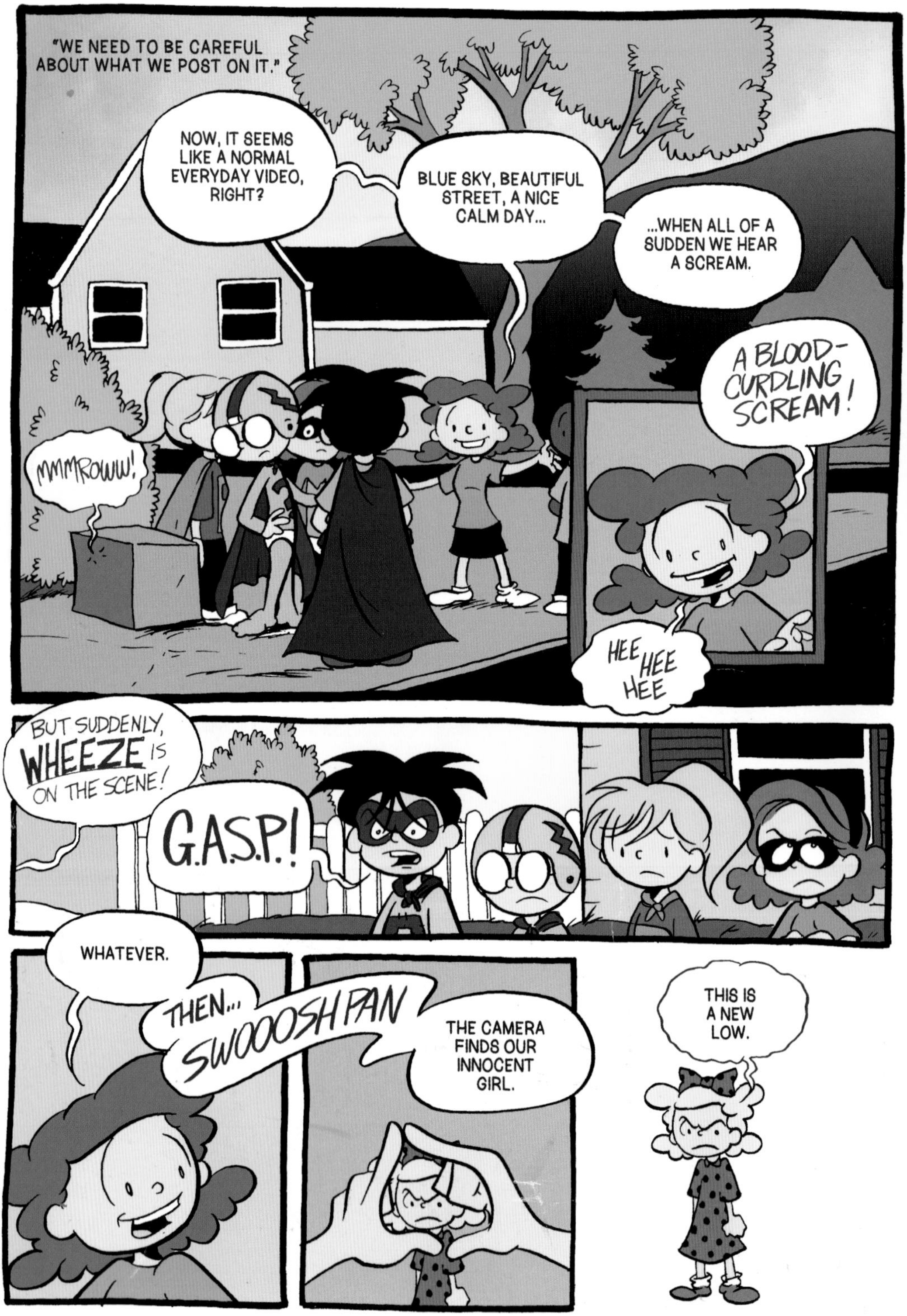
"WE NEED TO BE CAREFUL ABOUT WHAT WE POST ON IT."
NOW, IT SEEMS LIKE A NORMAL EVERYDAY VIDEO, RIGHT?
BLUE SKY, BEAUTIFUL STREET, A NICE CALM DAY...
...WHEN ALL OF A SUDDEN WE HEAR A SCREAM.
A BLOOD-CURDLING SCREAM!
MMMROWW!
HEE HEE HEE
BUT SUDDENLY, WHEEZE IS ON THE SCENE!
G.A.S.P.!
WHATEVER.
THEN... SWOOOSH PAN
THE CAMERA FINDS OUR INNOCENT GIRL.
THIS IS A NEW LOW.

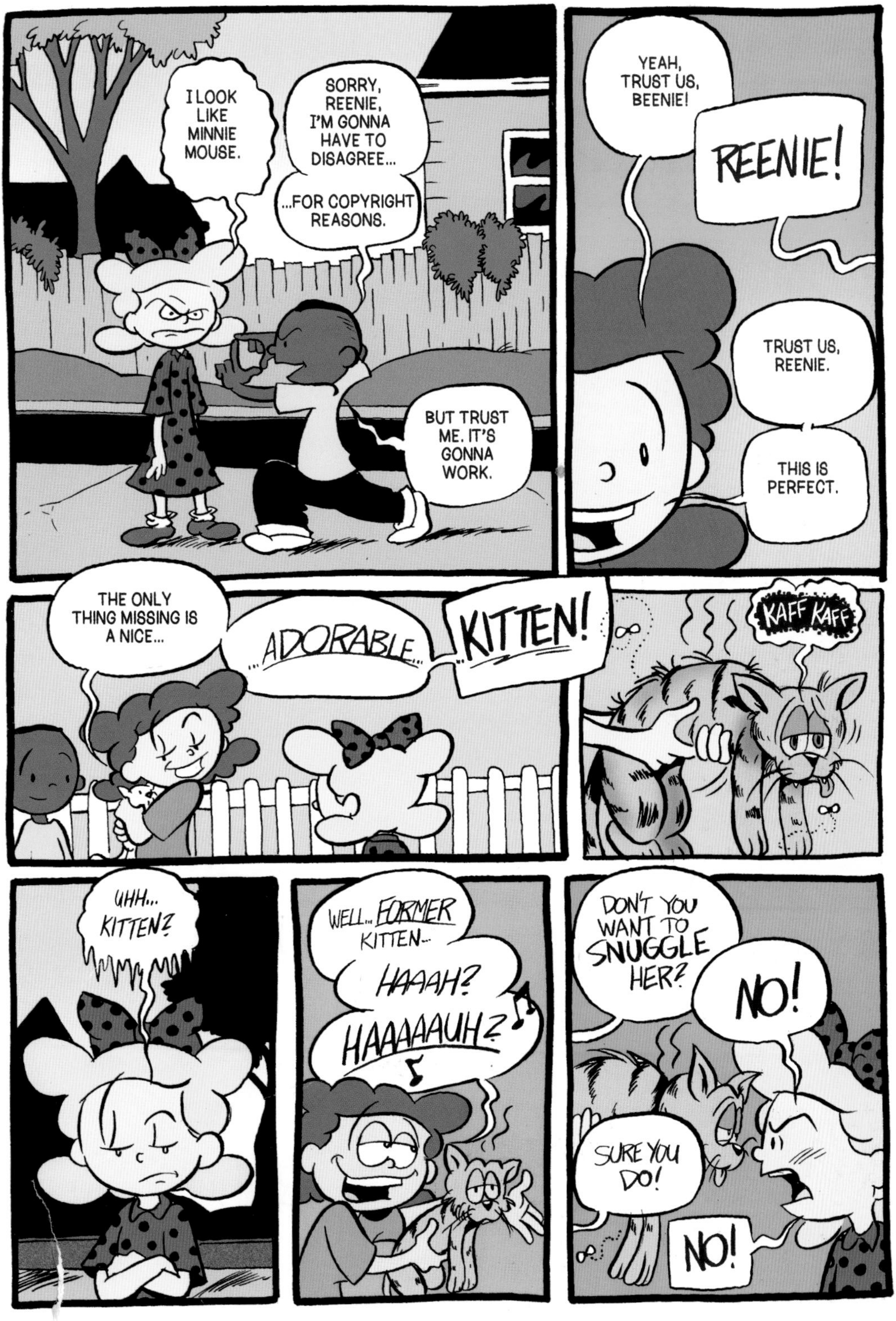

I LOOK LIKE MINNIE MOUSE.
SORRY, REENIE, I'M GONNA HAVE TO DISAGREE...
...FOR COPYRIGHT REASONS.
BUT TRUST ME. IT'S GONNA WORK.
YEAH, TRUST US, BEENIE!
REENIE!
TRUST US, REENIE.
THIS IS PERFECT.
THE ONLY THING MISSING IS A NICE...
...ADORABLE...
...KITTEN!
KAFF KAFF
UHH... KITTEN?
WELL... FORMER KITTEN...
HAAAH?
HAAAAAUH?
DON'T YOU WANT TO SNUGGLE HER?
NO!
SURE YOU DO!
NO!

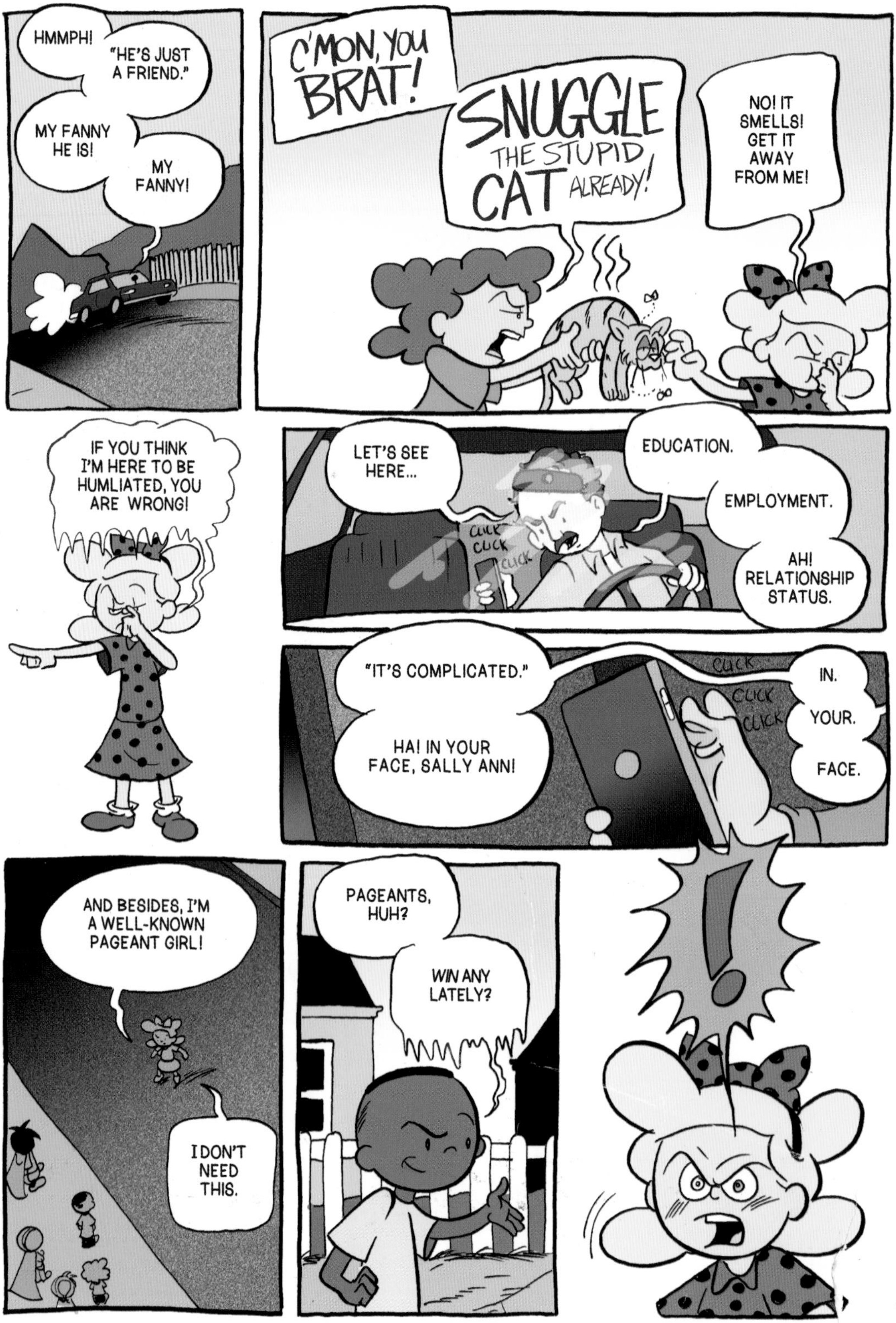
HMMPH!
"HE'S JUST A FRIEND."
MY FANNY HE IS!
MY FANNY!
C'MON, YOU BRAT!
SNUGGLE THE STUPID CAT ALREADY!
NO! IT SMELLS! GET IT AWAY FROM ME!
IF YOU THINK I'M HERE TO BE HUMLIATED, YOU ARE WRONG!
LET'S SEE HERE...
CLICK CLICK CLICK
EDUCATION.
EMPLOYMENT.
AH! RELATIONSHIP STATUS.
"IT'S COMPLICATED."
HA! IN YOUR FACE, SALLY ANN!
CLICK CLICK CLICK
IN.
YOUR.
FACE.
AND BESIDES, I'M A WELL-KNOWN PAGEANT GIRL!
I DON'T NEED THIS.
PAGEANTS, HUH?
WIN ANY LATELY?
!

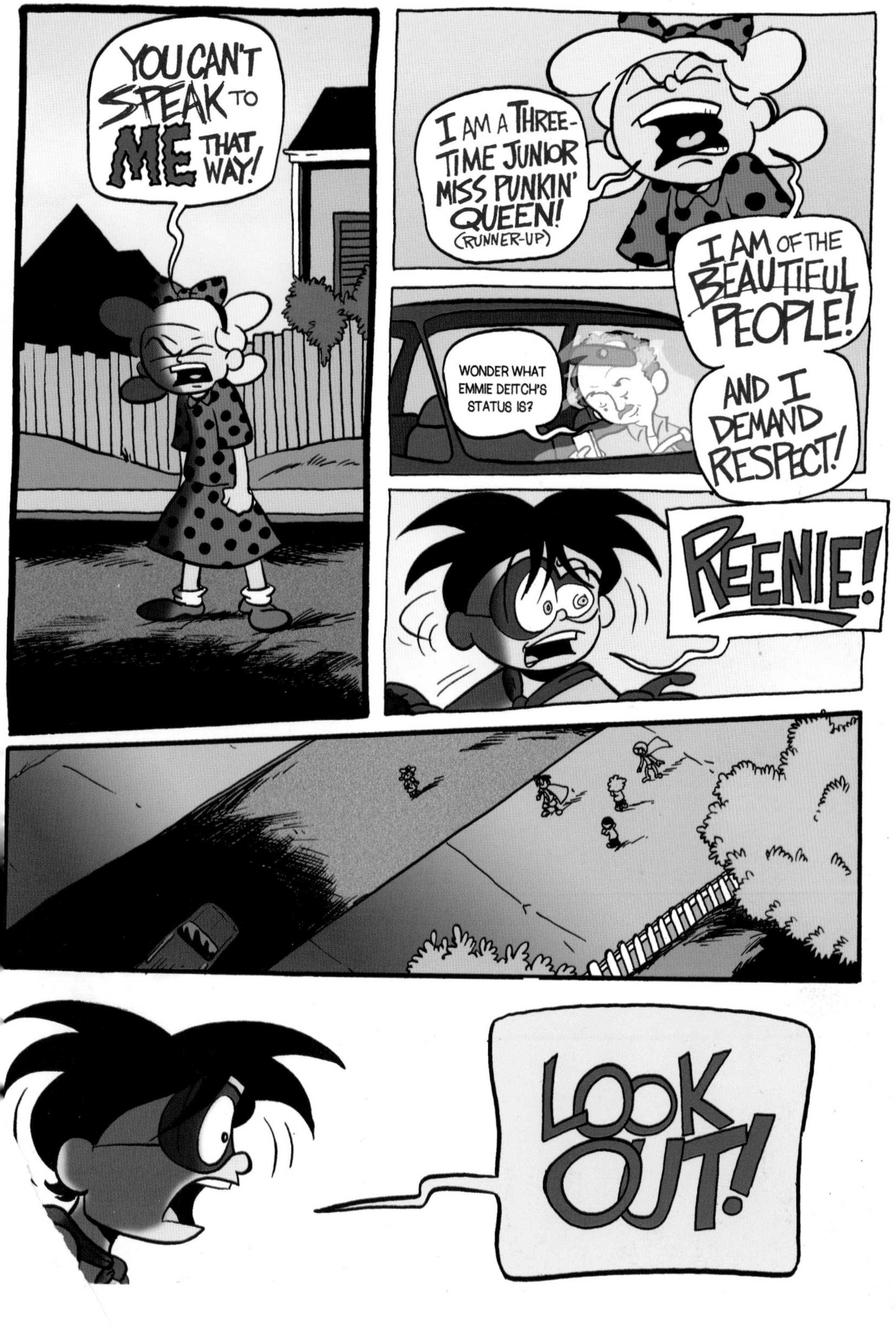
YOU CAN'T SPEAK TO ME THAT WAY!
I AM A THREE-TIME JUNIOR MISS PUNKIN' QUEEN! (RUNNER-UP)
I AM OF THE BEAUTIFUL PEOPLE!
AND I DEMAND RESPECT!
WONDER WHAT EMMIE DEITCH'S STATUS IS?
REENIE!
LOOK OUT!

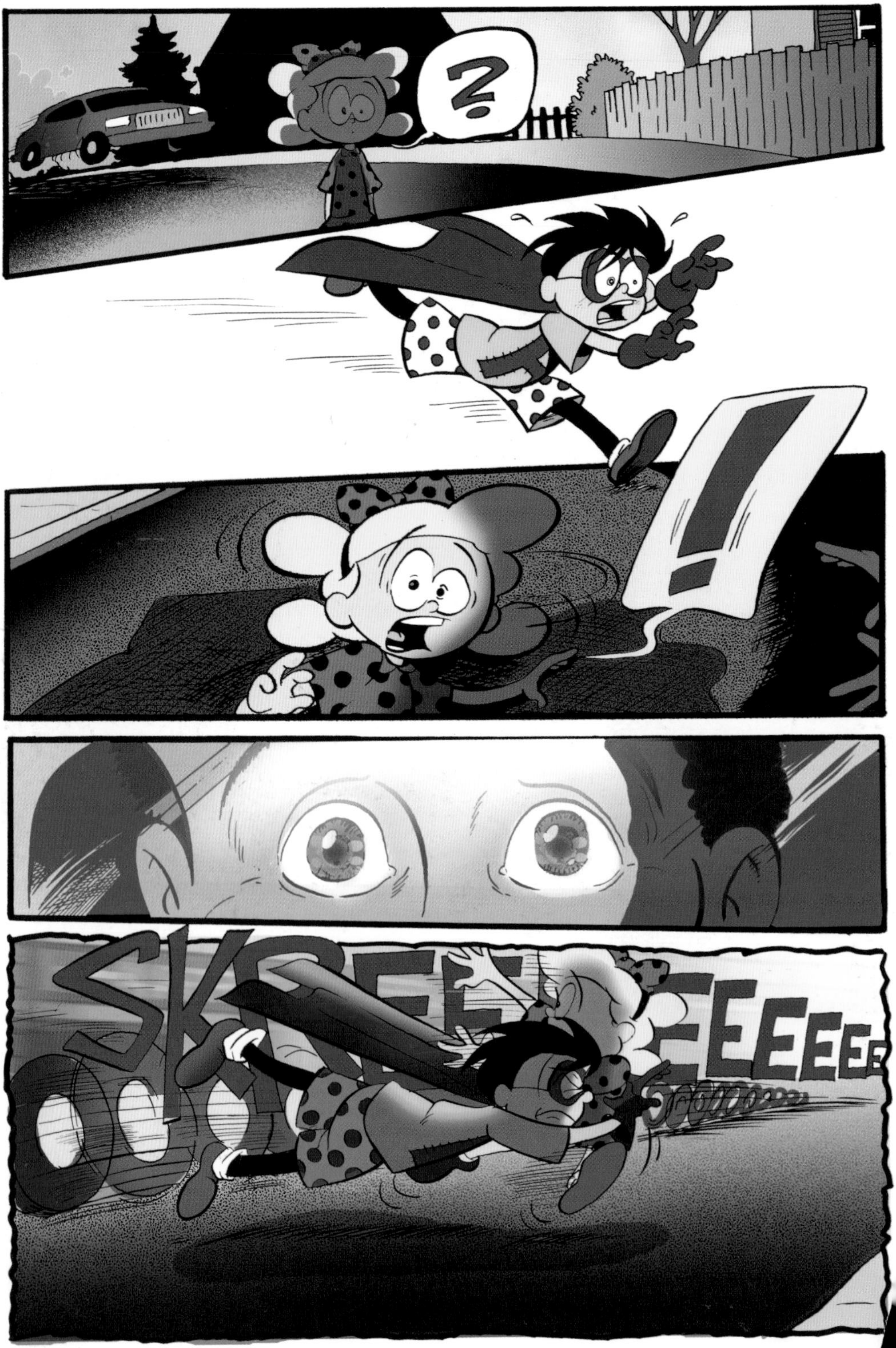
?
!

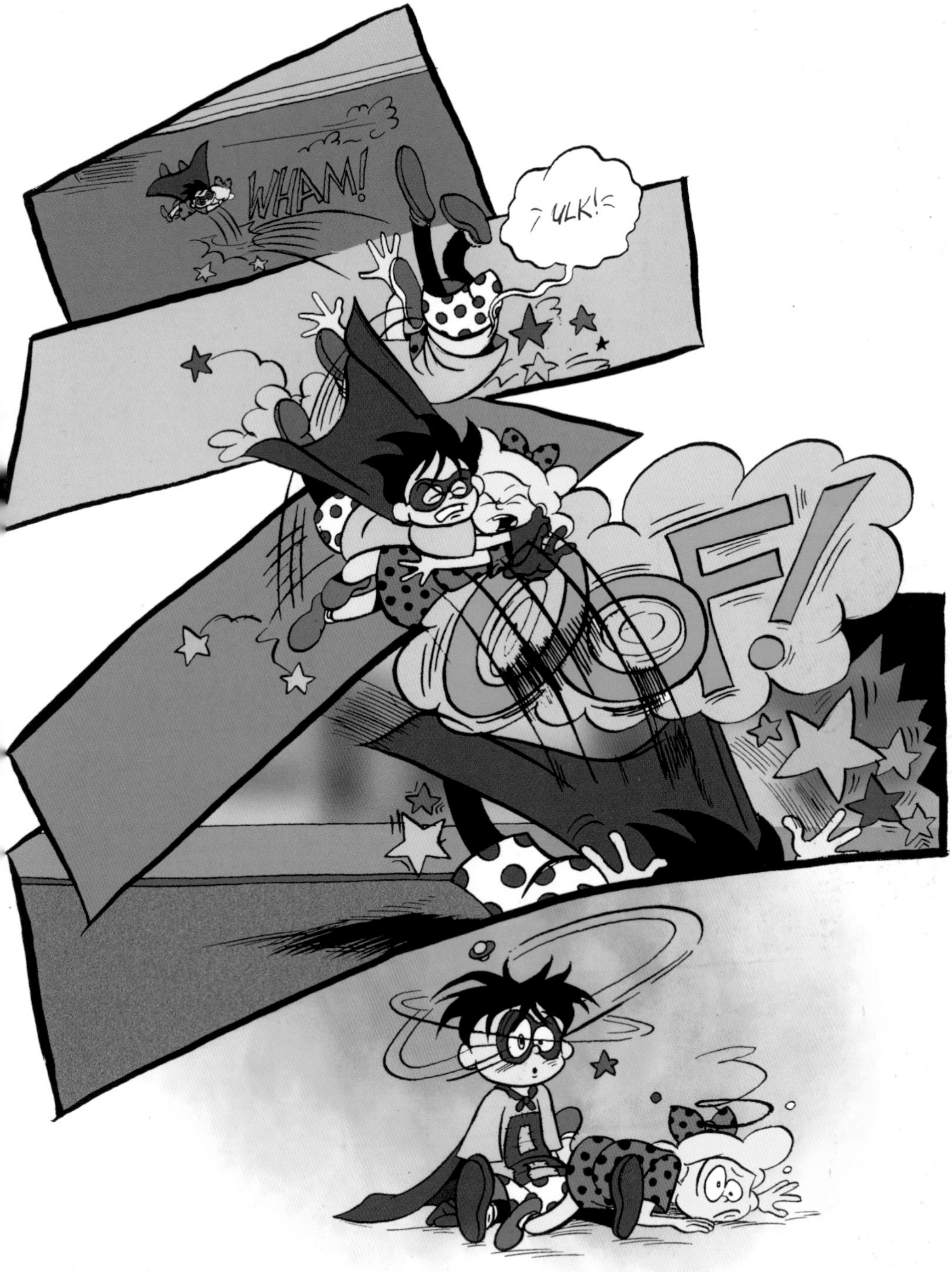
WHAM!
ULK!
OOF!

JACKPOT.

AND SHE WAS RIGHT!

ONCE HANNIGAN POSTED THE VIDEO ON TWEENIEZEENIE.COM, IT BECAME A SENSATION!

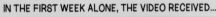

IN THE FIRST WEEK ALONE, THE VIDEO RECEIVED...

175,000 HITS!

WHICH, AFTER SOMEONE PHOTOSHOPPED IN SOME LIGHTSABERS, CLIMBED TO...

648,000 HITS!

AND FINALLY, ONCE HANNIGAN GOT HER KITTEN IN...

2,000,000 HITS!

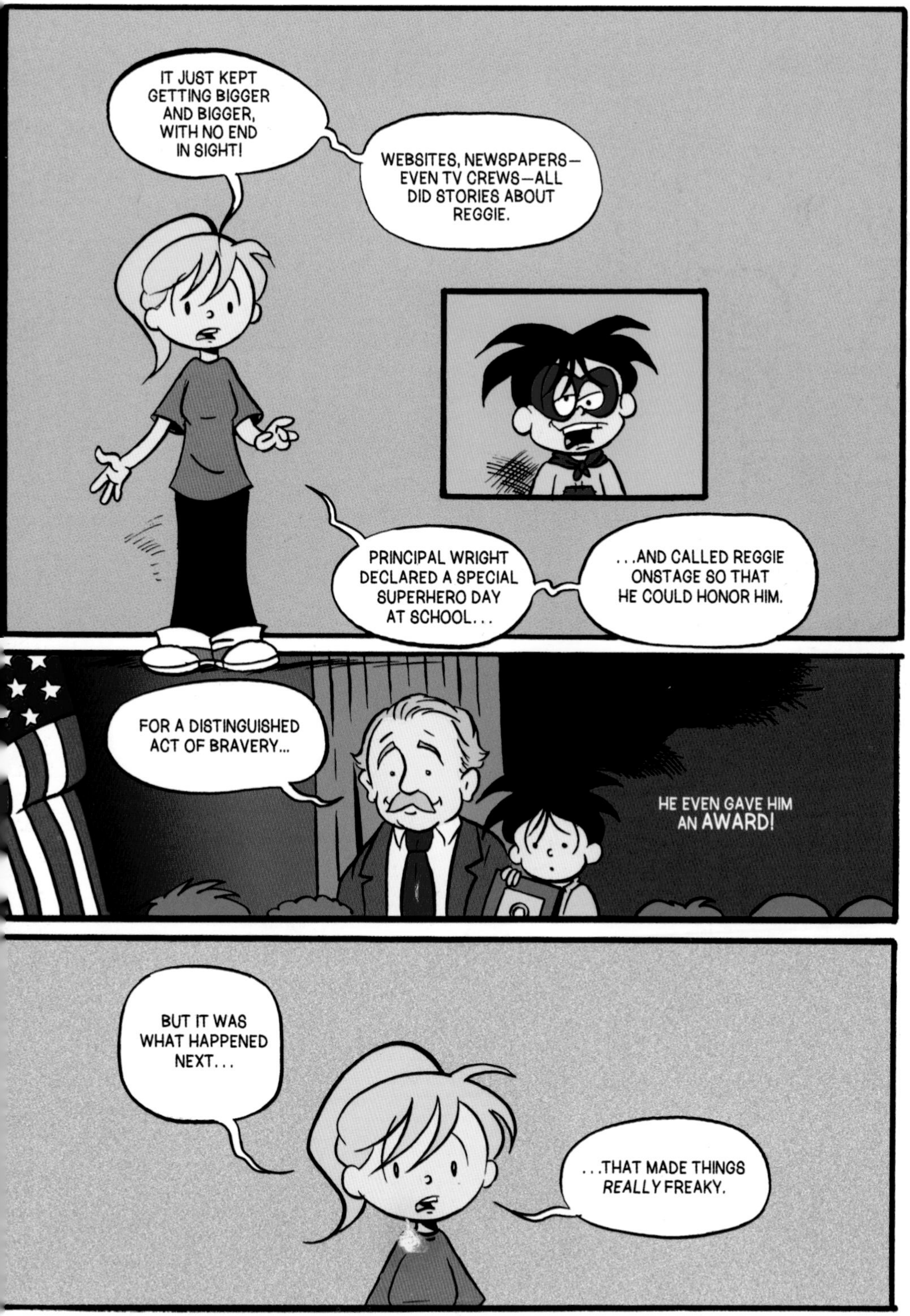
IT JUST KEPT GETTING BIGGER AND BIGGER, WITH NO END IN SIGHT!
WEBSITES, NEWSPAPERS—EVEN TV CREWS—ALL DID STORIES ABOUT REGGIE.
PRINCIPAL WRIGHT DECLARED A SPECIAL SUPERHERO DAY AT SCHOOL...
...AND CALLED REGGIE ONSTAGE SO THAT HE COULD HONOR HIM.
FOR A DISTINGUISHED ACT OF BRAVERY...
HE EVEN GAVE HIM AN AWARD!
BUT IT WAS WHAT HAPPENED NEXT...
...THAT MADE THINGS *REALLY* FREAKY.

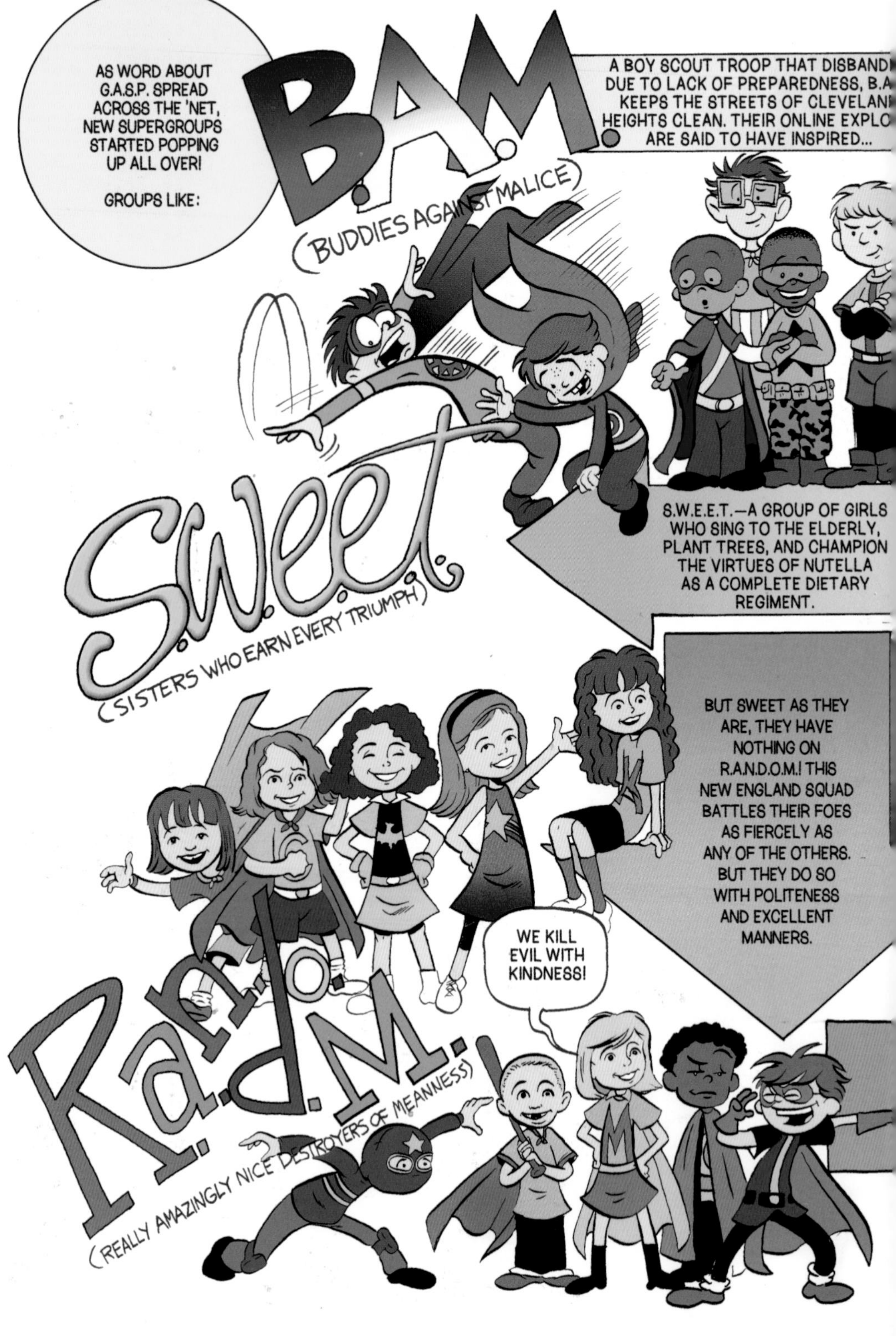
AS WORD ABOUT G.A.S.P. SPREAD ACROSS THE 'NET, NEW SUPERGROUPS STARTED POPPING UP ALL OVER!
GROUPS LIKE:
B.A.M.
(BUDDIES AGAINST MALICE)
A BOY SCOUT TROOP THAT DISBAND DUE TO LACK OF PREPAREDNESS, B.A KEEPS THE STREETS OF CLEVELAN HEIGHTS CLEAN. THEIR ONLINE EXPLO ARE SAID TO HAVE INSPIRED...
S.W.E.E.T.
(SISTERS WHO EARN EVERY TRIUMPH)
S.W.E.E.T.—A GROUP OF GIRLS WHO SING TO THE ELDERLY, PLANT TREES, AND CHAMPION THE VIRTUES OF NUTELLA AS A COMPLETE DIETARY REGIMENT.
BUT SWEET AS THEY ARE, THEY HAVE NOTHING ON R.A.N.D.O.M.! THIS NEW ENGLAND SQUAD BATTLES THEIR FOES AS FIERCELY AS ANY OF THE OTHERS. BUT THEY DO SO WITH POLITENESS AND EXCELLENT MANNERS.
R.A.N.D.O.M.
(REALLY AMAZINGLY NICE DESTROYERS OF MEANNESS)
WE KILL EVIL WITH KINDNESS!

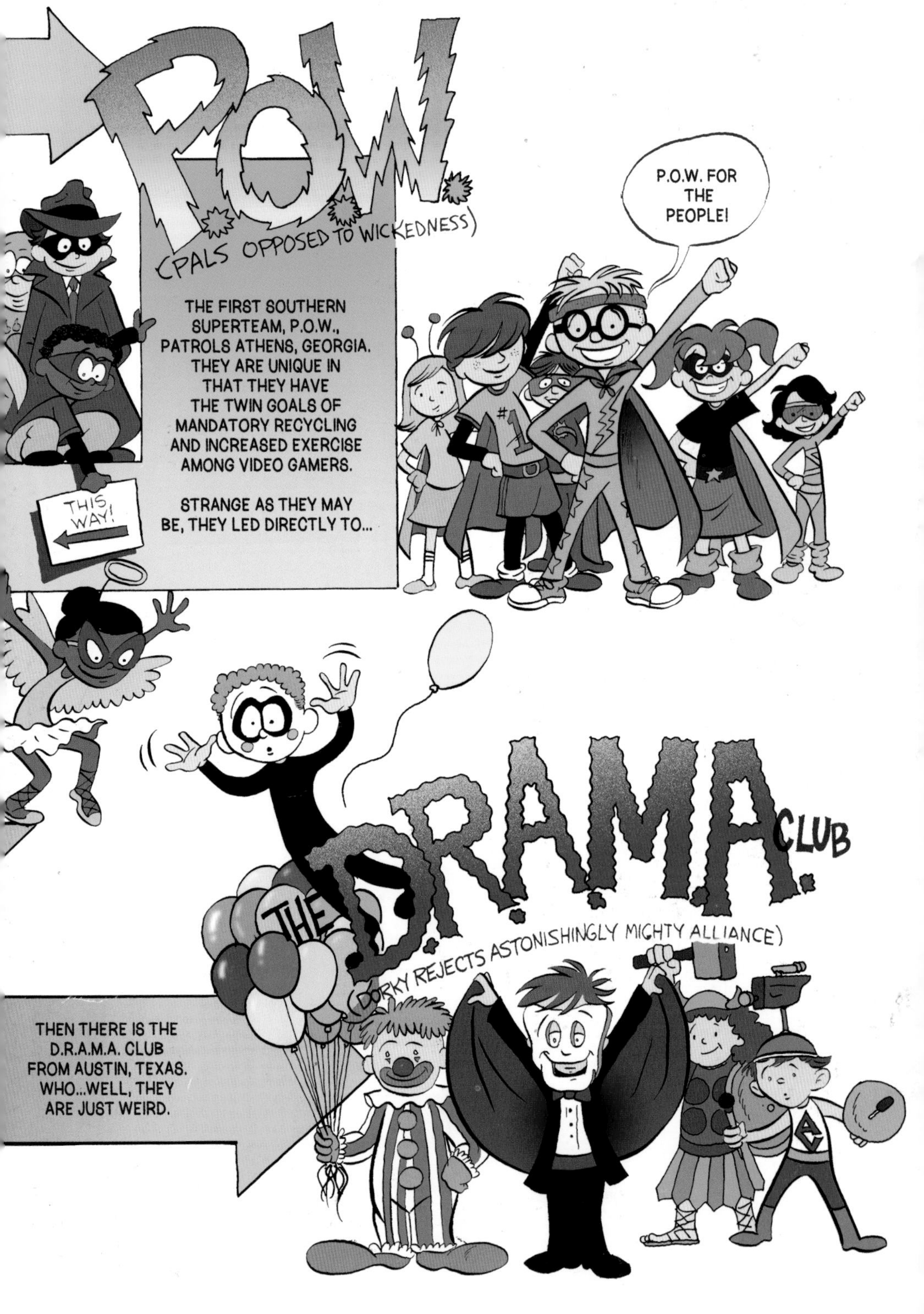
P.O.W.
(PALS OPPOSED TO WICKEDNESS)
THE FIRST SOUTHERN SUPERTEAM, P.O.W., PATROLS ATHENS, GEORGIA. THEY ARE UNIQUE IN THAT THEY HAVE THE TWIN GOALS OF MANDATORY RECYCLING AND INCREASED EXERCISE AMONG VIDEO GAMERS.
STRANGE AS THEY MAY BE, THEY LED DIRECTLY TO...
THIS WAY!
P.O.W. FOR THE PEOPLE!
THE D.R.A.M.A. CLUB
(DORKY REJECTS ASTONISHINGLY MIGHTY ALLIANCE)
THEN THERE IS THE D.R.A.M.A. CLUB FROM AUSTIN, TEXAS. WHO...WELL, THEY ARE JUST WEIRD.

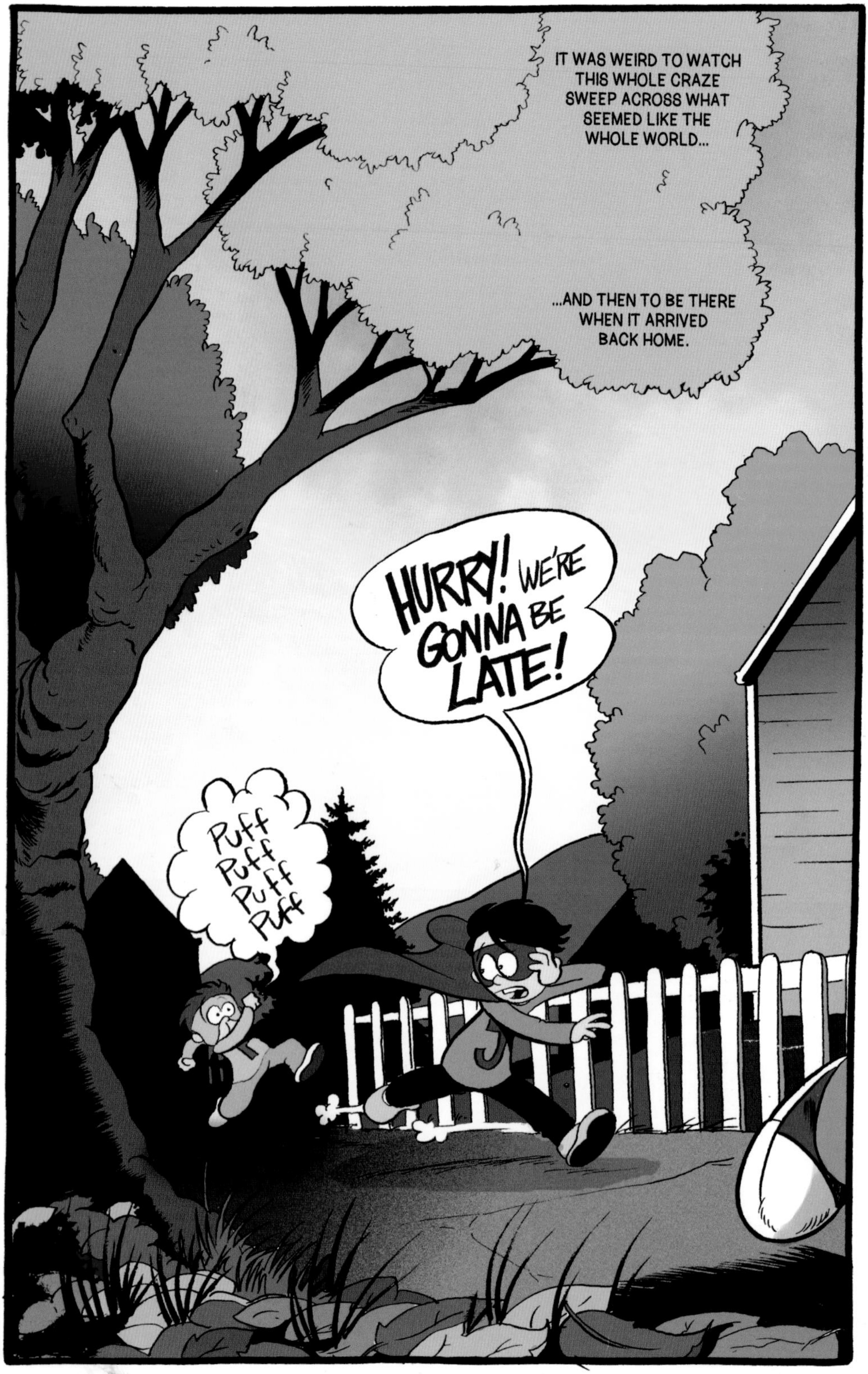
IT WAS WEIRD TO WATCH THIS WHOLE CRAZE SWEEP ACROSS WHAT SEEMED LIKE THE WHOLE WORLD...
...AND THEN TO BE THERE WHEN IT ARRIVED BACK HOME.
HURRY! WE'RE GONNA BE LATE!
Puff Puff Puff Puff

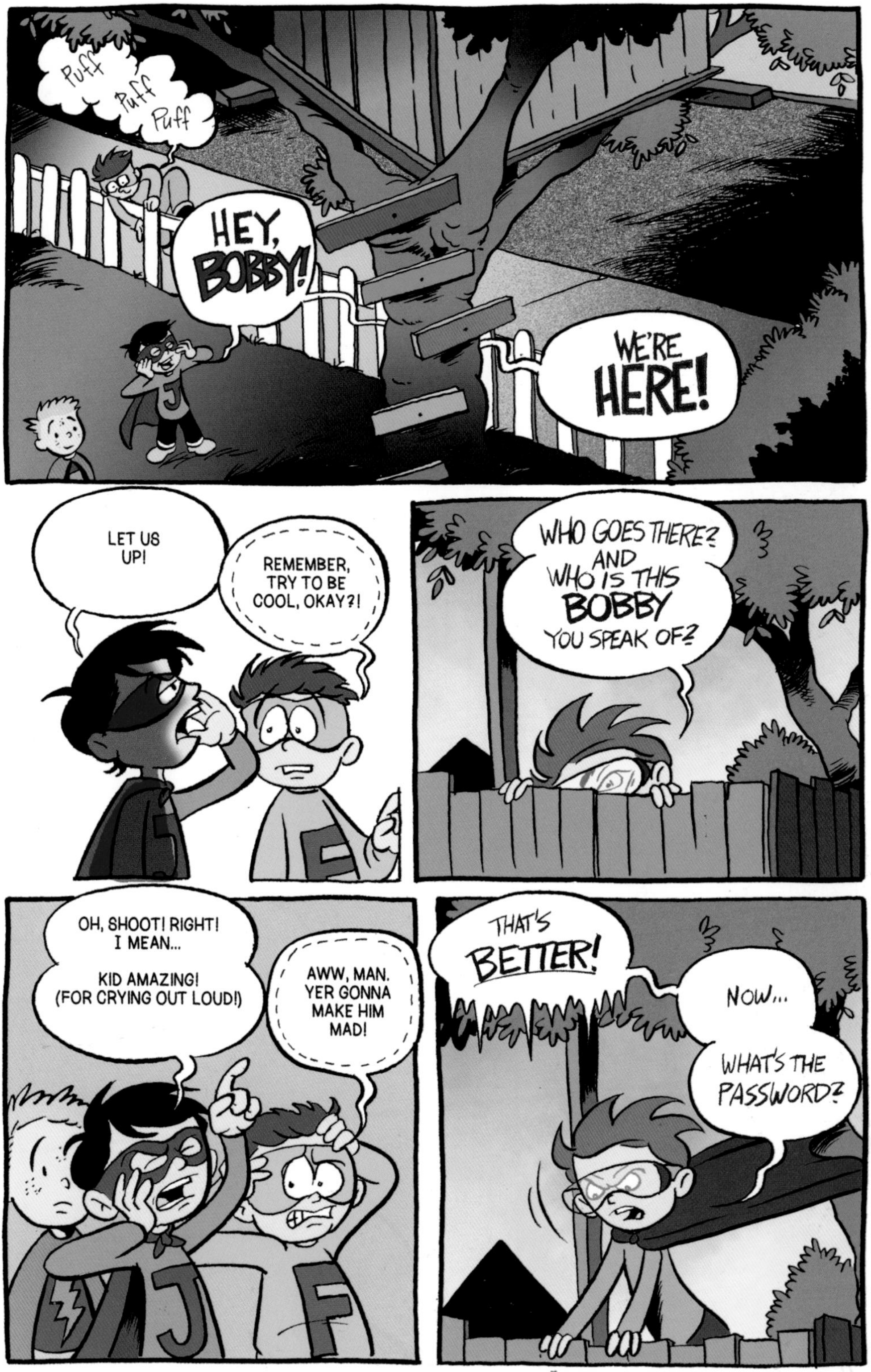
Puff Puff Puff
HEY, BOBBY!
WE'RE HERE!
LET US UP!
REMEMBER, TRY TO BE COOL, OKAY?!
WHO GOES THERE? AND WHO IS THIS BOBBY YOU SPEAK OF?
OH, SHOOT! RIGHT! I MEAN...
KID AMAZING! (FOR CRYING OUT LOUD!)
AWW, MAN. YER GONNA MAKE HIM MAD!
THAT'S BETTER!
NOW...
WHAT'S THE PASSWORD?

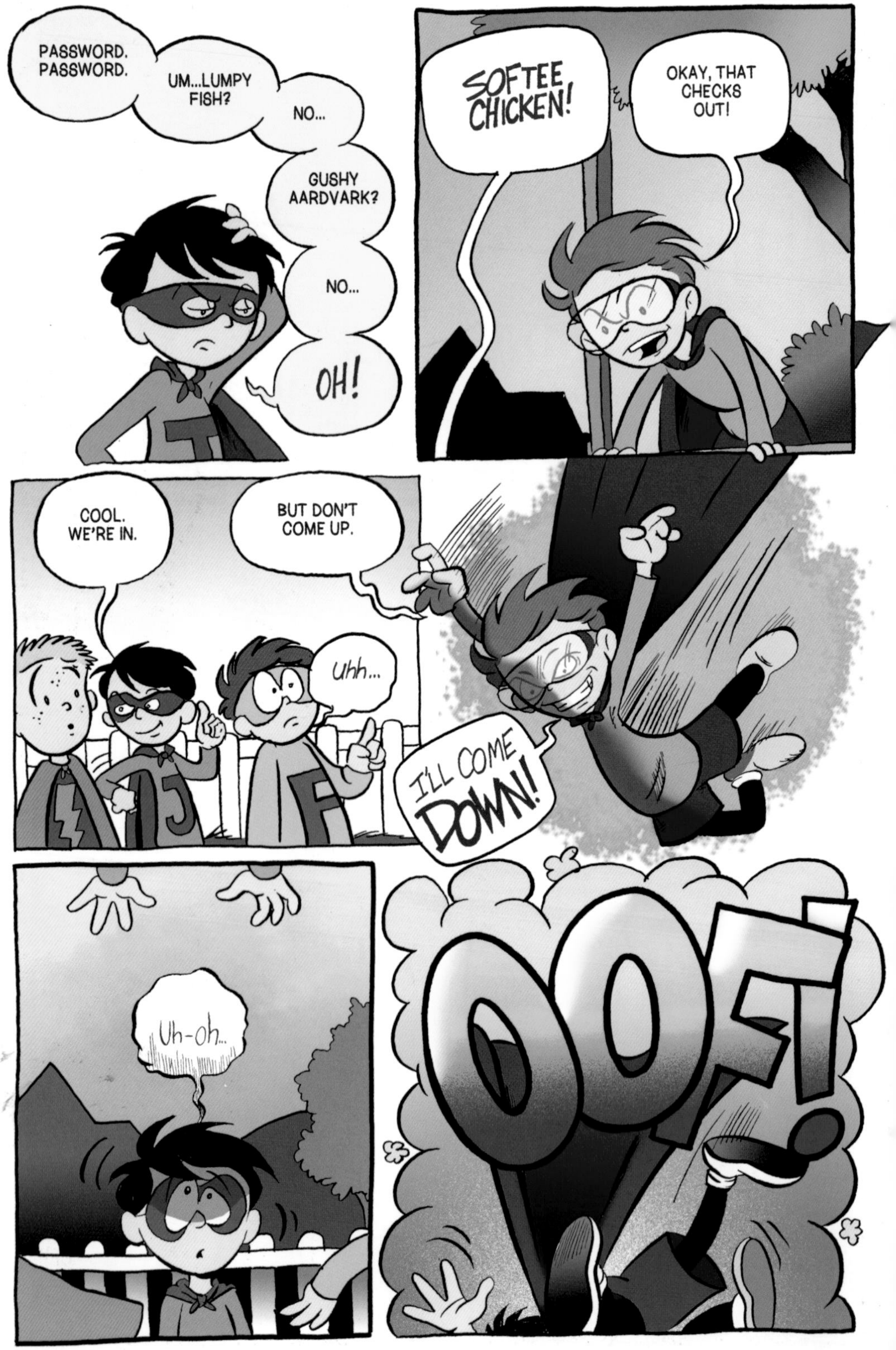
PASSWORD. PASSWORD.
UM...LUMPY FISH?
NO...
GUSHY AARDVARK?
NO...
OH!
SOFTEE CHICKEN!
OKAY, THAT CHECKS OUT!
COOL. WE'RE IN.
BUT DON'T COME UP.
Uhh...
I'LL COME DOWN!
Uh-oh...
OOF!

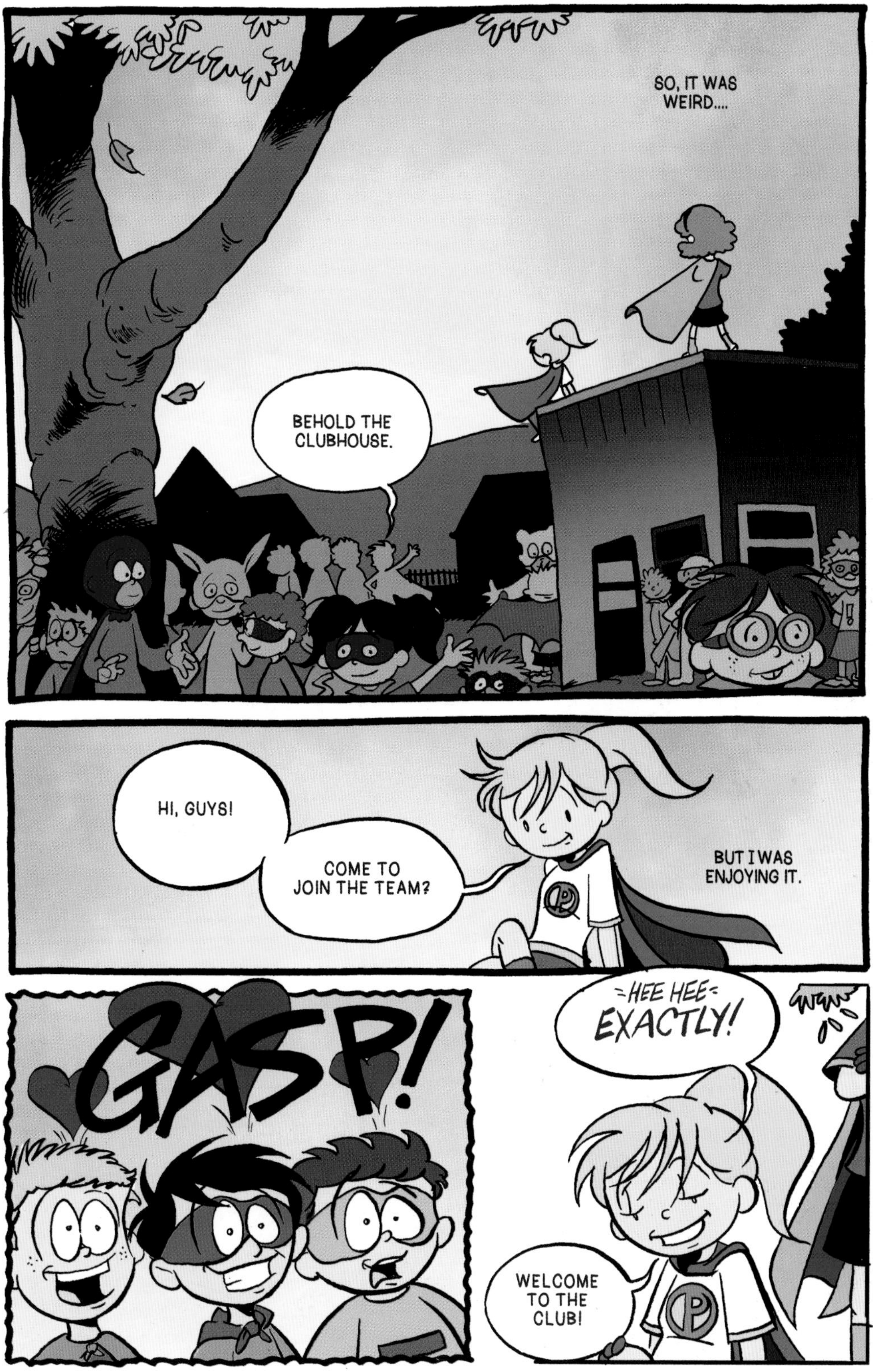
SO, IT WAS WEIRD....
BEHOLD THE CLUBHOUSE.
HI, GUYS!
COME TO JOIN THE TEAM?
BUT I WAS ENJOYING IT.
GASP!
HEE HEE EXACTLY!
WELCOME TO THE CLUB!

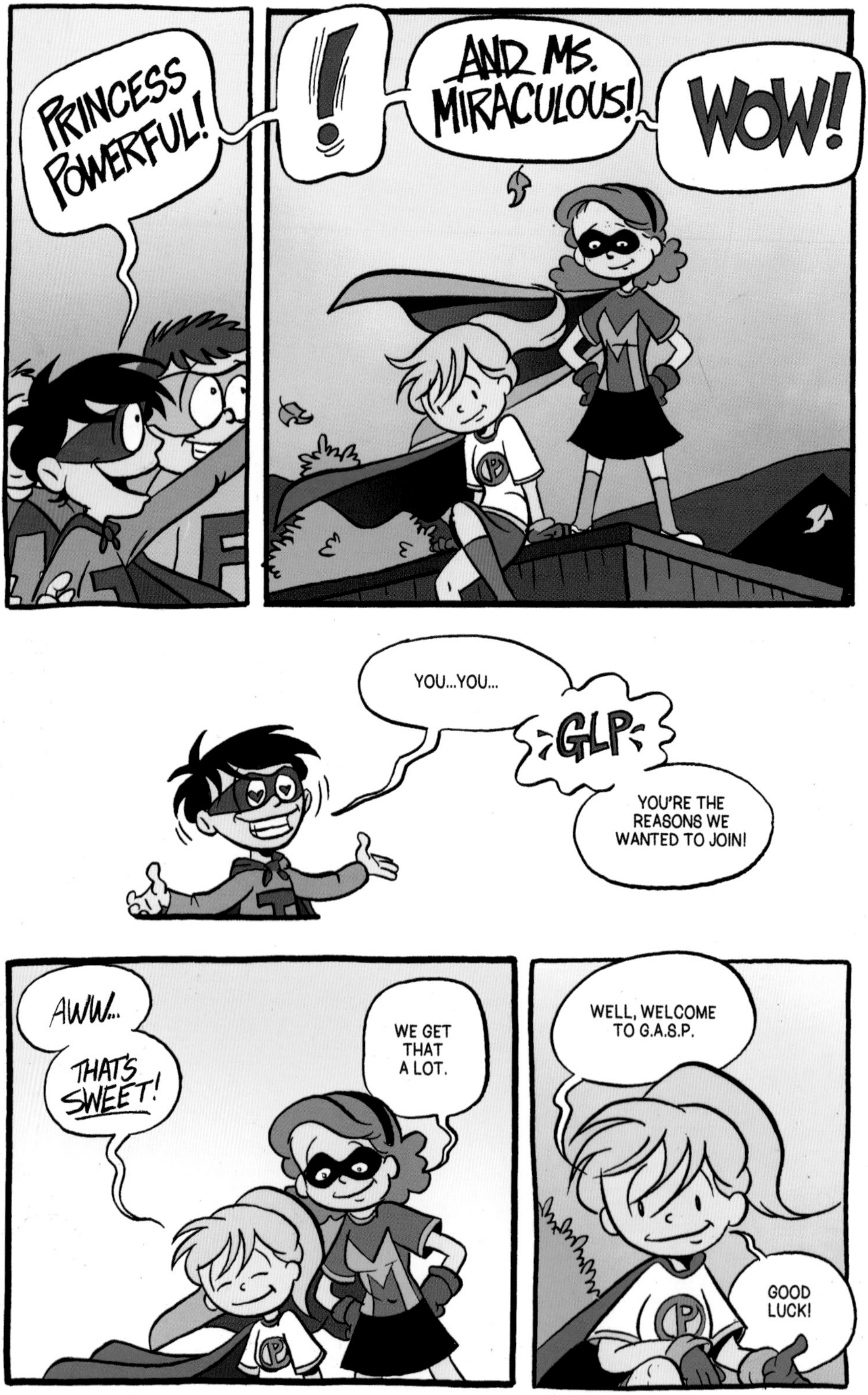
PRINCESS POWERFUL!
!
AND MS. MIRACULOUS!
WOW!
YOU...YOU...
GLP
YOU'RE THE REASONS WE WANTED TO JOIN!
AWW...
THAT'S SWEET!
WE GET THAT A LOT.
WELL, WELCOME TO G.A.S.P.
GOOD LUCK!

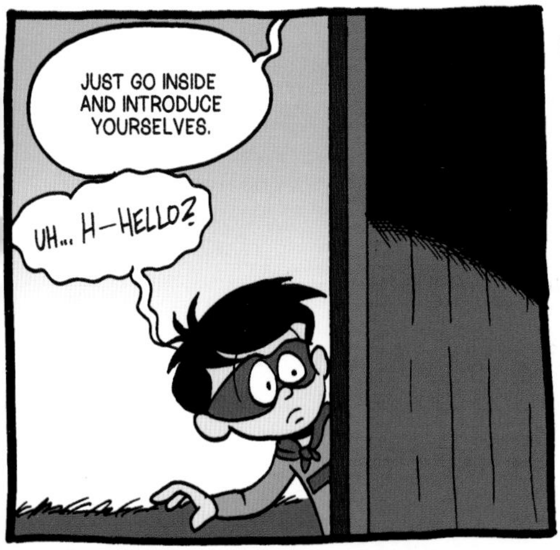
JUST GO INSIDE AND INTRODUCE YOURSELVES.
UH... H-HELLO?

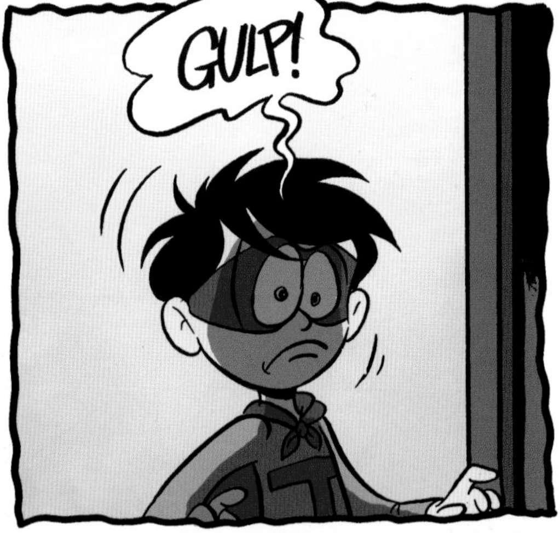
GULP!

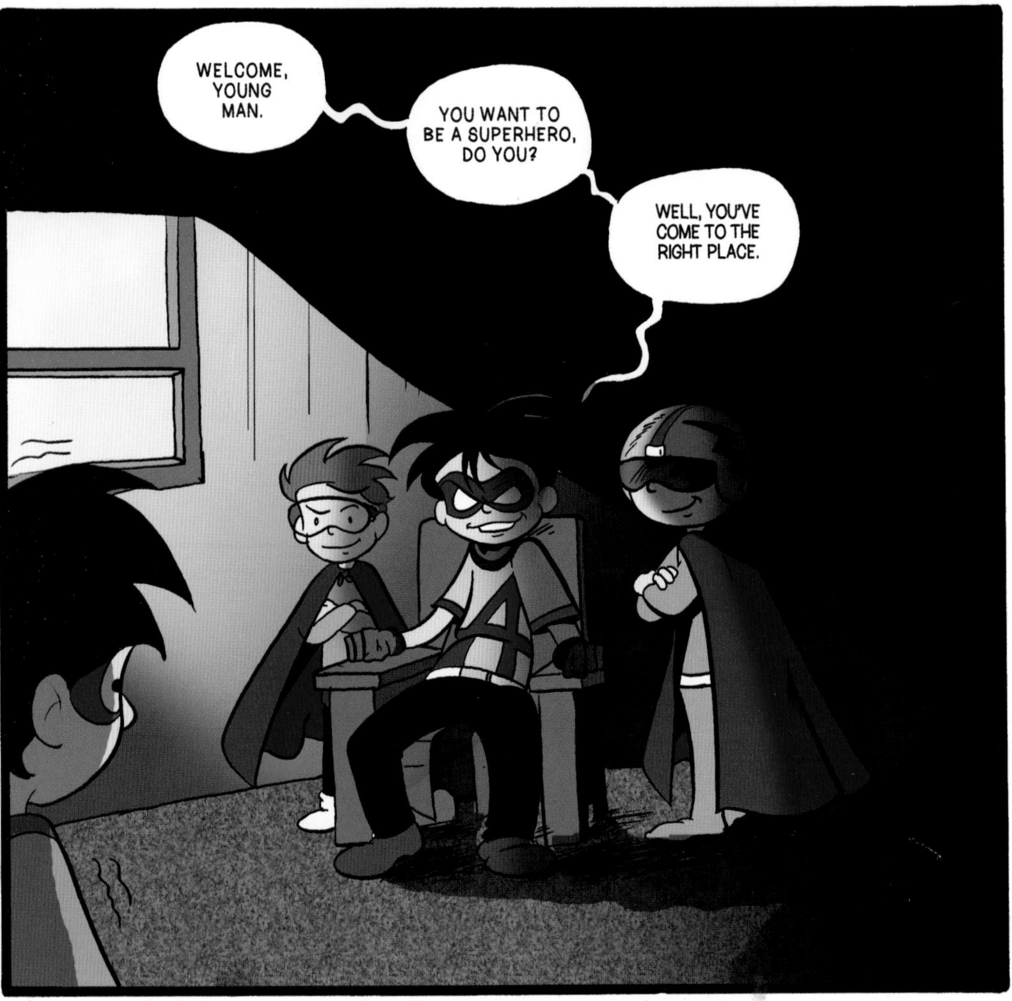
WELCOME, YOUNG MAN.
YOU WANT TO BE A SUPERHERO, DO YOU?
WELL, YOU'VE COME TO THE RIGHT PLACE.

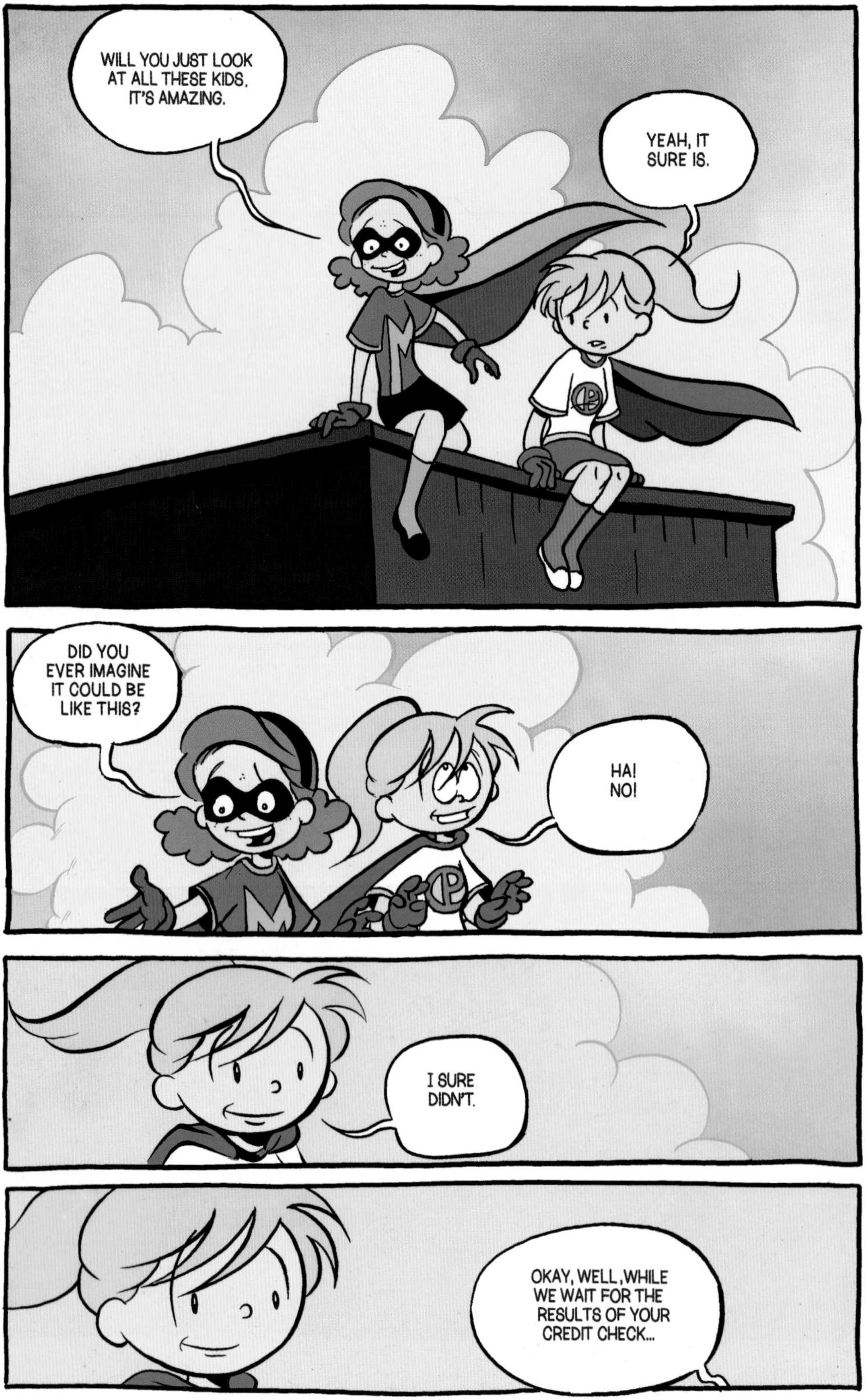
WILL YOU JUST LOOK AT ALL THESE KIDS. IT'S AMAZING.
YEAH, IT SURE IS.
DID YOU EVER IMAGINE IT COULD BE LIKE THIS?
HA! NO!
I SURE DIDN'T.
OKAY, WELL, WHILE WE WAIT FOR THE RESULTS OF YOUR CREDIT CHECK...

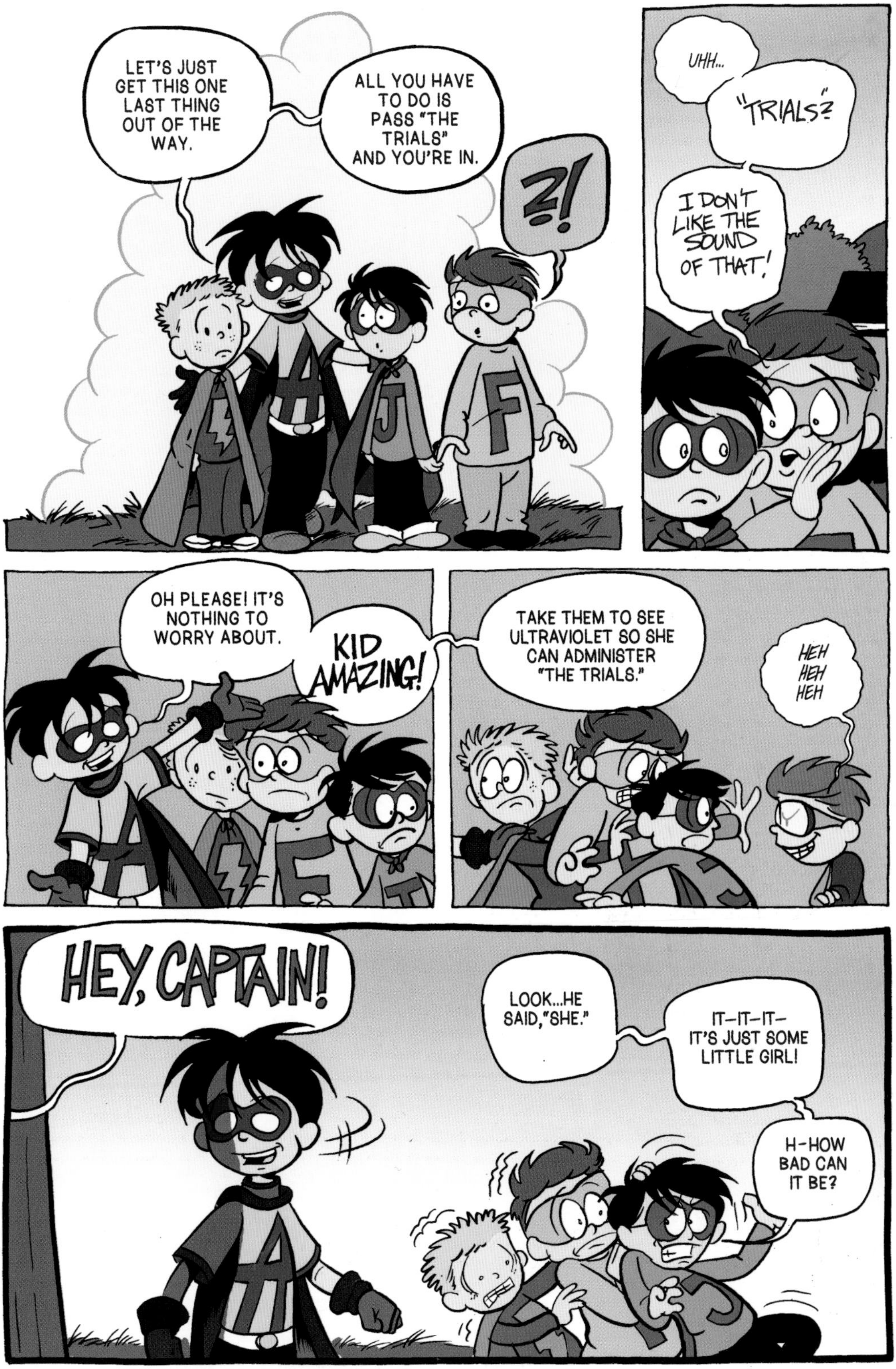
LET'S JUST GET THIS ONE LAST THING OUT OF THE WAY.
ALL YOU HAVE TO DO IS PASS "THE TRIALS" AND YOU'RE IN.
?!
UHH...
"TRIALS?"
I DON'T LIKE THE SOUND OF THAT!
OH PLEASE! IT'S NOTHING TO WORRY ABOUT.
KID AMAZING!
TAKE THEM TO SEE ULTRAVIOLET SO SHE CAN ADMINISTER "THE TRIALS."
HEH HEH HEH
HEY, CAPTAIN!
LOOK...HE SAID, "SHE."
IT-IT-IT-IT'S JUST SOME LITTLE GIRL!
H-HOW BAD CAN IT BE?

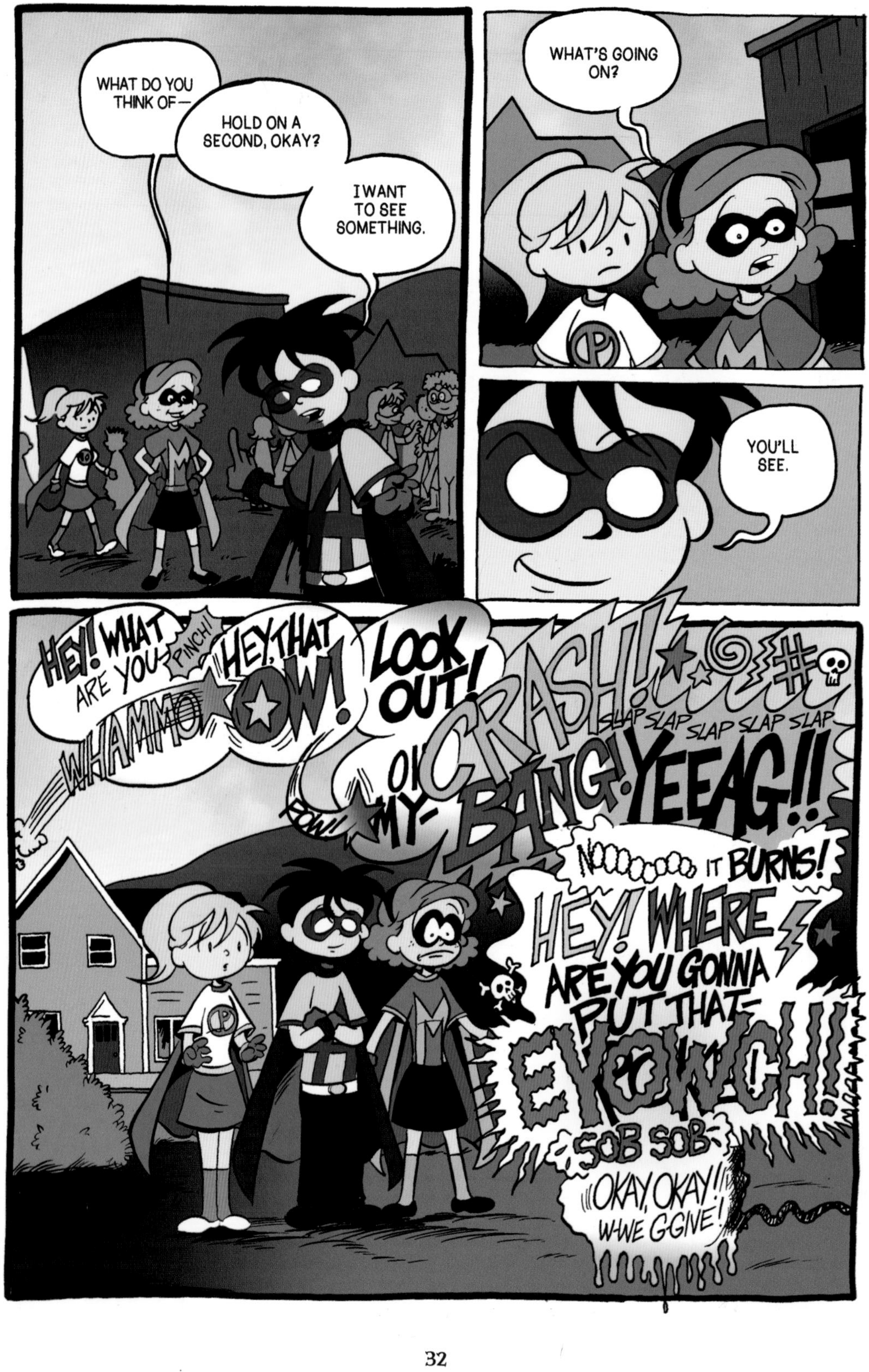
WHAT DO YOU THINK OF—
HOLD ON A SECOND, OKAY?
I WANT TO SEE SOMETHING.
WHAT'S GOING ON?
YOU'LL SEE.
HEY! WHAT ARE YOU-
PINCH!
HEY, THAT
WHAMMO
OW!
LOOK OUT!
OI MY-
POW!
CRASH!
SLAP SLAP SLAP SLAP SLAP
BANG!
YEEAG!!
NOOOOOOOOO IT BURNS!
HEY! WHERE ARE YOU GONNA PUT THAT-
EYOWCH!!
SOB SOB
OKAY, OKAY! W-WE G-GIVE!

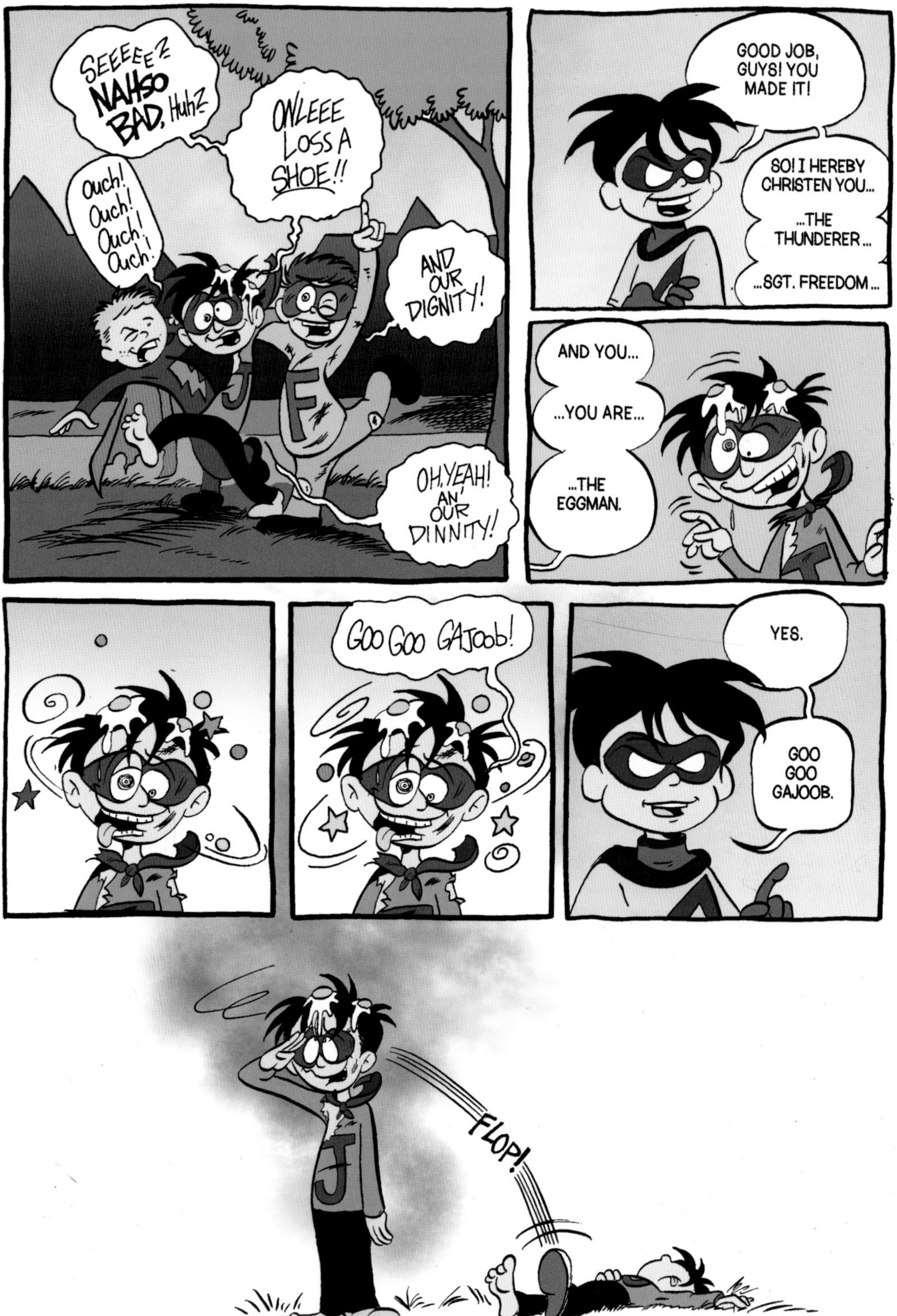
SEEEEEZ NAHSO BAD, Huh?
ONLEEE LOSS A SHOE!!
Ouch! Ouch! Ouch! Ouch!
AND OUR DIGNITY!
OH, YEAH! AN' OUR DINNITY!
GOOD JOB, GUYS! YOU MADE IT!
SO! I HEREBY CHRISTEN YOU...
...THE THUNDERER...
...SGT. FREEDOM...
AND YOU...
...YOU ARE...
...THE EGGMAN.
GOO GOO GAJOOB!
YES.
GOO GOO GAJOOB.
FLOP!

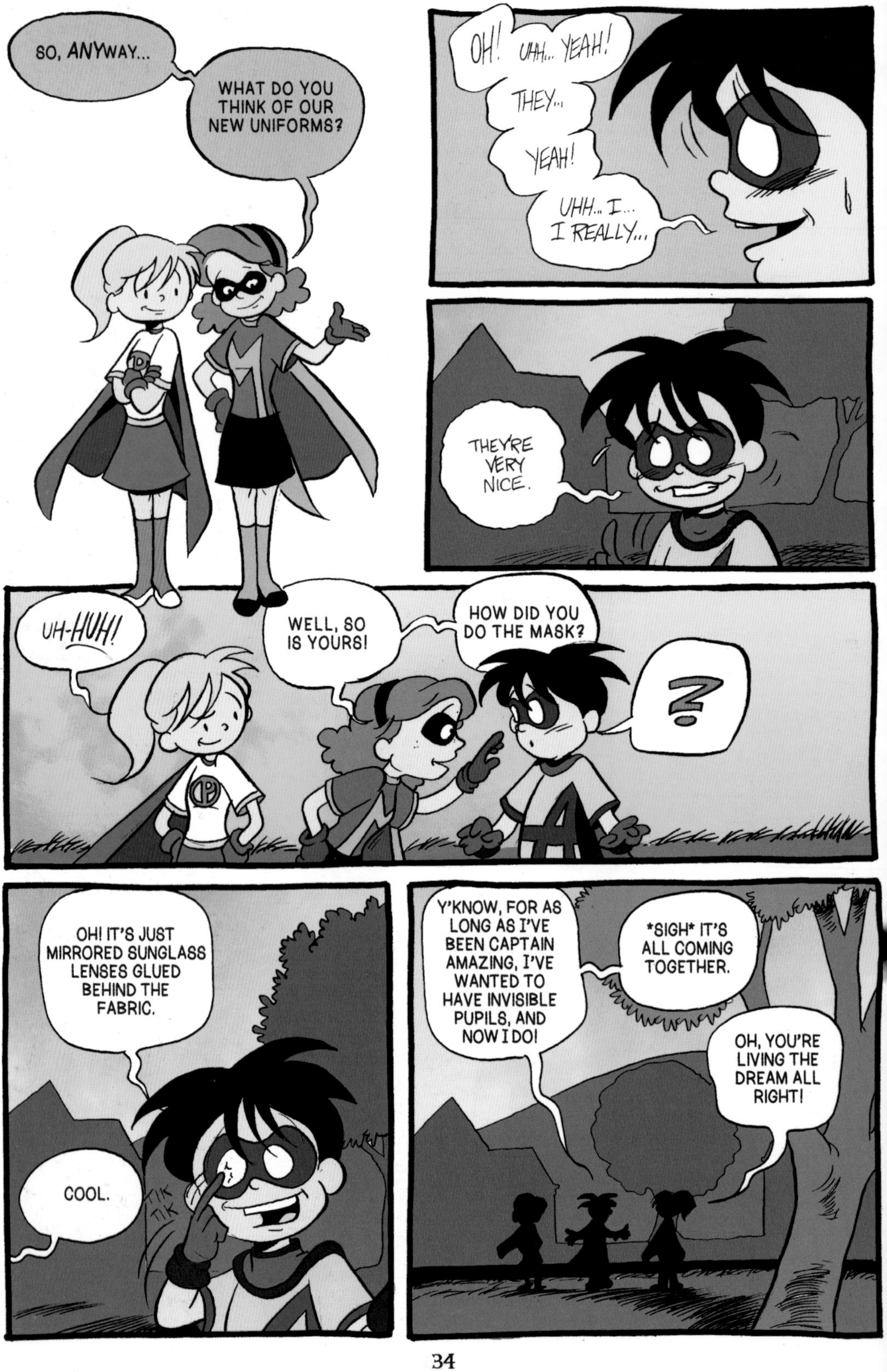
SO, ANYWAY...
WHAT DO YOU THINK OF OUR NEW UNIFORMS?
OH! UHH... YEAH!
THEY...
YEAH!
UHH... I... I REALLY...
THEY'RE VERY NICE.
UH-HUH!
WELL, SO IS YOURS!
HOW DID YOU DO THE MASK?
?
OH! IT'S JUST MIRRORED SUNGLASS LENSES GLUED BEHIND THE FABRIC.
TIK TIK
COOL.
Y'KNOW, FOR AS LONG AS I'VE BEEN CAPTAIN AMAZING, I'VE WANTED TO HAVE INVISIBLE PUPILS, AND NOW I DO!
SIGH IT'S ALL COMING TOGETHER.
OH, YOU'RE LIVING THE DREAM ALL RIGHT!

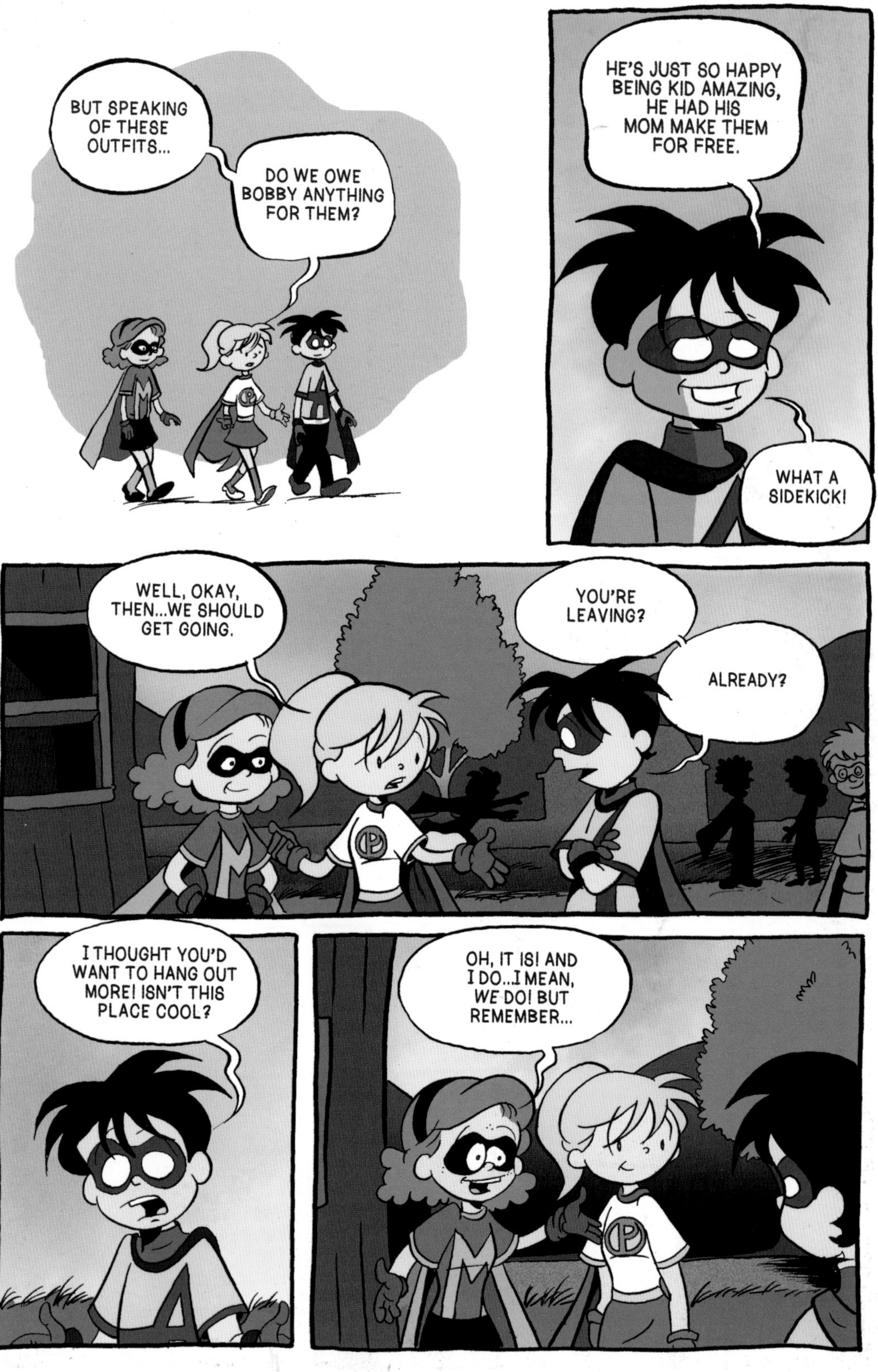
BUT SPEAKING OF THESE OUTFITS...
DO WE OWE BOBBY ANYTHING FOR THEM?
HE'S JUST SO HAPPY BEING KID AMAZING, HE HAD HIS MOM MAKE THEM FOR FREE.
WHAT A SIDEKICK!
WELL, OKAY, THEN...WE SHOULD GET GOING.
YOU'RE LEAVING?
ALREADY?
I THOUGHT YOU'D WANT TO HANG OUT MORE! ISN'T THIS PLACE COOL?
OH, IT IS! AND I DO...I MEAN, WE DO! BUT REMEMBER...

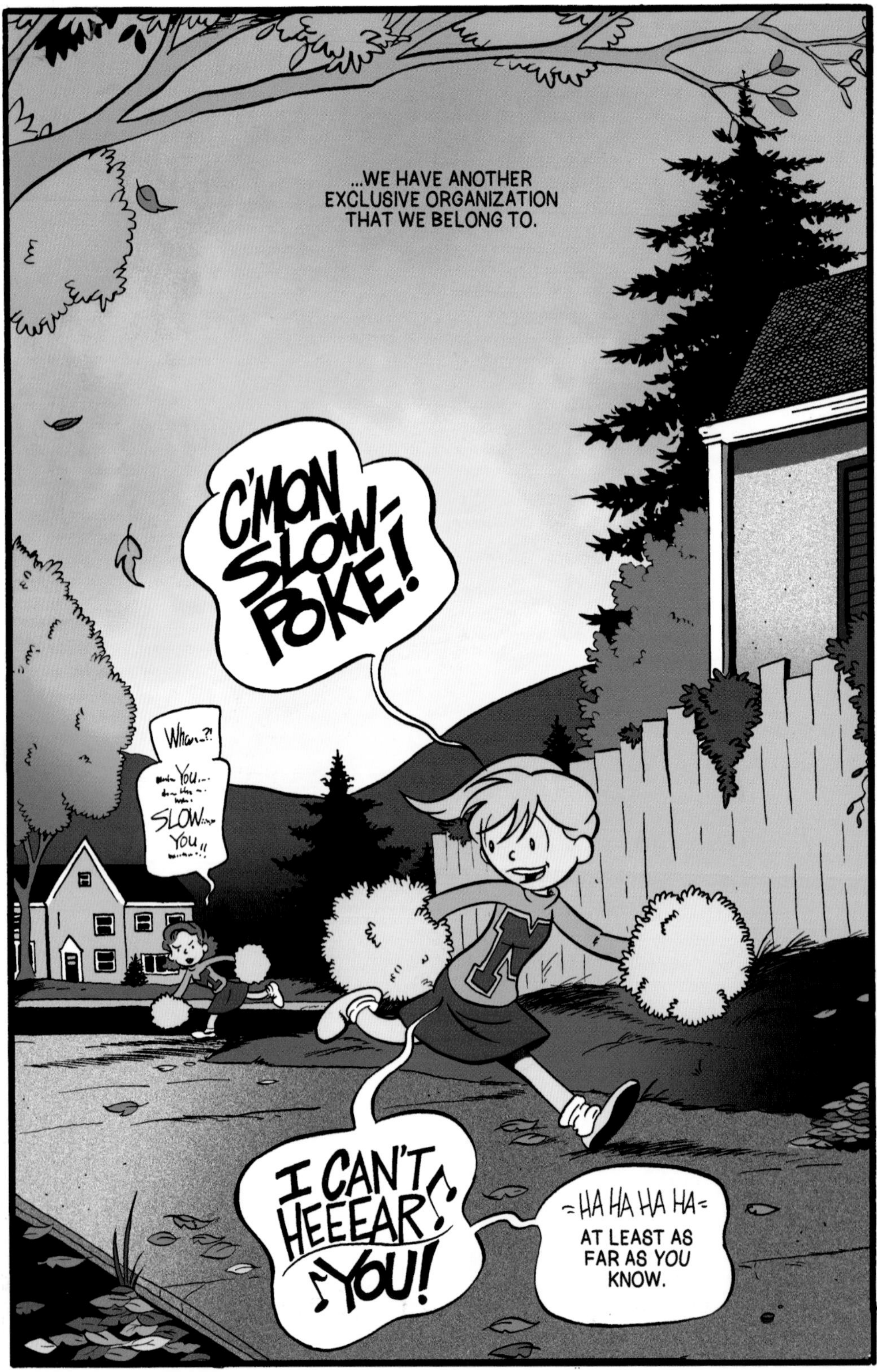
...WE HAVE ANOTHER EXCLUSIVE ORGANIZATION THAT WE BELONG TO.
C'MON SLOW-POKE!
Whaa...?!
YOU...
SLOW...
YOU!!
I CAN'T HEEEAR YOU!
=HA HA HA HA=
AT LEAST AS FAR AS YOU KNOW.

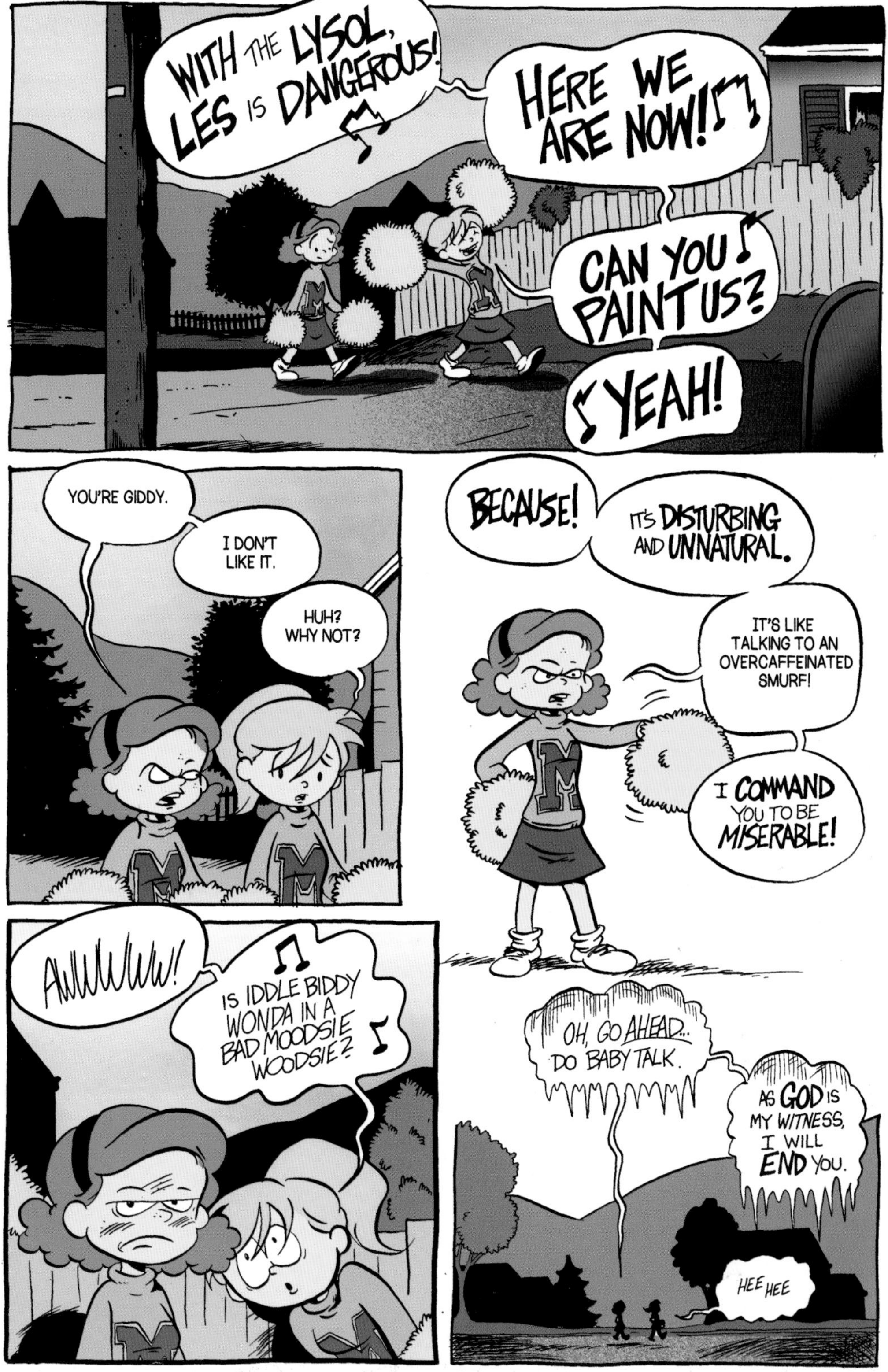
WITH THE LYSOL, LES IS DANGEROUS!
HERE WE ARE NOW!
CAN YOU PAINT US?
YEAH!
YOU'RE GIDDY.
I DON'T LIKE IT.
HUH? WHY NOT?
BECAUSE!
IT'S DISTURBING AND UNNATURAL.
IT'S LIKE TALKING TO AN OVERCAFFEINATED SMURF!
I COMMAND YOU TO BE MISERABLE!
AWWWWW!
IS IDDLE BIDDY WONDA IN A BAD MOODSIE WOODSIE?
OH, GO AHEAD... DO BABY TALK.
AS GOD IS MY WITNESS, I WILL END YOU.
HEE HEE

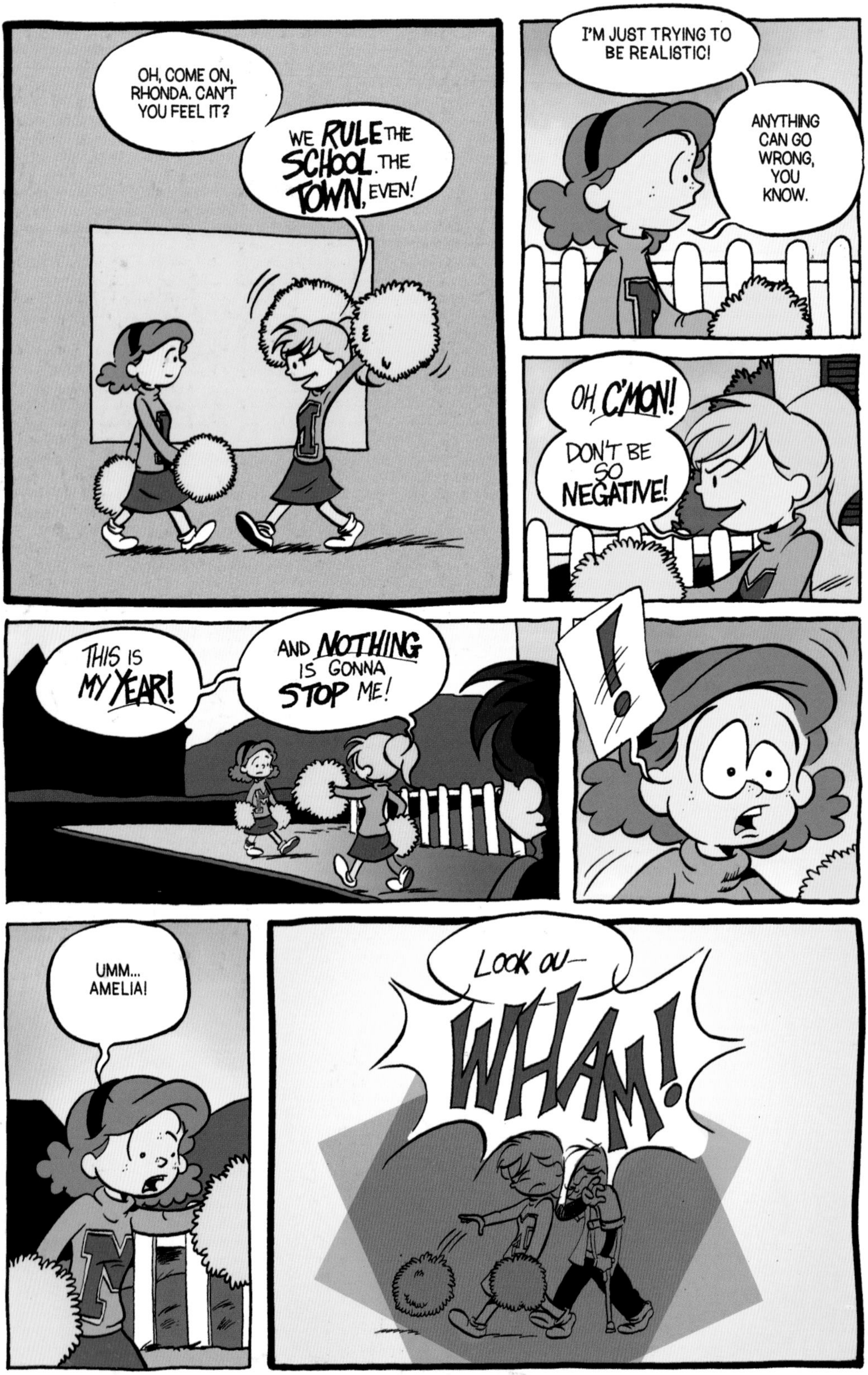
OH, COME ON, RHONDA. CAN'T YOU FEEL IT?
WE RULE THE SCHOOL. THE TOWN, EVEN!
I'M JUST TRYING TO BE REALISTIC!
ANYTHING CAN GO WRONG, YOU KNOW.
OH, C'MON!
DON'T BE SO NEGATIVE!
THIS IS MY YEAR!
AND NOTHING IS GONNA STOP ME!
!
UMM... AMELIA!
LOOK OU—
WHAM!

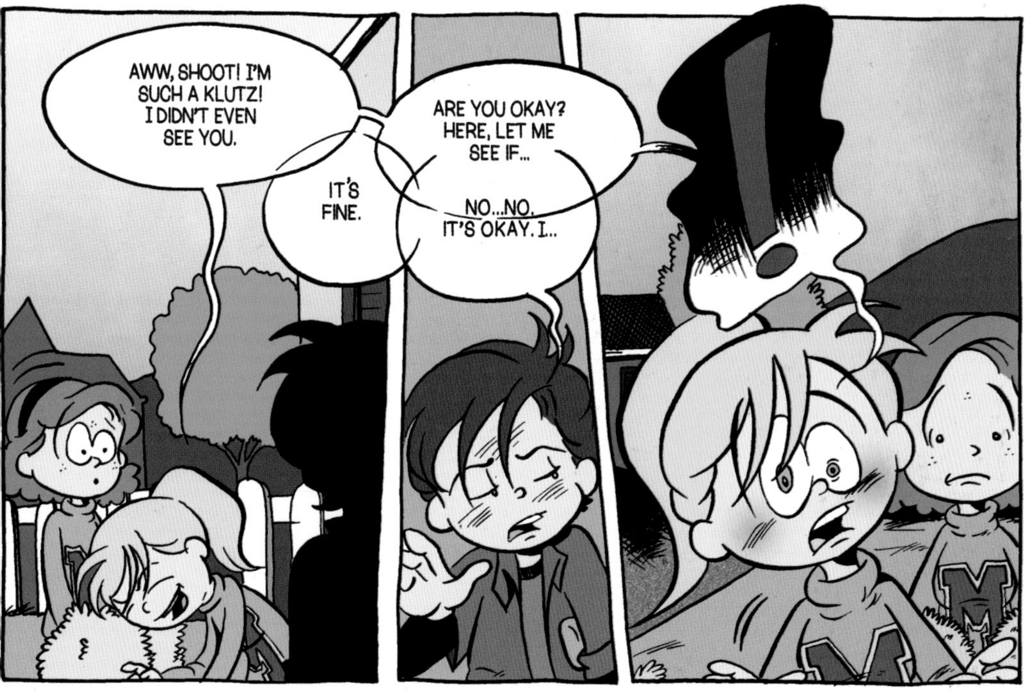

AWW, SHOOT! I'M SUCH A KLUTZ! I DIDN'T EVEN SEE YOU.
IT'S FINE.
ARE YOU OKAY? HERE, LET ME SEE IF...
NO...NO. IT'S OKAY. I...

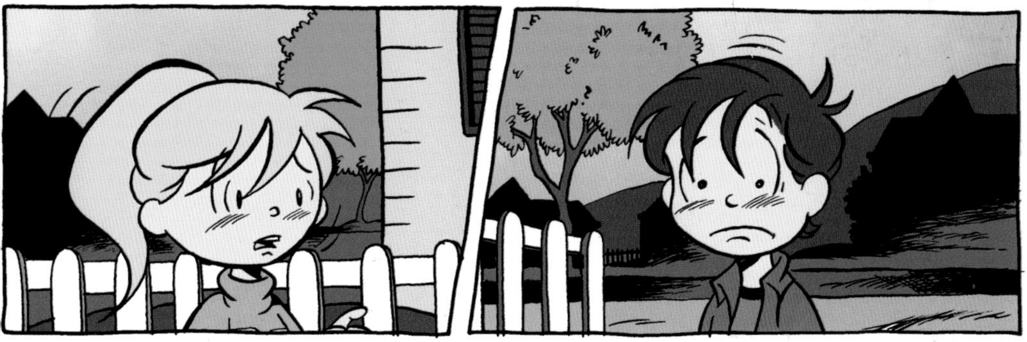

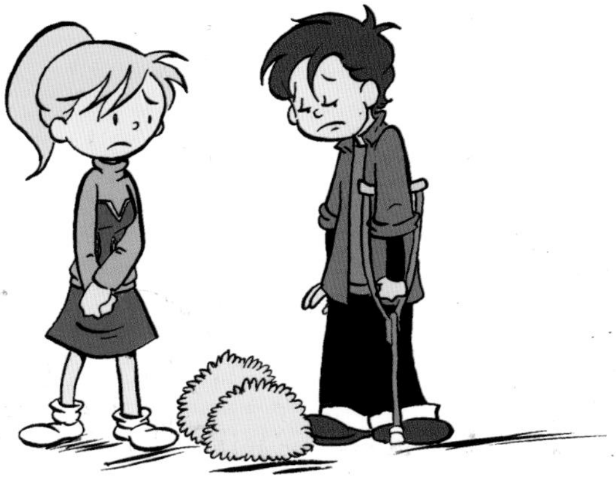

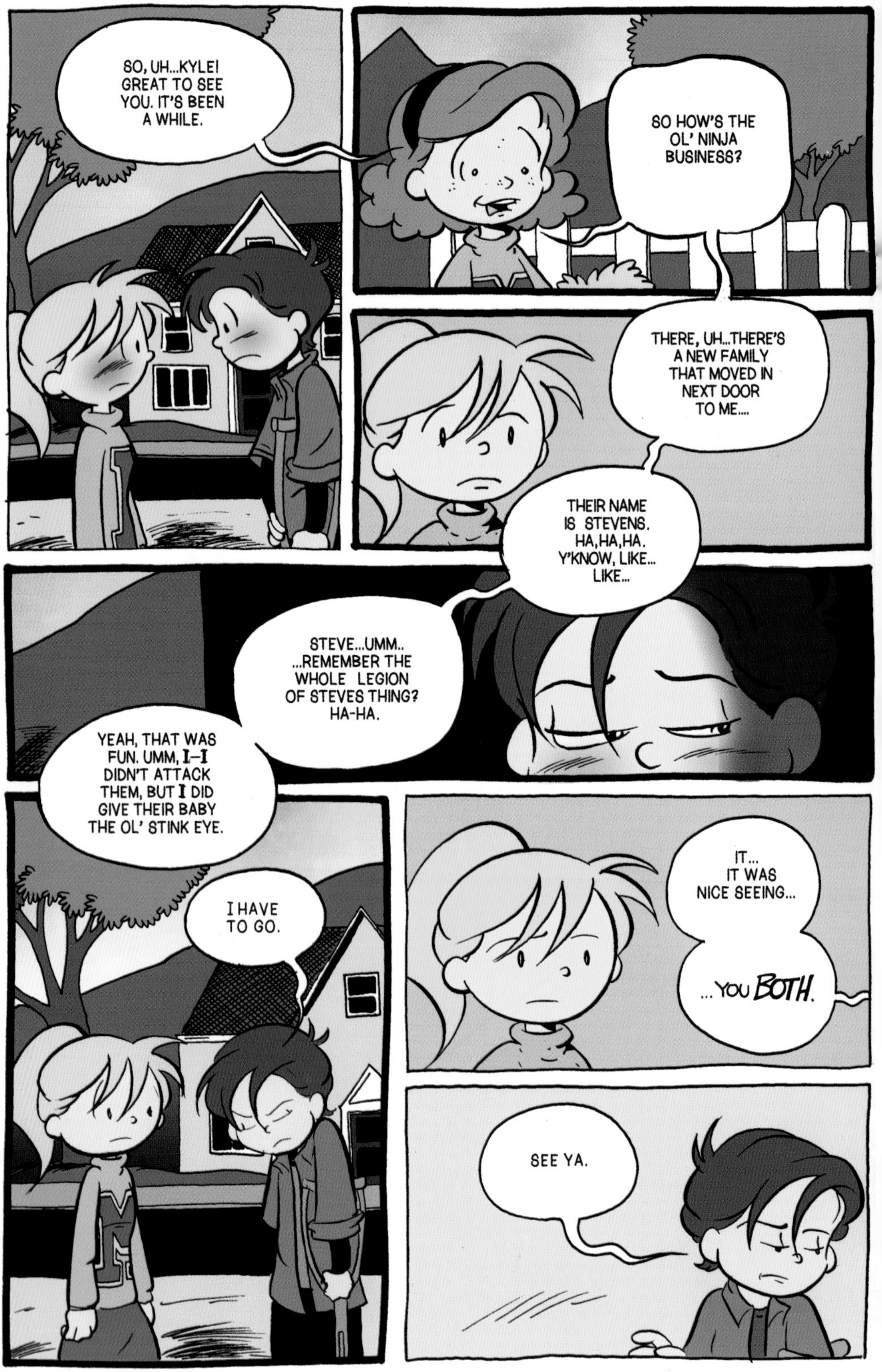
SO, UH...KYLE! GREAT TO SEE YOU. IT'S BEEN A WHILE.
SO HOW'S THE OL' NINJA BUSINESS?
THERE, UH...THERE'S A NEW FAMILY THAT MOVED IN NEXT DOOR TO ME....
THEIR NAME IS STEVENS. HA,HA,HA. Y'KNOW, LIKE... LIKE...
STEVE...UMM.. ...REMEMBER THE WHOLE LEGION OF STEVES THING? HA-HA.
YEAH, THAT WAS FUN. UMM, I—I DIDN'T ATTACK THEM, BUT I DID GIVE THEIR BABY THE OL' STINK EYE.
I HAVE TO GO.
IT... IT WAS NICE SEEING...
...YOU BOTH.
SEE YA.

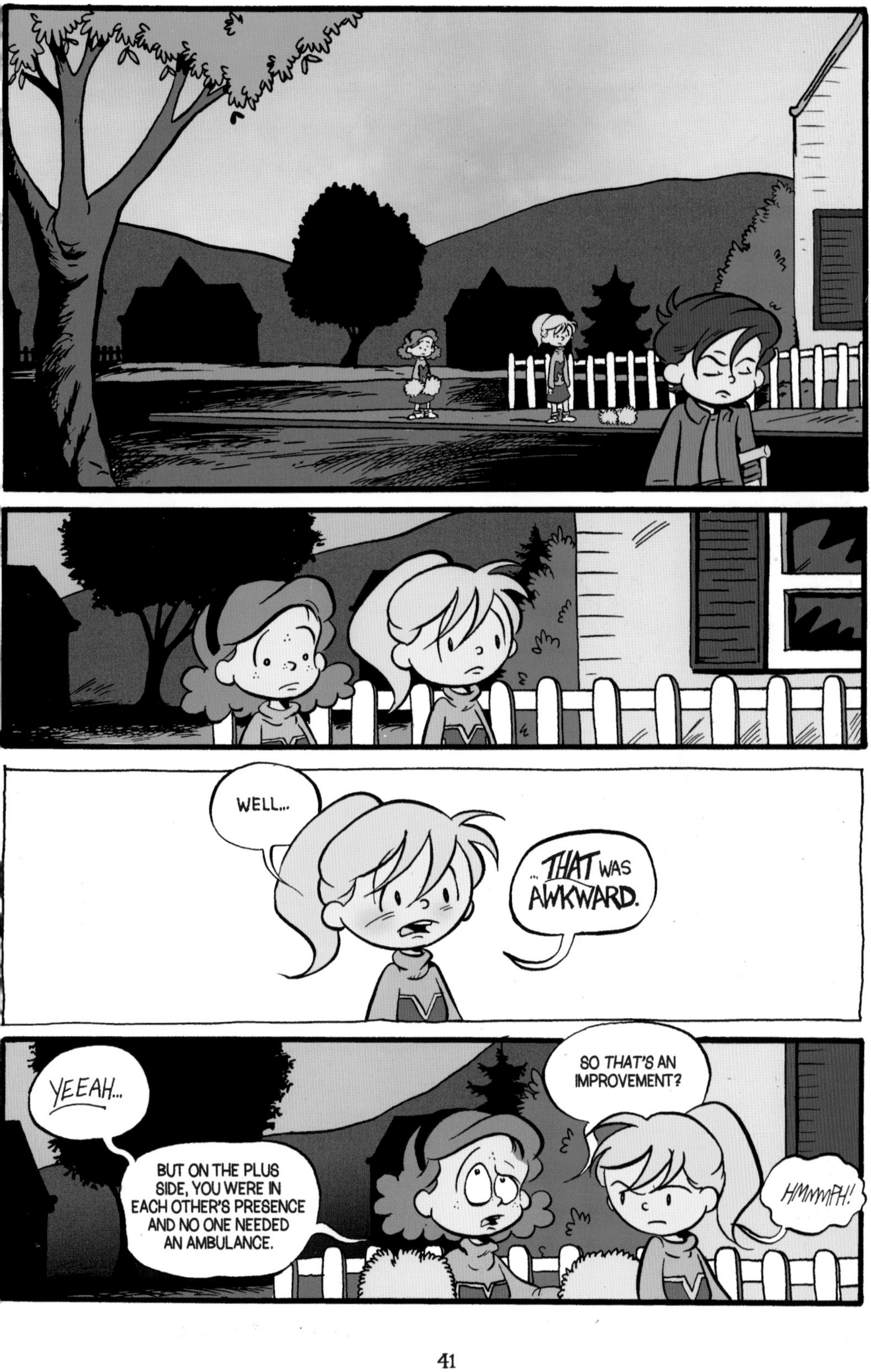
WELL...
...THAT WAS AWKWARD.
YEEAH...
BUT ON THE PLUS SIDE, YOU WERE IN EACH OTHER'S PRESENCE AND NO ONE NEEDED AN AMBULANCE.
SO THAT'S AN IMPROVEMENT?
HMMMPH!

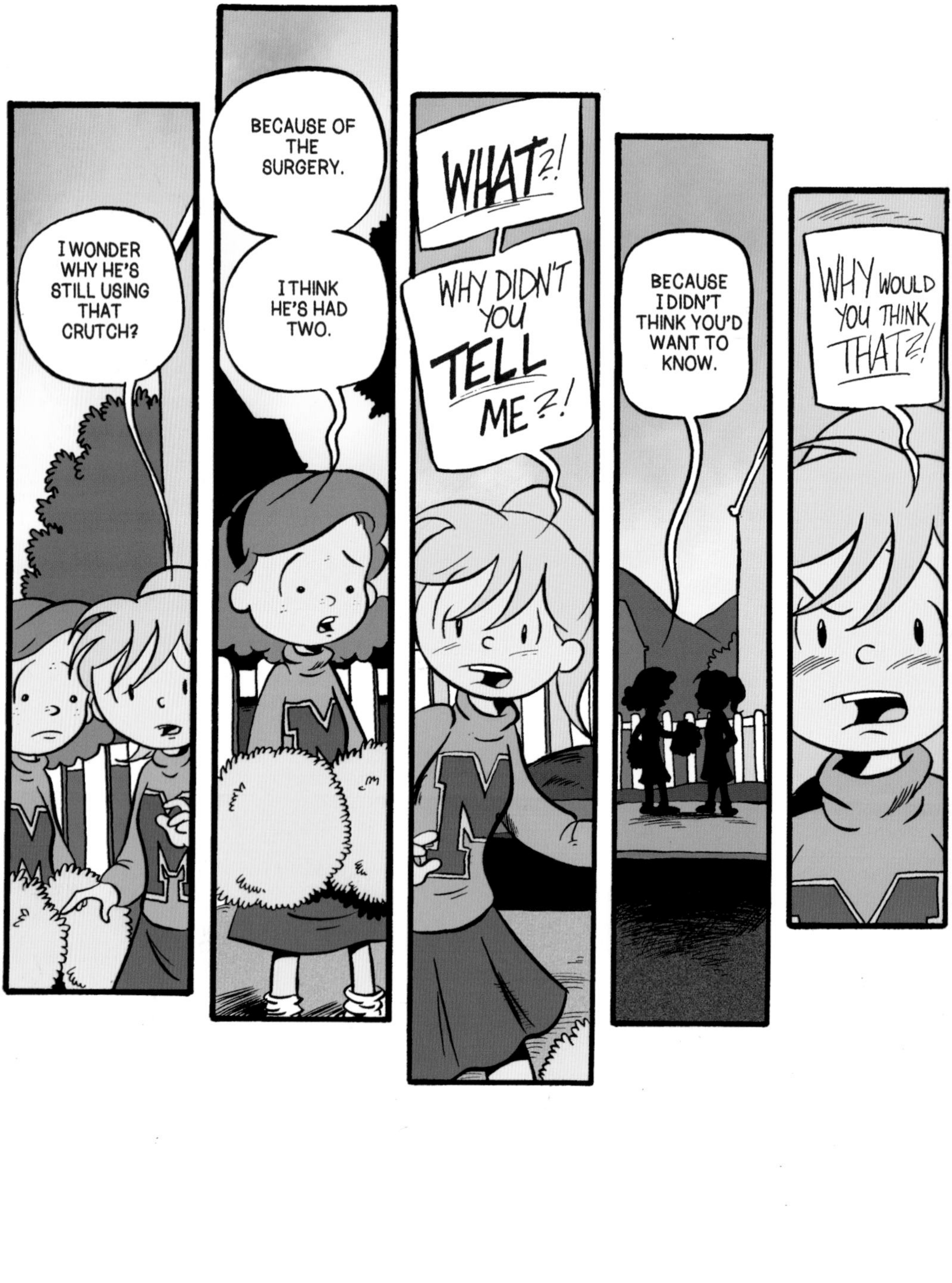
I WONDER WHY HE'S STILL USING THAT CRUTCH?
BECAUSE OF THE SURGERY.
I THINK HE'S HAD TWO.
WHAT?!
WHY DIDN'T YOU TELL ME?!
BECAUSE I DIDN'T THINK YOU'D WANT TO KNOW.
WHY WOULD YOU THINK THAT?!

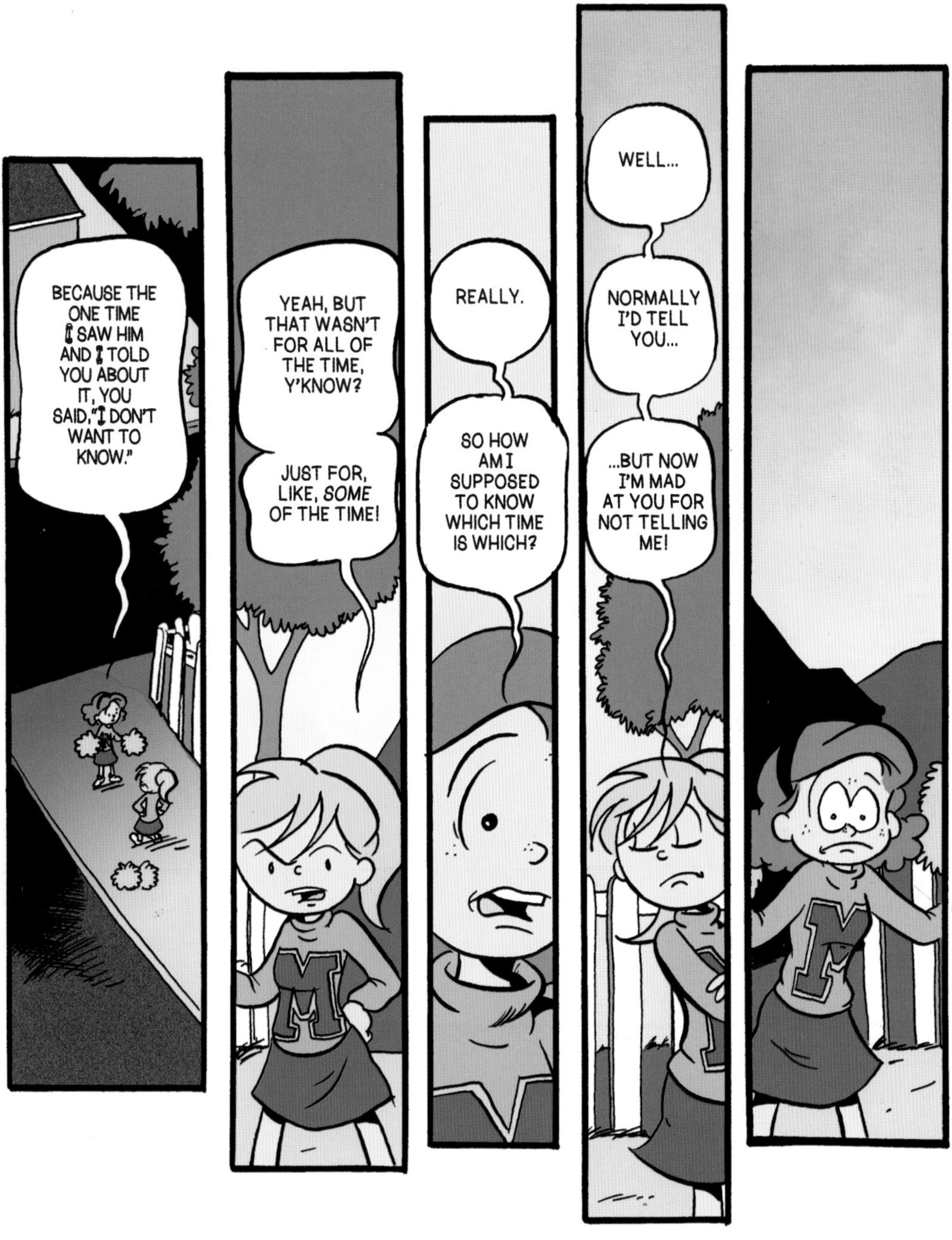

BECAUSE THE ONE TIME I SAW HIM AND I TOLD YOU ABOUT IT, YOU SAID, "I DON'T WANT TO KNOW."
YEAH, BUT THAT WASN'T FOR ALL OF THE TIME, Y'KNOW?
JUST FOR, LIKE, *SOME* OF THE TIME!
REALLY.
SO HOW AM I SUPPOSED TO KNOW WHICH TIME IS WHICH?
WELL...
NORMALLY I'D TELL YOU...
...BUT NOW I'M MAD AT YOU FOR NOT TELLING ME!

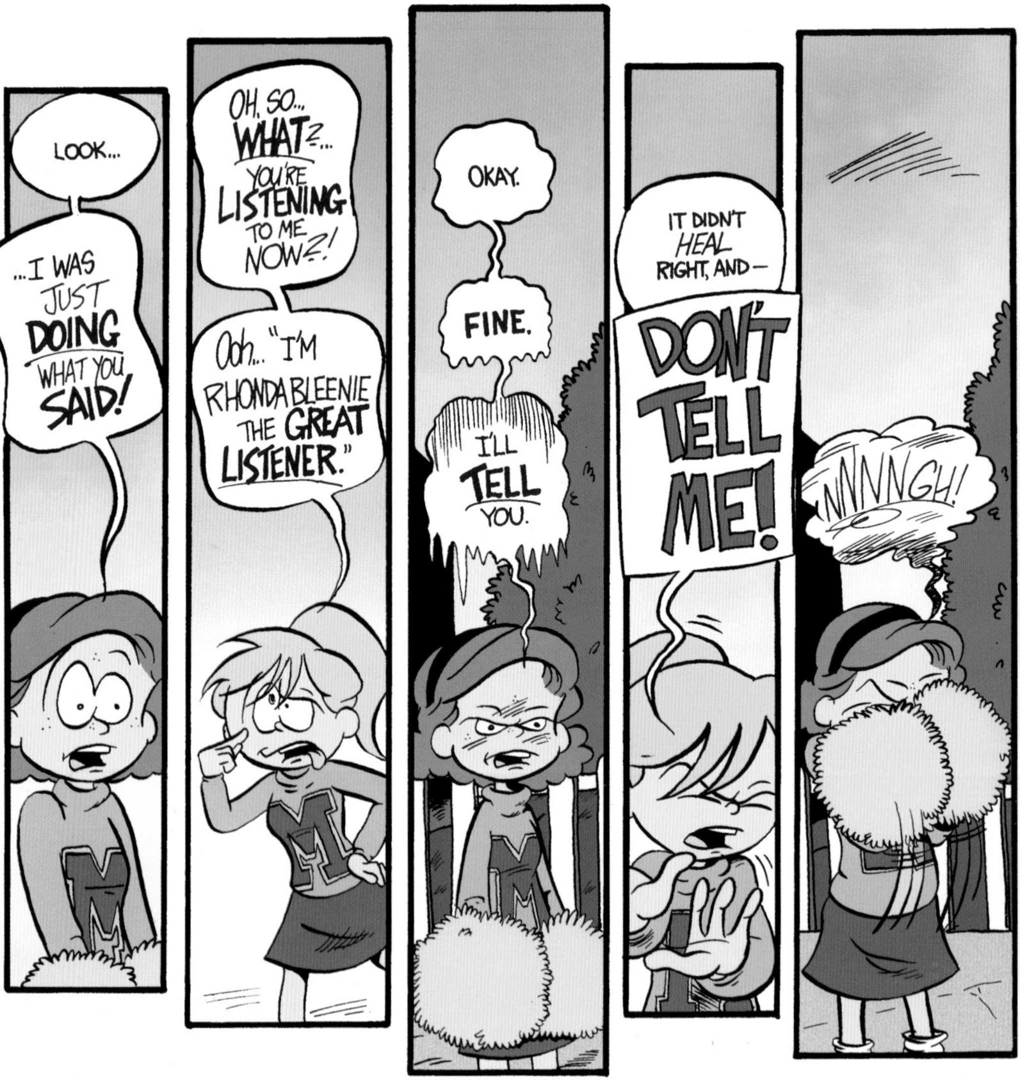
LOOK...
...I WAS JUST DOING WHAT YOU SAID!
OH, SO... WHAT?... YOU'RE LISTENING TO ME NOW?!
Ooh... "I'M RHONDA BLEENIE THE GREAT LISTENER."
OKAY.
FINE.
I'LL TELL YOU.
IT DIDN'T HEAL RIGHT, AND—
DON'T TELL ME!
NNNNGH!

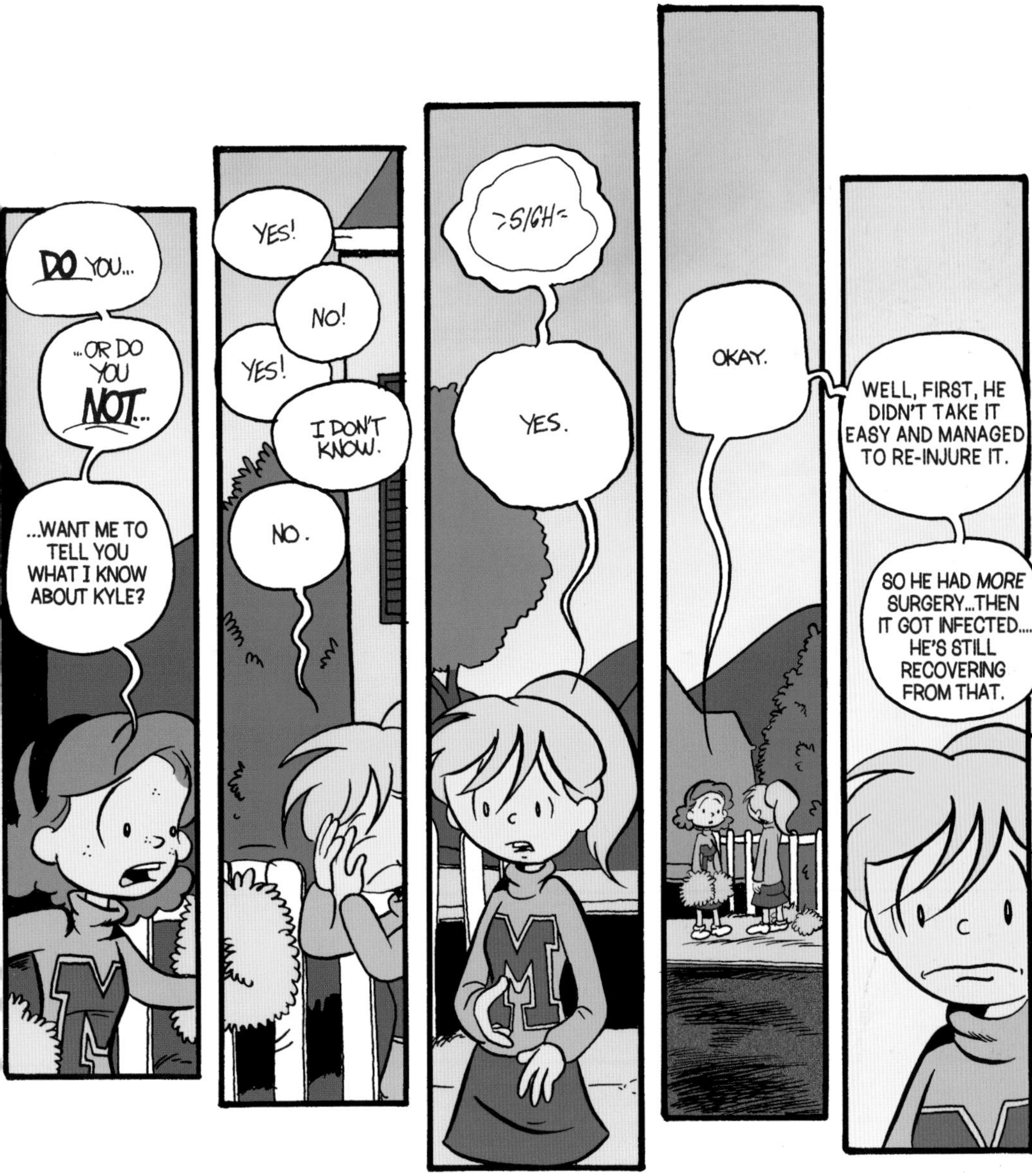
DO YOU...
...OR DO YOU NOT...
...WANT ME TO TELL YOU WHAT I KNOW ABOUT KYLE?
YES!
NO!
YES!
I DON'T KNOW.
NO.
~SIGH~
YES.
OKAY.
WELL, FIRST, HE DIDN'T TAKE IT EASY AND MANAGED TO RE-INJURE IT.
SO HE HAD MORE SURGERY...THEN IT GOT INFECTED.... HE'S STILL RECOVERING FROM THAT.

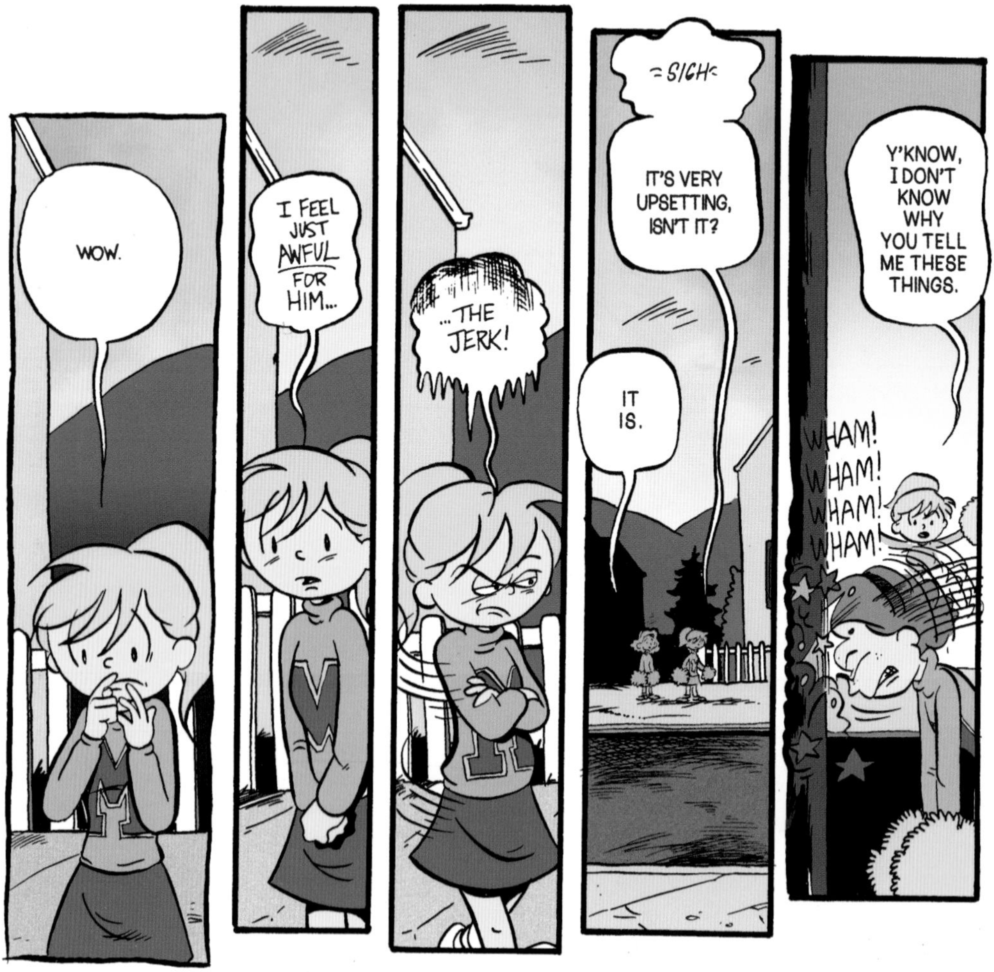
WOW.
I FEEL JUST AWFUL FOR HIM...
...THE JERK!
=SIGH=
IT'S VERY UPSETTING, ISN'T IT?
IT IS.
Y'KNOW, I DON'T KNOW WHY YOU TELL ME THESE THINGS.
WHAM! WHAM! WHAM! WHAM!

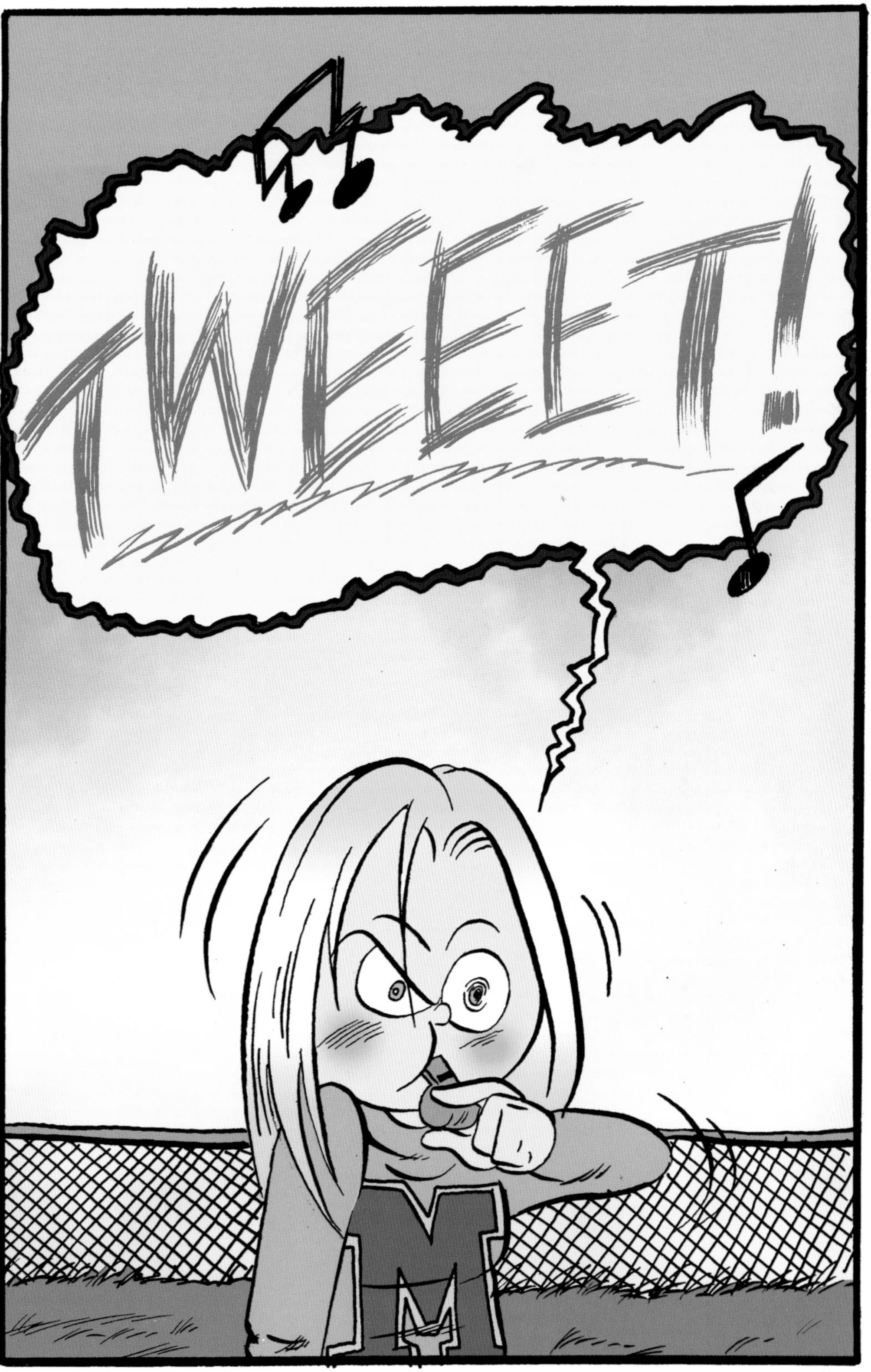
TWEET!

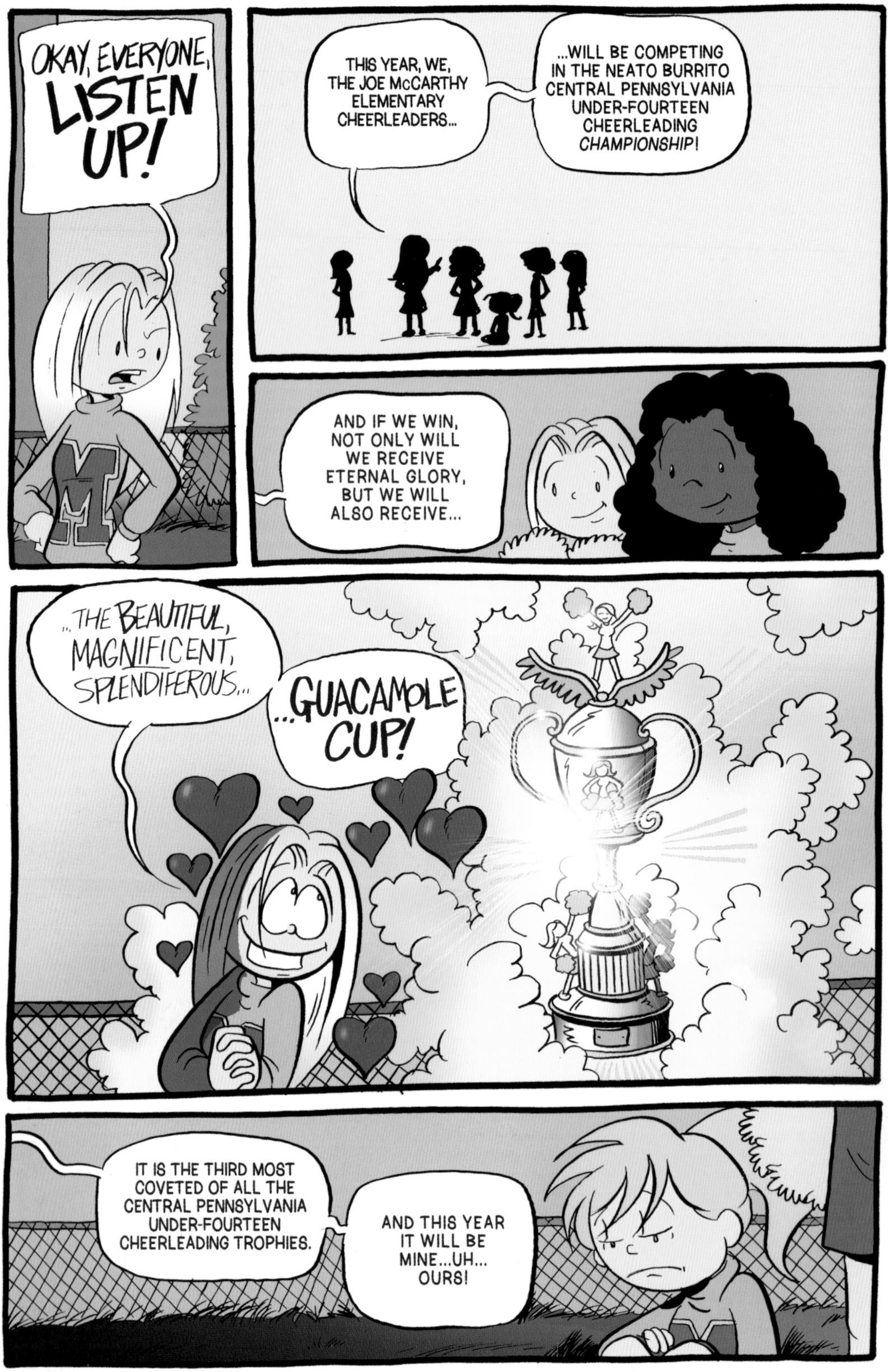
OKAY, EVERYONE, LISTEN UP!
THIS YEAR, WE, THE JOE McCARTHY ELEMENTARY CHEERLEADERS...
...WILL BE COMPETING IN THE NEATO BURRITO CENTRAL PENNSYLVANIA UNDER-FOURTEEN CHEERLEADING *CHAMPIONSHIP*!
AND IF WE WIN, NOT ONLY WILL WE RECEIVE ETERNAL GLORY, BUT WE WILL ALSO RECEIVE...
...THE BEAUTIFUL, MAGNIFICENT, SPLENDIFEROUS...
...GUACAMOLE CUP!
IT IS THE THIRD MOST COVETED OF ALL THE CENTRAL PENNSYLVANIA UNDER-FOURTEEN CHEERLEADING TROPHIES.
AND THIS YEAR IT WILL BE MINE...UH... OURS!

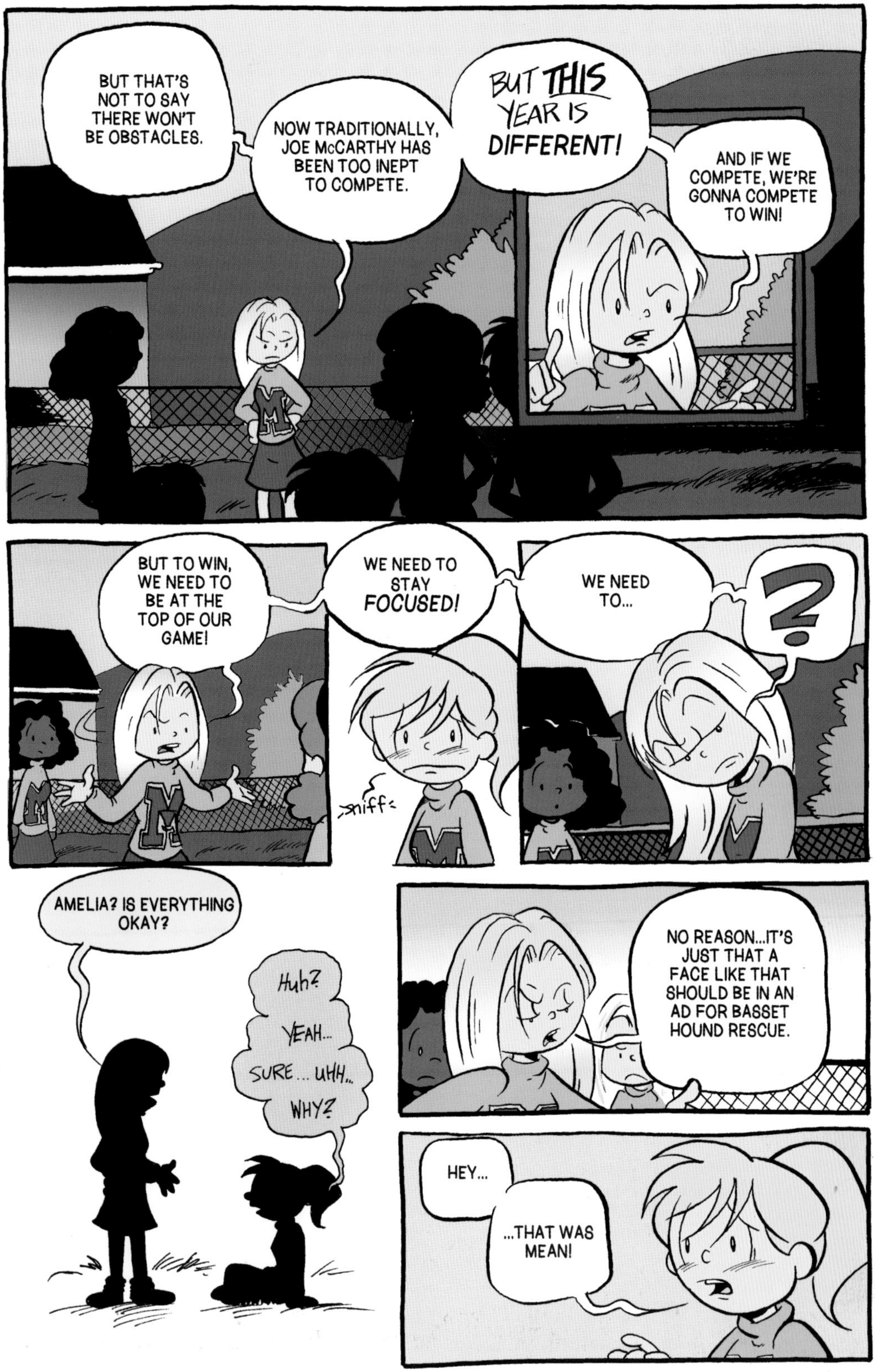
BUT THAT'S NOT TO SAY THERE WON'T BE OBSTACLES.
NOW TRADITIONALLY, JOE McCARTHY HAS BEEN TOO INEPT TO COMPETE.
BUT THIS YEAR IS DIFFERENT!
AND IF WE COMPETE, WE'RE GONNA COMPETE TO WIN!
BUT TO WIN, WE NEED TO BE AT THE TOP OF OUR GAME!
WE NEED TO STAY FOCUSED!
sniff
WE NEED TO...
?
AMELIA? IS EVERYTHING OKAY?
Huh? YEAH... SURE... UHH... WHY?
NO REASON...IT'S JUST THAT A FACE LIKE THAT SHOULD BE IN AN AD FOR BASSET HOUND RESCUE.
HEY...
...THAT WAS MEAN!

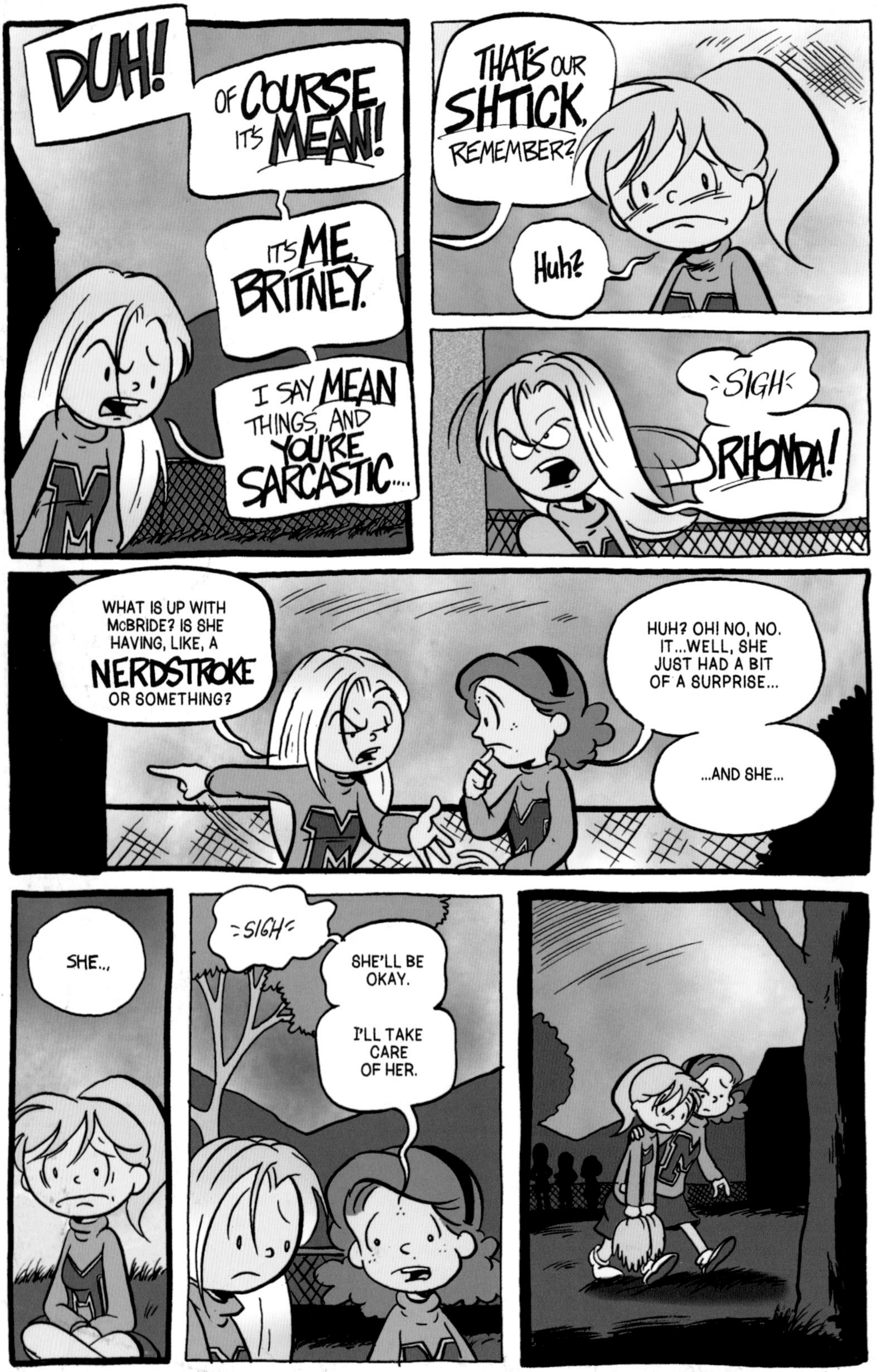

DUH!
OF COURSE IT'S MEAN!
IT'S ME, BRITNEY.
I SAY MEAN THINGS, AND YOU'RE SARCASTIC....
THAT'S OUR SHTICK, REMEMBER?
Huh?
SIGH
RHONDA!
WHAT IS UP WITH McBRIDE? IS SHE HAVING, LIKE, A NERDSTROKE OR SOMETHING?
HUH? OH! NO, NO. IT...WELL, SHE JUST HAD A BIT OF A SURPRISE...
...AND SHE...
SHE...,
SIGH
SHE'LL BE OKAY.
I'LL TAKE CARE OF HER.

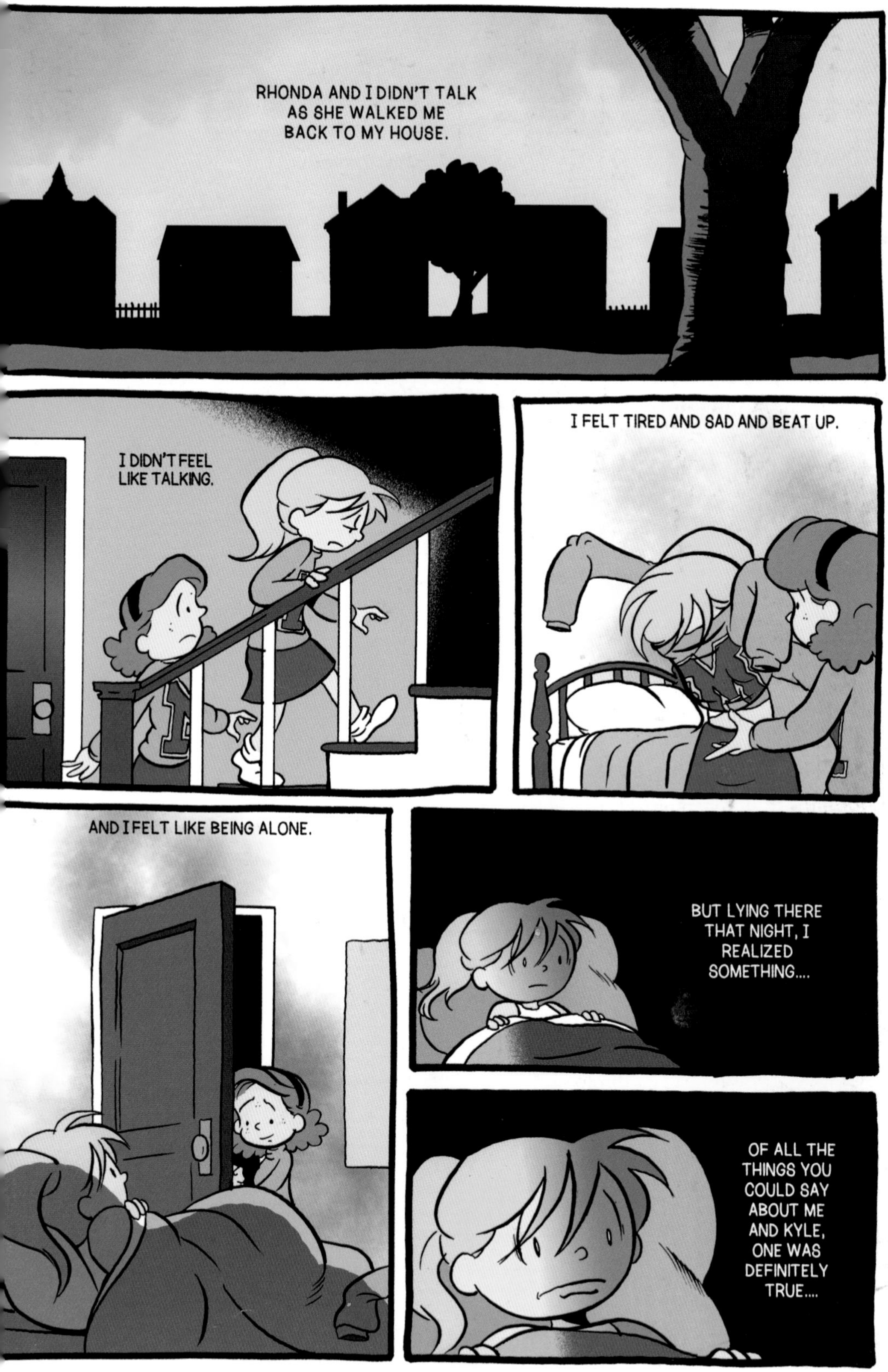
RHONDA AND I DIDN'T TALK AS SHE WALKED ME BACK TO MY HOUSE.
I DIDN'T FEEL LIKE TALKING.
I FELT TIRED AND SAD AND BEAT UP.
AND I FELT LIKE BEING ALONE.
BUT LYING THERE THAT NIGHT, I REALIZED SOMETHING....
OF ALL THE THINGS YOU COULD SAY ABOUT ME AND KYLE, ONE WAS DEFINITELY TRUE....

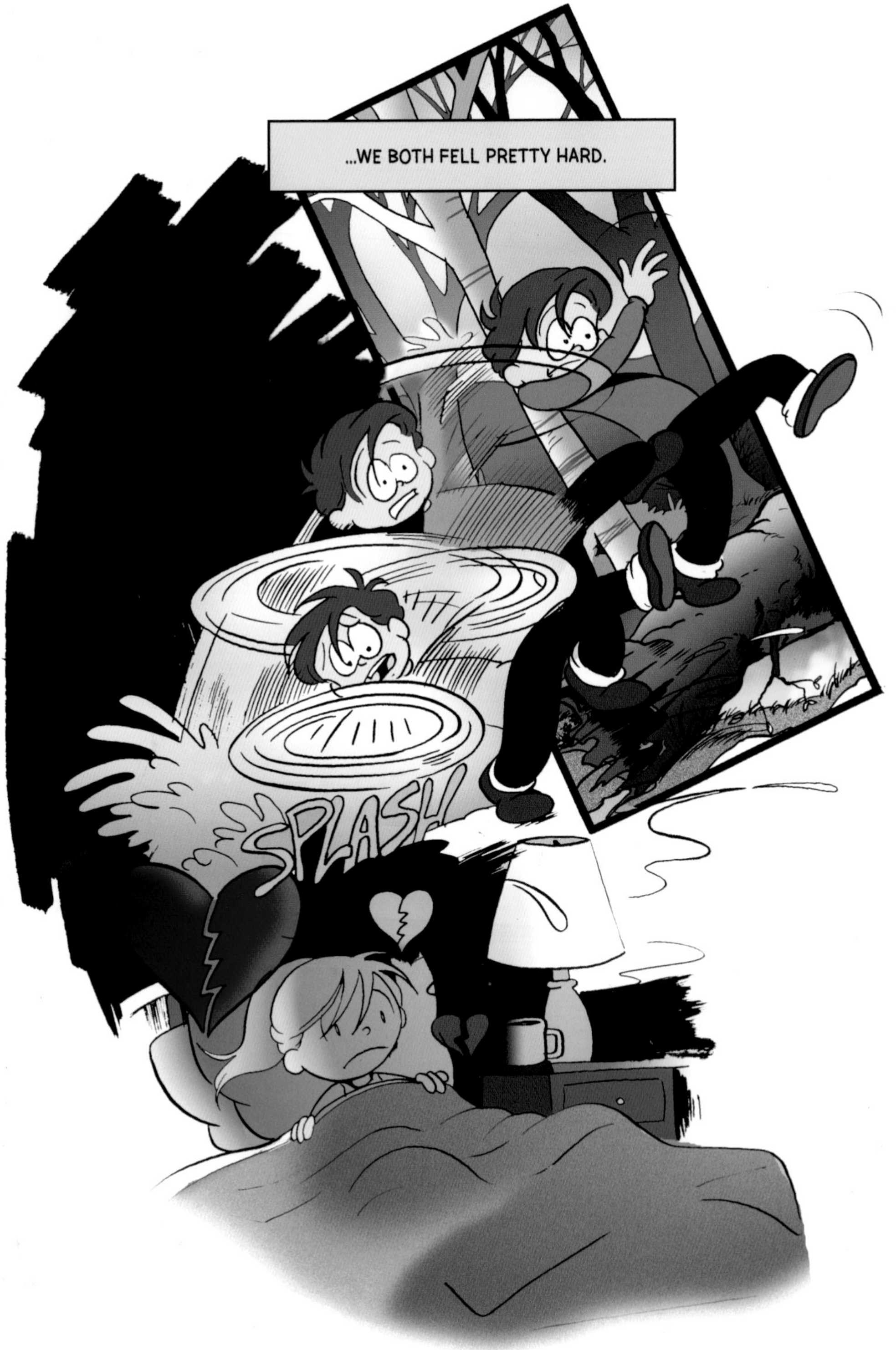
...WE BOTH FELL PRETTY HARD.
SPLASH

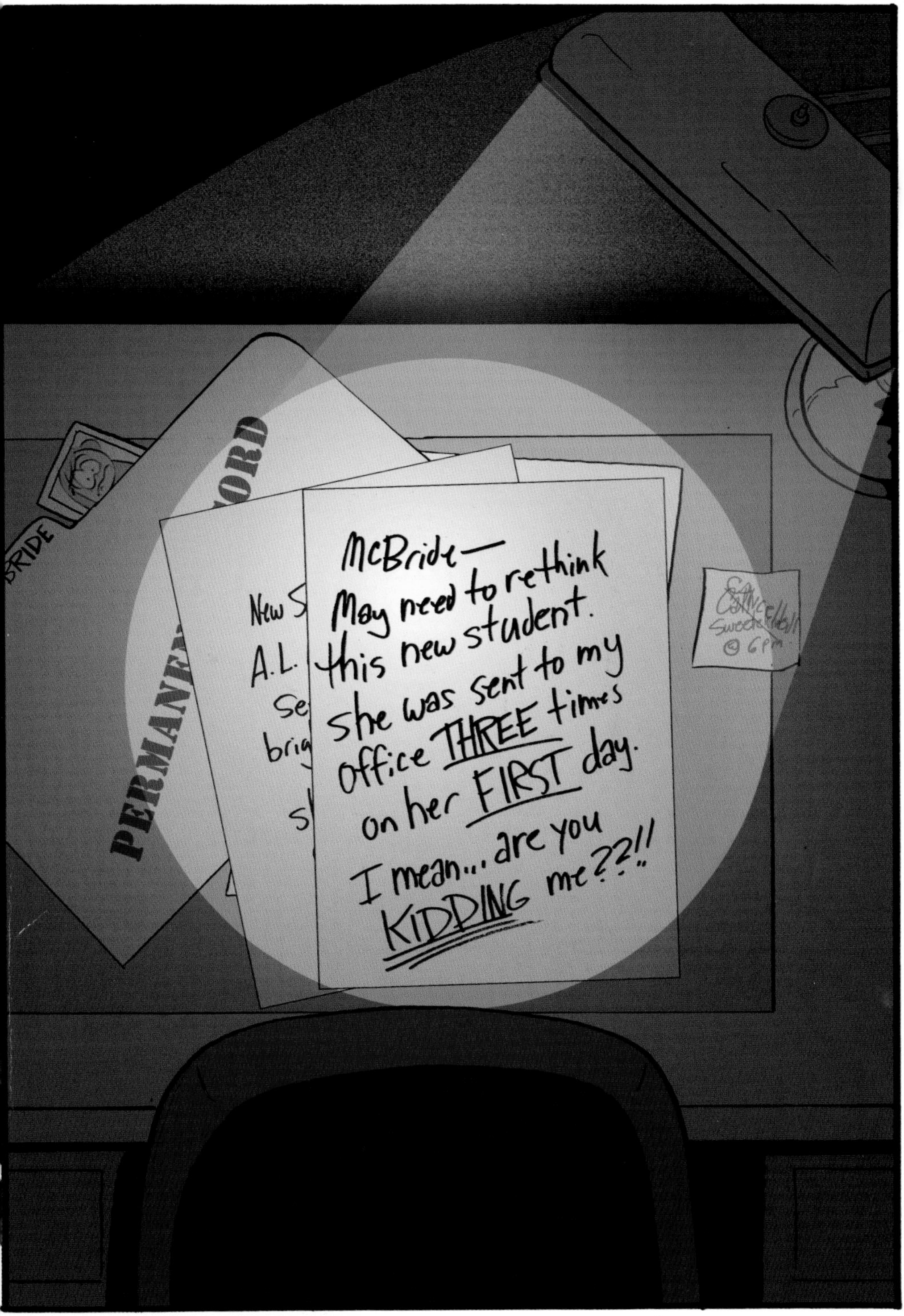
McBride—
May need to rethink
this new student.
she was sent to my
office THREE times
on her FIRST day.
I mean... are you
KIDDING me??!!

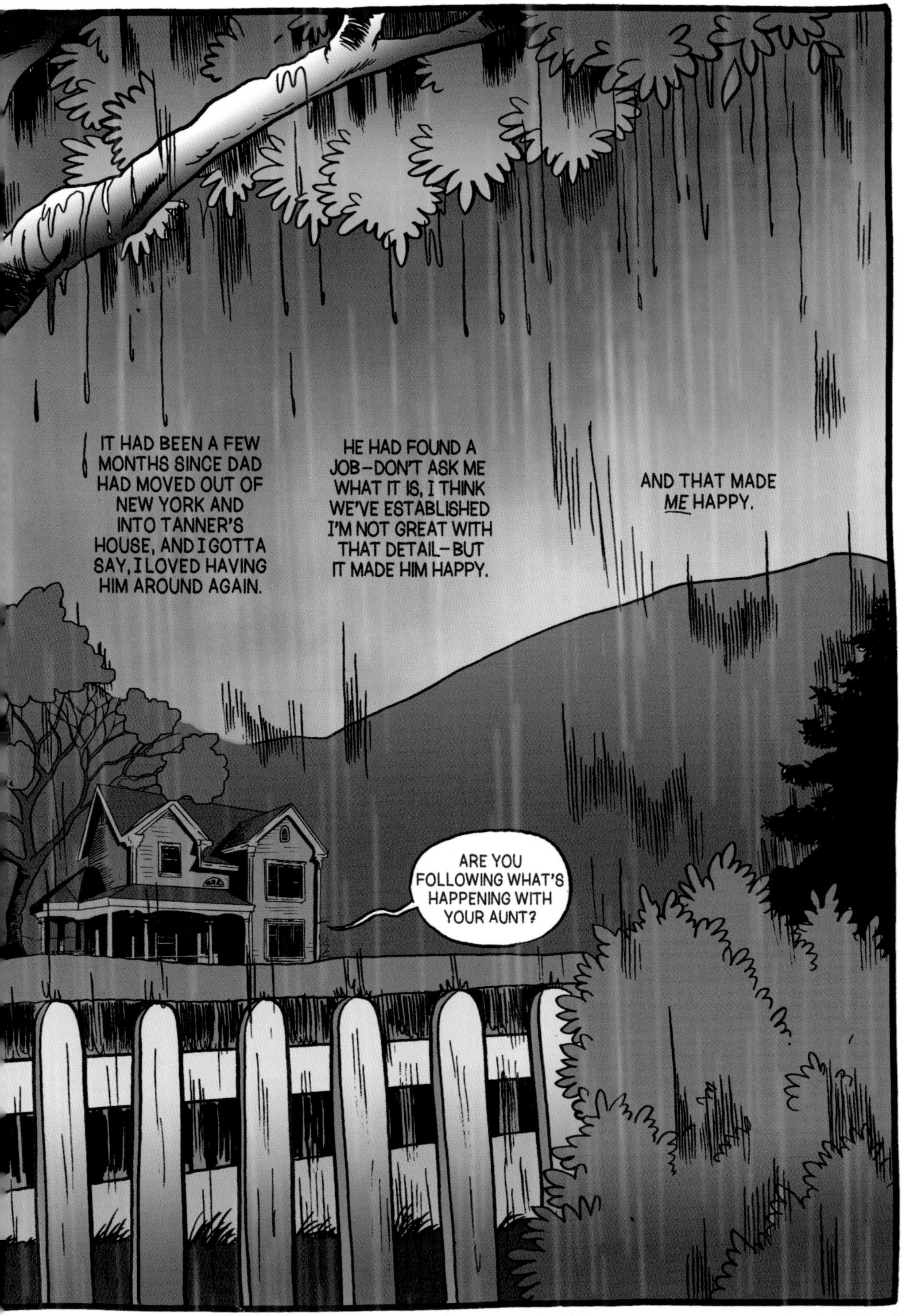
IT HAD BEEN A FEW MONTHS SINCE DAD HAD MOVED OUT OF NEW YORK AND INTO TANNER'S HOUSE, AND I GOTTA SAY, I LOVED HAVING HIM AROUND AGAIN.
HE HAD FOUND A JOB—DON'T ASK ME WHAT IT IS, I THINK WE'VE ESTABLISHED I'M NOT GREAT WITH THAT DETAIL—BUT IT MADE HIM HAPPY.
AND THAT MADE ME HAPPY.
ARE YOU FOLLOWING WHAT'S HAPPENING WITH YOUR AUNT?

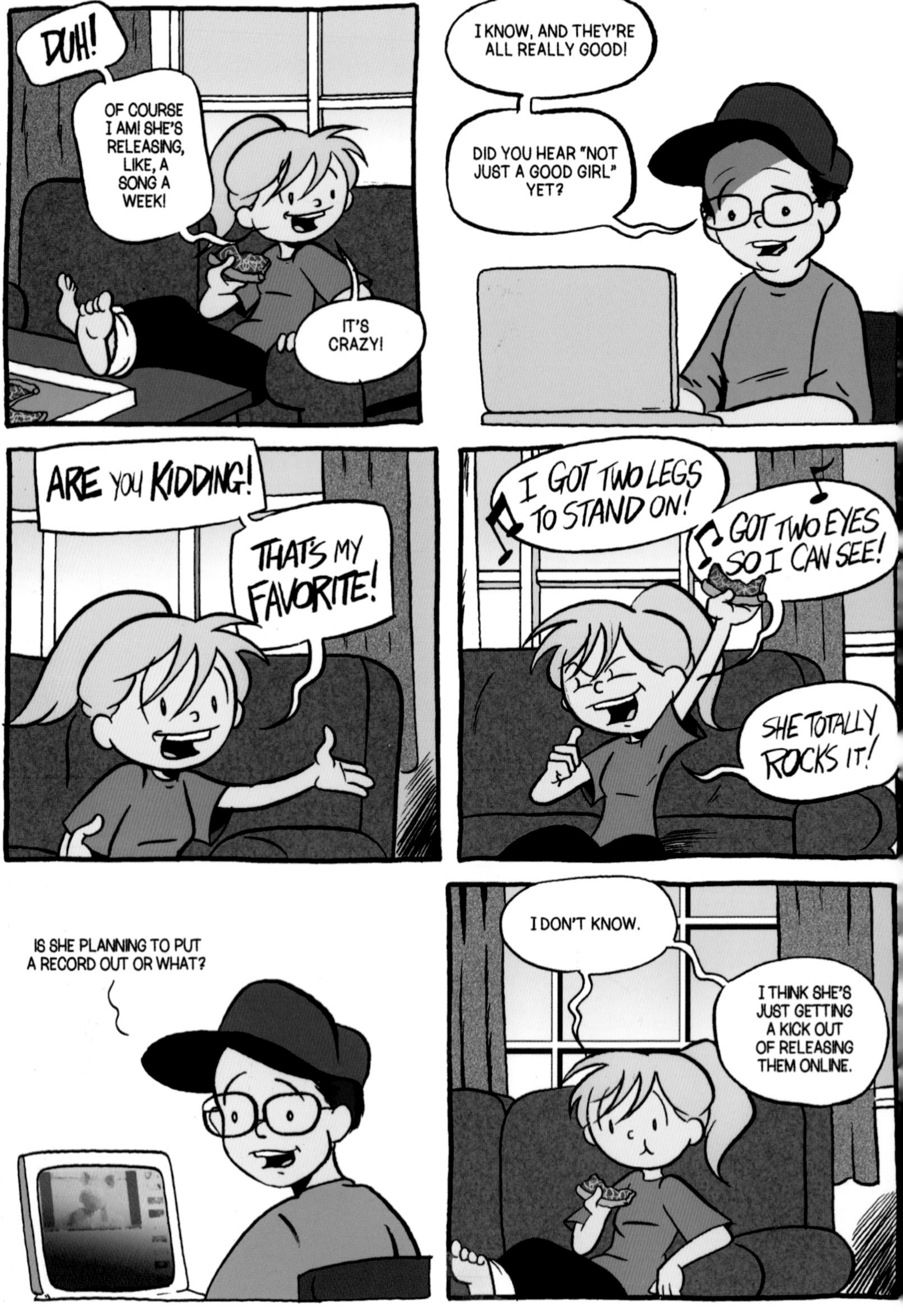
DUH!
OF COURSE I AM! SHE'S RELEASING, LIKE, A SONG A WEEK!
IT'S CRAZY!
I KNOW, AND THEY'RE ALL REALLY GOOD!
DID YOU HEAR "NOT JUST A GOOD GIRL" YET?
ARE YOU KIDDING!
THAT'S MY FAVORITE!
I GOT TWO LEGS TO STAND ON!
GOT TWO EYES SO I CAN SEE!
SHE TOTALLY ROCKS IT!
IS SHE PLANNING TO PUT A RECORD OUT OR WHAT?
I DON'T KNOW.
I THINK SHE'S JUST GETTING A KICK OUT OF RELEASING THEM ONLINE.

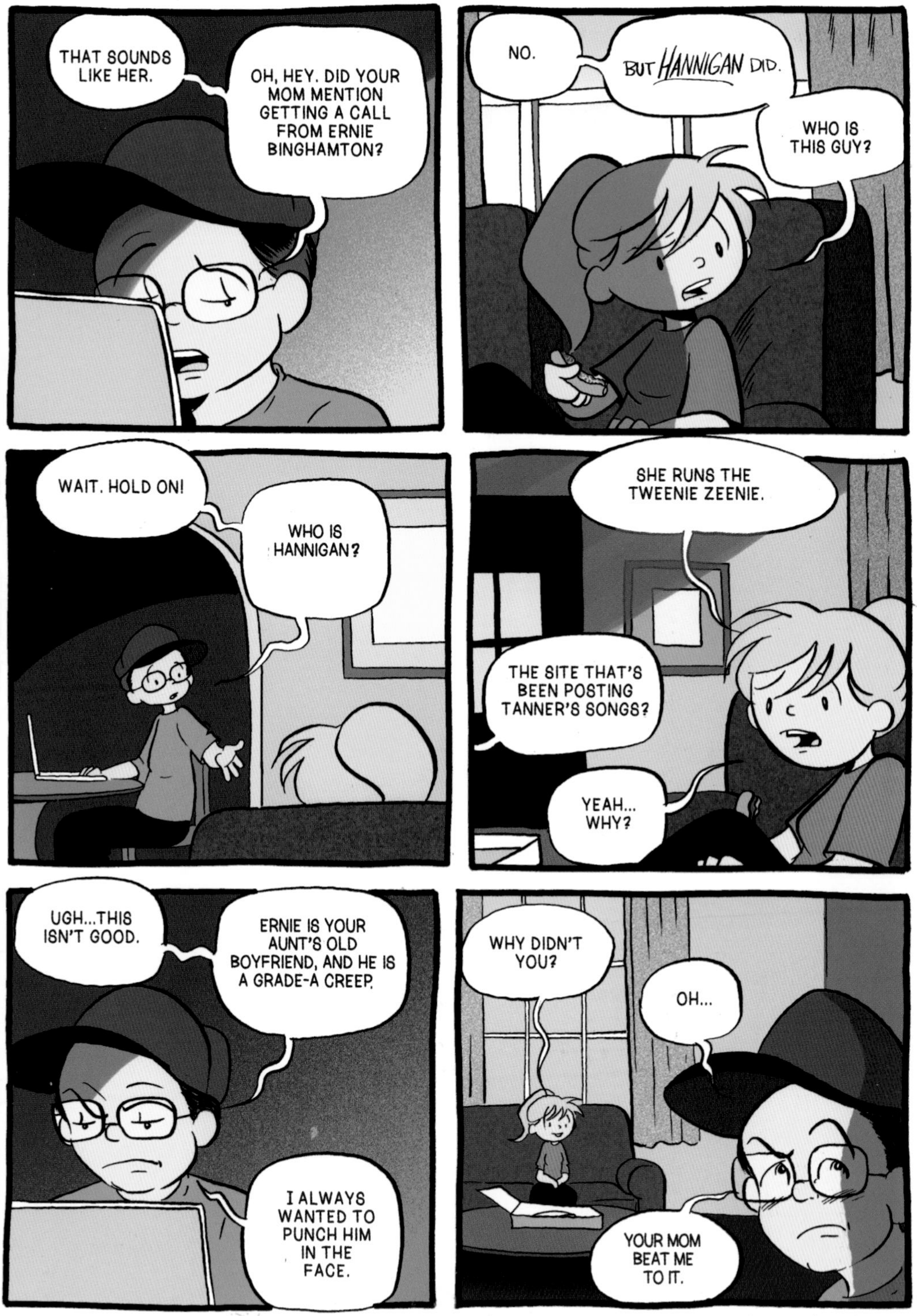
THAT SOUNDS LIKE HER.
OH, HEY. DID YOUR MOM MENTION GETTING A CALL FROM ERNIE BINGHAMTON?
NO.
BUT HANNIGAN DID.
WHO IS THIS GUY?
WAIT. HOLD ON!
WHO IS HANNIGAN?
SHE RUNS THE TWEENIE ZEENIE.
THE SITE THAT'S BEEN POSTING TANNER'S SONGS?
YEAH... WHY?
UGH...THIS ISN'T GOOD.
ERNIE IS YOUR AUNT'S OLD BOYFRIEND, AND HE IS A GRADE-A CREEP.
I ALWAYS WANTED TO PUNCH HIM IN THE FACE.
WHY DIDN'T YOU?
OH...
YOUR MOM BEAT ME TO IT.

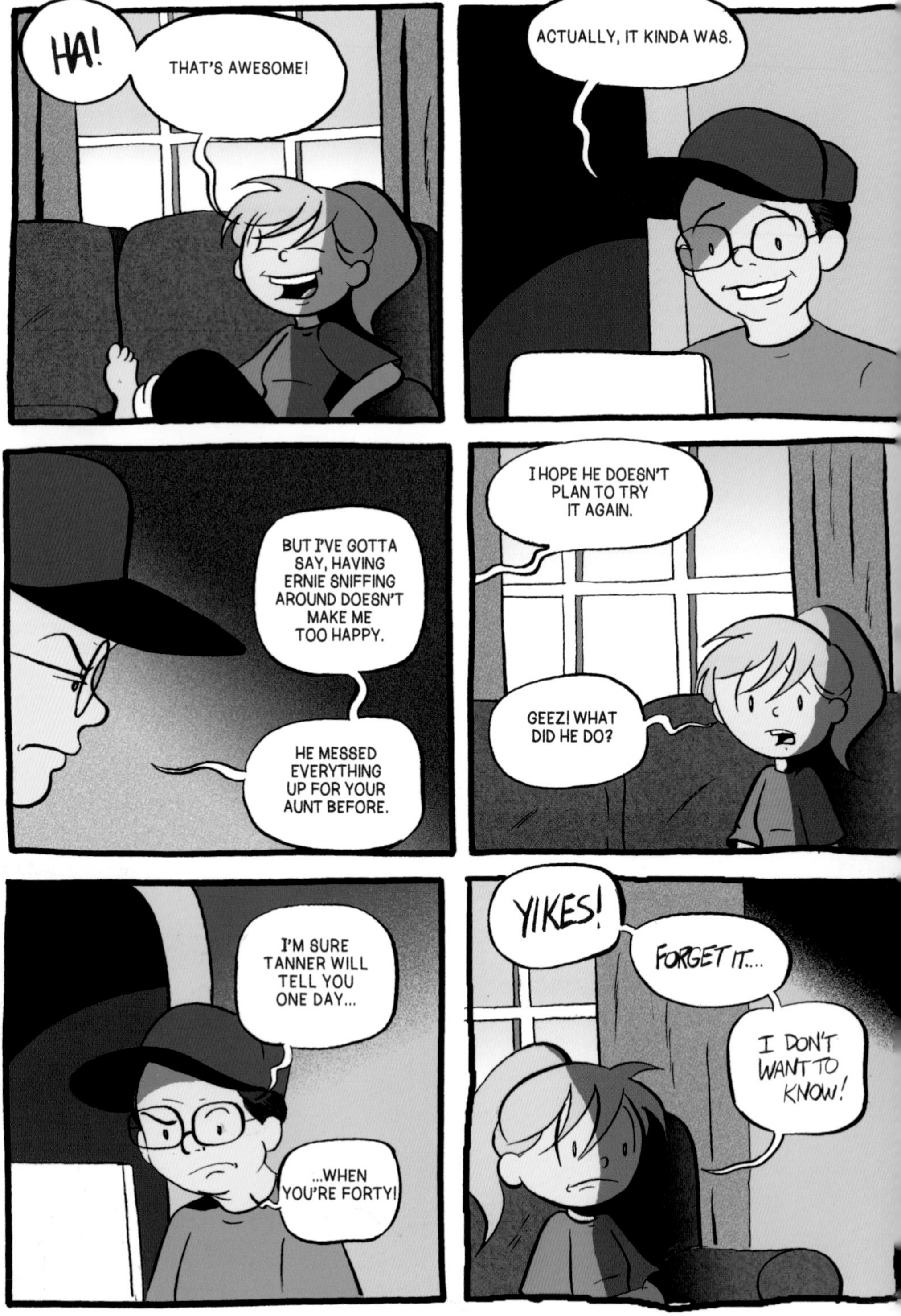
HA!
THAT'S AWESOME!
ACTUALLY, IT KINDA WAS.
BUT I'VE GOTTA SAY, HAVING ERNIE SNIFFING AROUND DOESN'T MAKE ME TOO HAPPY.
HE MESSED EVERYTHING UP FOR YOUR AUNT BEFORE.
I HOPE HE DOESN'T PLAN TO TRY IT AGAIN.
GEEZ! WHAT DID HE DO?
I'M SURE TANNER WILL TELL YOU ONE DAY...
...WHEN YOU'RE FORTY!
YIKES!
FORGET IT....
I DON'T WANT TO KNOW!

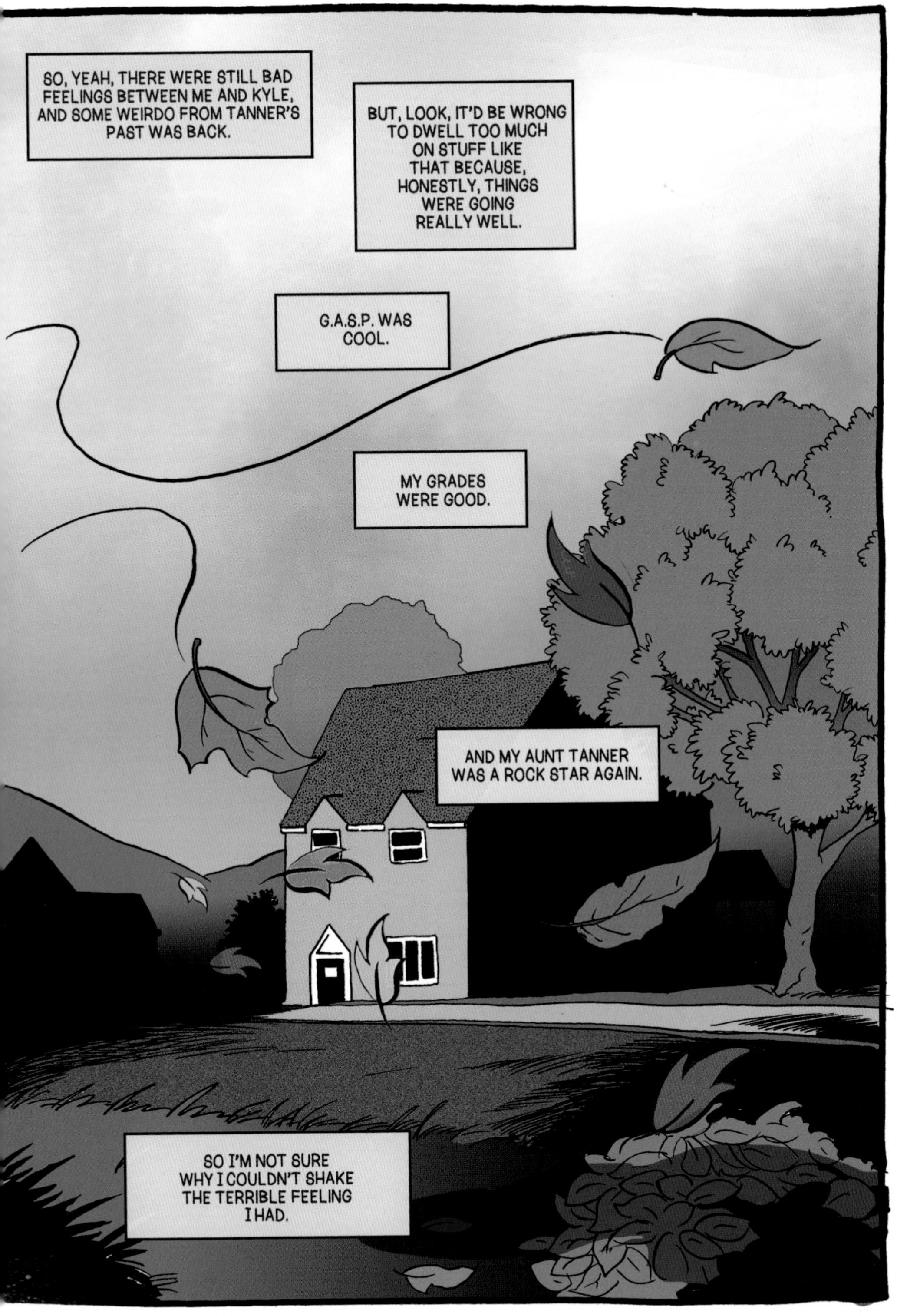
SO, YEAH, THERE WERE STILL BAD FEELINGS BETWEEN ME AND KYLE, AND SOME WEIRDO FROM TANNER'S PAST WAS BACK.
BUT, LOOK, IT'D BE WRONG TO DWELL TOO MUCH ON STUFF LIKE THAT BECAUSE, HONESTLY, THINGS WERE GOING REALLY WELL.
G.A.S.P. WAS COOL.
MY GRADES WERE GOOD.
AND MY AUNT TANNER WAS A ROCK STAR AGAIN.
SO I'M NOT SURE WHY I COULDN'T SHAKE THE TERRIBLE FEELING I HAD.

HEY, GUYS!

WHAT'S GOIN' ON?

WE'RE PUTTING TOGETHER A CARE PACKAGE FOR YOUR AUNT TANNER.

OH! HI, AMELIA!

I HOPE IT'S NOT WEIRD FOR YOU....MY BEING HERE, I MEAN.

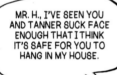

MR. H., I'VE SEEN YOU AND TANNER SUCK FACE ENOUGH THAT I THINK IT'S SAFE FOR YOU TO HANG IN MY HOUSE.

BESIDES, YOU'RE NOT MY TEACHER ANYMORE.

THAT'S TRUE.

HOW ARE THINGS WITH MISS BOODSKY?

OKAY, I GUESS....

BUT WHY DOES SHE SMELL LIKE PEANUTS AND LISTERINE?

BECAUSE SHE EATS PB&J FOR LUNCH, AND THEN SHE GARGLES.

OH.

WELL, ASK A STUPID QUESTION!

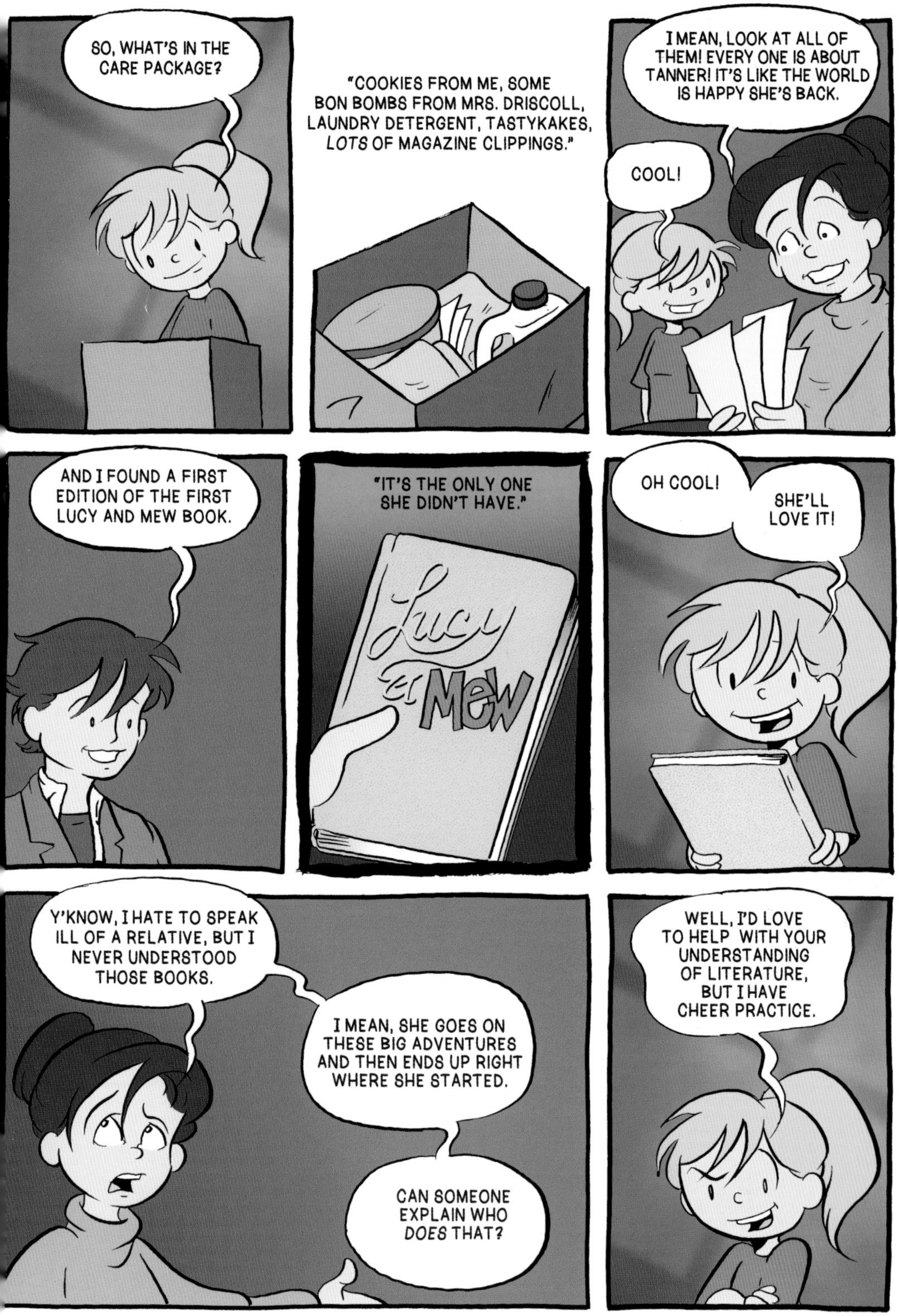

SO, WHAT'S IN THE CARE PACKAGE?
"COOKIES FROM ME, SOME BON BOMBS FROM MRS. DRISCOLL, LAUNDRY DETERGENT, TASTYKAKES, *LOTS* OF MAGAZINE CLIPPINGS."
I MEAN, LOOK AT ALL OF THEM! EVERY ONE IS ABOUT TANNER! IT'S LIKE THE WORLD IS HAPPY SHE'S BACK.
COOL!
AND I FOUND A FIRST EDITION OF THE FIRST LUCY AND MEW BOOK.
"IT'S THE ONLY ONE SHE DIDN'T HAVE."
Lucy and Mew
OH COOL!
SHE'LL LOVE IT!
Y'KNOW, I HATE TO SPEAK ILL OF A RELATIVE, BUT I NEVER UNDERSTOOD THOSE BOOKS.
I MEAN, SHE GOES ON THESE BIG ADVENTURES AND THEN ENDS UP RIGHT WHERE SHE STARTED.
CAN SOMEONE EXPLAIN WHO *DOES* THAT?
WELL, I'D LOVE TO HELP WITH YOUR UNDERSTANDING OF LITERATURE, BUT I HAVE CHEER PRACTICE.

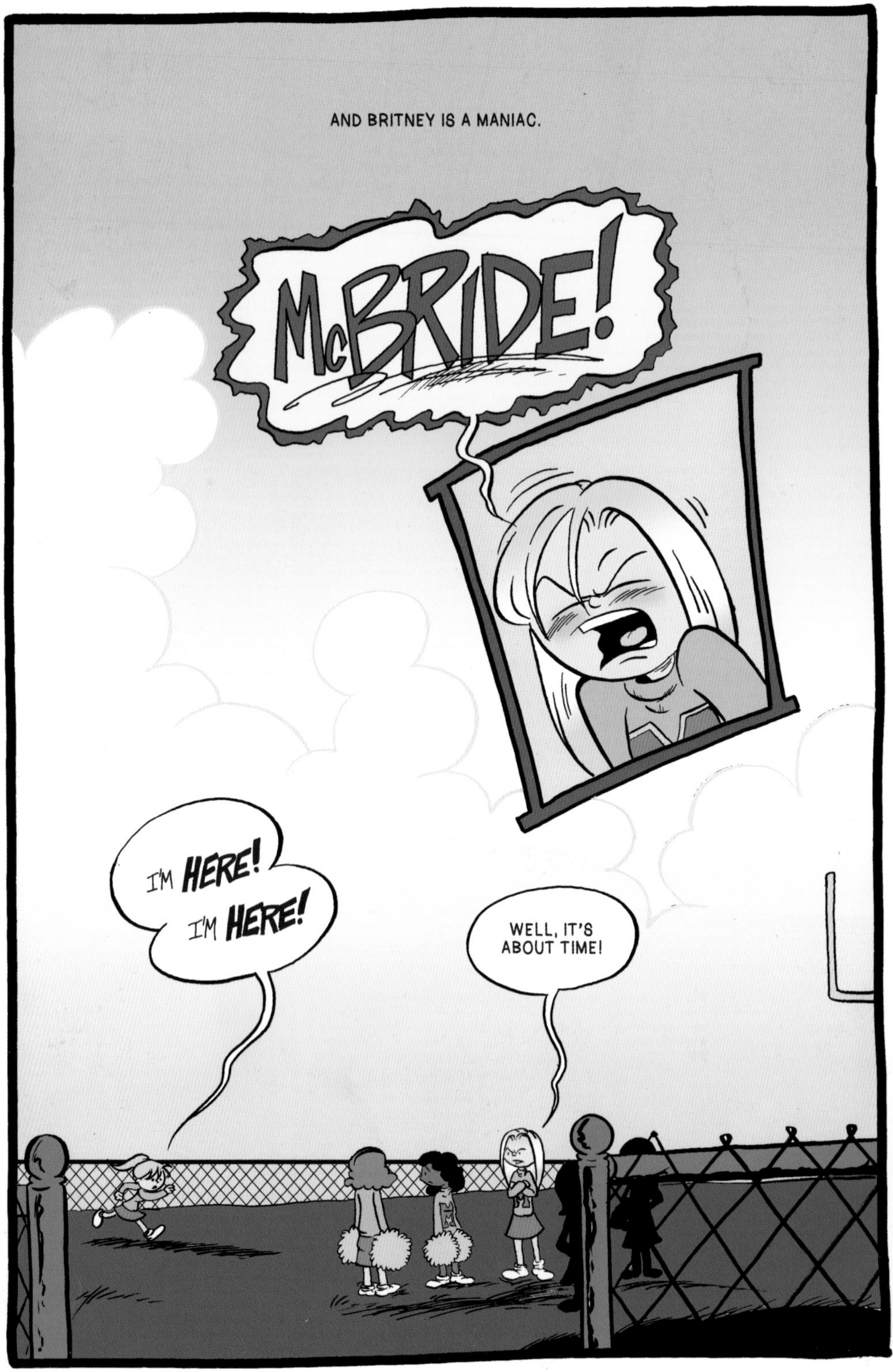
AND BRITNEY IS A MANIAC.
McBRIDE!
I'M HERE! I'M HERE!
WELL, IT'S ABOUT TIME!

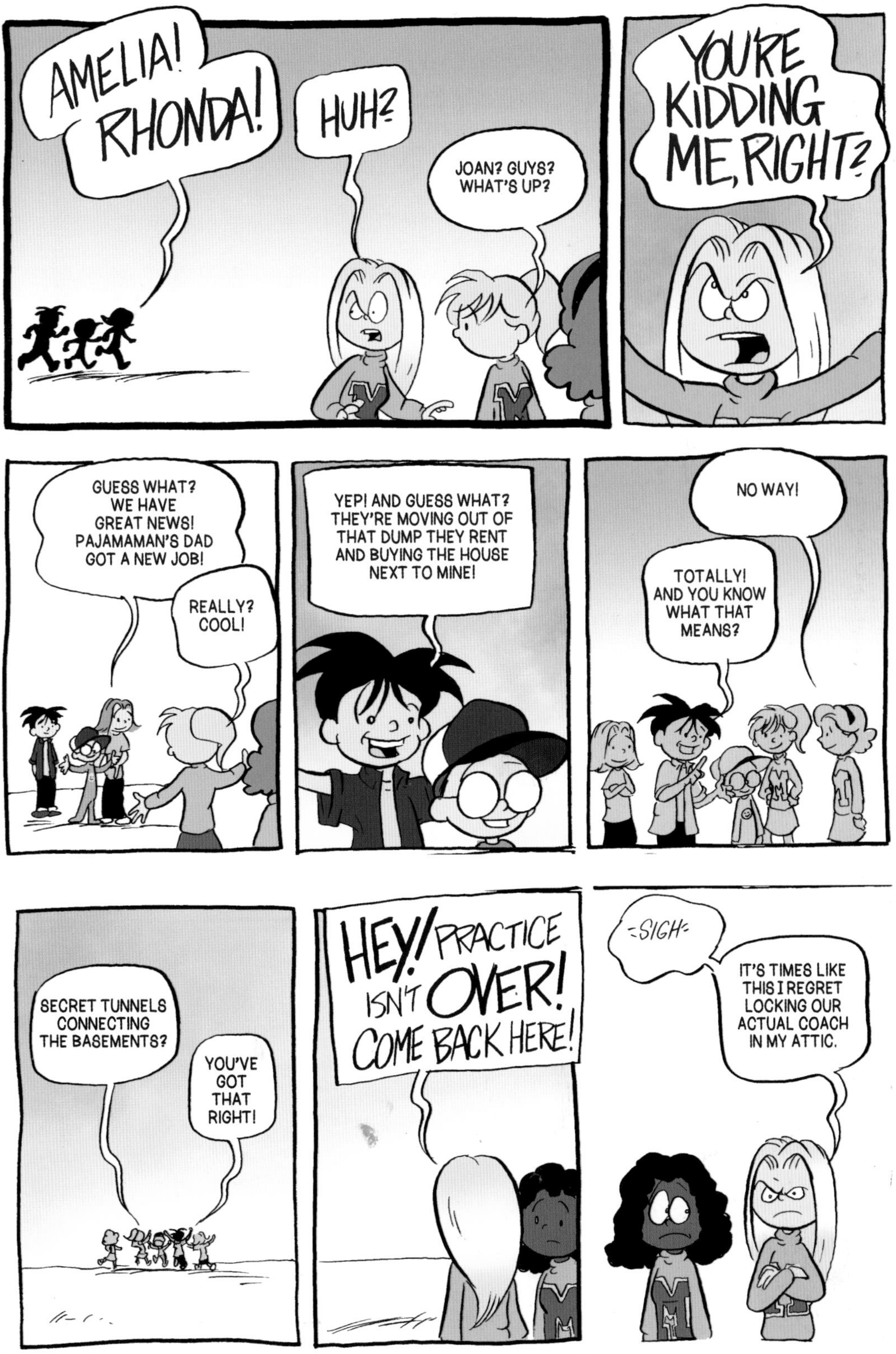
AMELIA! RHONDA!
HUH?
JOAN? GUYS? WHAT'S UP?
YOU'RE KIDDING ME, RIGHT?
GUESS WHAT? WE HAVE GREAT NEWS! PAJAMAMAN'S DAD GOT A NEW JOB!
REALLY? COOL!
YEP! AND GUESS WHAT? THEY'RE MOVING OUT OF THAT DUMP THEY RENT AND BUYING THE HOUSE NEXT TO MINE!
NO WAY!
TOTALLY! AND YOU KNOW WHAT THAT MEANS?
SECRET TUNNELS CONNECTING THE BASEMENTS?
YOU'VE GOT THAT RIGHT!
HEY! PRACTICE ISN'T OVER! COME BACK HERE!
-SIGH-
IT'S TIMES LIKE THIS I REGRET LOCKING OUR ACTUAL COACH IN MY ATTIC.

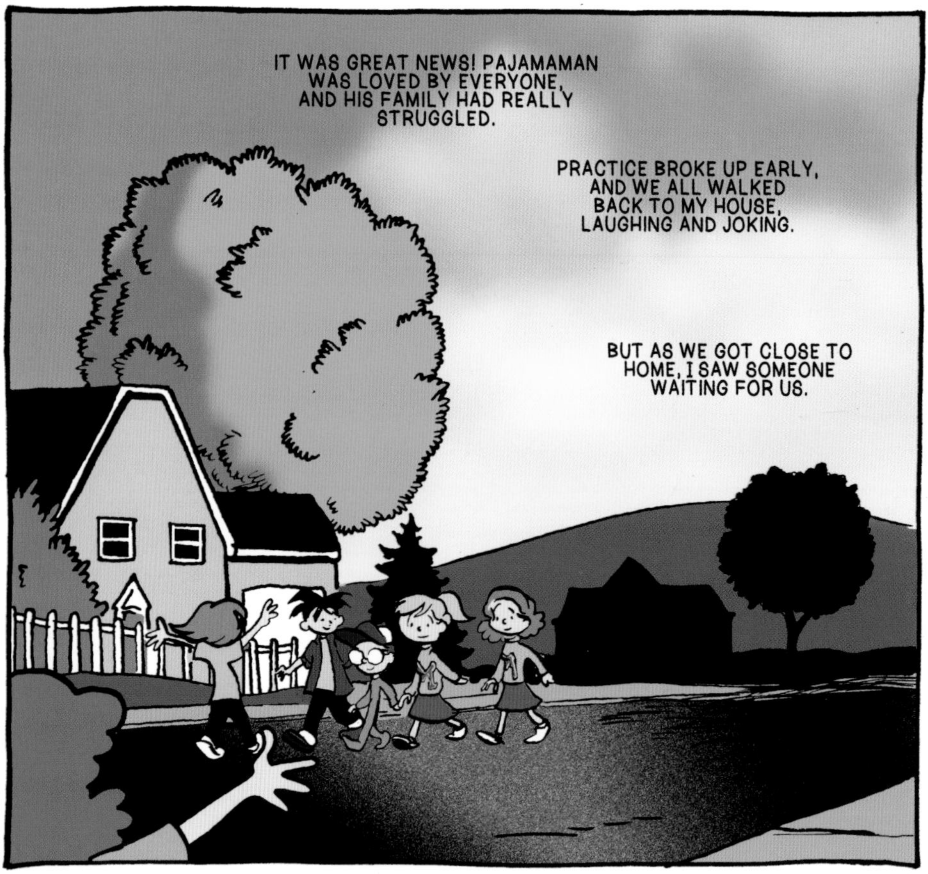
IT WAS GREAT NEWS! PAJAMAMAN WAS LOVED BY EVERYONE, AND HIS FAMILY HAD REALLY STRUGGLED.
PRACTICE BROKE UP EARLY, AND WE ALL WALKED BACK TO MY HOUSE, LAUGHING AND JOKING.
BUT AS WE GOT CLOSE TO HOME, I SAW SOMEONE WAITING FOR US.

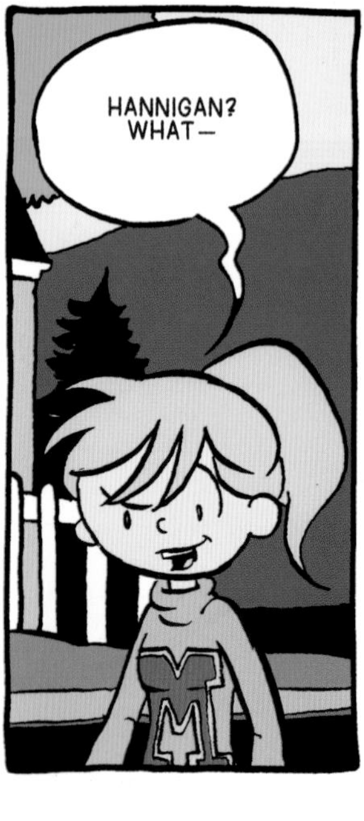
HANNIGAN? WHAT—

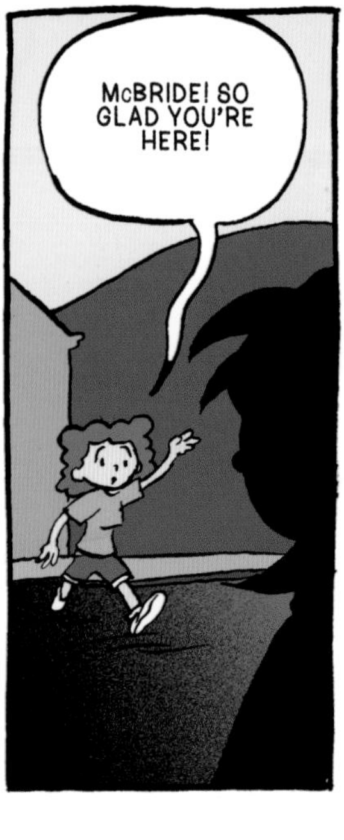
McBRIDE! SO GLAD YOU'RE HERE!

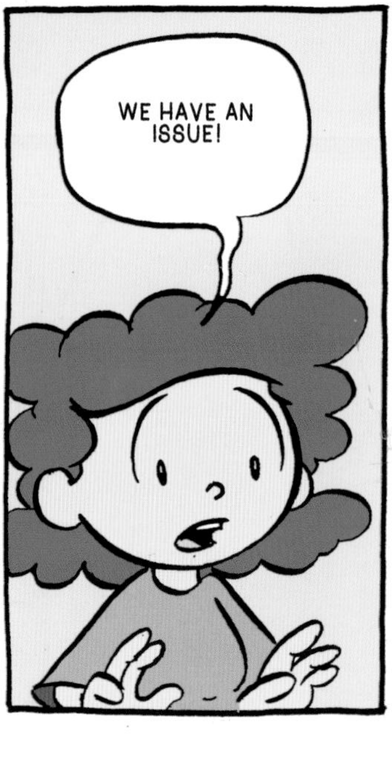
WE HAVE AN ISSUE!

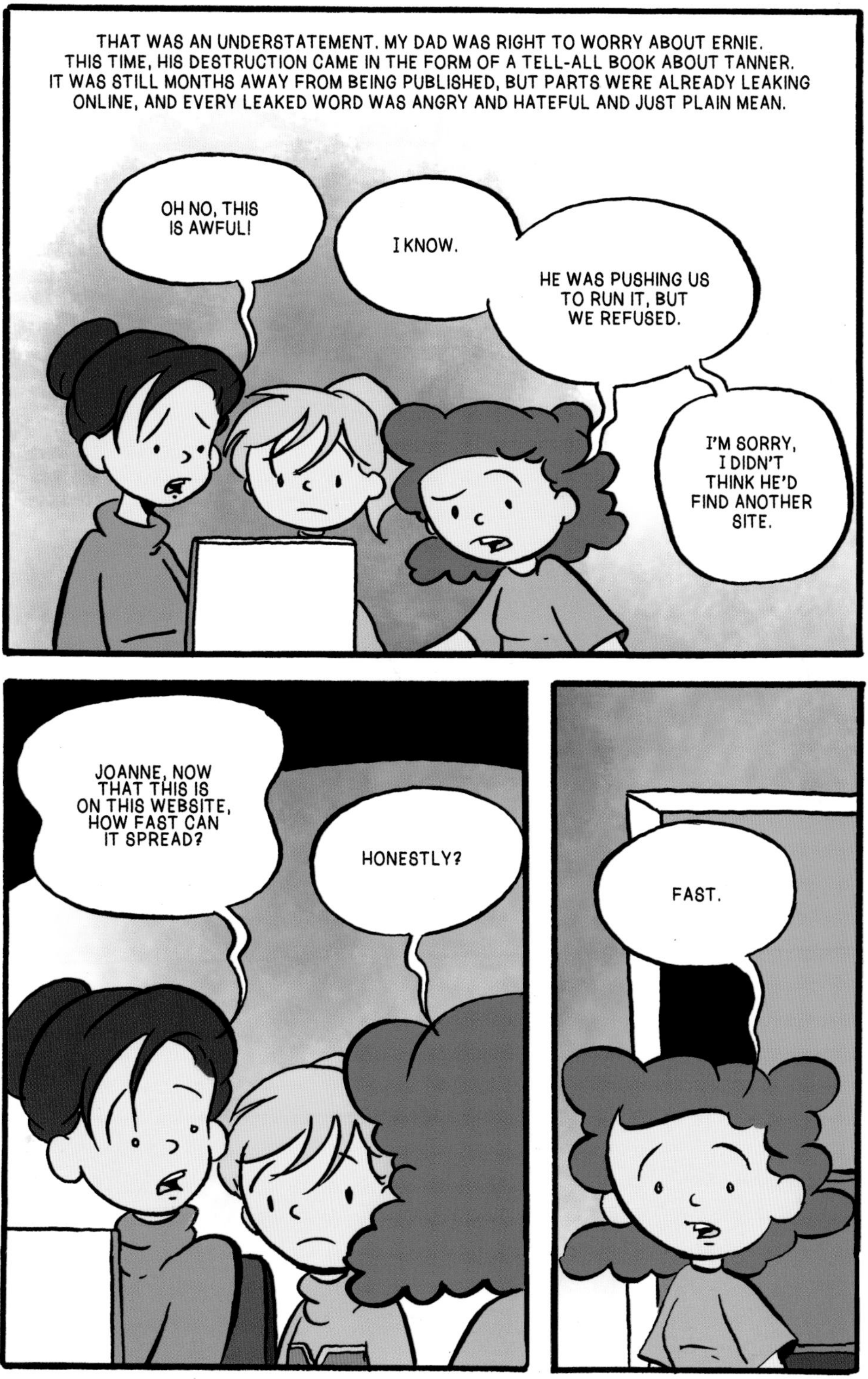
THAT WAS AN UNDERSTATEMENT. MY DAD WAS RIGHT TO WORRY ABOUT ERNIE. THIS TIME, HIS DESTRUCTION CAME IN THE FORM OF A TELL-ALL BOOK ABOUT TANNER. IT WAS STILL MONTHS AWAY FROM BEING PUBLISHED, BUT PARTS WERE ALREADY LEAKING ONLINE, AND EVERY LEAKED WORD WAS ANGRY AND HATEFUL AND JUST PLAIN MEAN.
OH NO, THIS IS AWFUL!
I KNOW.
HE WAS PUSHING US TO RUN IT, BUT WE REFUSED.
I'M SORRY, I DIDN'T THINK HE'D FIND ANOTHER SITE.
JOANNE, NOW THAT THIS IS ON THIS WEBSITE, HOW FAST CAN IT SPREAD?
HONESTLY?
FAST.

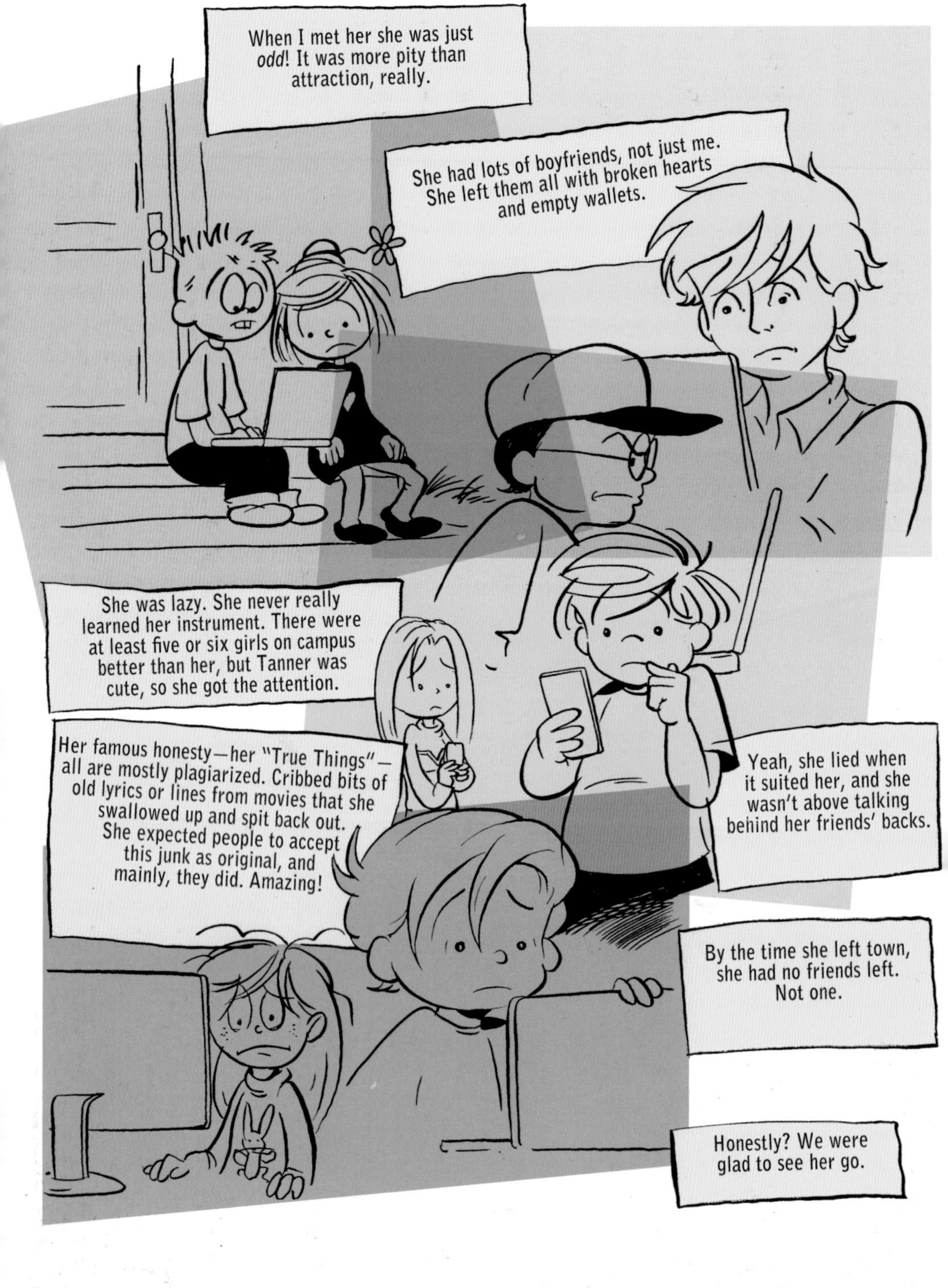
When I met her she was just *odd*! It was more pity than attraction, really.
She had lots of boyfriends, not just me. She left them all with broken hearts and empty wallets.
She was lazy. She never really learned her instrument. There were at least five or six girls on campus better than her, but Tanner was cute, so she got the attention.
Her famous honesty—her "True Things"—all are mostly plagiarized. Cribbed bits of old lyrics or lines from movies that she swallowed up and spit back out. She expected people to accept this junk as original, and mainly, they did. Amazing!
Yeah, she lied when it suited her, and she wasn't above talking behind her friends' backs.
By the time she left town, she had no friends left. Not one.
Honestly? We were glad to see her go.

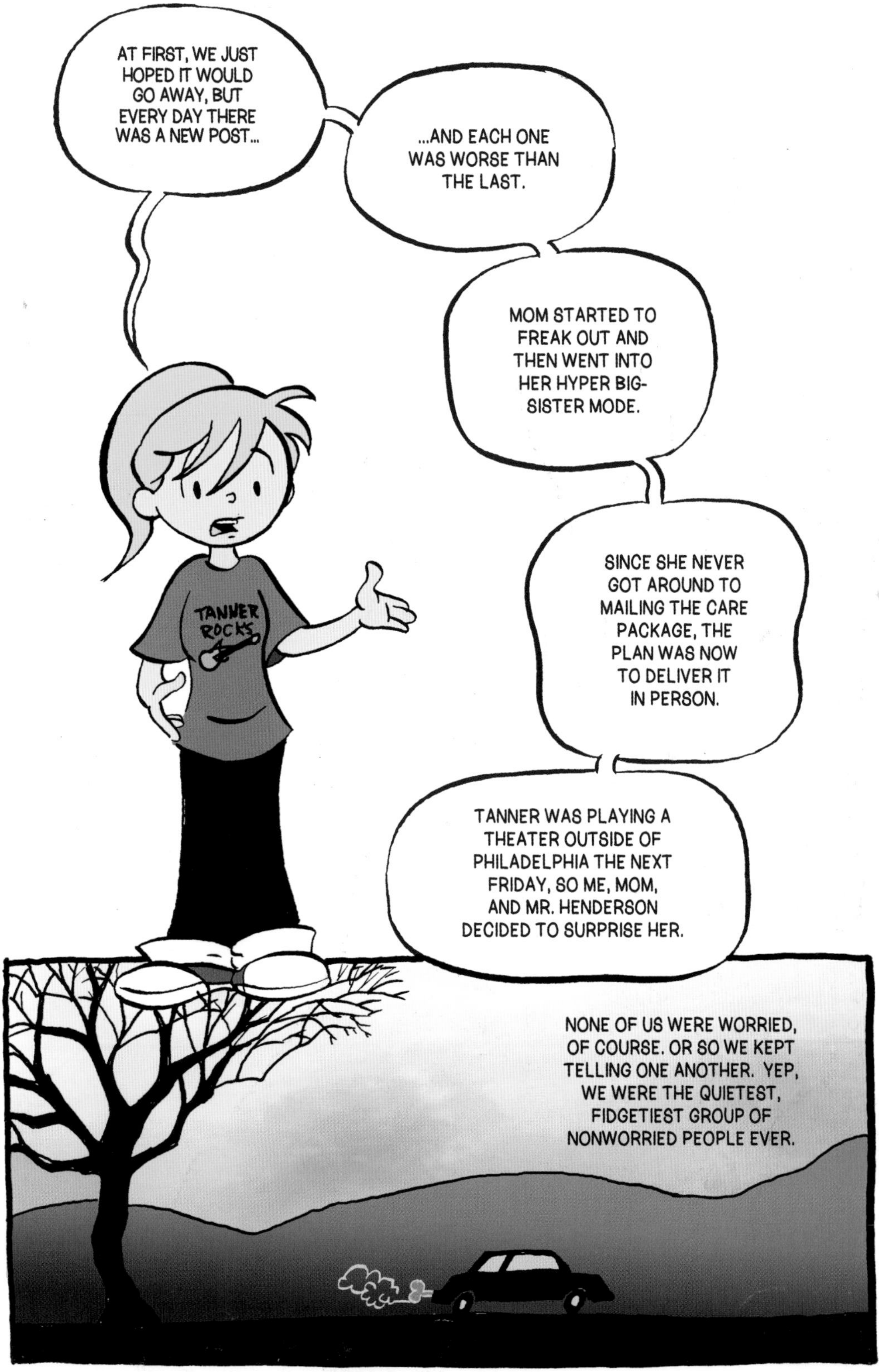
AT FIRST, WE JUST HOPED IT WOULD GO AWAY, BUT EVERY DAY THERE WAS A NEW POST...
...AND EACH ONE WAS WORSE THAN THE LAST.
MOM STARTED TO FREAK OUT AND THEN WENT INTO HER HYPER BIG-SISTER MODE.
SINCE SHE NEVER GOT AROUND TO MAILING THE CARE PACKAGE, THE PLAN WAS NOW TO DELIVER IT IN PERSON.
TANNER WAS PLAYING A THEATER OUTSIDE OF PHILADELPHIA THE NEXT FRIDAY, SO ME, MOM, AND MR. HENDERSON DECIDED TO SURPRISE HER.
TANNER ROCKS
NONE OF US WERE WORRIED, OF COURSE. OR SO WE KEPT TELLING ONE ANOTHER. YEP, WE WERE THE QUIETEST, FIDGETIEST GROUP OF NONWORRIED PEOPLE EVER.

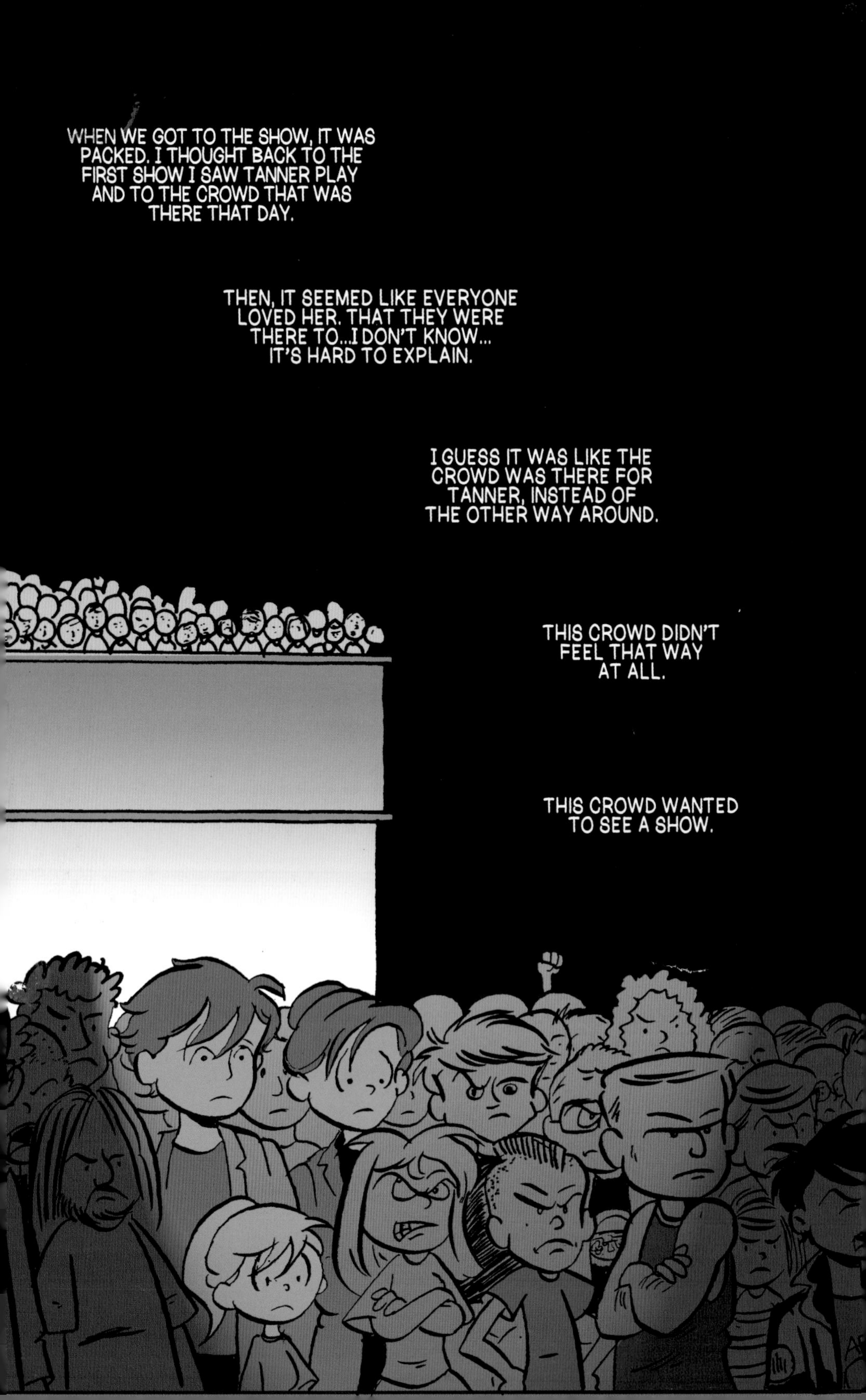
WHEN WE GOT TO THE SHOW, IT WAS PACKED. I THOUGHT BACK TO THE FIRST SHOW I SAW TANNER PLAY AND TO THE CROWD THAT WAS THERE THAT DAY.
THEN, IT SEEMED LIKE EVERYONE LOVED HER. THAT THEY WERE THERE TO...I DON'T KNOW... IT'S HARD TO EXPLAIN.
I GUESS IT WAS LIKE THE CROWD WAS THERE FOR TANNER, INSTEAD OF THE OTHER WAY AROUND.
THIS CROWD DIDN'T FEEL THAT WAY AT ALL.
THIS CROWD WANTED TO SEE A SHOW.

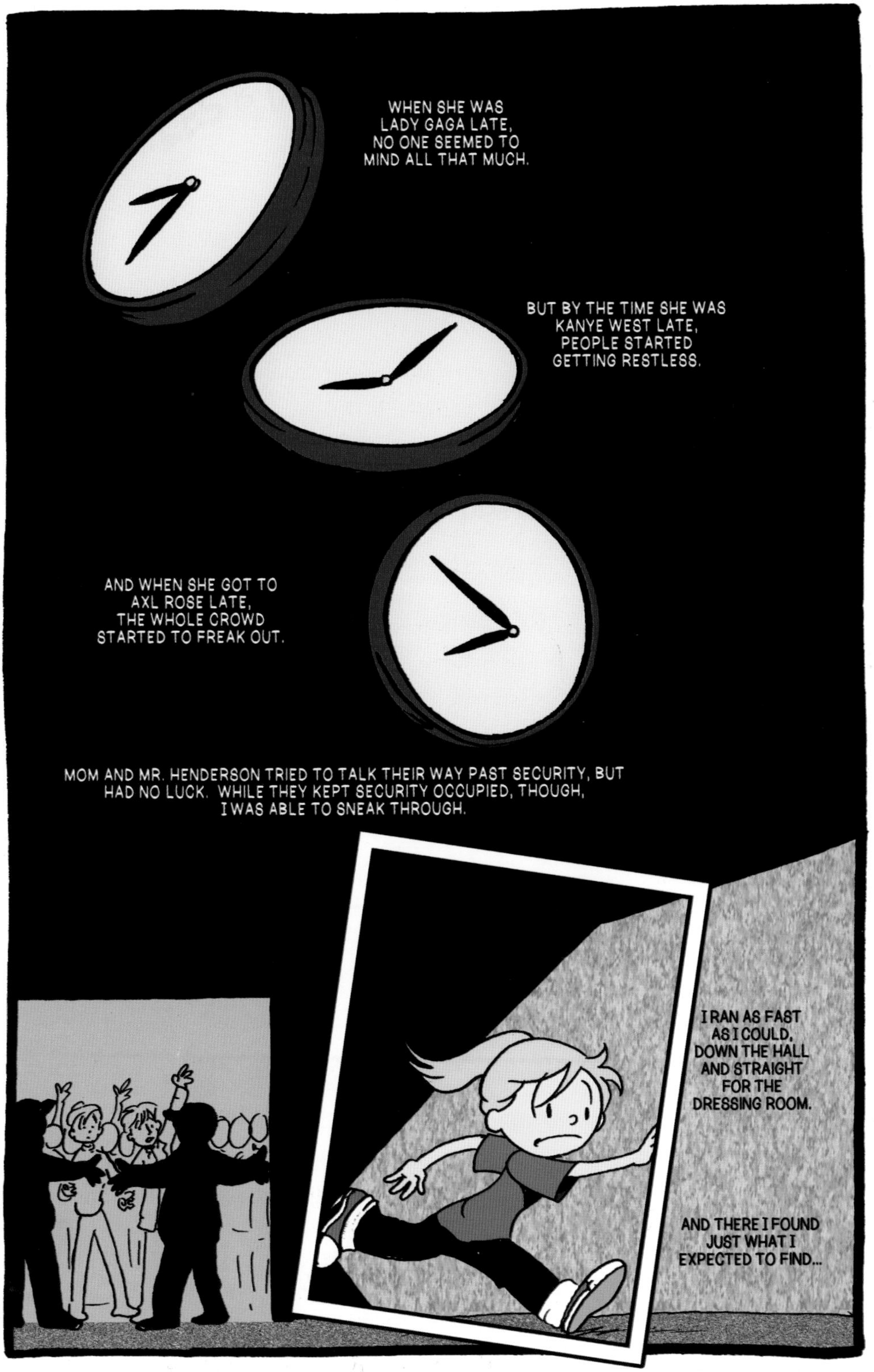
WHEN SHE WAS
LADY GAGA LATE,
NO ONE SEEMED TO
MIND ALL THAT MUCH.
BUT BY THE TIME SHE WAS
KANYE WEST LATE,
PEOPLE STARTED
GETTING RESTLESS.
AND WHEN SHE GOT TO
AXL ROSE LATE,
THE WHOLE CROWD
STARTED TO FREAK OUT.
MOM AND MR. HENDERSON TRIED TO TALK THEIR WAY PAST SECURITY, BUT
HAD NO LUCK. WHILE THEY KEPT SECURITY OCCUPIED, THOUGH,
I WAS ABLE TO SNEAK THROUGH.
I RAN AS FAST
AS I COULD,
DOWN THE HALL
AND STRAIGHT
FOR THE
DRESSING ROOM.
AND THERE I FOUND
JUST WHAT I
EXPECTED TO FIND...

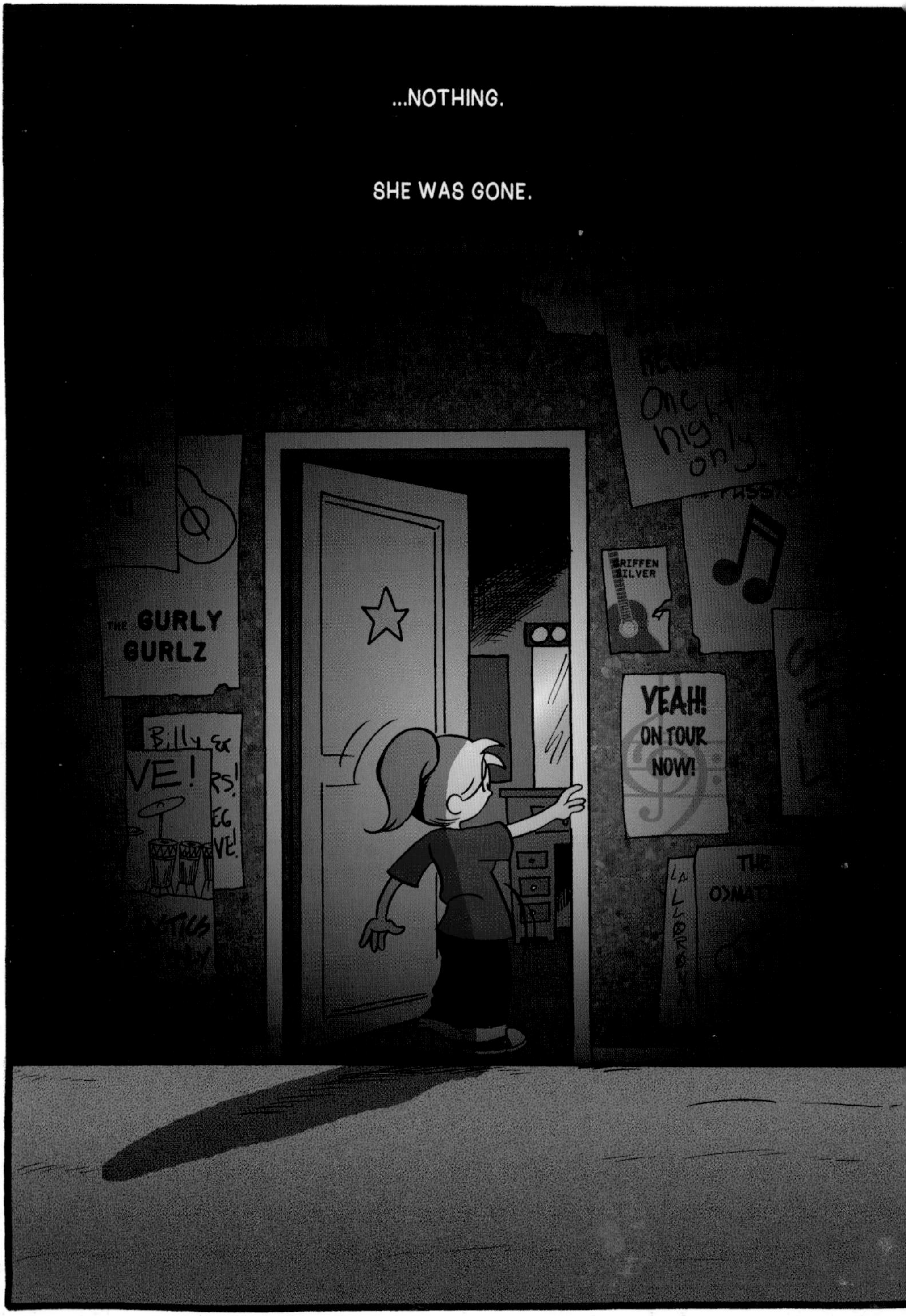
...NOTHING.
SHE WAS GONE.
THE GURLY GURLZ
YEAH! ON TOUR NOW!

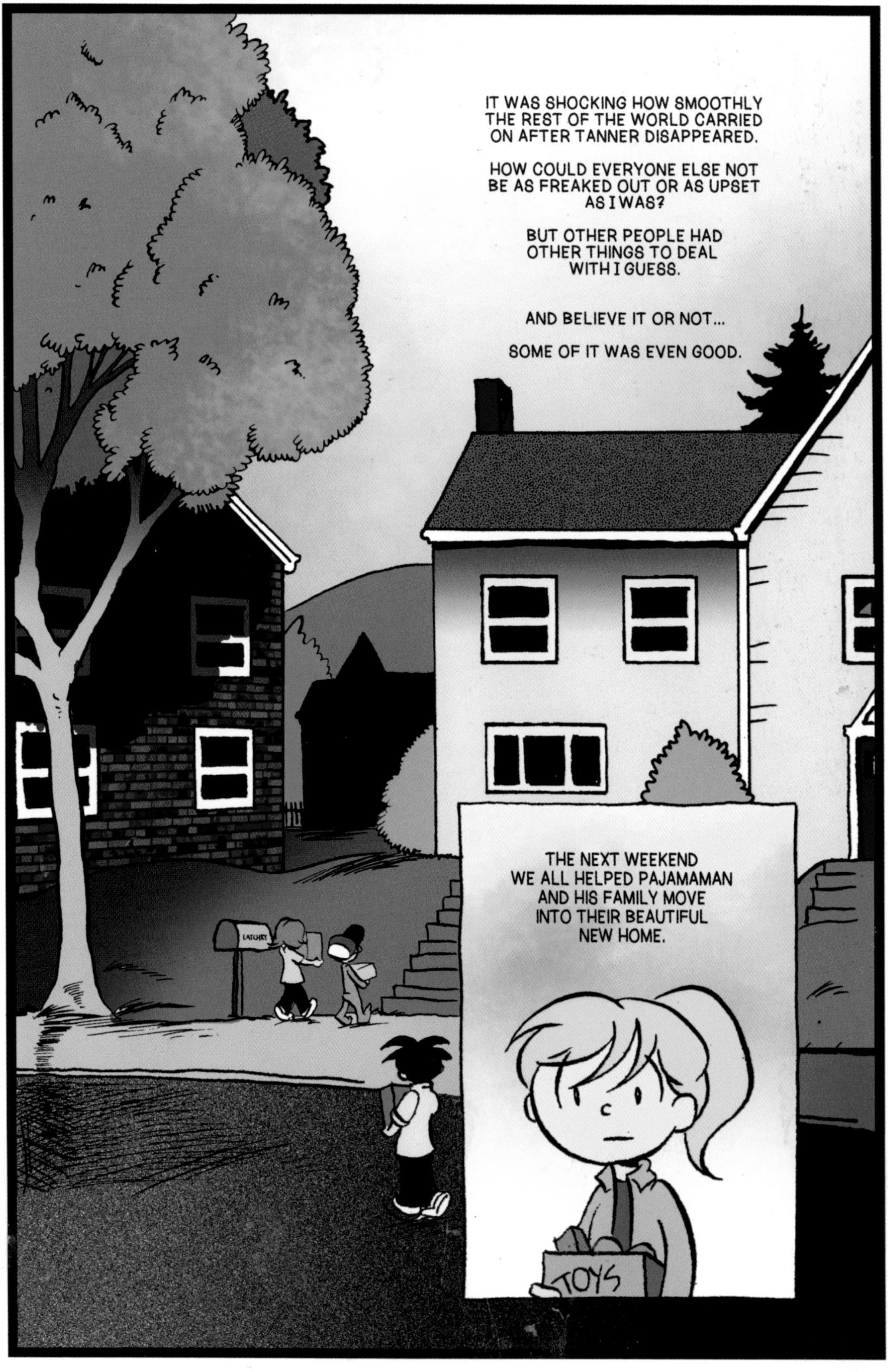
IT WAS SHOCKING HOW SMOOTHLY THE REST OF THE WORLD CARRIED ON AFTER TANNER DISAPPEARED.
HOW COULD EVERYONE ELSE NOT BE AS FREAKED OUT OR AS UPSET AS I WAS?
BUT OTHER PEOPLE HAD OTHER THINGS TO DEAL WITH I GUESS.
AND BELIEVE IT OR NOT...
SOME OF IT WAS EVEN GOOD.
LATCHET
THE NEXT WEEKEND WE ALL HELPED PAJAMAMAN AND HIS FAMILY MOVE INTO THEIR BEAUTIFUL NEW HOME.
TOYS

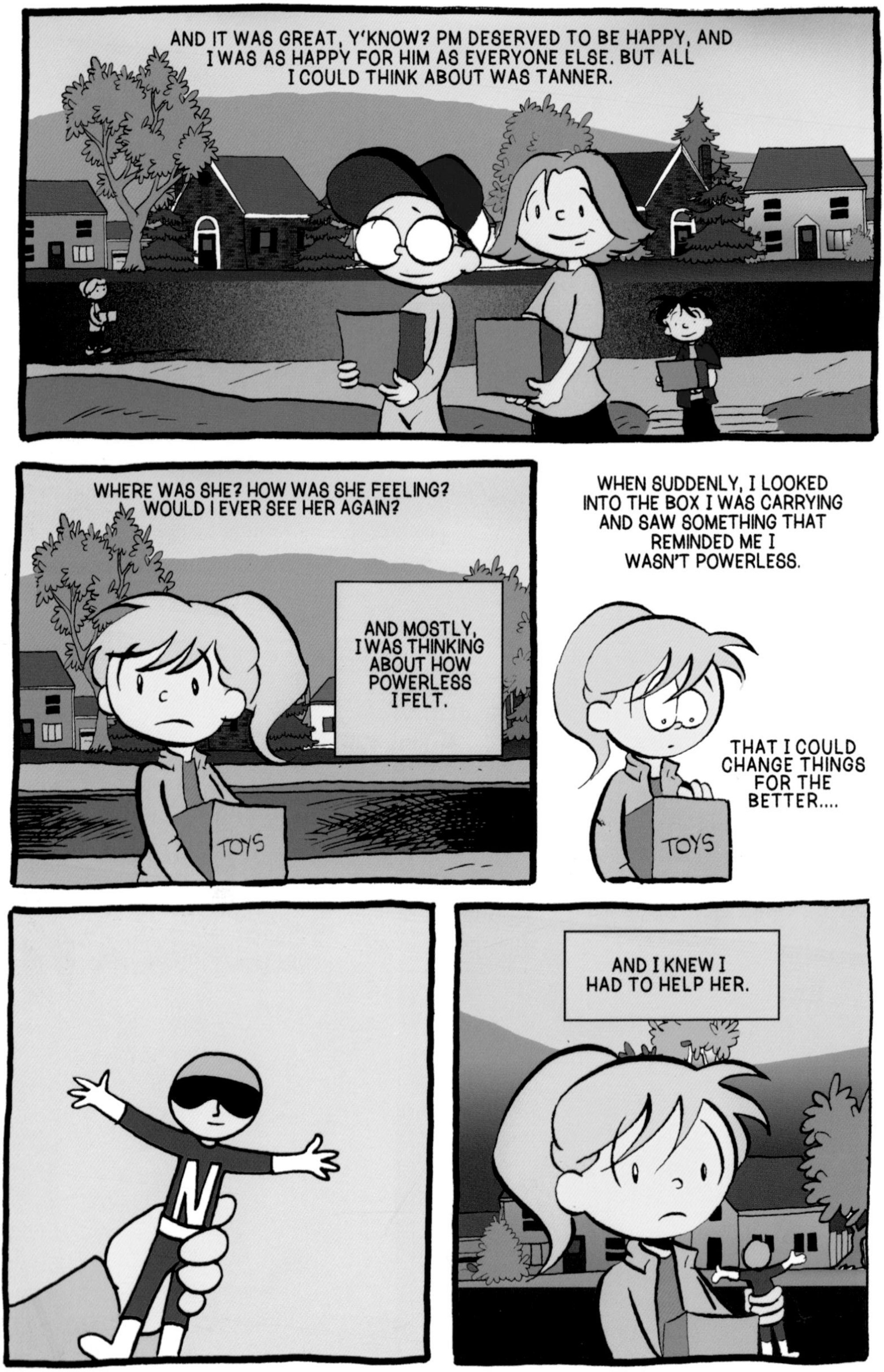
AND IT WAS GREAT, Y'KNOW? PM DESERVED TO BE HAPPY, AND I WAS AS HAPPY FOR HIM AS EVERYONE ELSE. BUT ALL I COULD THINK ABOUT WAS TANNER.
WHERE WAS SHE? HOW WAS SHE FEELING? WOULD I EVER SEE HER AGAIN?
AND MOSTLY, I WAS THINKING ABOUT HOW POWERLESS I FELT.
TOYS
WHEN SUDDENLY, I LOOKED INTO THE BOX I WAS CARRYING AND SAW SOMETHING THAT REMINDED ME I WASN'T POWERLESS.
THAT I COULD CHANGE THINGS FOR THE BETTER....
TOYS
N
AND I KNEW I HAD TO HELP HER.

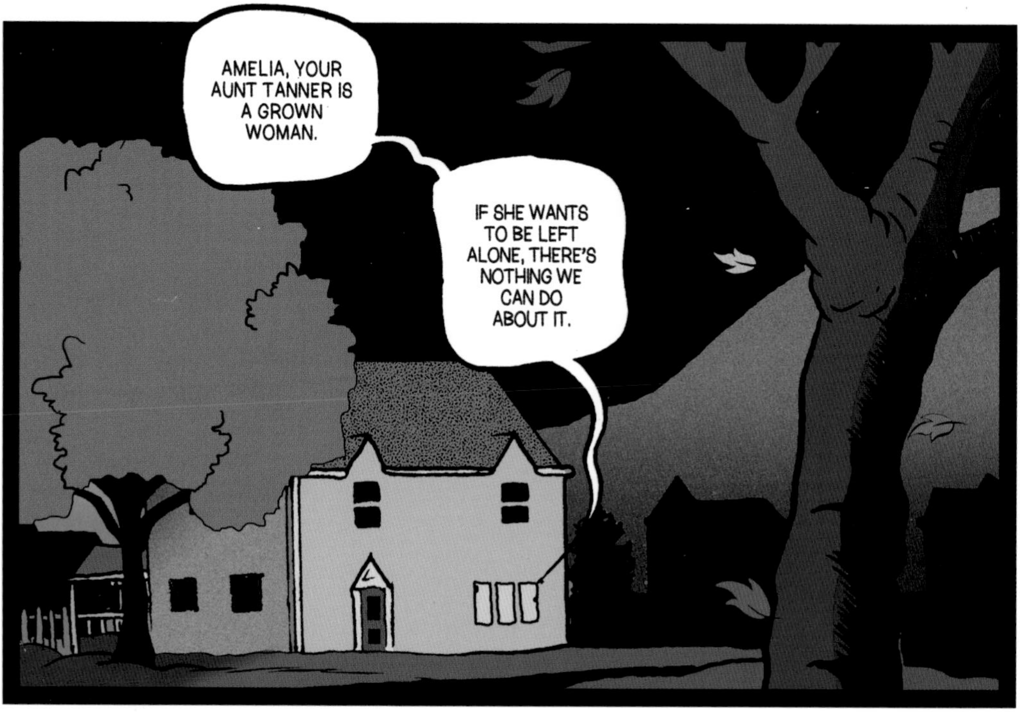
AMELIA, YOUR AUNT TANNER IS A GROWN WOMAN.
IF SHE WANTS TO BE LEFT ALONE, THERE'S NOTHING WE CAN DO ABOUT IT.

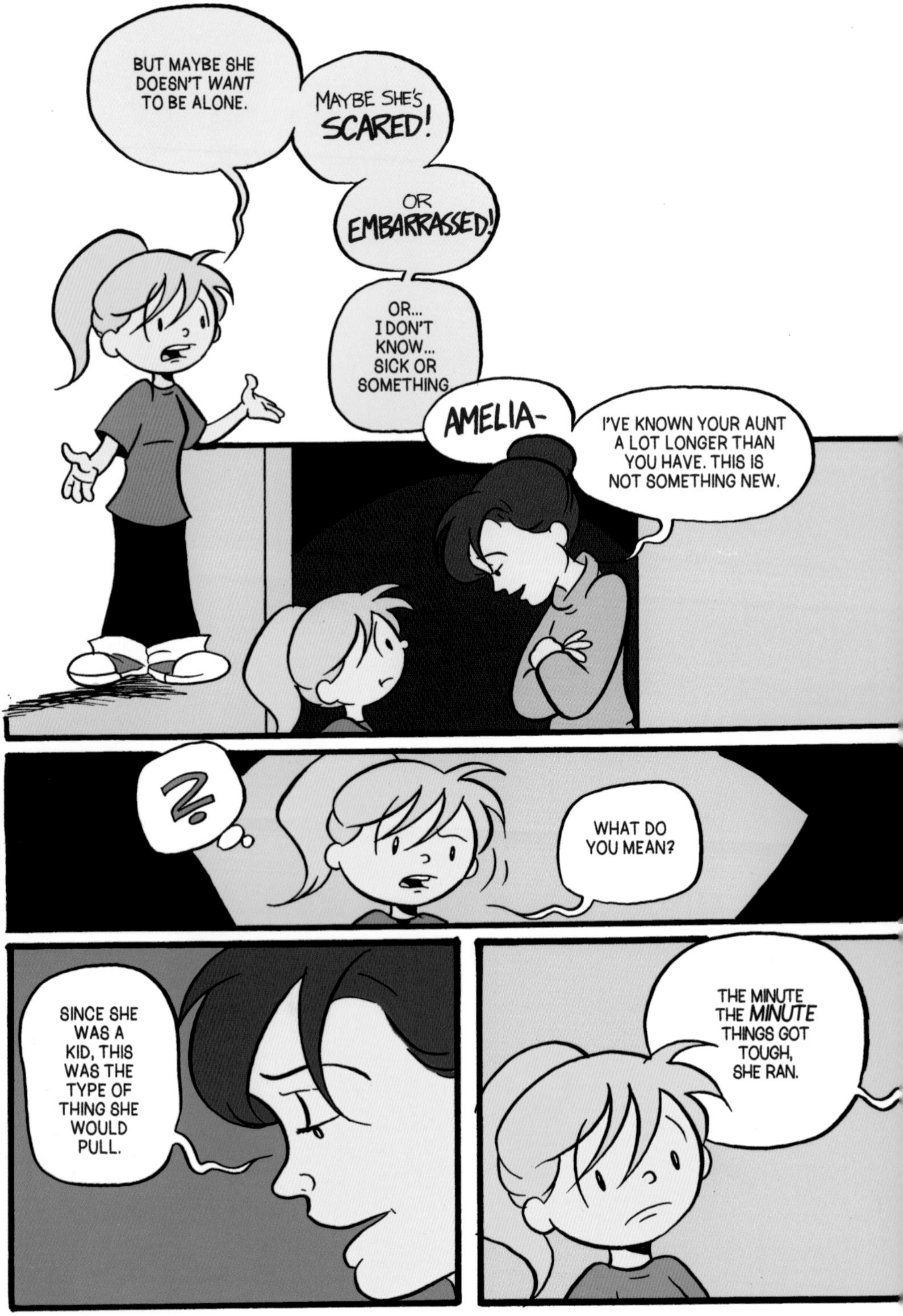
BUT MAYBE SHE DOESN'T WANT TO BE ALONE.
MAYBE SHE'S SCARED!
OR EMBARRASSED!
OR... I DON'T KNOW... SICK OR SOMETHING.
AMELIA-
I'VE KNOWN YOUR AUNT A LOT LONGER THAN YOU HAVE. THIS IS NOT SOMETHING NEW.
?
WHAT DO YOU MEAN?
SINCE SHE WAS A KID, THIS WAS THE TYPE OF THING SHE WOULD PULL.
THE MINUTE THE MINUTE THINGS GOT TOUGH, SHE RAN.

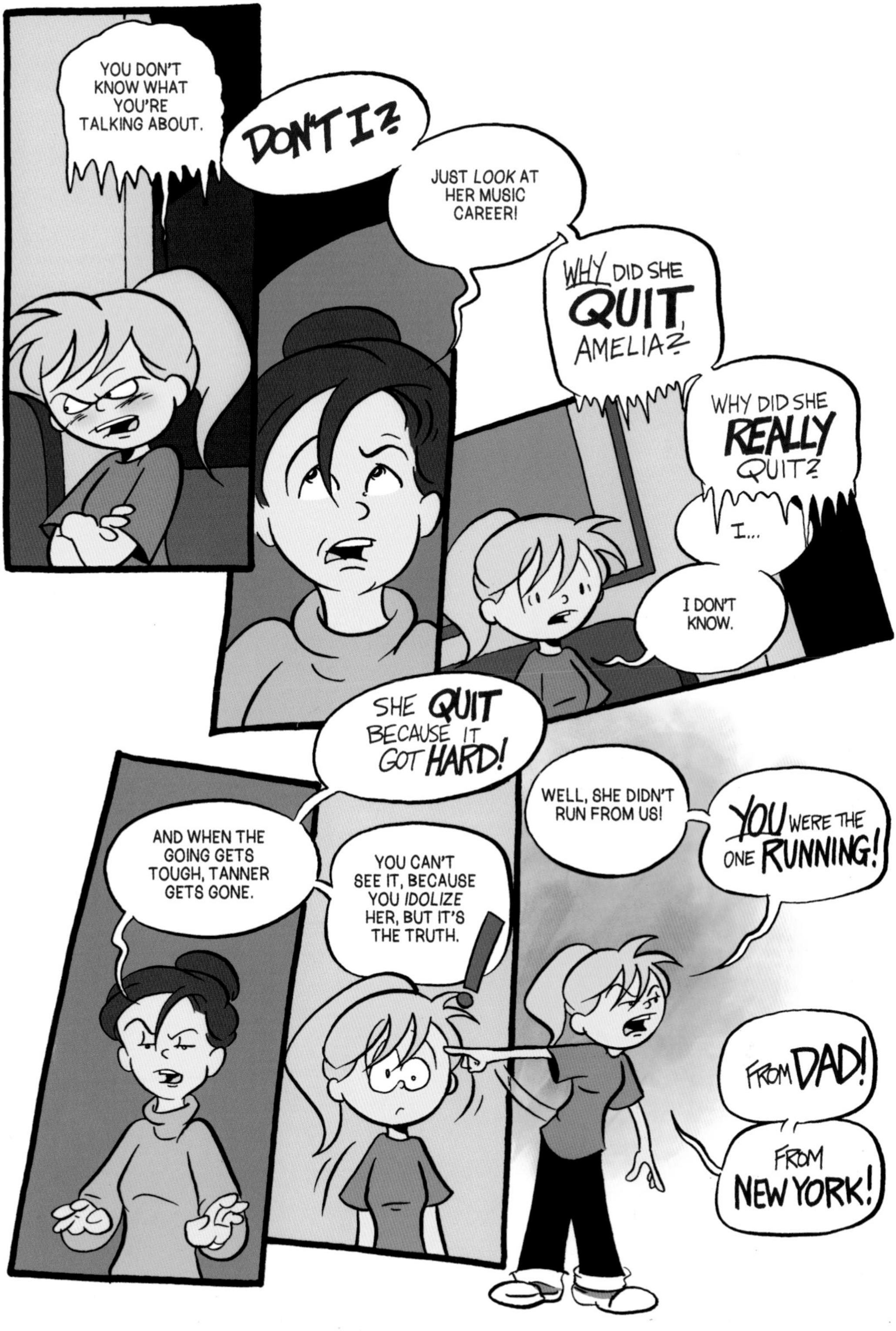
YOU DON'T KNOW WHAT YOU'RE TALKING ABOUT.
DON'T I?
JUST LOOK AT HER MUSIC CAREER!
WHY DID SHE QUIT, AMELIA?
WHY DID SHE REALLY QUIT?
I...
I DON'T KNOW.
SHE QUIT BECAUSE IT GOT HARD!
AND WHEN THE GOING GETS TOUGH, TANNER GETS GONE.
YOU CAN'T SEE IT, BECAUSE YOU IDOLIZE HER, BUT IT'S THE TRUTH.
!
WELL, SHE DIDN'T RUN FROM US!
YOU WERE THE ONE RUNNING!
FROM DAD!
FROM NEW YORK!

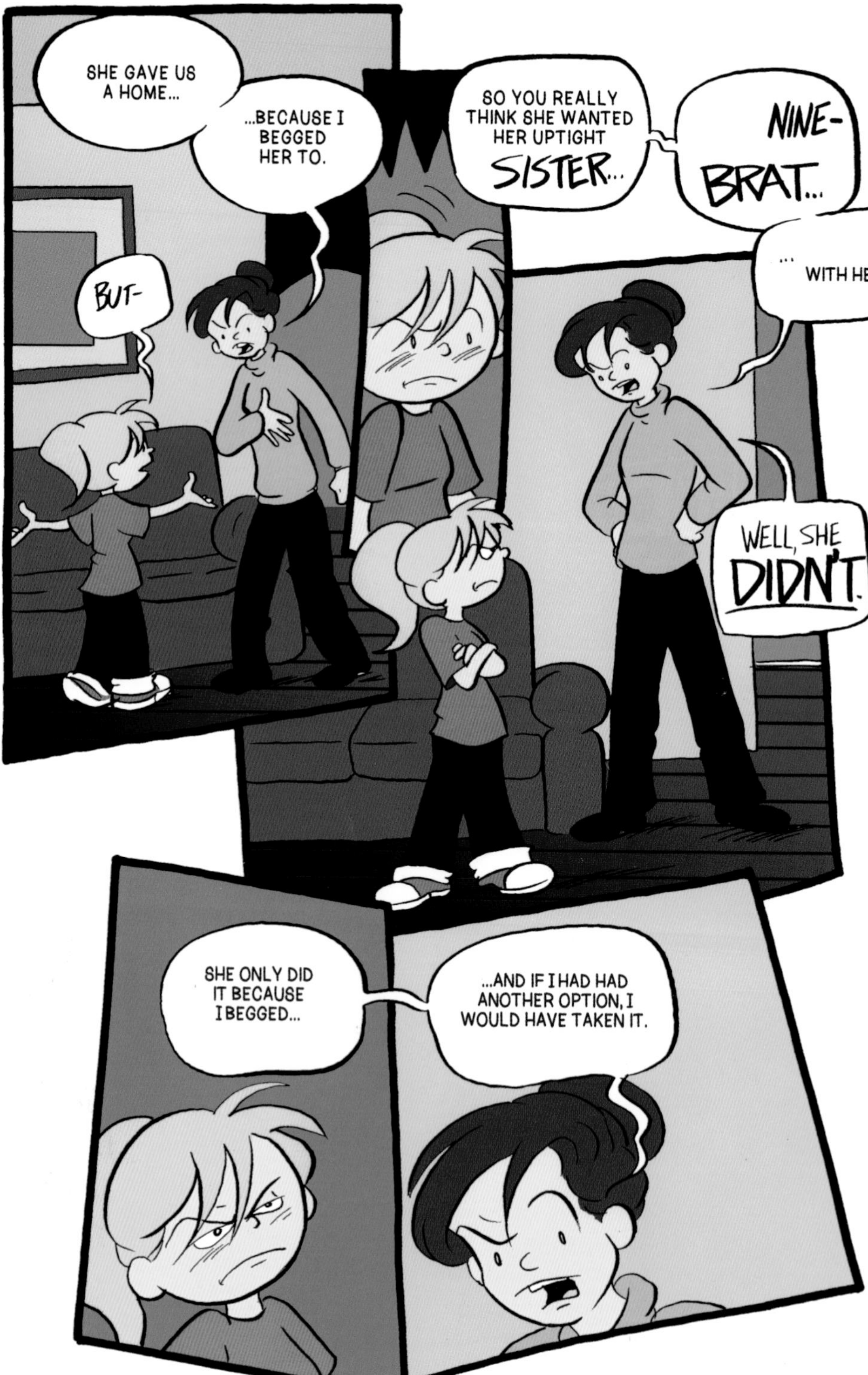
SHE GAVE US A HOME...
...BECAUSE I BEGGED HER TO.
BUT-
SO YOU REALLY THINK SHE WANTED HER UPTIGHT SISTER...
NINE-BRAT...
... IN WITH HER?
WELL, SHE DIDN'T.
SHE ONLY DID IT BECAUSE I BEGGED...
...AND IF I HAD HAD ANOTHER OPTION, I WOULD HAVE TAKEN IT.

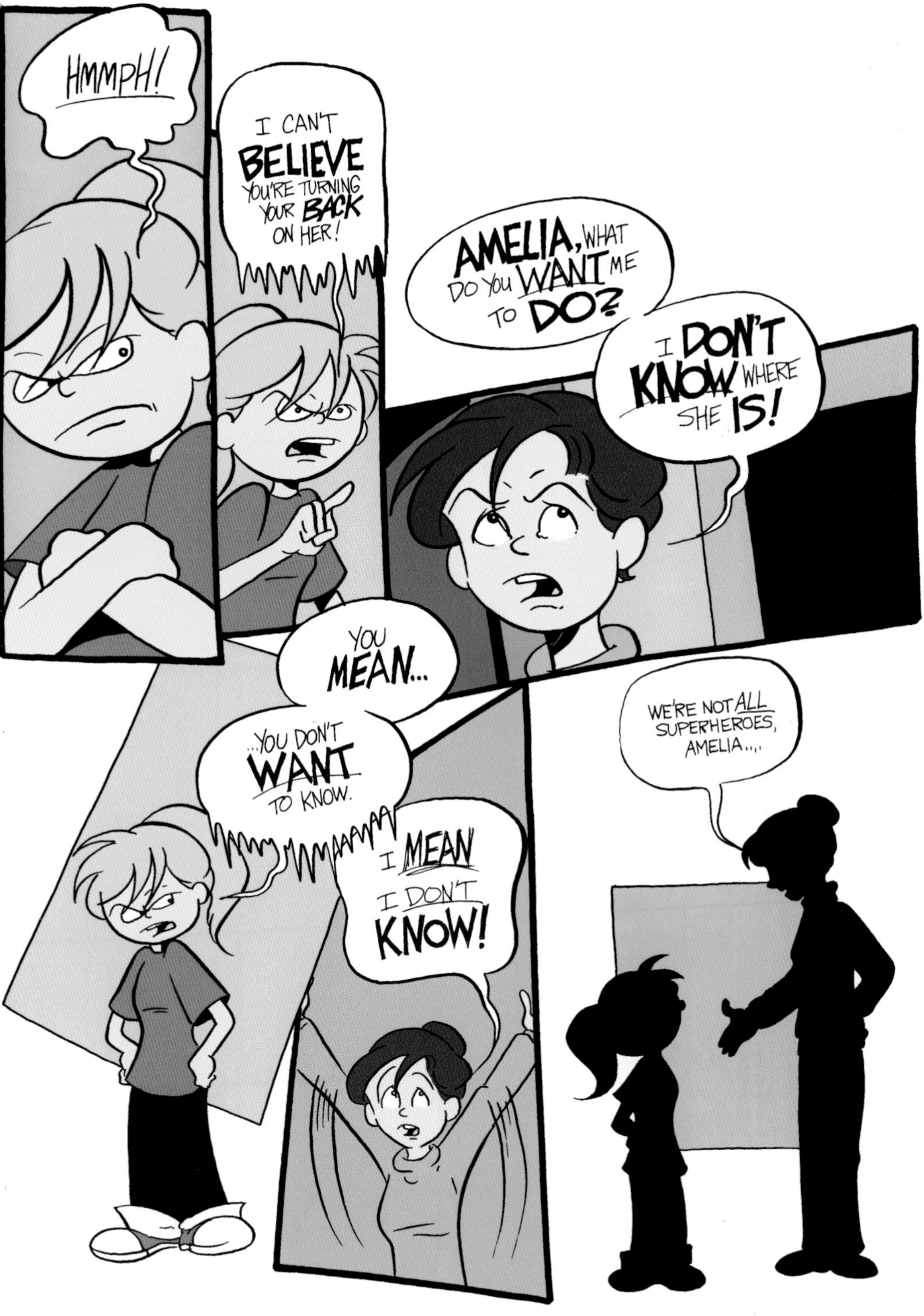
HMMPH!
I CAN'T BELIEVE YOU'RE TURNING YOUR BACK ON HER!
AMELIA, WHAT DO YOU WANT ME TO DO?
I DON'T KNOW WHERE SHE IS!
YOU MEAN...
...YOU DON'T WANT TO KNOW.
I MEAN I DON'T KNOW!
WE'RE NOT ALL SUPERHEROES, AMELIA....

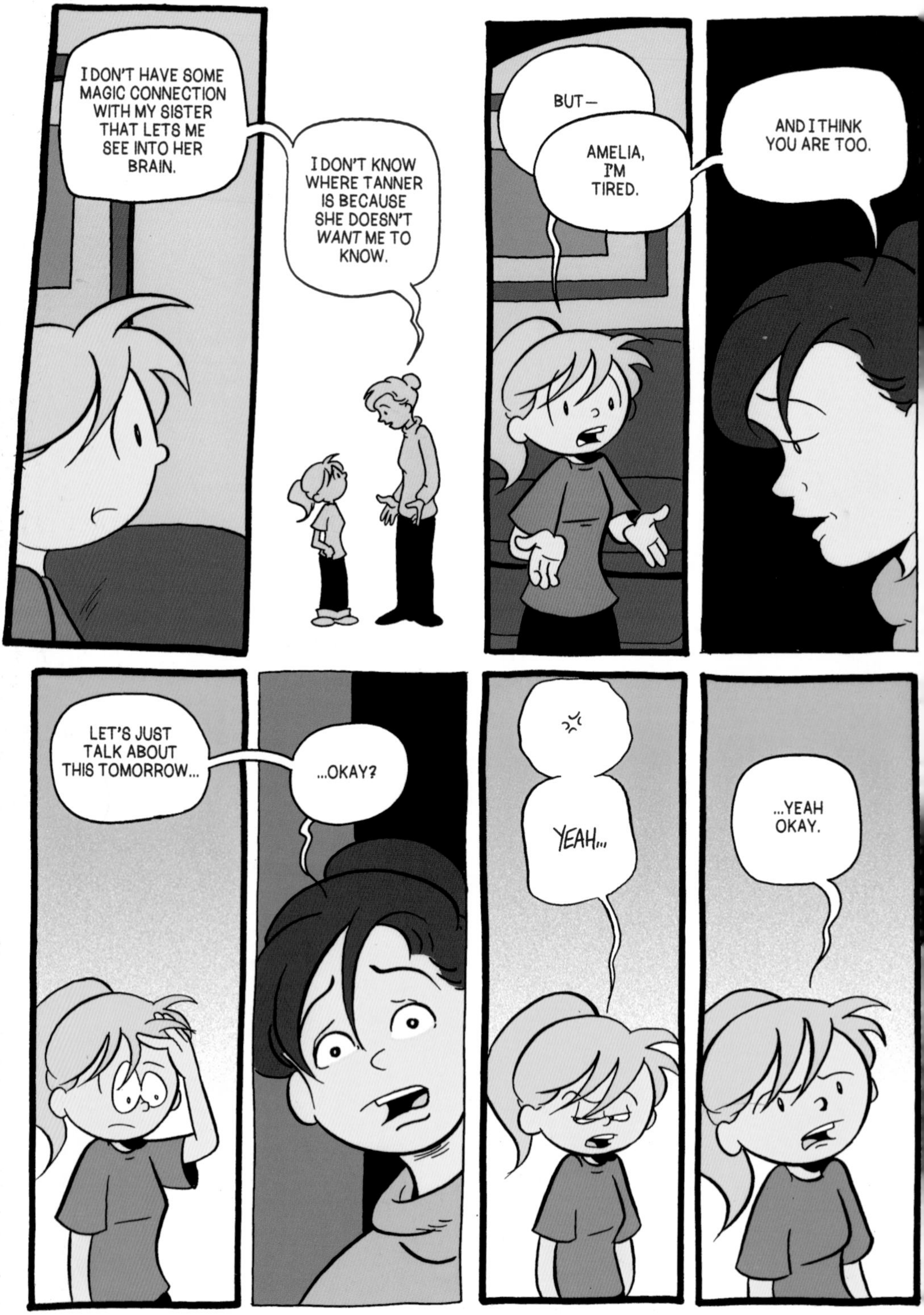
I DON'T HAVE SOME MAGIC CONNECTION WITH MY SISTER THAT LETS ME SEE INTO HER BRAIN.
I DON'T KNOW WHERE TANNER IS BECAUSE SHE DOESN'T *WANT* ME TO KNOW.
BUT—
AMELIA, I'M TIRED.
AND I THINK YOU ARE TOO.
LET'S JUST TALK ABOUT THIS TOMORROW...
...OKAY?
YEAH...
...YEAH OKAY.

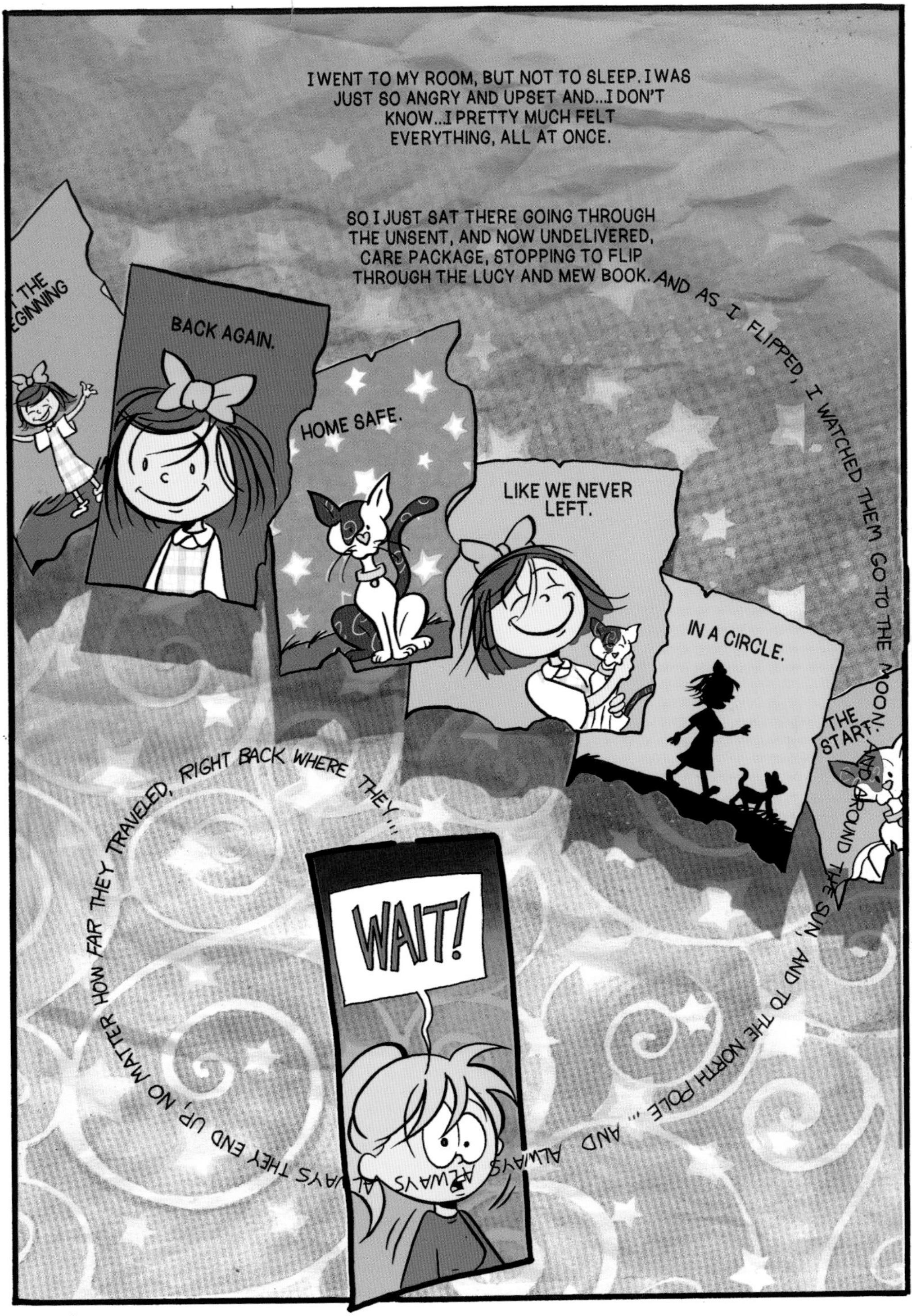
I WENT TO MY ROOM, BUT NOT TO SLEEP. I WAS JUST SO ANGRY AND UPSET AND...I DON'T KNOW...I PRETTY MUCH FELT EVERYTHING, ALL AT ONCE.
SO I JUST SAT THERE GOING THROUGH THE UNSENT, AND NOW UNDELIVERED, CARE PACKAGE, STOPPING TO FLIP THROUGH THE LUCY AND MEW BOOK.
BACK AGAIN.
HOME SAFE.
LIKE WE NEVER LEFT.
IN A CIRCLE.
THE START.
AND AS I FLIPPED, I WATCHED THEM GO TO THE MOON, AND AROUND THE SUN, AND TO THE NORTH POLE... AND ALWAYS ALWAYS ALWAYS THEY END UP, NO MATTER HOW FAR THEY TRAVELED, RIGHT BACK WHERE THEY...
WAIT!

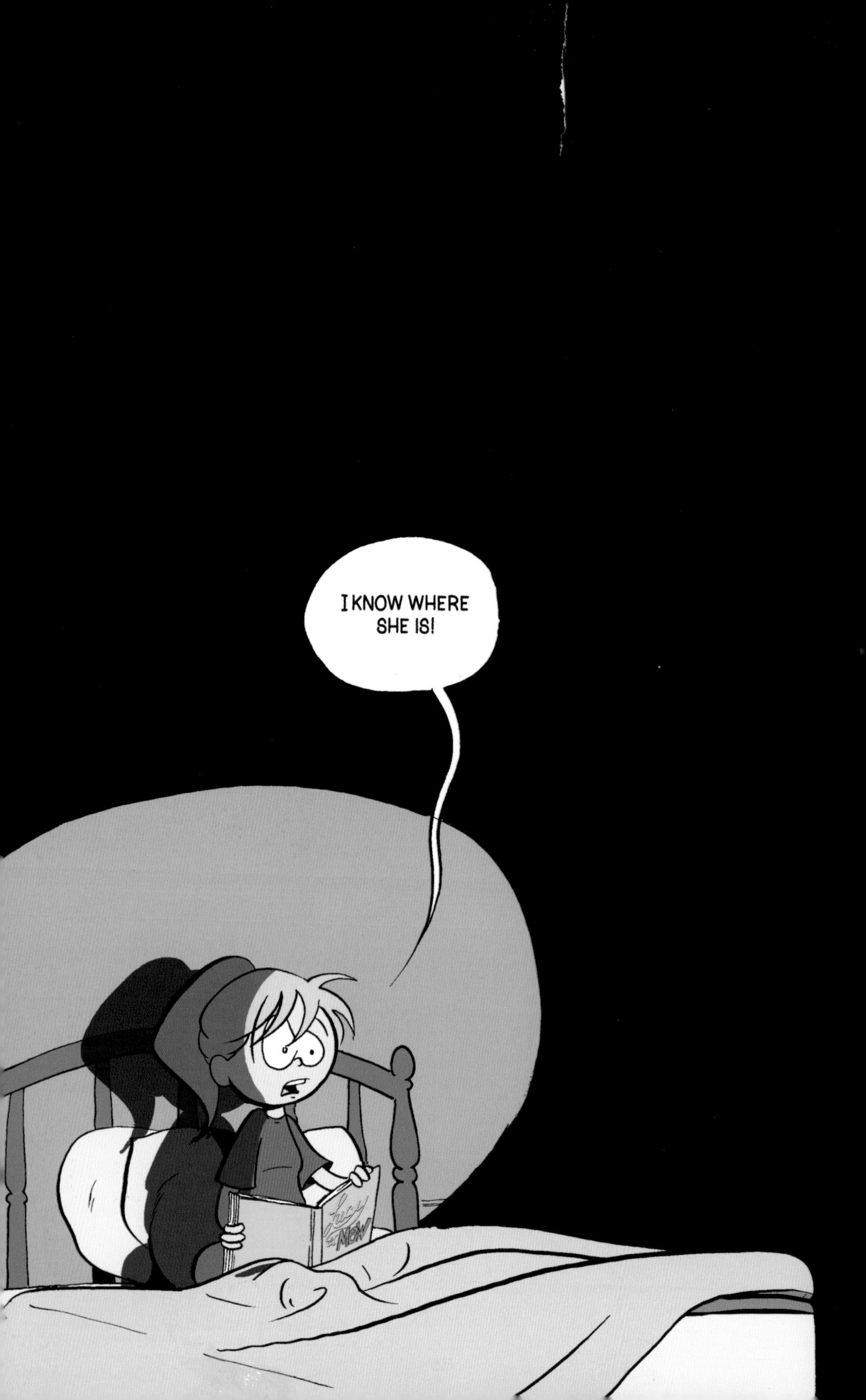
I KNOW WHERE SHE IS!

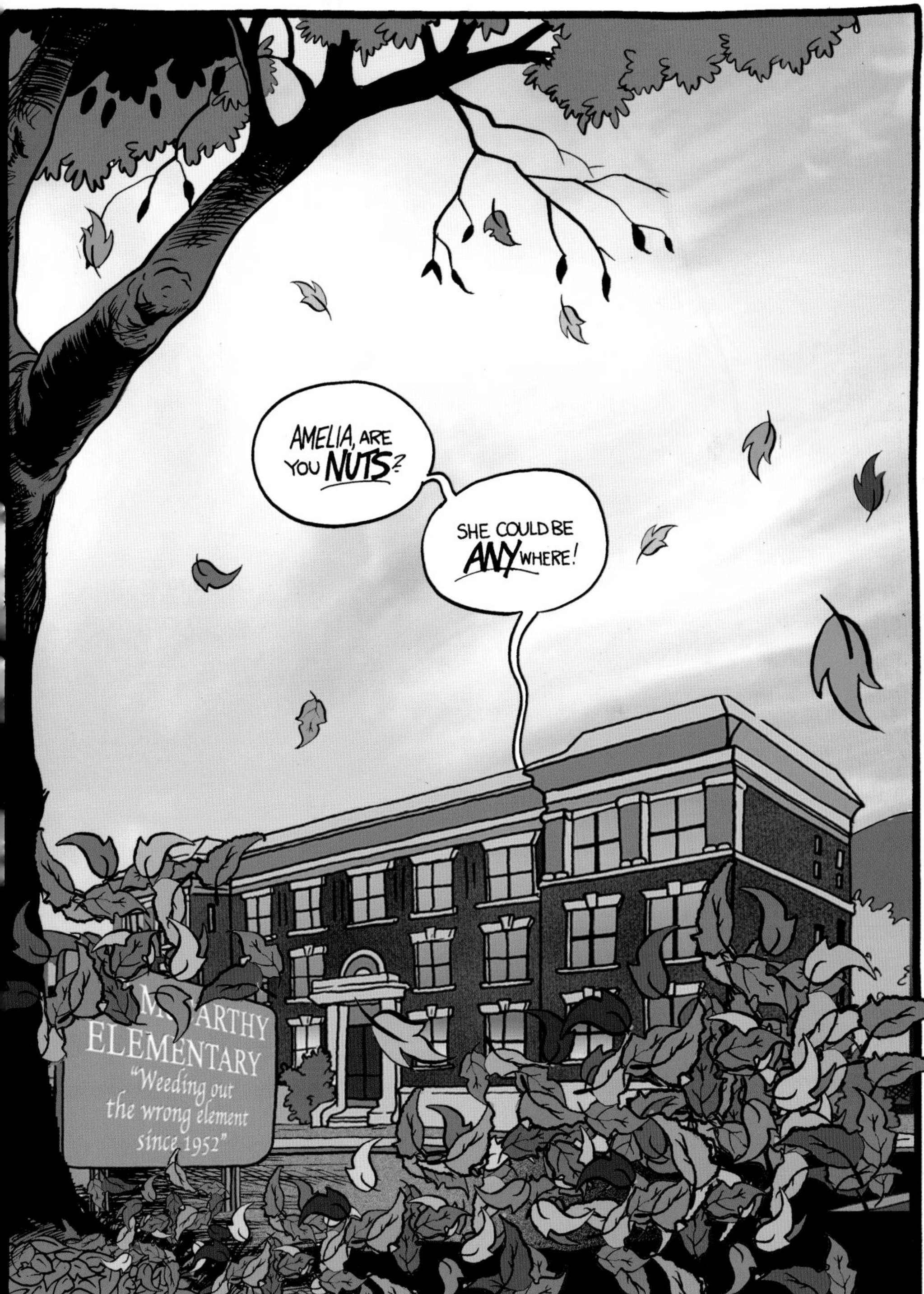
AMELIA, ARE YOU NUTS?
SHE COULD BE ANYWHERE!
ELEMENTARY
"Weeding out the wrong element since 1952"

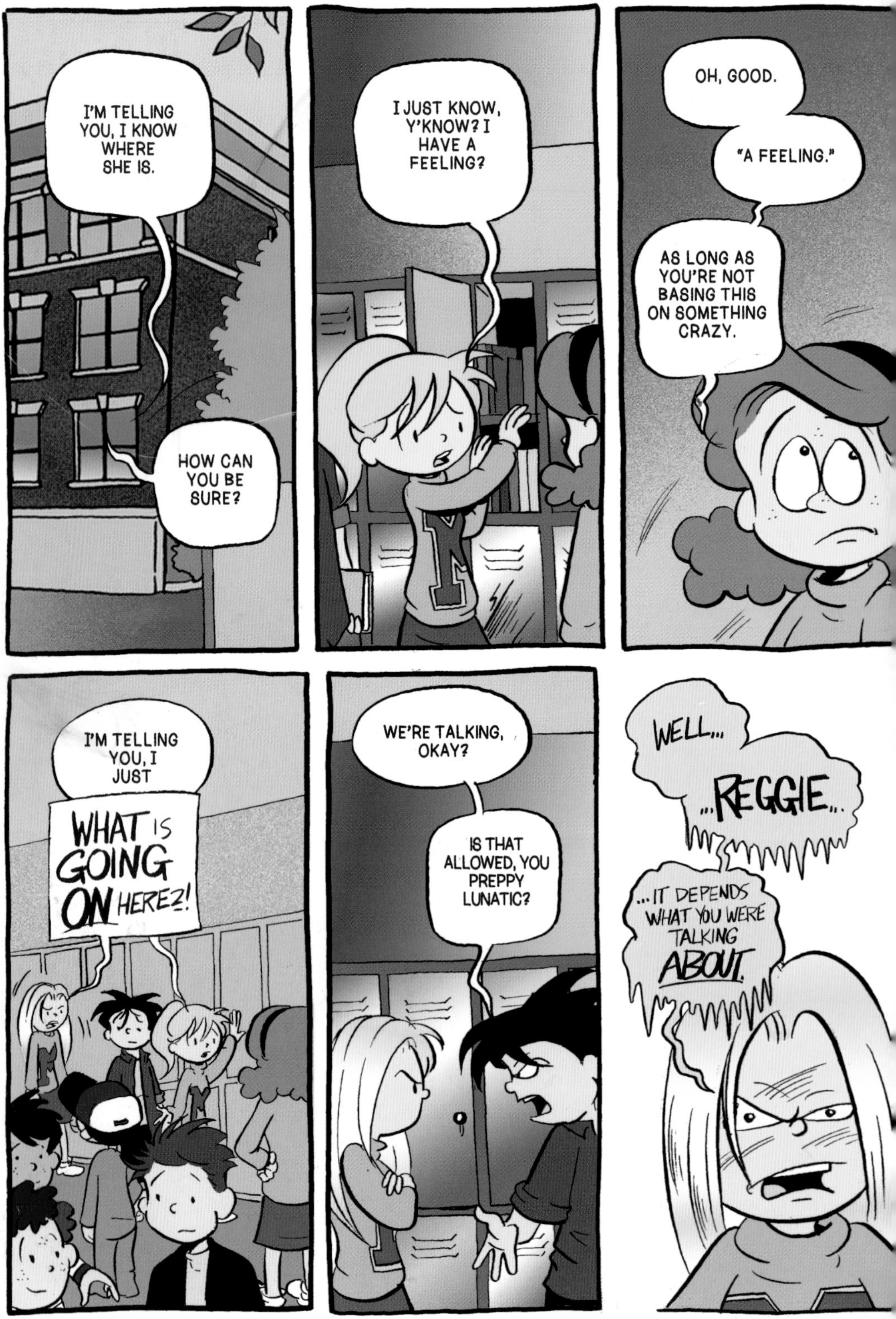
I'M TELLING YOU, I KNOW WHERE SHE IS.
HOW CAN YOU BE SURE?
I JUST KNOW, Y'KNOW? I HAVE A FEELING?
OH, GOOD.
"A FEELING."
AS LONG AS YOU'RE NOT BASING THIS ON SOMETHING CRAZY.
I'M TELLING YOU, I JUST
WHAT IS GOING ON HERE?!
WE'RE TALKING, OKAY?
IS THAT ALLOWED, YOU PREPPY LUNATIC?
WELL...
...REGGIE...
...IT DEPENDS WHAT YOU WERE TALKING ABOUT.

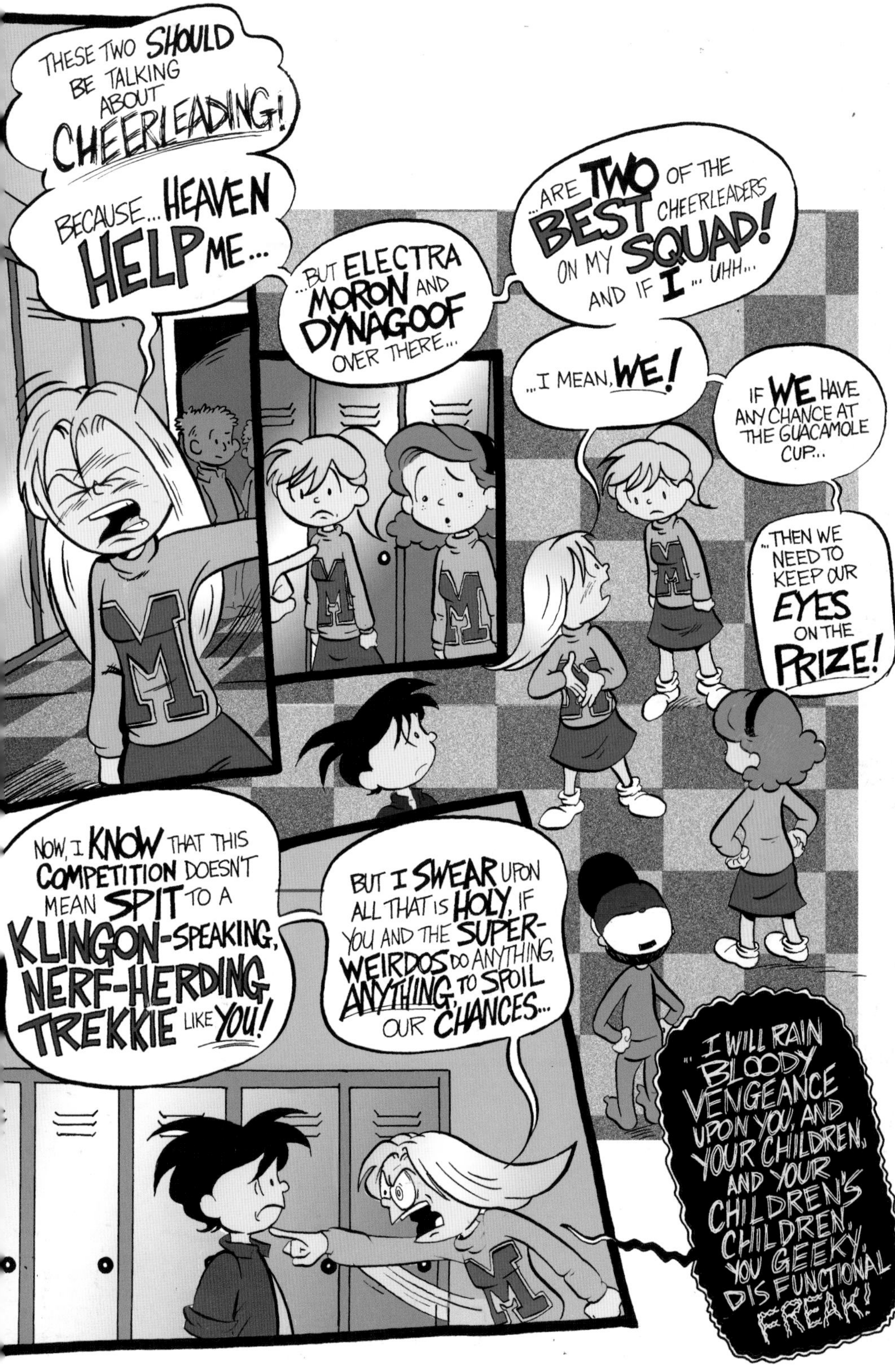
THESE TWO SHOULD BE TALKING ABOUT CHEERLEADING!
BECAUSE... HEAVEN HELP ME...
...BUT ELECTRA MORON AND DYNAGOOF OVER THERE...
...ARE TWO OF THE BEST CHEERLEADERS ON MY SQUAD! AND IF I... UHH...
...I MEAN, WE!
IF WE HAVE ANY CHANCE AT THE GUACAMOLE CUP...
...THEN WE NEED TO KEEP OUR EYES ON THE PRIZE!
NOW, I KNOW THAT THIS COMPETITION DOESN'T MEAN SPIT TO A KLINGON-SPEAKING, NERF-HERDING TREKKIE LIKE YOU!
BUT I SWEAR UPON ALL THAT IS HOLY, IF YOU AND THE SUPER-WEIRDOS DO ANYTHING, ANYTHING, TO SPOIL OUR CHANCES...
...I WILL RAIN BLOODY VENGEANCE UPON YOU, AND YOUR CHILDREN, AND YOUR CHILDREN'S CHILDREN, YOU GEEKY, DISFUNCTIONAL FREAK!

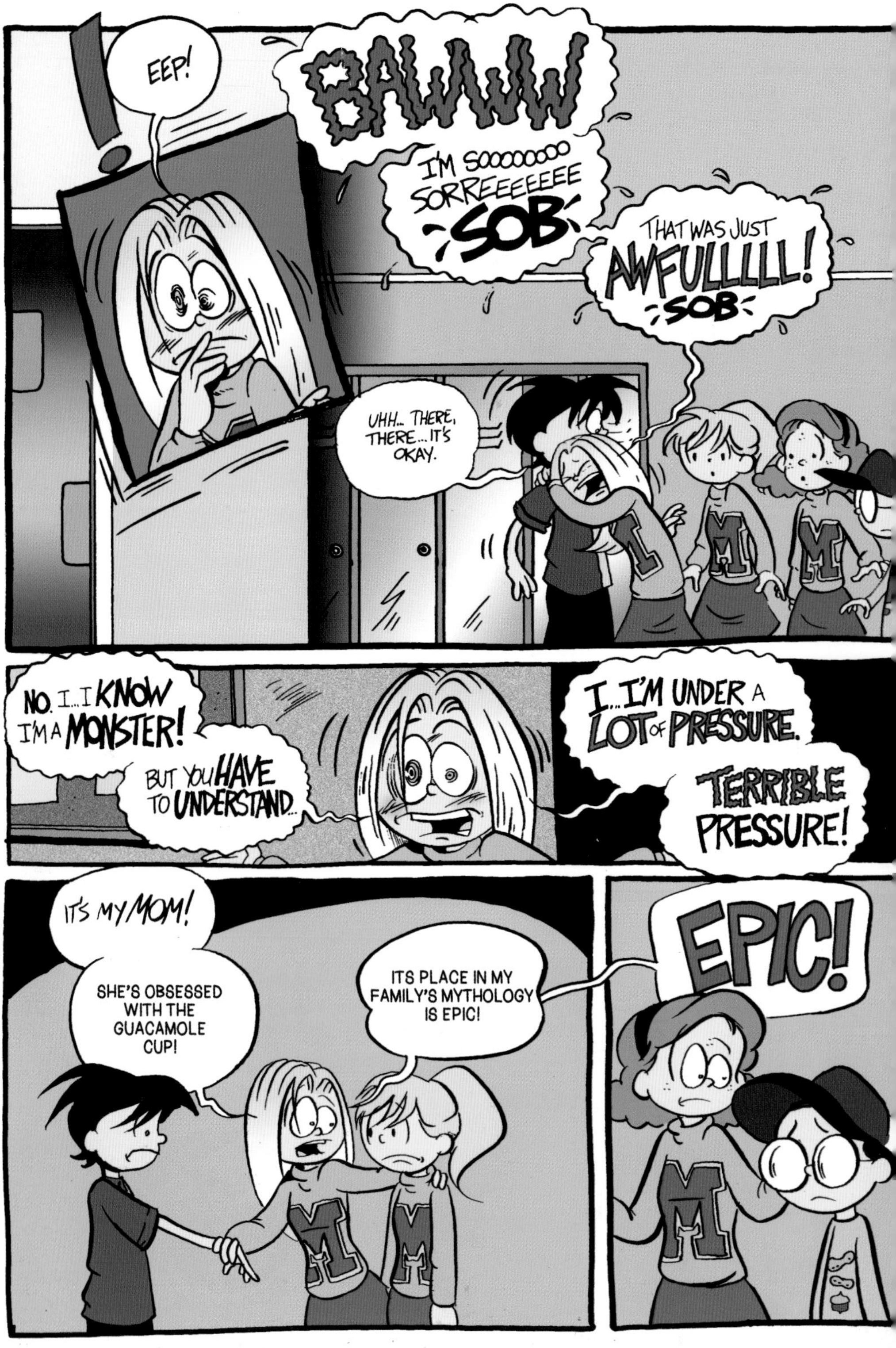
!
EEP!
BAWWW
I'M SOOOOOOOO SORREEEEEEE
SOB
THAT WAS JUST AWFULLLLL!
SOB
UHH... THERE, THERE... IT'S OKAY.
NO. I... I KNOW I'M A MONSTER!
BUT YOU HAVE TO UNDERSTAND...
I... I'M UNDER A LOT OF PRESSURE.
TERRIBLE PRESSURE!
IT'S MY MOM!
SHE'S OBSESSED WITH THE GUACAMOLE CUP!
ITS PLACE IN MY FAMILY'S MYTHOLOGY IS EPIC!
EPIC!

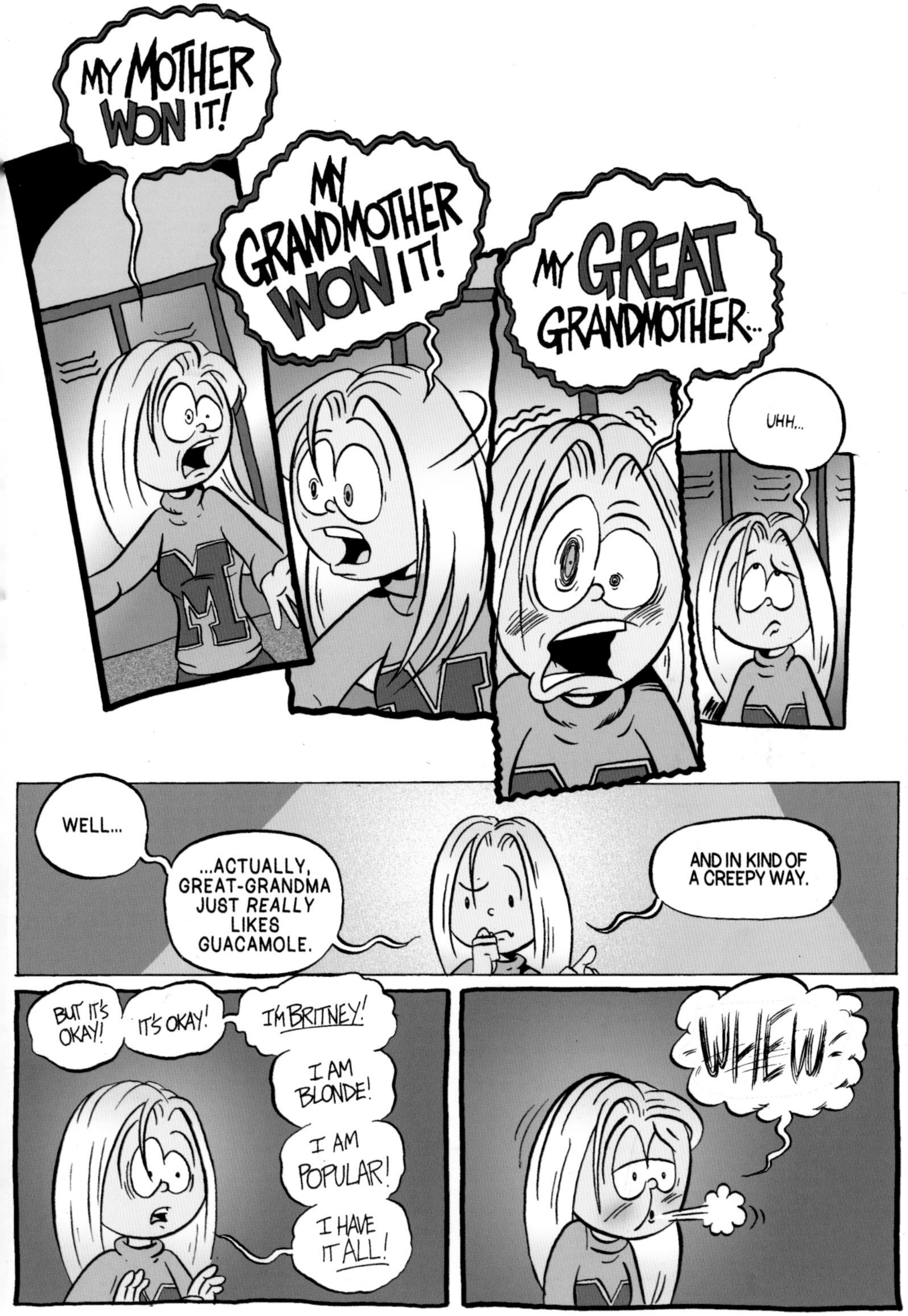
MY MOTHER WON IT!
MY GRANDMOTHER WON IT!
MY GREAT GRANDMOTHER...
UHH...
WELL...
...ACTUALLY, GREAT-GRANDMA JUST *REALLY* LIKES GUACAMOLE.
AND IN KIND OF A CREEPY WAY.
BUT IT'S OKAY!
IT'S OKAY!
I'M BRITNEY!
I AM BLONDE!
I AM POPULAR!
I HAVE IT ALL!
WHEW

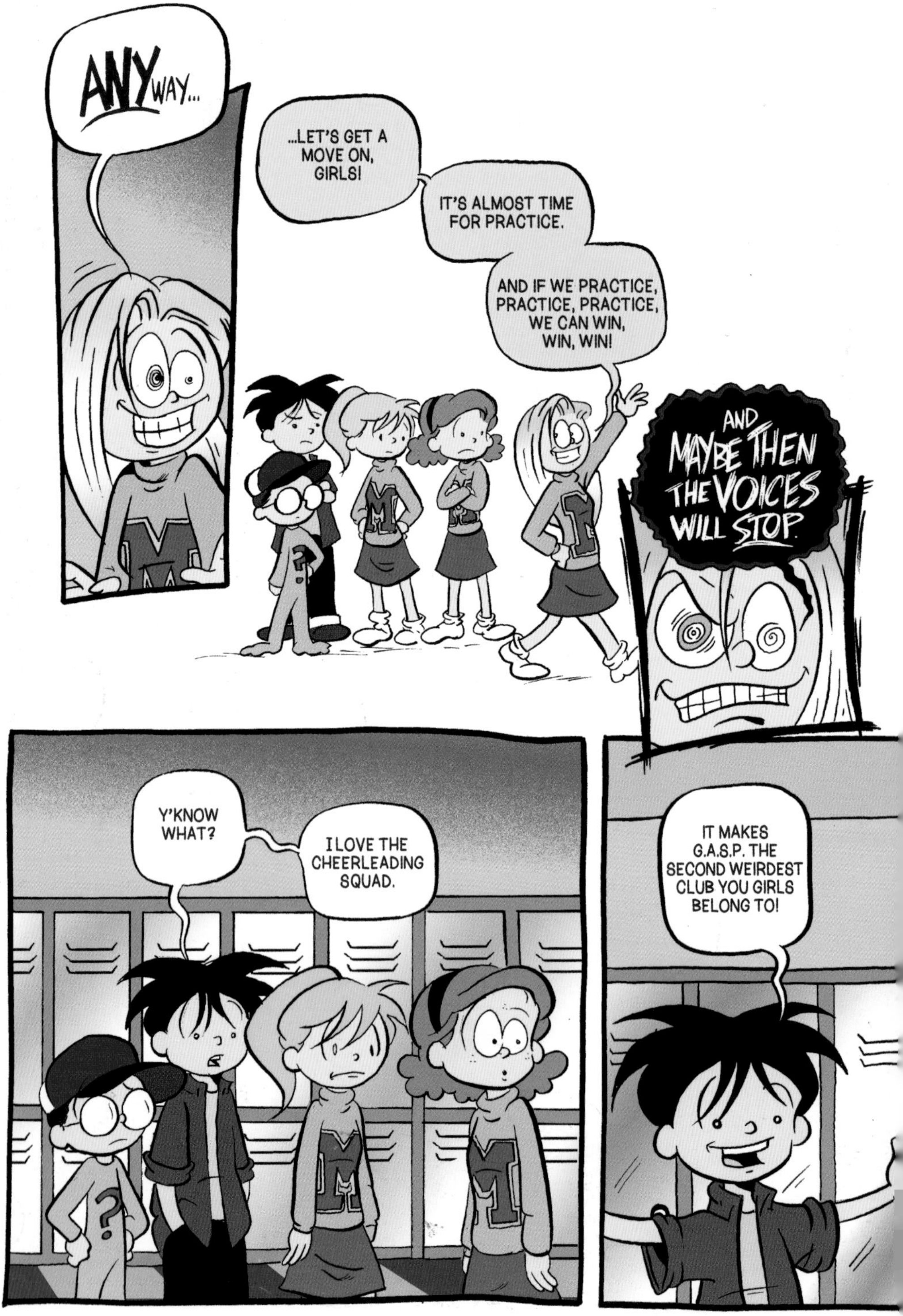
ANYWAY...
...LET'S GET A MOVE ON, GIRLS!
IT'S ALMOST TIME FOR PRACTICE.
AND IF WE PRACTICE, PRACTICE, PRACTICE, WE CAN WIN, WIN, WIN!
AND MAYBE THEN THE VOICES WILL STOP.
Y'KNOW WHAT?
I LOVE THE CHEERLEADING SQUAD.
IT MAKES G.A.S.P. THE SECOND WEIRDEST CLUB YOU GIRLS BELONG TO!

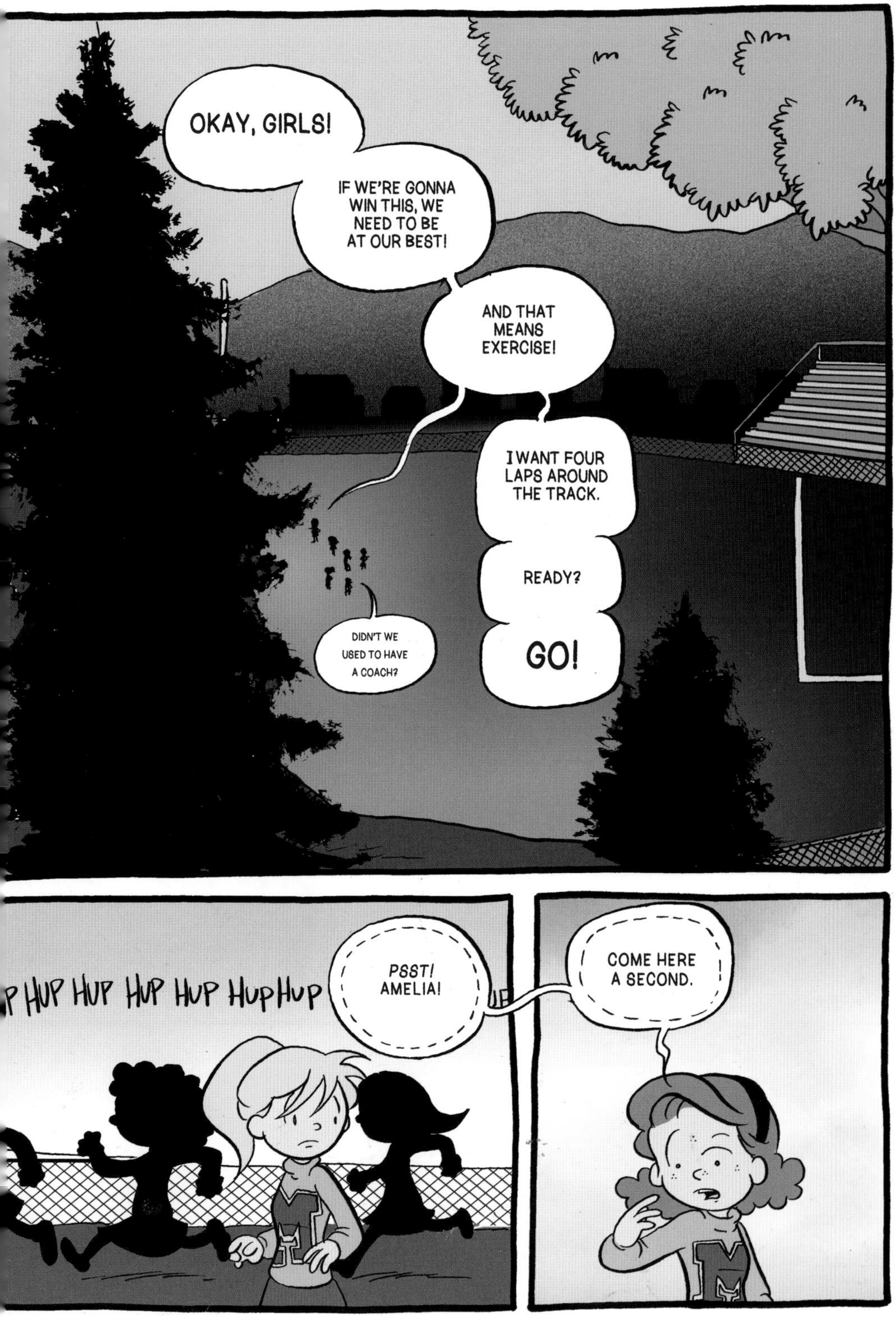
OKAY, GIRLS!
IF WE'RE GONNA WIN THIS, WE NEED TO BE AT OUR BEST!
AND THAT MEANS EXERCISE!
I WANT FOUR LAPS AROUND THE TRACK.
READY?
GO!
DIDN'T WE USED TO HAVE A COACH?
HUP HUP HUP HUP HUP HUP
PSST! AMELIA!
COME HERE A SECOND.

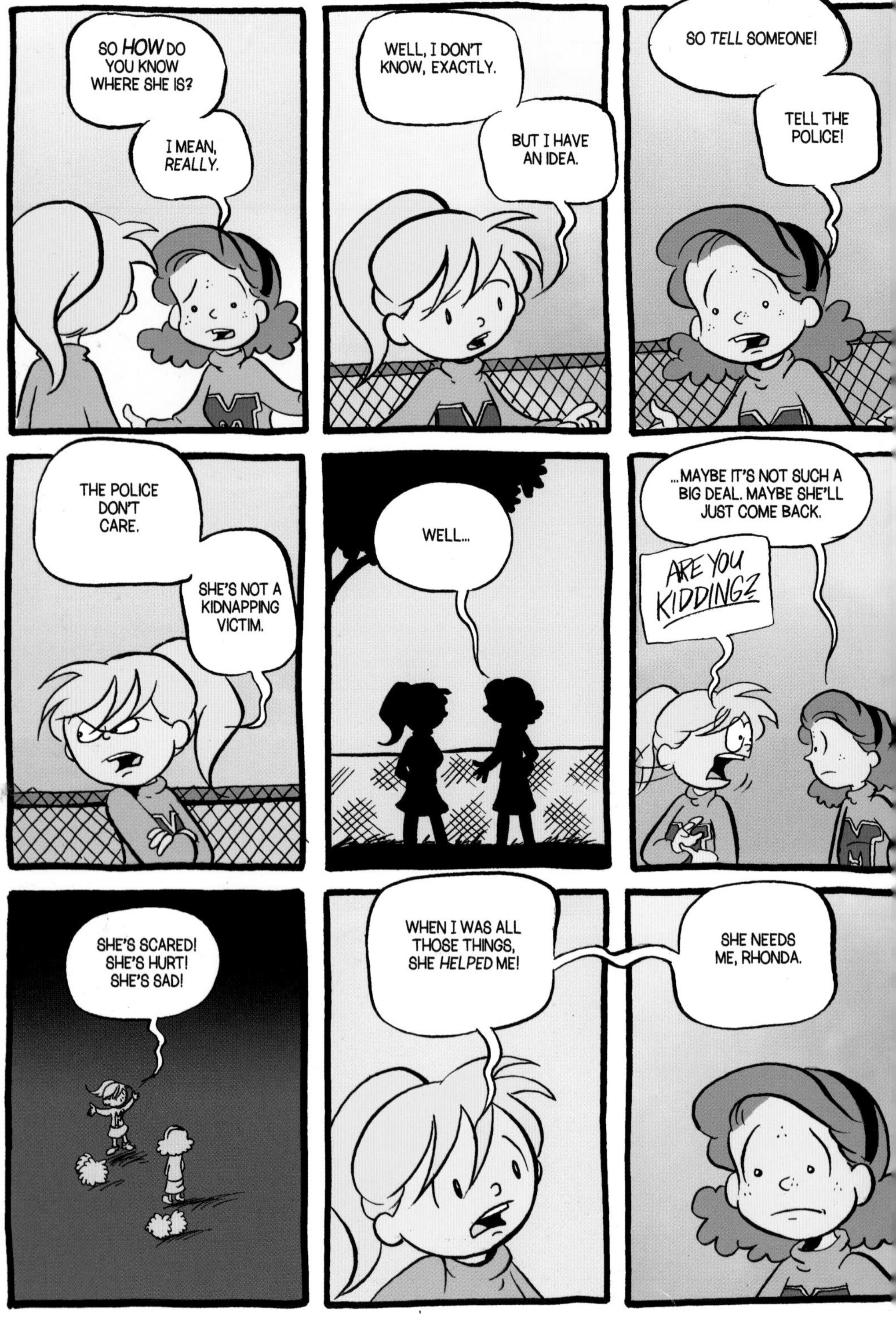
SO *HOW* DO YOU KNOW WHERE SHE IS?
I MEAN, *REALLY*.
WELL, I DON'T KNOW, EXACTLY.
BUT I HAVE AN IDEA.
SO *TELL* SOMEONE!
TELL THE POLICE!
THE POLICE DON'T CARE.
SHE'S NOT A KIDNAPPING VICTIM.
WELL...
...MAYBE IT'S NOT SUCH A BIG DEAL. MAYBE SHE'LL JUST COME BACK.
ARE YOU KIDDING?
SHE'S SCARED! SHE'S HURT! SHE'S SAD!
WHEN I WAS ALL THOSE THINGS, SHE *HELPED* ME!
SHE NEEDS ME, RHONDA.

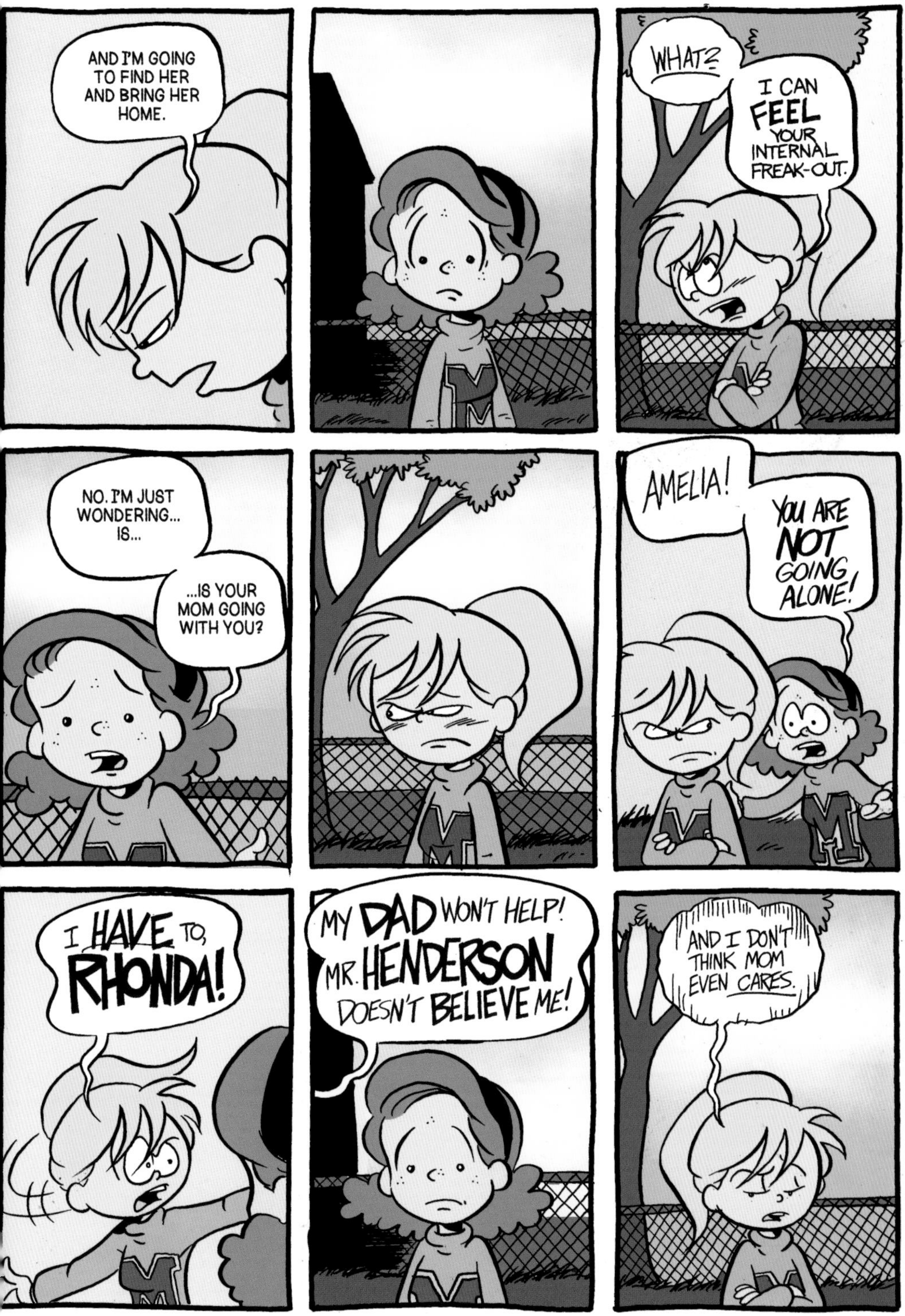
AND I'M GOING TO FIND HER AND BRING HER HOME.
WHAT?
I CAN FEEL YOUR INTERNAL FREAK-OUT.
NO. I'M JUST WONDERING... IS...
...IS YOUR MOM GOING WITH YOU?
AMELIA!
YOU ARE NOT GOING ALONE!
I HAVE TO, RHONDA!
MY DAD WON'T HELP! MR. HENDERSON DOESN'T BELIEVE ME!
AND I DON'T THINK MOM EVEN CARES.

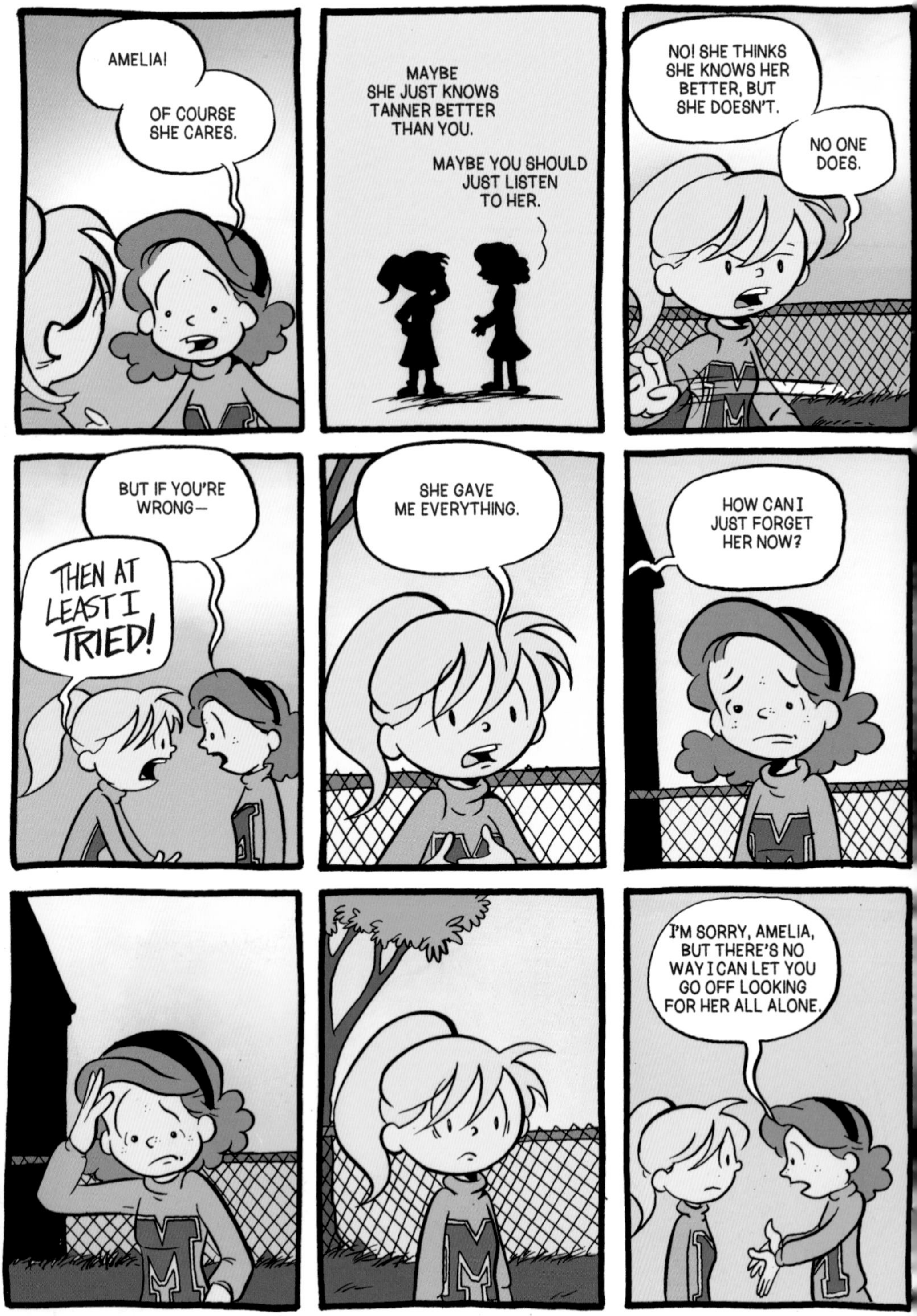
AMELIA!
OF COURSE SHE CARES.
MAYBE SHE JUST KNOWS TANNER BETTER THAN YOU.
MAYBE YOU SHOULD JUST LISTEN TO HER.
NO! SHE THINKS SHE KNOWS HER BETTER, BUT SHE DOESN'T.
NO ONE DOES.
BUT IF YOU'RE WRONG—
THEN AT LEAST I TRIED!
SHE GAVE ME EVERYTHING.
HOW CAN I JUST FORGET HER NOW?
I'M SORRY, AMELIA, BUT THERE'S NO WAY I CAN LET YOU GO OFF LOOKING FOR HER ALL ALONE.

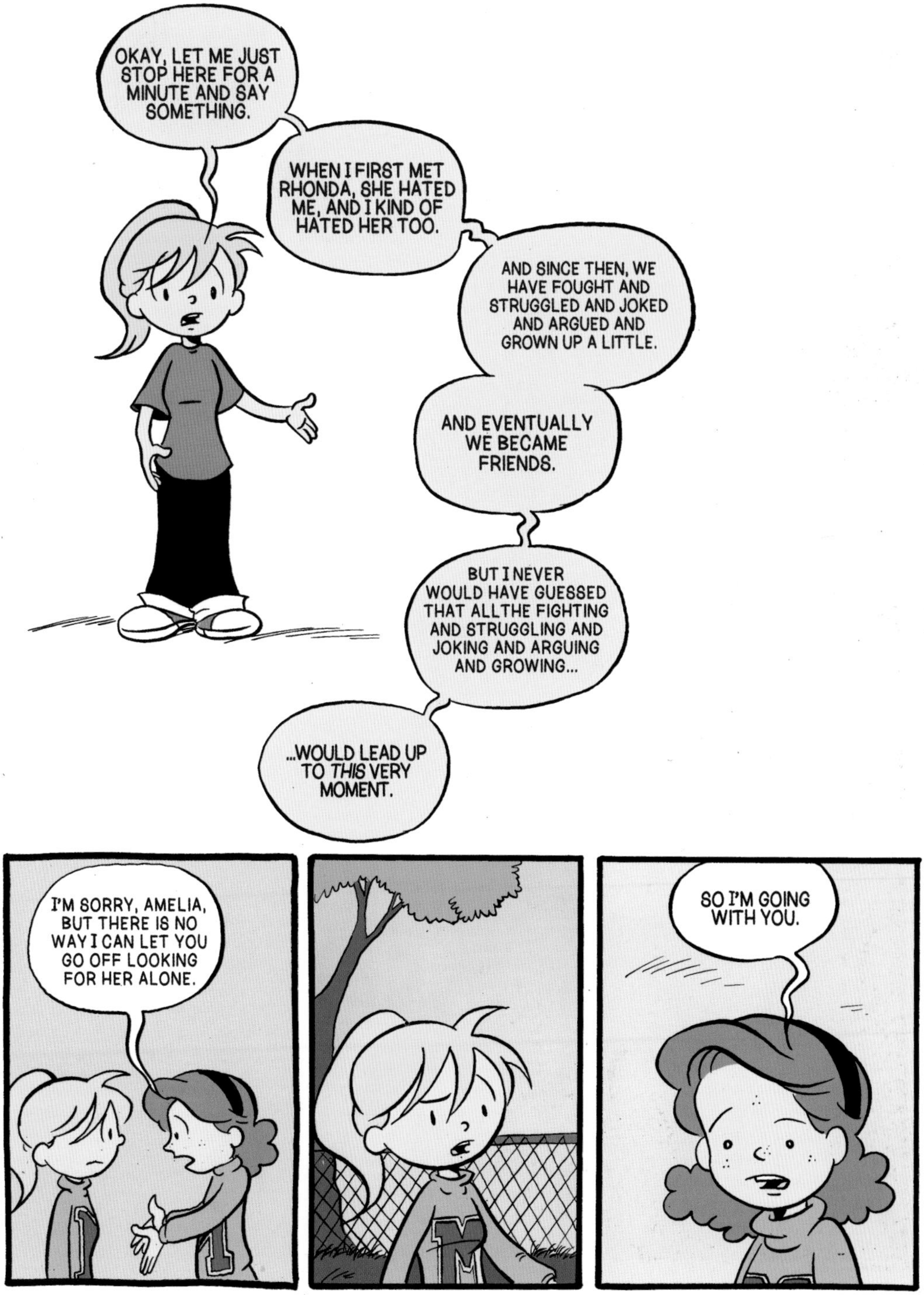
OKAY, LET ME JUST STOP HERE FOR A MINUTE AND SAY SOMETHING.
WHEN I FIRST MET RHONDA, SHE HATED ME, AND I KIND OF HATED HER TOO.
AND SINCE THEN, WE HAVE FOUGHT AND STRUGGLED AND JOKED AND ARGUED AND GROWN UP A LITTLE.
AND EVENTUALLY WE BECAME FRIENDS.
BUT I NEVER WOULD HAVE GUESSED THAT ALL THE FIGHTING AND STRUGGLING AND JOKING AND ARGUING AND GROWING...
...WOULD LEAD UP TO *THIS* VERY MOMENT.
I'M SORRY, AMELIA, BUT THERE IS NO WAY I CAN LET YOU GO OFF LOOKING FOR HER ALONE.
SO I'M GOING WITH YOU.

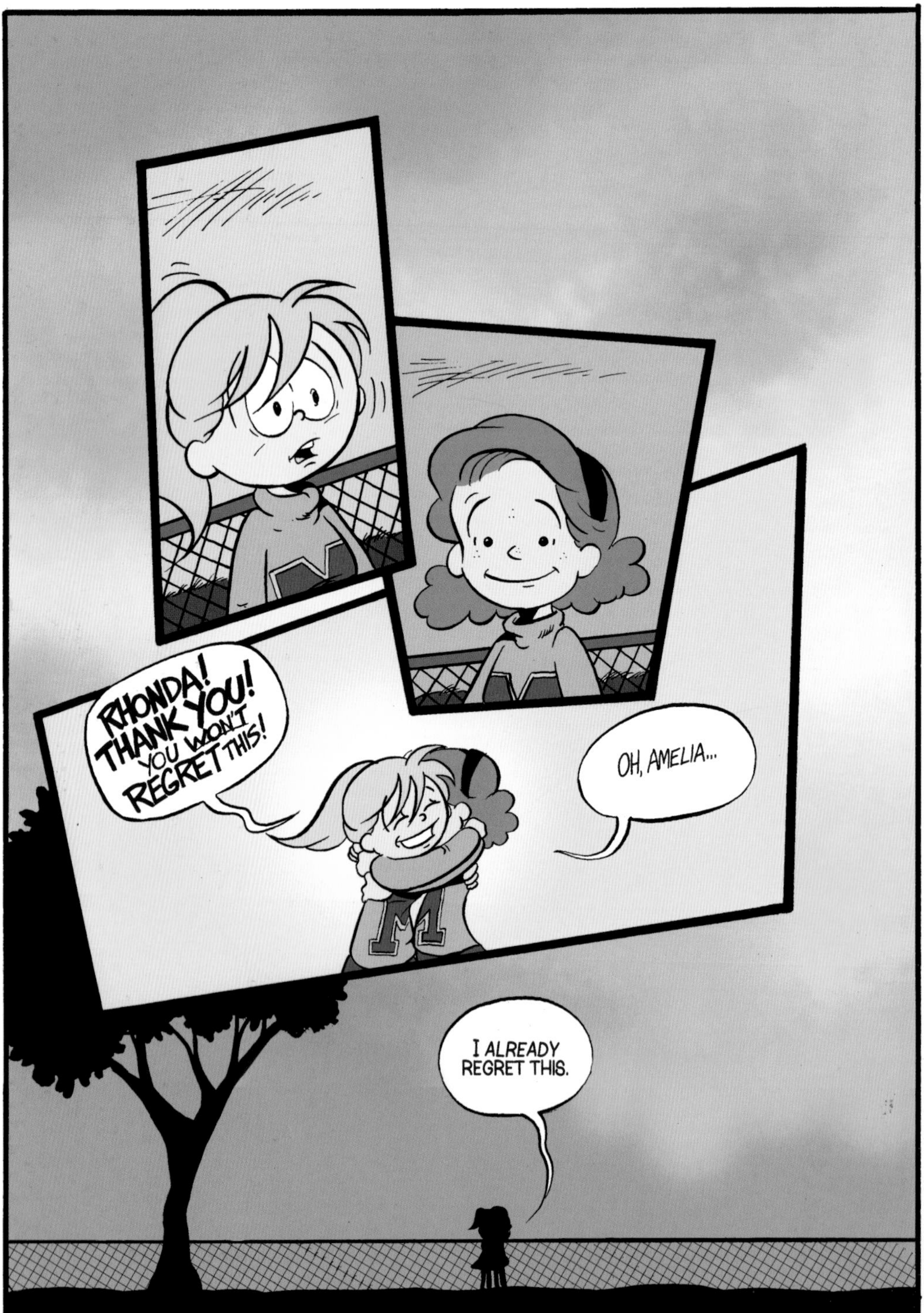
RHONDA! THANK YOU! YOU WON'T REGRET THIS!
OH, AMELIA...
I ALREADY REGRET THIS.

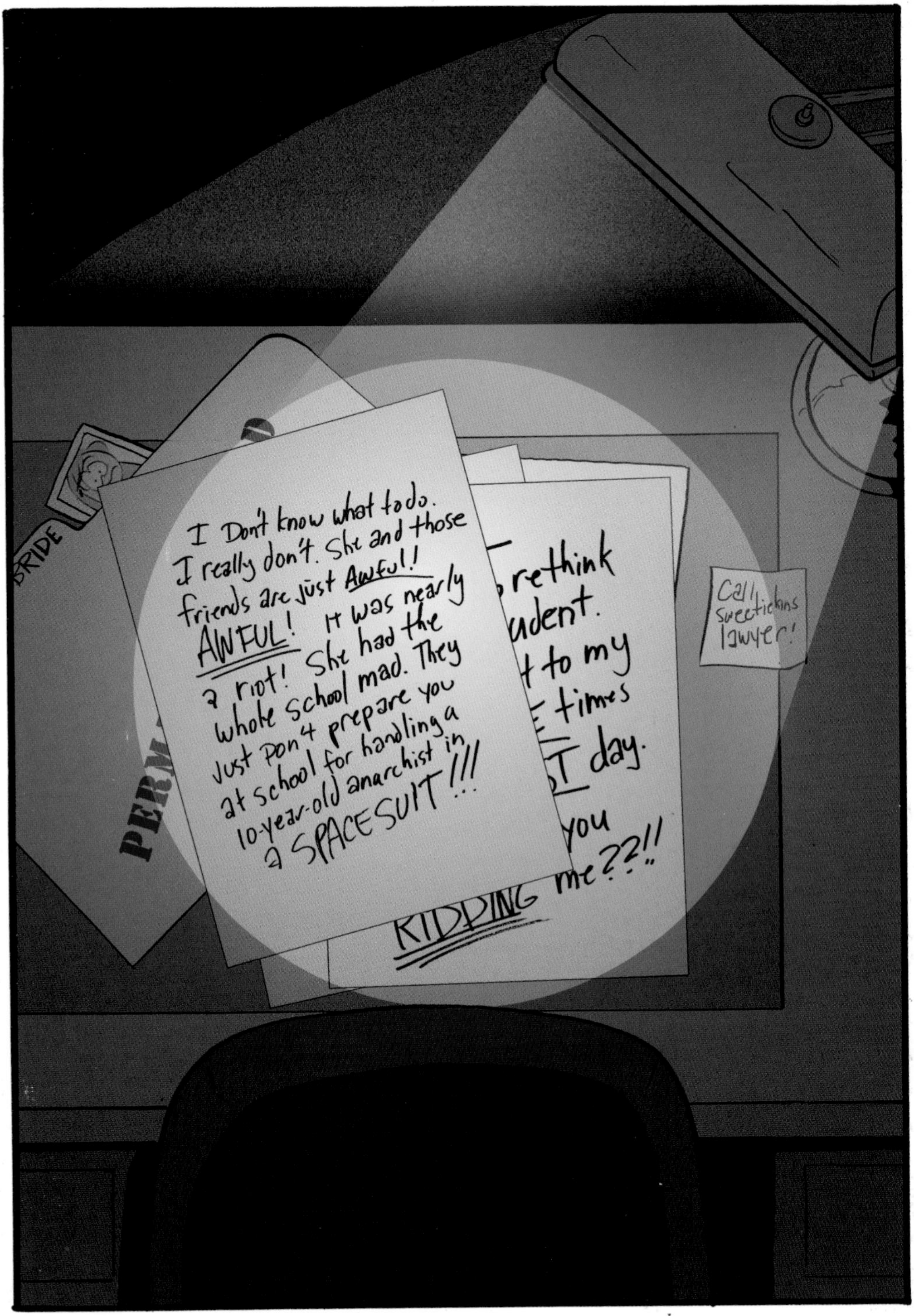

I Don't know what to do.
I really don't. She and those
friends are just AWFUL!
AWFUL! It was nearly
a riot! She had the
whole school mad. They
just Don't prepare you
at school for handling a
10-year-old anarchist in
a SPACESUIT!!!
rethink
day.
you
KIDDING me??!!
Call sweetickins lawyer!
BRIDE
PERM

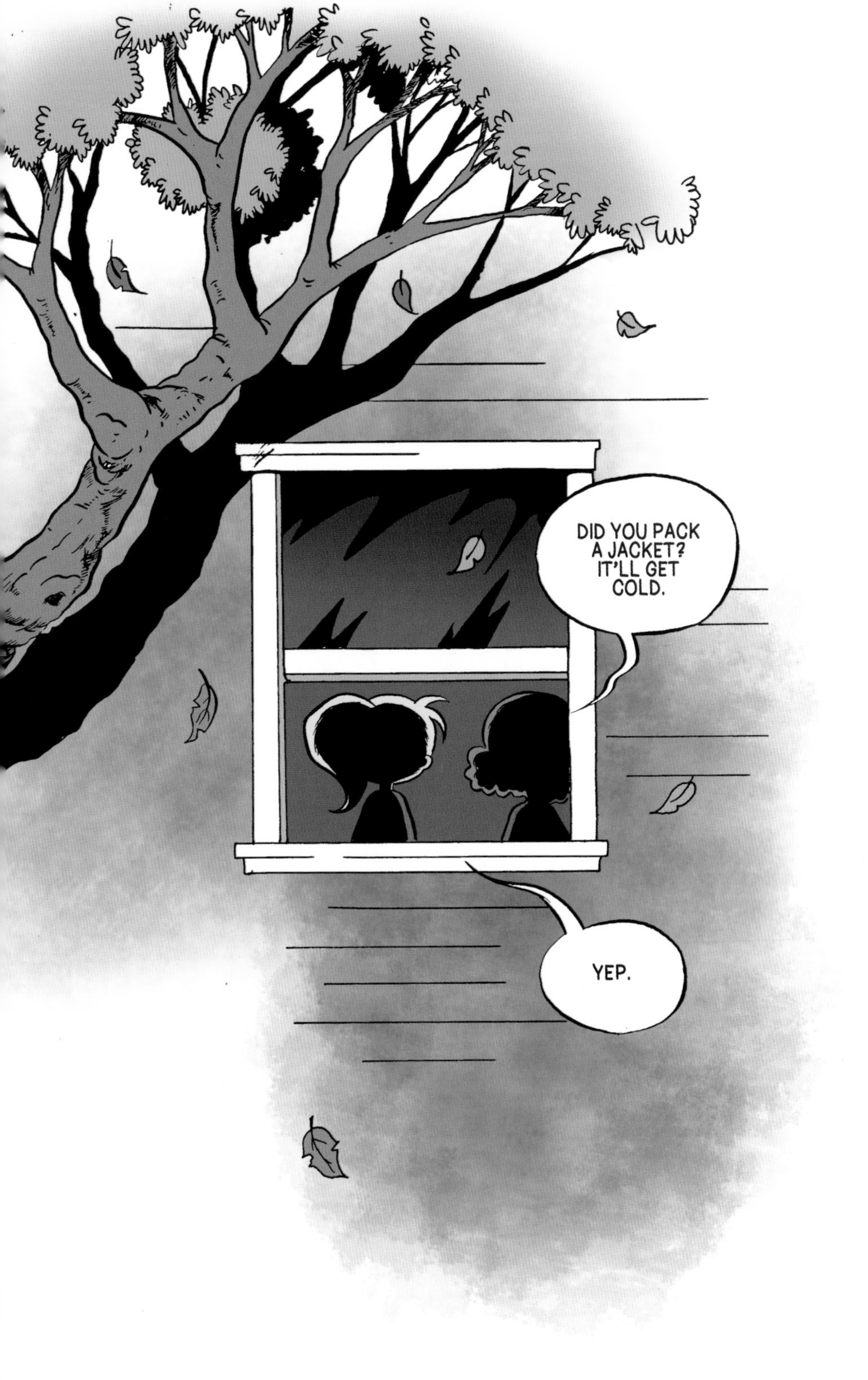
DID YOU PACK A JACKET? IT'LL GET COLD.
YEP.

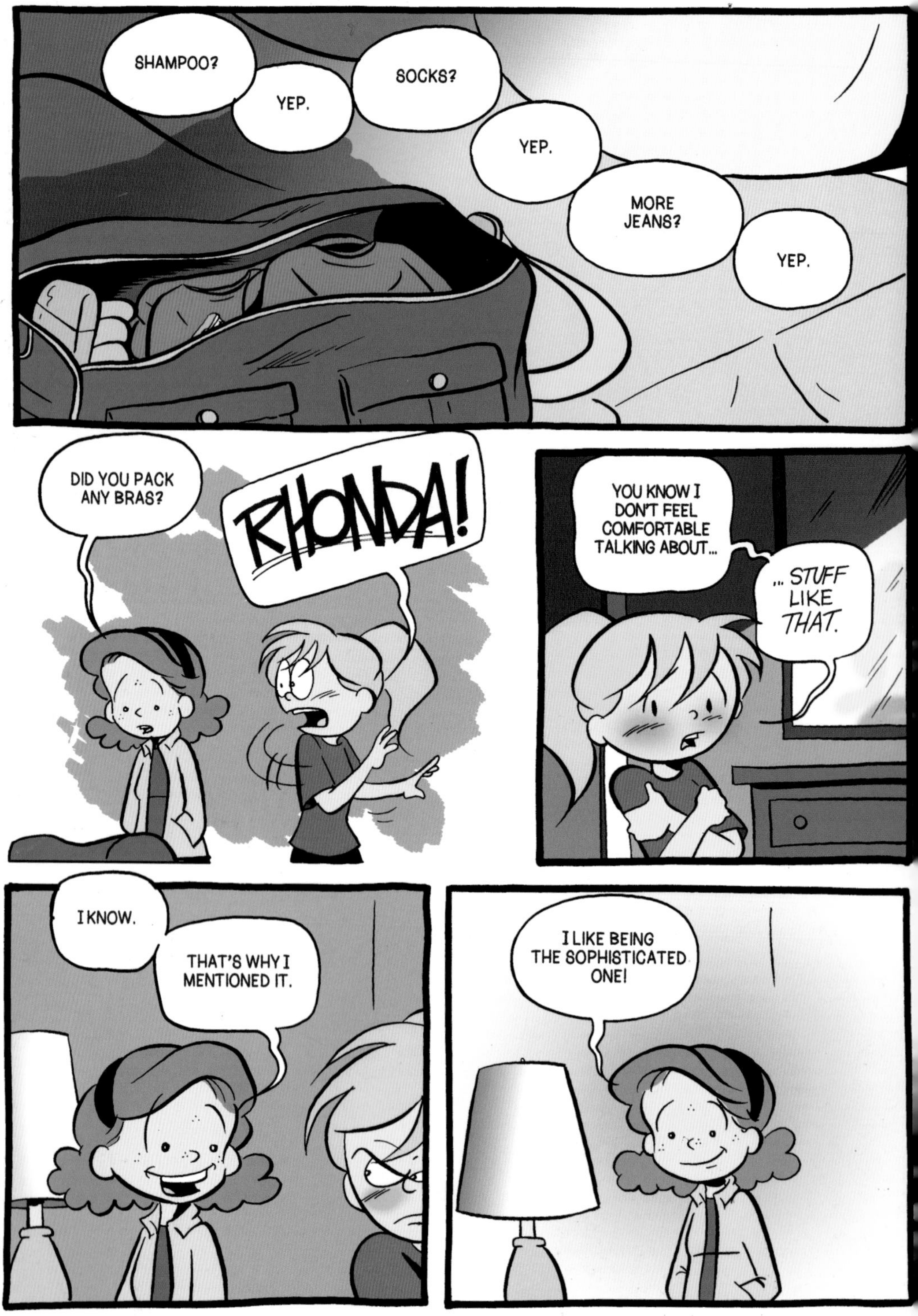
SHAMPOO?
YEP.
SOCKS?
YEP.
MORE JEANS?
YEP.
DID YOU PACK ANY BRAS?
RHONDA!
YOU KNOW I DON'T FEEL COMFORTABLE TALKING ABOUT...
... STUFF LIKE THAT.
I KNOW.
THAT'S WHY I MENTIONED IT.
I LIKE BEING THE SOPHISTICATED ONE!

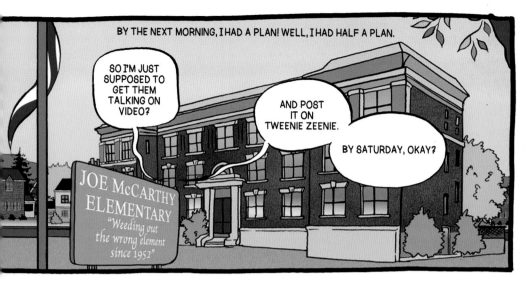

BY THE NEXT MORNING, I HAD A PLAN! WELL, I HAD HALF A PLAN.

SO I'M JUST SUPPOSED TO GET THEM TALKING ON VIDEO?

AND POST IT ON TWEENIE ZEENIE.

BY SATURDAY, OKAY?

JOE McCARTHY ELEMENTARY
"Weeding out the wrong element since 1952"

SATURDAY, GOT IT.

AND SPEAKING OF SATURDAY...

...THAT'S THE DAY OF THE CHEERLEADING COMPETITION. YOU NEED TO STOP IT.

STOP IT? HOW DO I DO THAT?

I DON'T KNOW, YOU'RE YOU.

DO SOMETHING YOU-ESQUE.

MISS McBRIDE!

CAN YOU SEE ME IN MY OFFICE?

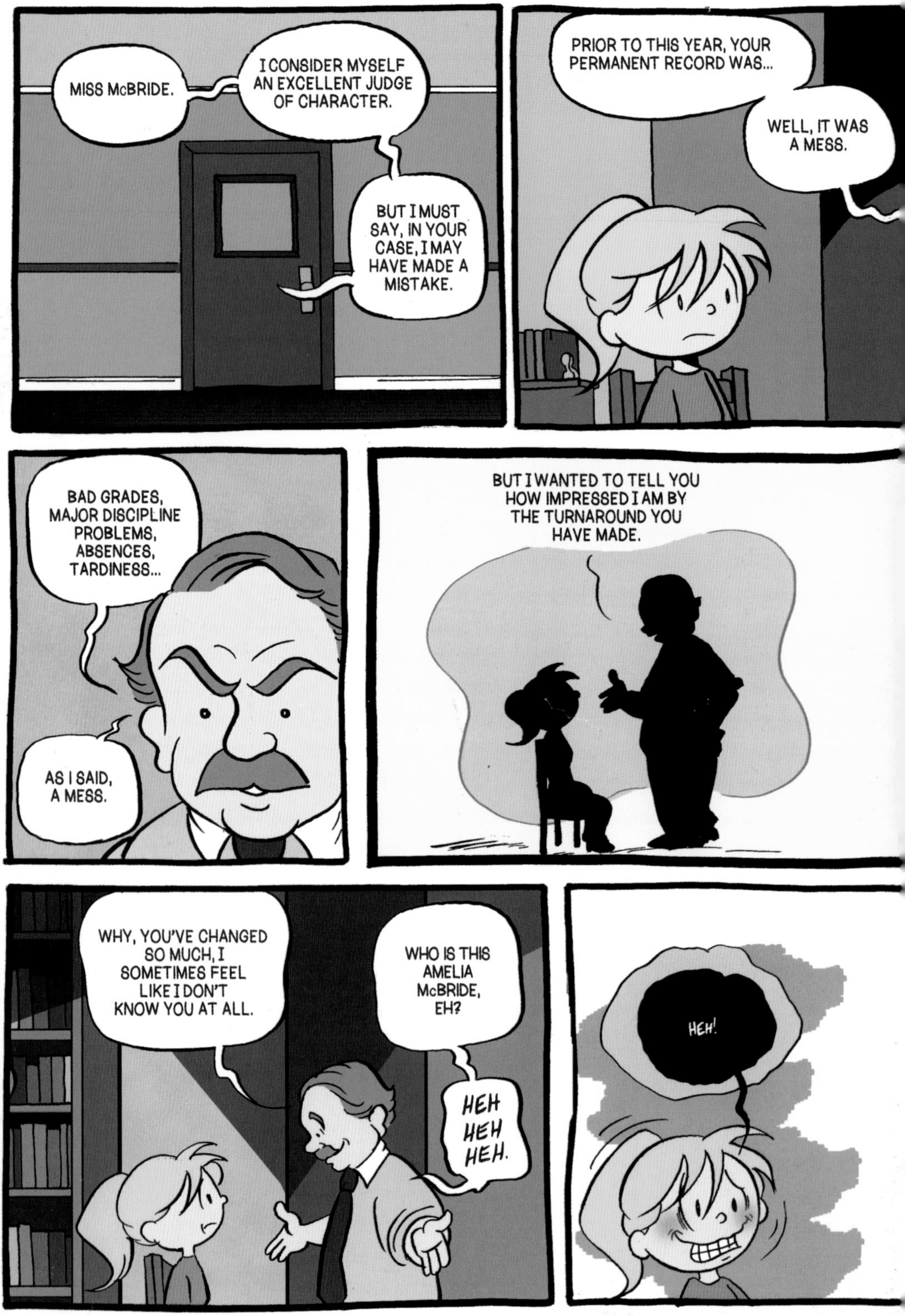
MISS McBRIDE.
I CONSIDER MYSELF AN EXCELLENT JUDGE OF CHARACTER.
BUT I MUST SAY, IN YOUR CASE, I MAY HAVE MADE A MISTAKE.
PRIOR TO THIS YEAR, YOUR PERMANENT RECORD WAS...
WELL, IT WAS A MESS.
BAD GRADES, MAJOR DISCIPLINE PROBLEMS, ABSENCES, TARDINESS...
AS I SAID, A MESS.
BUT I WANTED TO TELL YOU HOW IMPRESSED I AM BY THE TURNAROUND YOU HAVE MADE.
WHY, YOU'VE CHANGED SO MUCH, I SOMETIMES FEEL LIKE I DON'T KNOW YOU AT ALL.
WHO IS THIS AMELIA McBRIDE, EH?
HEH HEH HEH.
HEH!

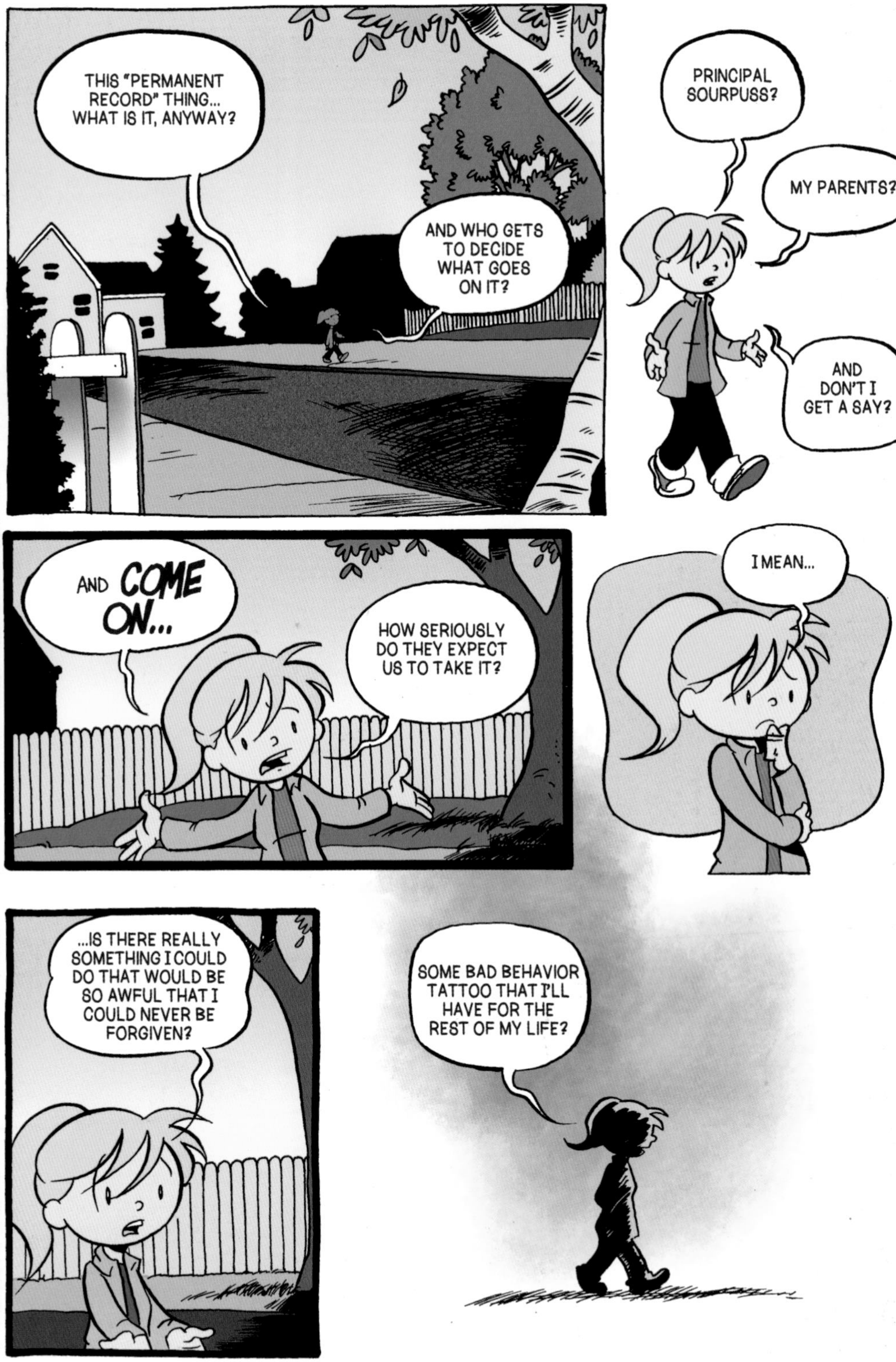
THIS "PERMANENT RECORD" THING... WHAT IS IT, ANYWAY?
AND WHO GETS TO DECIDE WHAT GOES ON IT?
PRINCIPAL SOURPUSS?
MY PARENTS?
AND DON'T I GET A SAY?
AND COME ON...
HOW SERIOUSLY DO THEY EXPECT US TO TAKE IT?
I MEAN...
...IS THERE REALLY SOMETHING I COULD DO THAT WOULD BE SO AWFUL THAT I COULD NEVER BE FORGIVEN?
SOME BAD BEHAVIOR TATTOO THAT I'LL HAVE FOR THE REST OF MY LIFE?

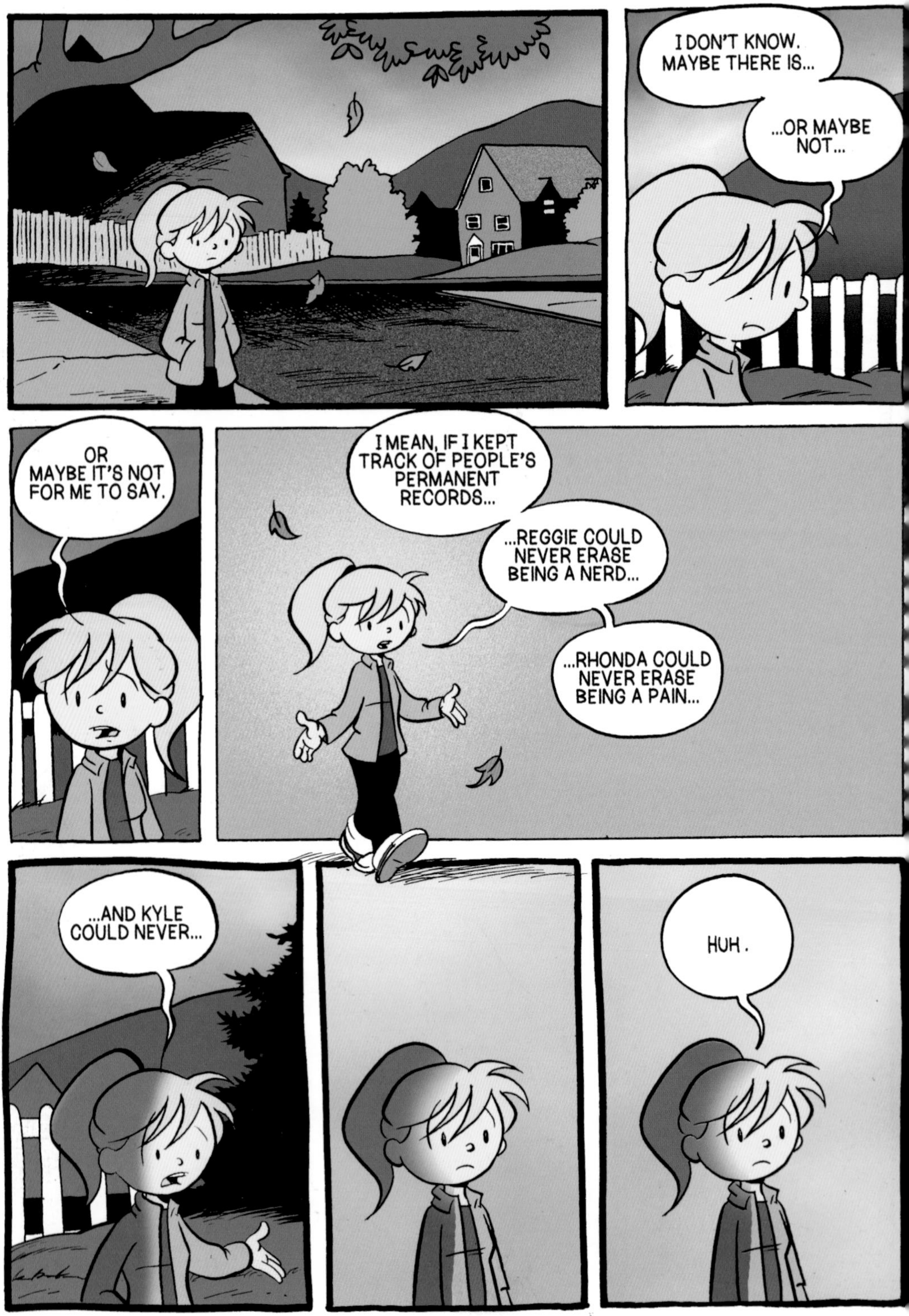
I DON'T KNOW. MAYBE THERE IS...
...OR MAYBE NOT...
OR MAYBE IT'S NOT FOR ME TO SAY.
I MEAN, IF I KEPT TRACK OF PEOPLE'S PERMANENT RECORDS...
...REGGIE COULD NEVER ERASE BEING A NERD...
...RHONDA COULD NEVER ERASE BEING A PAIN...
...AND KYLE COULD NEVER...
HUH.

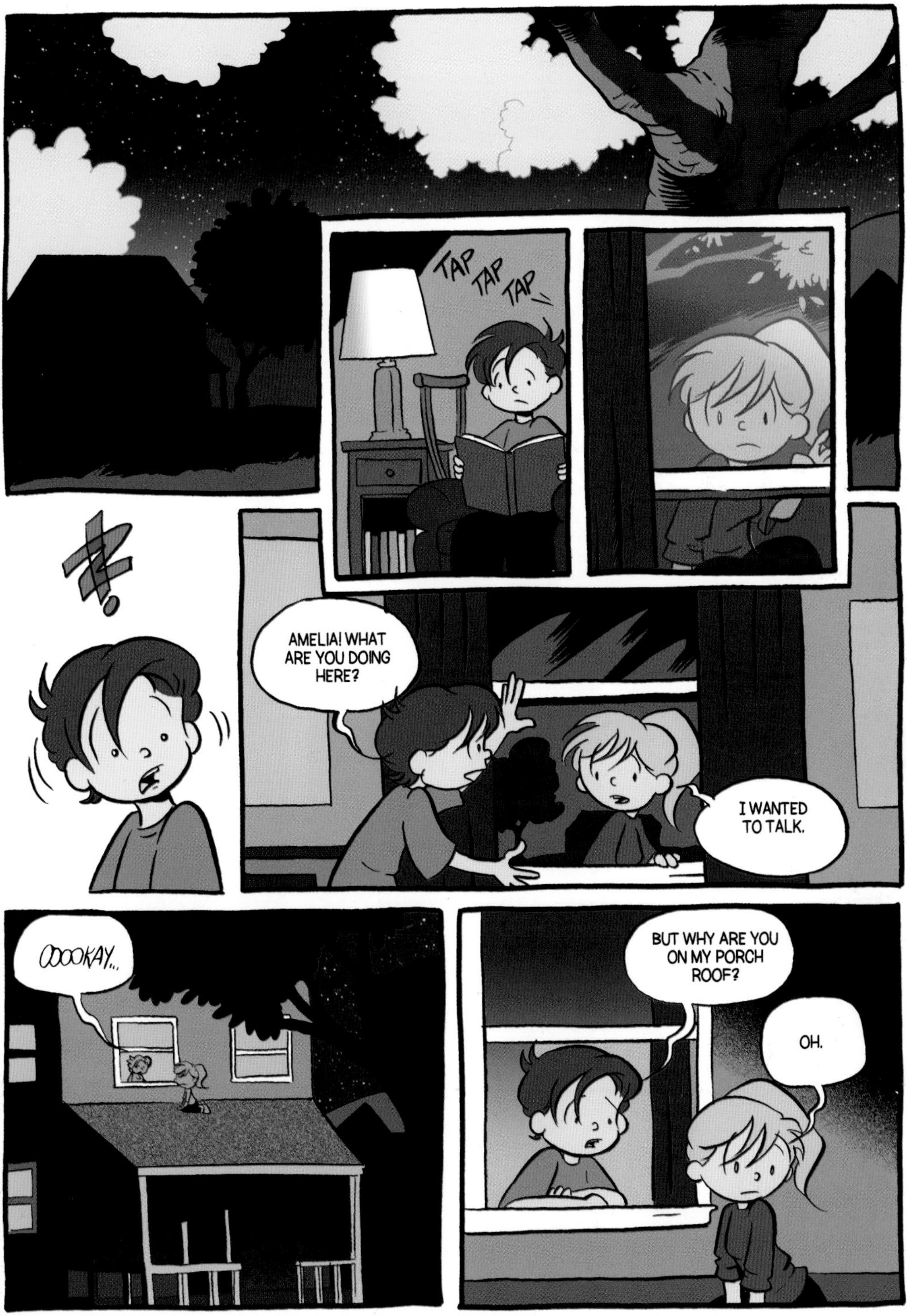
TAP TAP TAP
AMELIA! WHAT ARE YOU DOING HERE?
I WANTED TO TALK.
OOOOKAY...
BUT WHY ARE YOU ON MY PORCH ROOF?
OH.

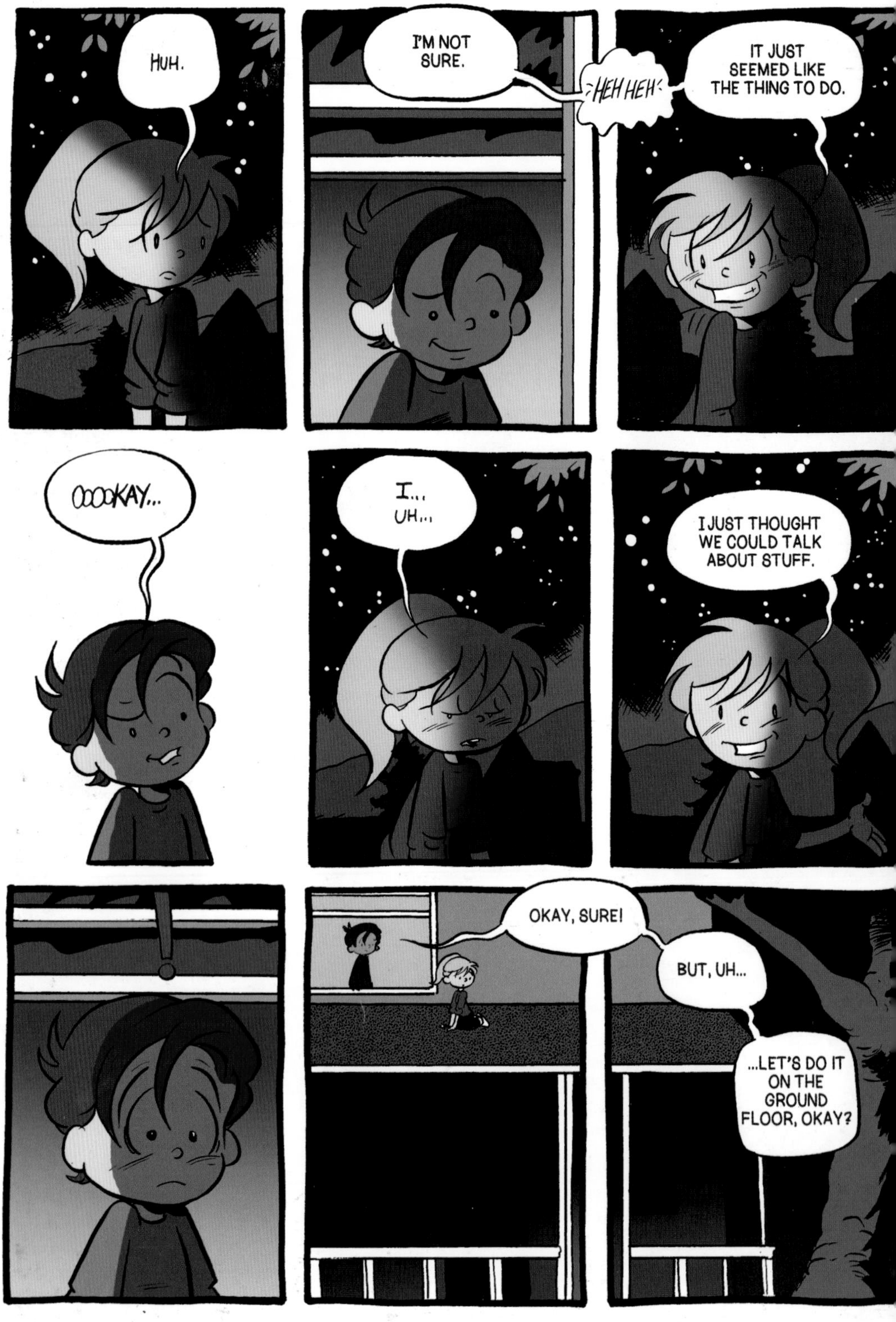
HUH.
I'M NOT SURE.
HEH HEH
IT JUST SEEMED LIKE THE THING TO DO.
OOOOKAY...
I... UH...
I JUST THOUGHT WE COULD TALK ABOUT STUFF.
!
OKAY, SURE!
BUT, UH...
...LET'S DO IT ON THE GROUND FLOOR, OKAY?

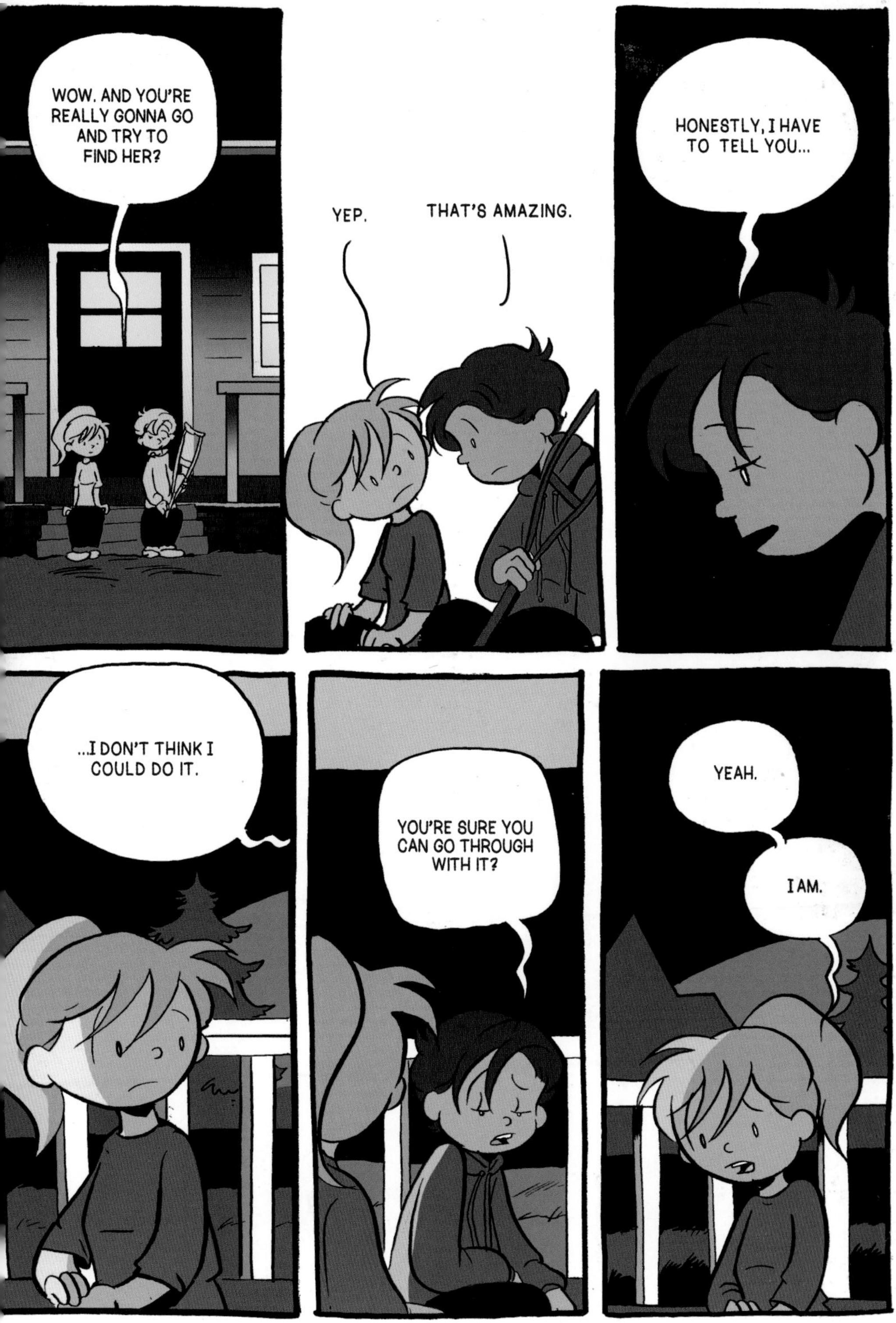

WOW. AND YOU'RE REALLY GONNA GO AND TRY TO FIND HER?
YEP.
THAT'S AMAZING.
HONESTLY, I HAVE TO TELL YOU...
...I DON'T THINK I COULD DO IT.
YOU'RE SURE YOU CAN GO THROUGH WITH IT?
YEAH.
I AM.

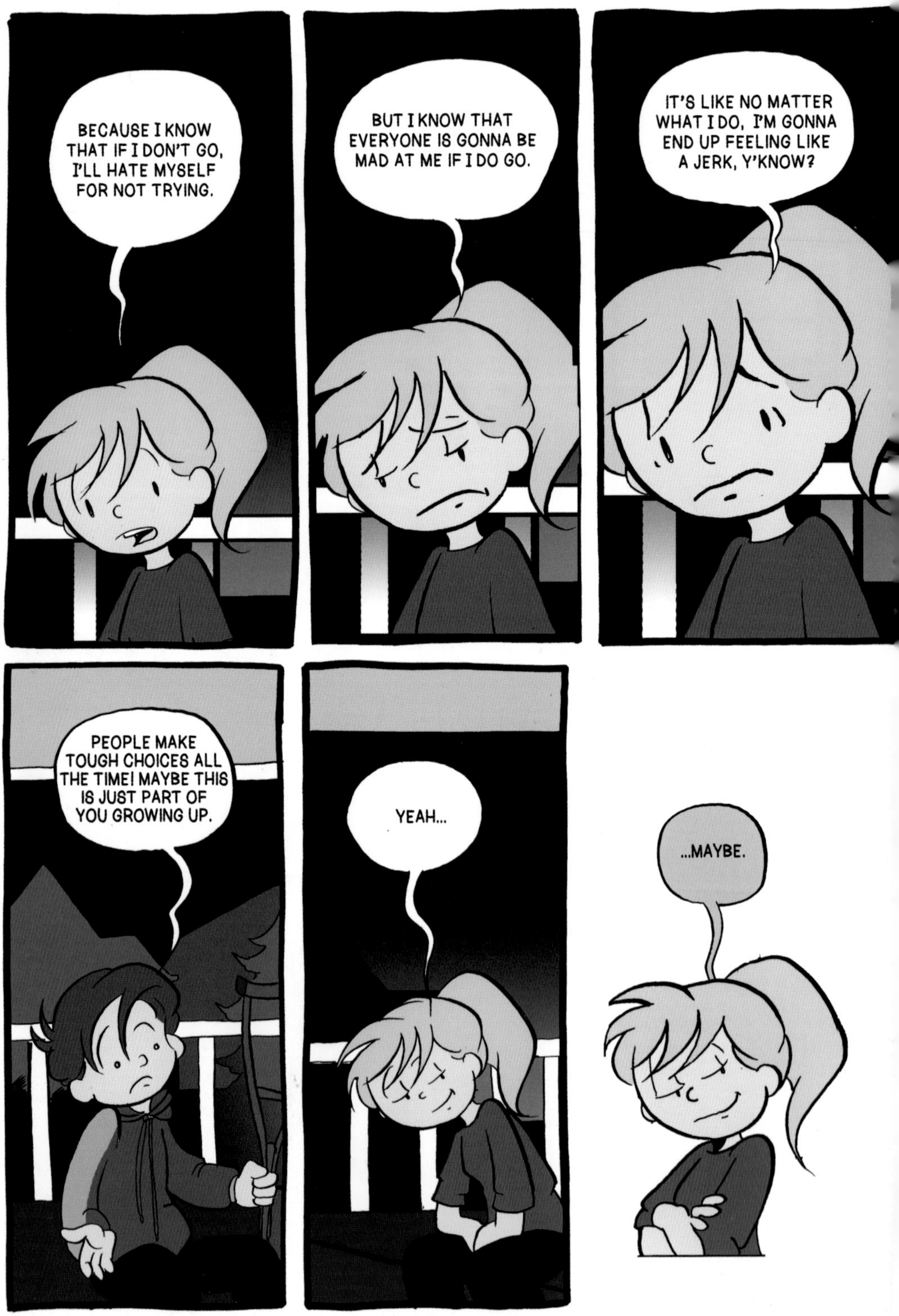
BECAUSE I KNOW THAT IF I DON'T GO, I'LL HATE MYSELF FOR NOT TRYING.
BUT I KNOW THAT EVERYONE IS GONNA BE MAD AT ME IF I DO GO.
IT'S LIKE NO MATTER WHAT I DO, I'M GONNA END UP FEELING LIKE A JERK, Y'KNOW?
PEOPLE MAKE TOUGH CHOICES ALL THE TIME! MAYBE THIS IS JUST PART OF YOU GROWING UP.
YEAH...
...MAYBE.

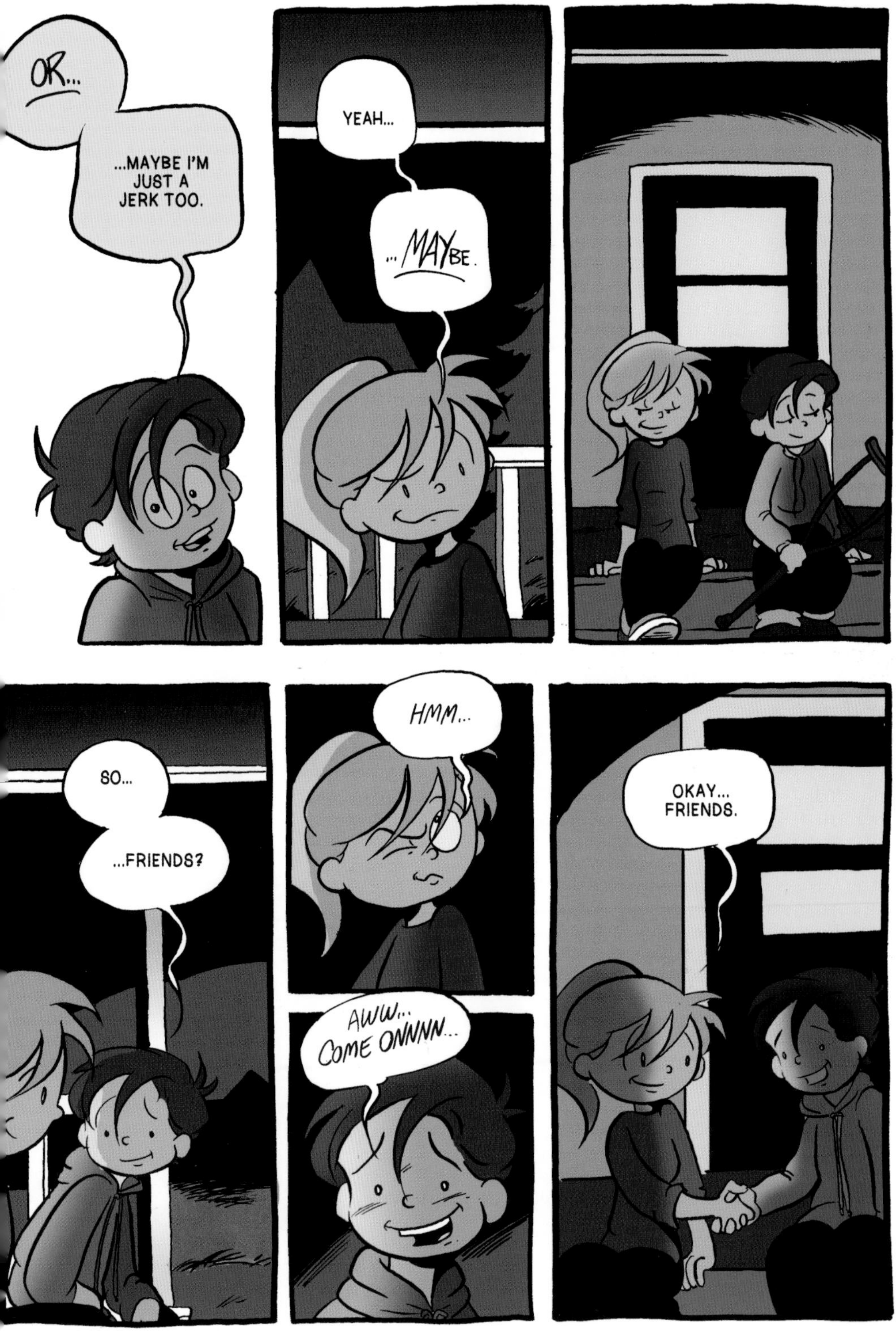
OR...
...MAYBE I'M JUST A JERK TOO.
YEAH...
...MAYBE.
SO...
...FRIENDS?
HMM...
AWW... COME ONNNN...
OKAY... FRIENDS.

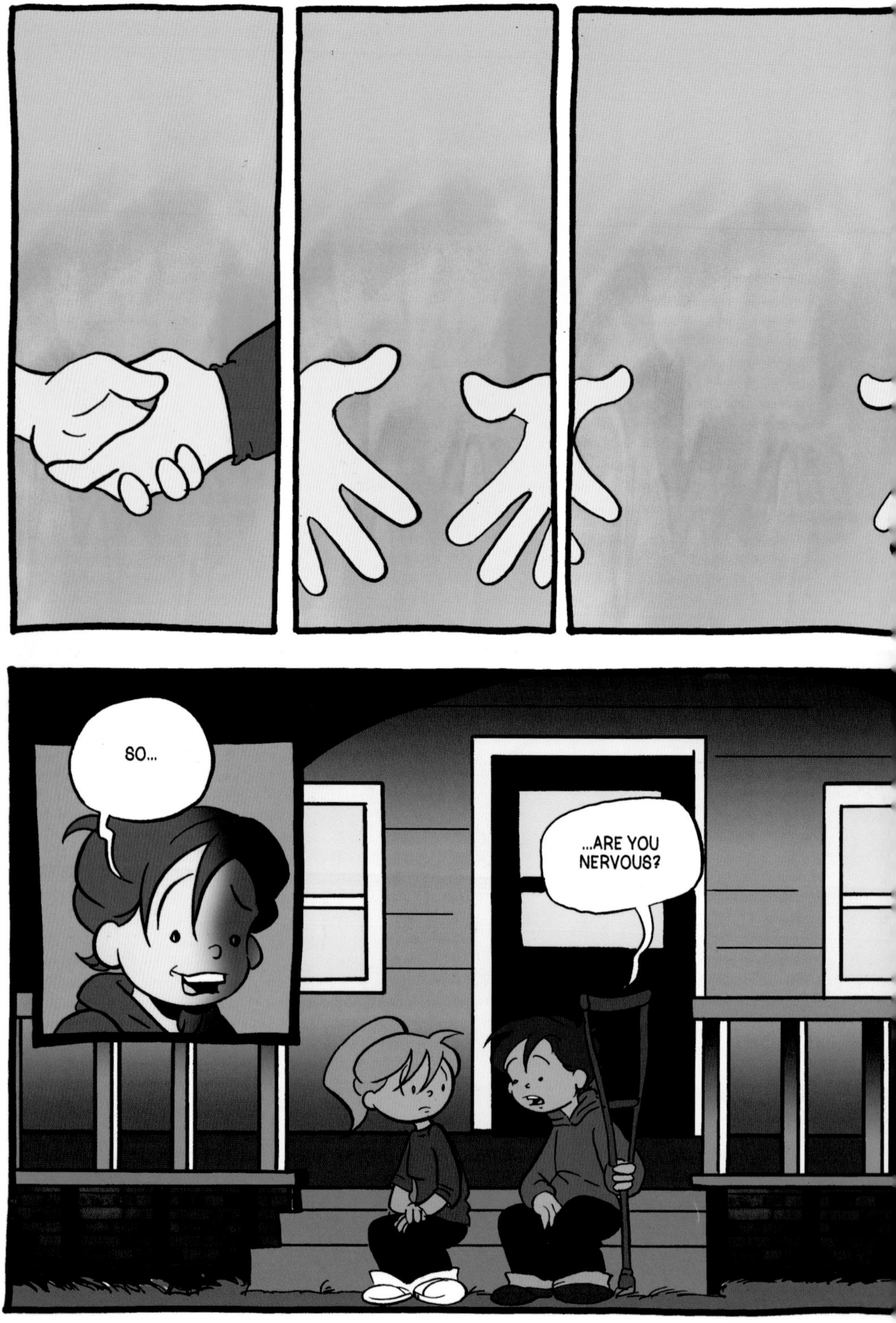
SO...
...ARE YOU NERVOUS?

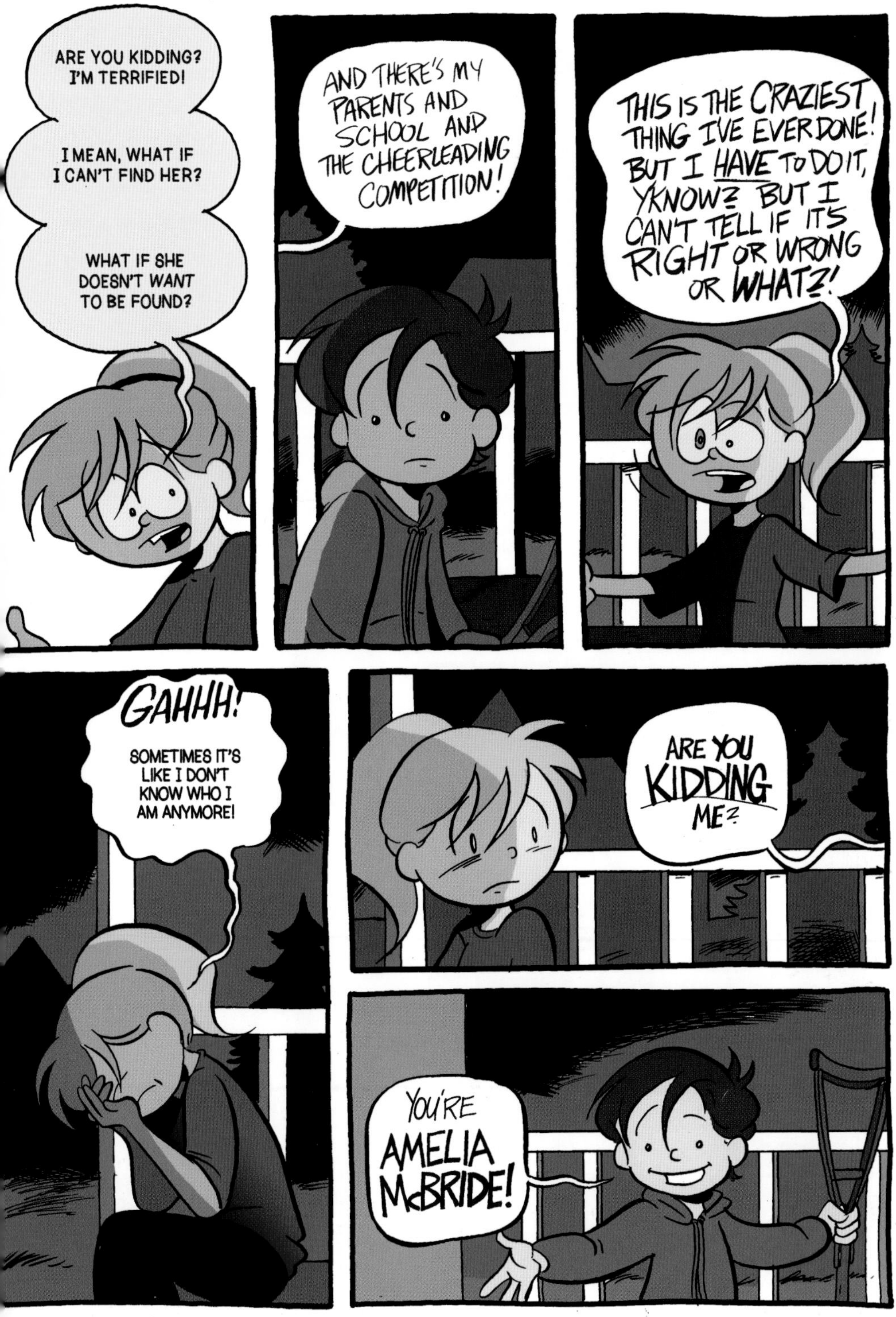
ARE YOU KIDDING? I'M TERRIFIED!
I MEAN, WHAT IF I CAN'T FIND HER?
WHAT IF SHE DOESN'T WANT TO BE FOUND?
AND THERE'S MY PARENTS AND SCHOOL AND THE CHEERLEADING COMPETITION!
THIS IS THE CRAZIEST THING I'VE EVER DONE! BUT I HAVE TO DO IT, Y'KNOW? BUT I CAN'T TELL IF IT'S RIGHT OR WRONG OR WHAT?!
GAHHH!
SOMETIMES IT'S LIKE I DON'T KNOW WHO I AM ANYMORE!
ARE YOU KIDDING ME?
YOU'RE AMELIA McBRIDE!

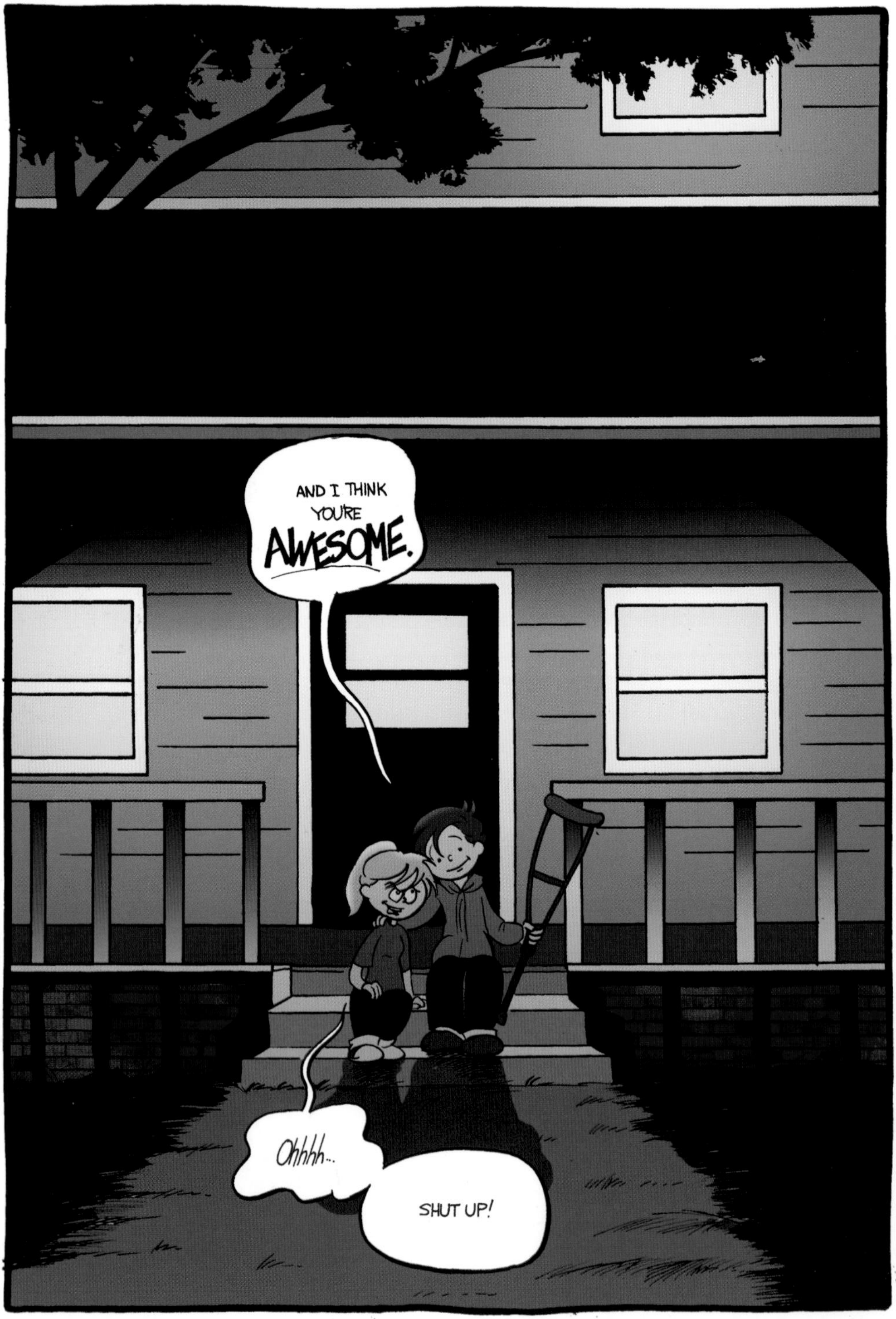
AND I THINK YOU'RE AWESOME.
Ohhhh..
SHUT UP!

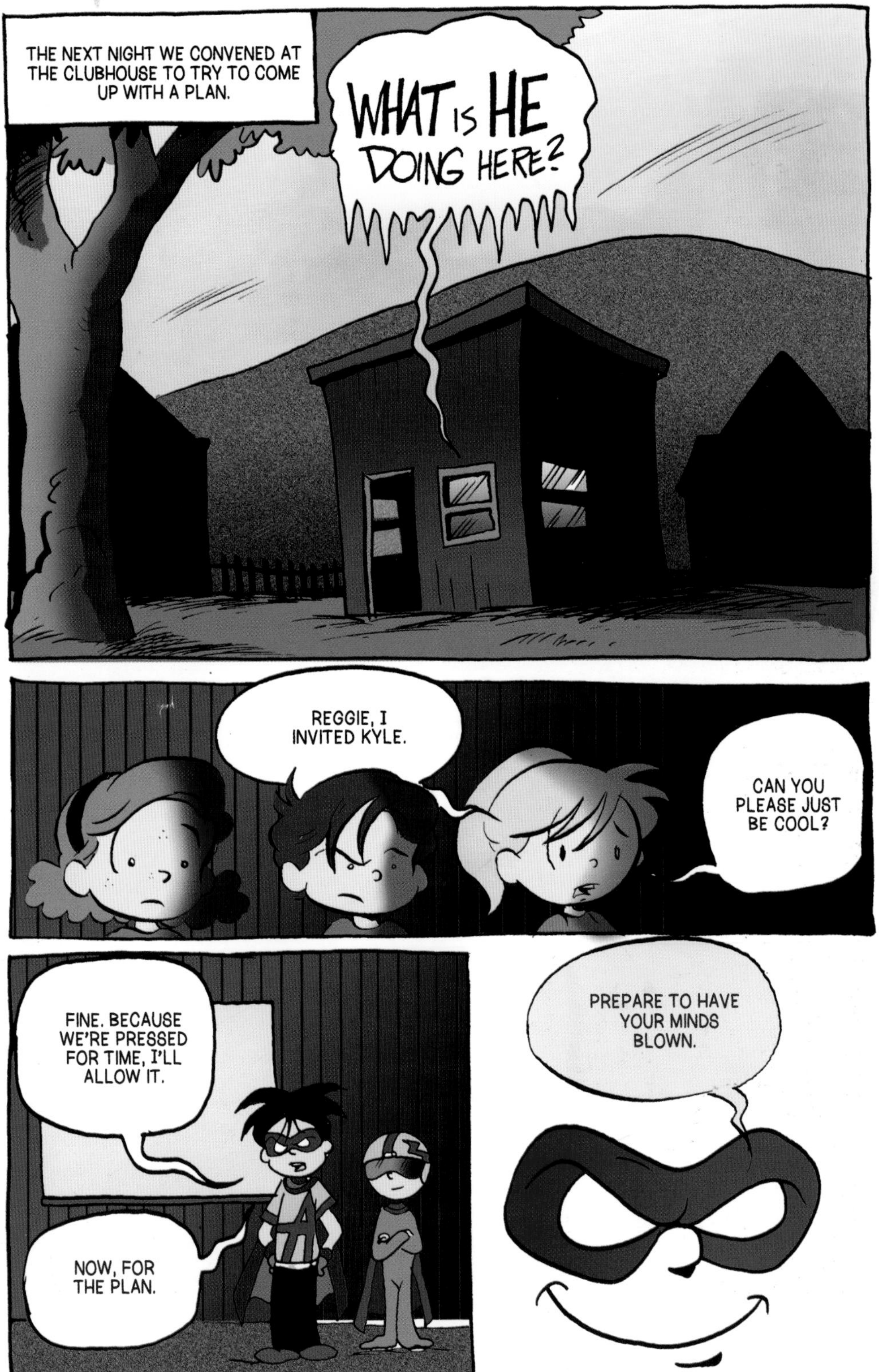
THE NEXT NIGHT WE CONVENED AT THE CLUBHOUSE TO TRY TO COME UP WITH A PLAN.
WHAT IS HE DOING HERE?
REGGIE, I INVITED KYLE.
CAN YOU PLEASE JUST BE COOL?
FINE. BECAUSE WE'RE PRESSED FOR TIME, I'LL ALLOW IT.
NOW, FOR THE PLAN.
PREPARE TO HAVE YOUR MINDS BLOWN.

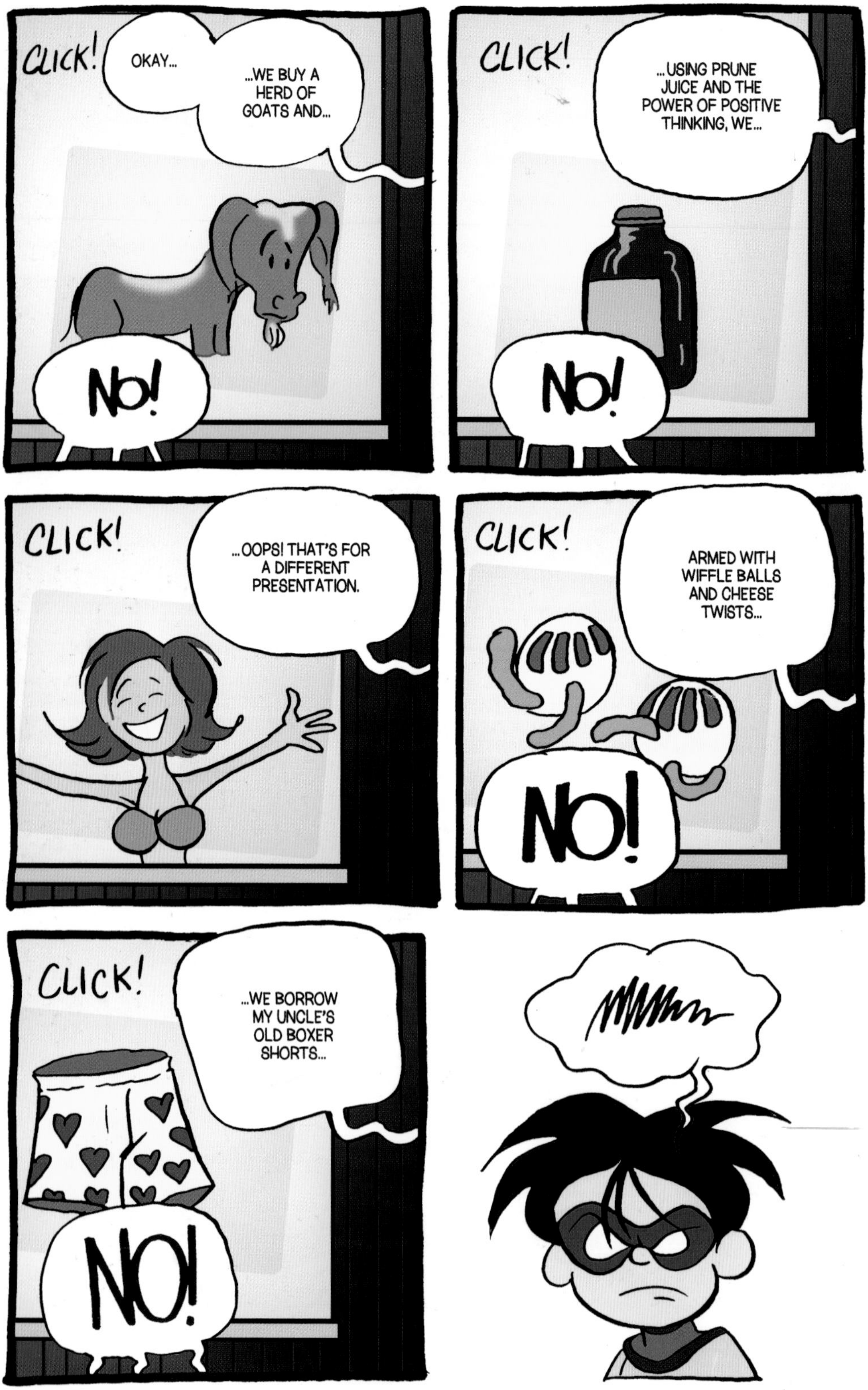
CLICK!
OKAY...
...WE BUY A HERD OF GOATS AND...
NO!
CLICK!
...USING PRUNE JUICE AND THE POWER OF POSITIVE THINKING, WE...
NO!
CLICK!
...OOPS! THAT'S FOR A DIFFERENT PRESENTATION.
CLICK!
ARMED WITH WIFFLE BALLS AND CHEESE TWISTS...
NO!
CLICK!
...WE BORROW MY UNCLE'S OLD BOXER SHORTS...
NO!

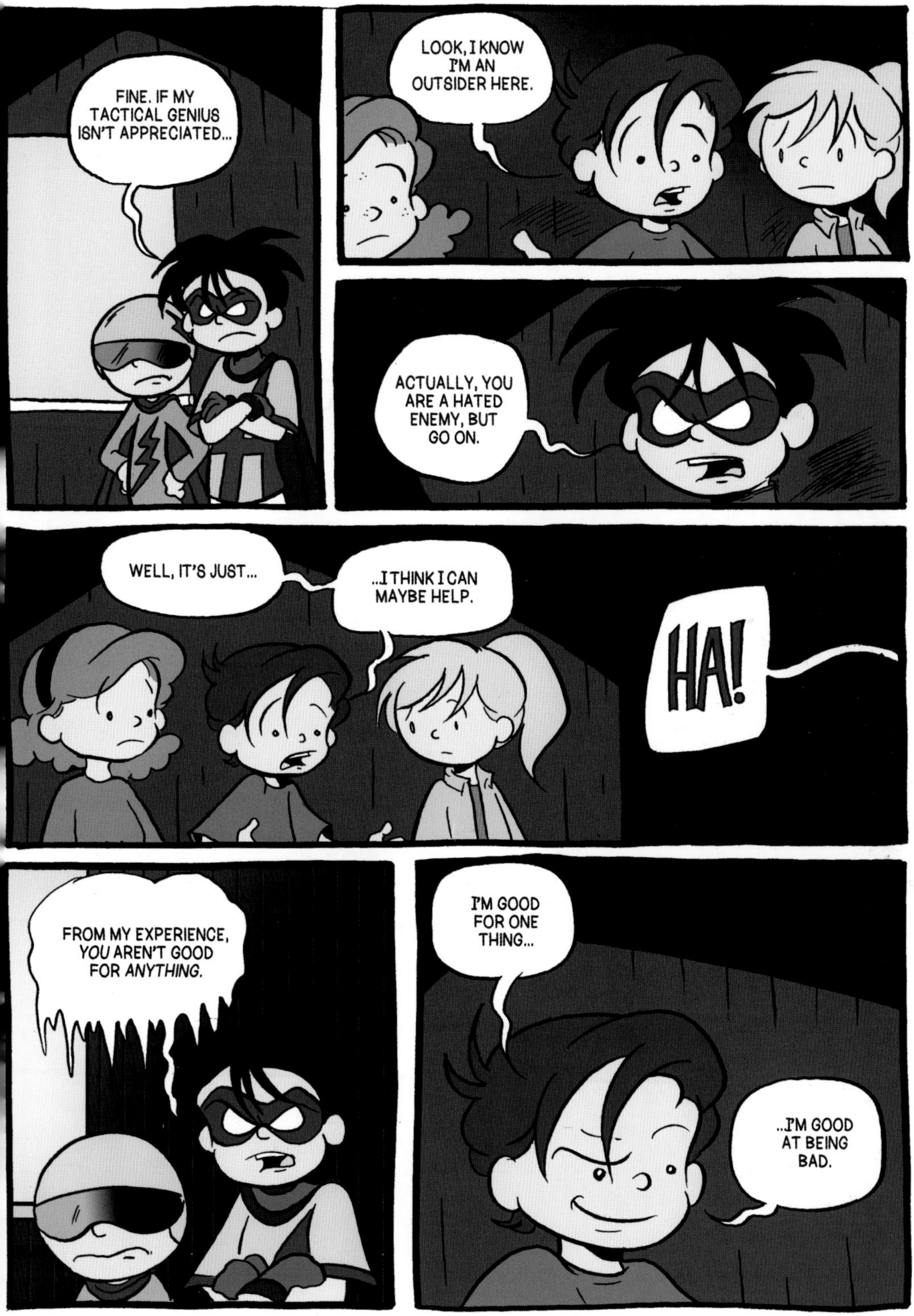
FINE. IF MY TACTICAL GENIUS ISN'T APPRECIATED...
LOOK, I KNOW I'M AN OUTSIDER HERE.
ACTUALLY, YOU ARE A HATED ENEMY, BUT GO ON.
WELL, IT'S JUST...
...I THINK I CAN MAYBE HELP.
HA!
FROM MY EXPERIENCE, *YOU* AREN'T GOOD FOR *ANYTHING.*
I'M GOOD FOR ONE THING...
...I'M GOOD AT BEING BAD.

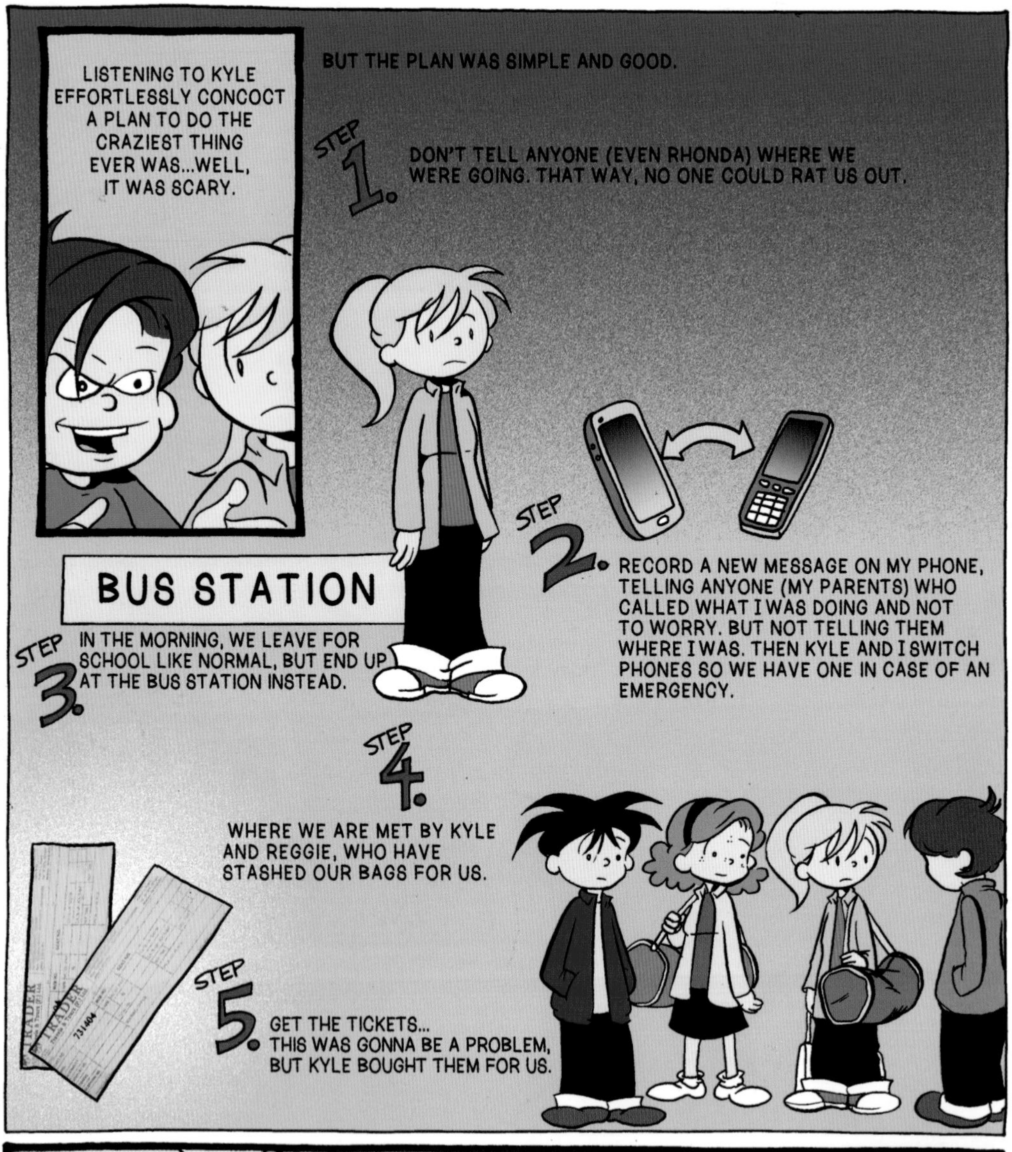
LISTENING TO KYLE EFFORTLESSLY CONCOCT A PLAN TO DO THE CRAZIEST THING EVER WAS...WELL, IT WAS SCARY.
BUT THE PLAN WAS SIMPLE AND GOOD.
STEP 1.
DON'T TELL ANYONE (EVEN RHONDA) WHERE WE WERE GOING. THAT WAY, NO ONE COULD RAT US OUT.
STEP 2.
RECORD A NEW MESSAGE ON MY PHONE, TELLING ANYONE (MY PARENTS) WHO CALLED WHAT I WAS DOING AND NOT TO WORRY. BUT NOT TELLING THEM WHERE I WAS. THEN KYLE AND I SWITCH PHONES SO WE HAVE ONE IN CASE OF AN EMERGENCY.
BUS STATION
STEP 3.
IN THE MORNING, WE LEAVE FOR SCHOOL LIKE NORMAL, BUT END UP AT THE BUS STATION INSTEAD.
STEP 4.
WHERE WE ARE MET BY KYLE AND REGGIE, WHO HAVE STASHED OUR BAGS FOR US.
STEP 5.
GET THE TICKETS... THIS WAS GONNA BE A PROBLEM, BUT KYLE BOUGHT THEM FOR US.

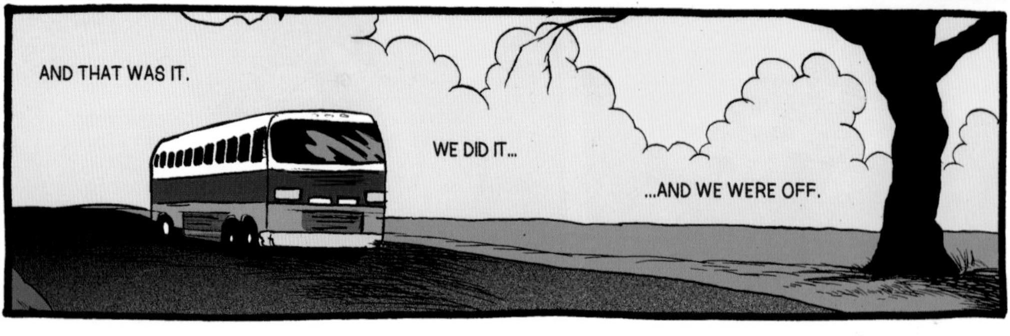
AND THAT WAS IT.
WE DID IT...
...AND WE WERE OFF.

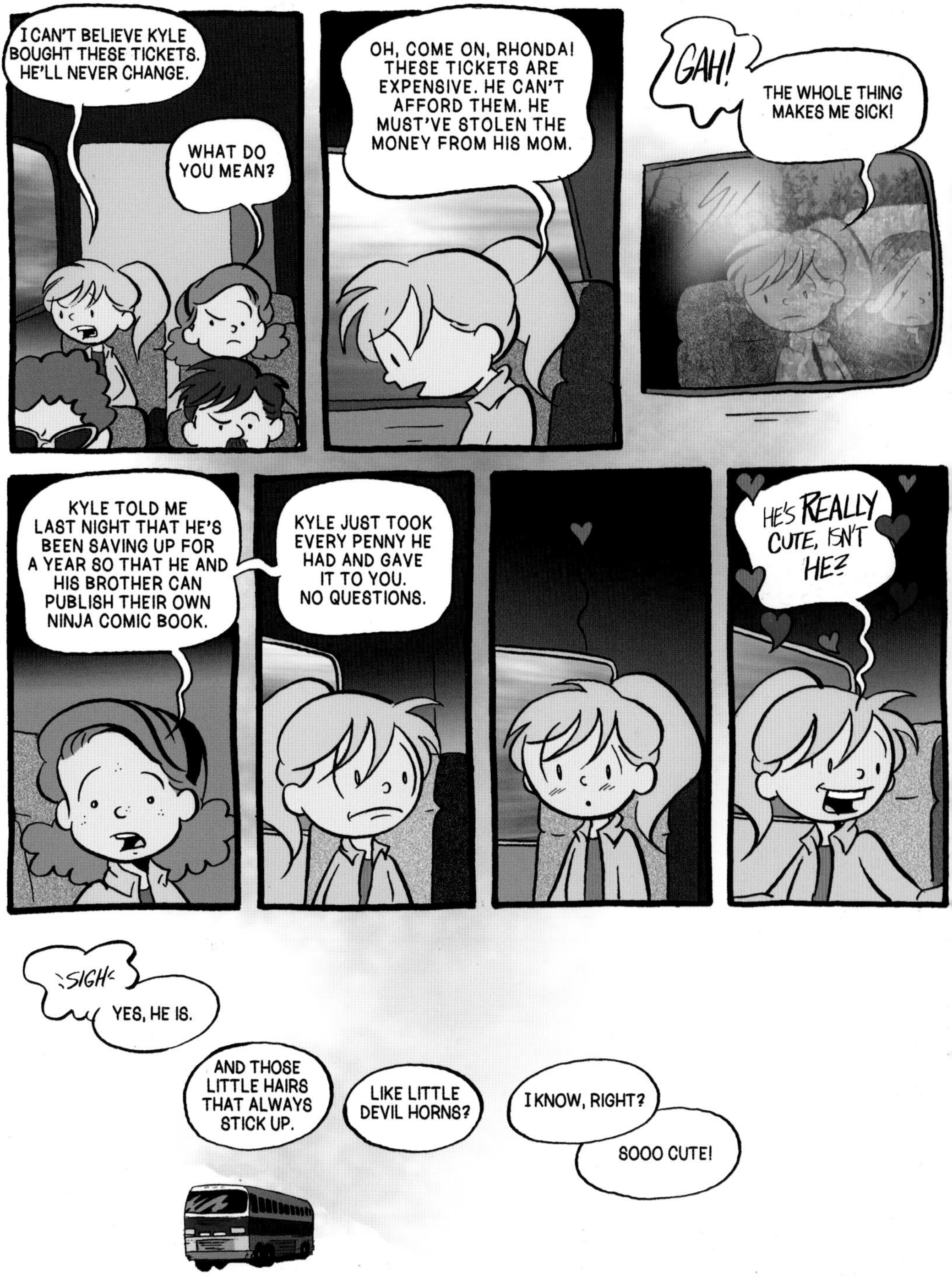
I CAN'T BELIEVE KYLE BOUGHT THESE TICKETS. HE'LL NEVER CHANGE.
WHAT DO YOU MEAN?
OH, COME ON, RHONDA! THESE TICKETS ARE EXPENSIVE. HE CAN'T AFFORD THEM. HE MUST'VE STOLEN THE MONEY FROM HIS MOM.
GAH!
THE WHOLE THING MAKES ME SICK!
KYLE TOLD ME LAST NIGHT THAT HE'S BEEN SAVING UP FOR A YEAR SO THAT HE AND HIS BROTHER CAN PUBLISH THEIR OWN NINJA COMIC BOOK.
KYLE JUST TOOK EVERY PENNY HE HAD AND GAVE IT TO YOU. NO QUESTIONS.
HE'S REALLY CUTE, ISN'T HE?
SIGH
YES, HE IS.
AND THOSE LITTLE HAIRS THAT ALWAYS STICK UP.
LIKE LITTLE DEVIL HORNS?
I KNOW, RIGHT?
SOOO CUTE!

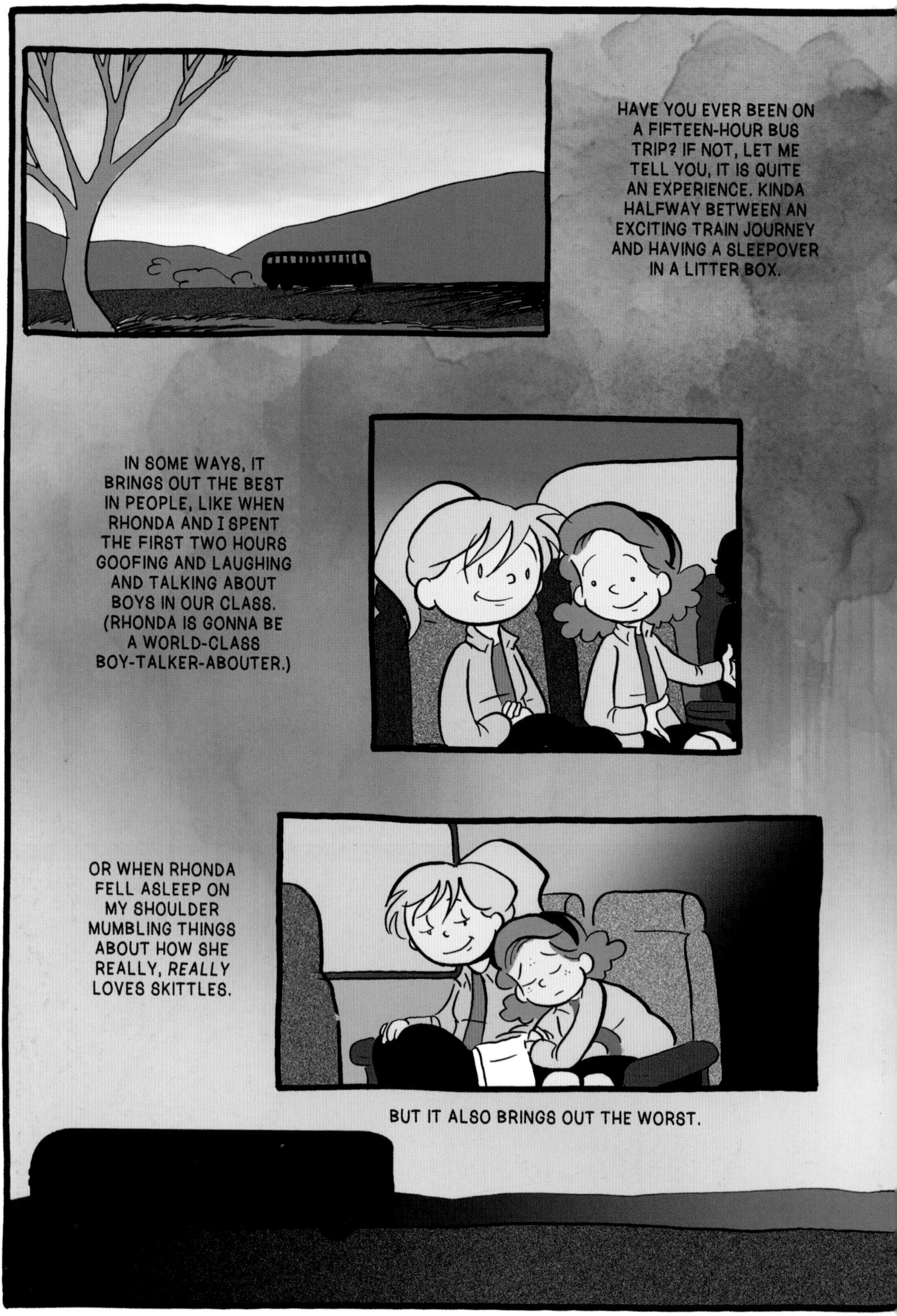
HAVE YOU EVER BEEN ON A FIFTEEN-HOUR BUS TRIP? IF NOT, LET ME TELL YOU, IT IS QUITE AN EXPERIENCE. KINDA HALFWAY BETWEEN AN EXCITING TRAIN JOURNEY AND HAVING A SLEEPOVER IN A LITTER BOX.
IN SOME WAYS, IT BRINGS OUT THE BEST IN PEOPLE, LIKE WHEN RHONDA AND I SPENT THE FIRST TWO HOURS GOOFING AND LAUGHING AND TALKING ABOUT BOYS IN OUR CLASS. (RHONDA IS GONNA BE A WORLD-CLASS BOY-TALKER-ABOUTER.)
OR WHEN RHONDA FELL ASLEEP ON MY SHOULDER MUMBLING THINGS ABOUT HOW SHE REALLY, *REALLY* LOVES SKITTLES.
BUT IT ALSO BRINGS OUT THE WORST.

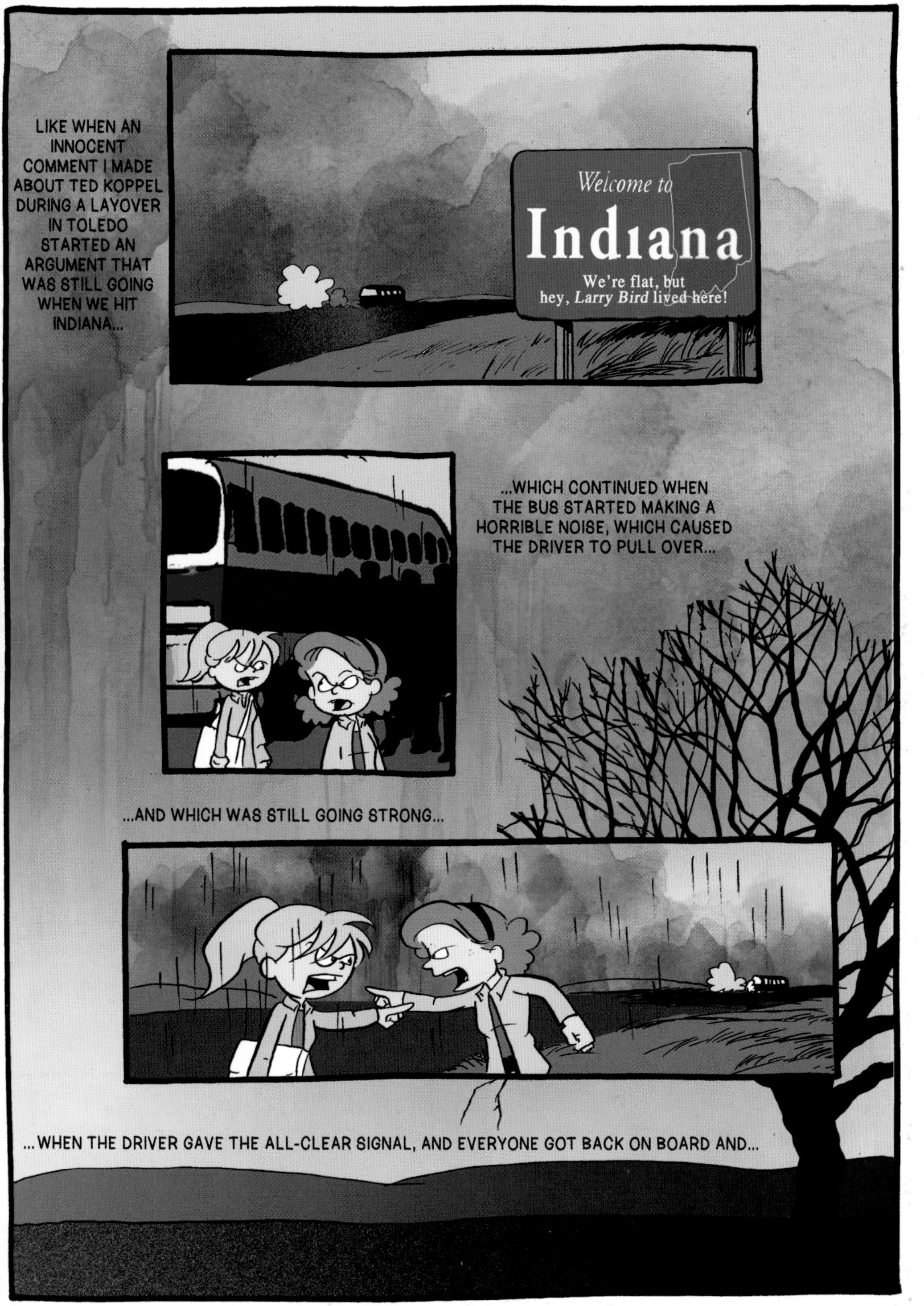
LIKE WHEN AN INNOCENT COMMENT I MADE ABOUT TED KOPPEL DURING A LAYOVER IN TOLEDO STARTED AN ARGUMENT THAT WAS STILL GOING WHEN WE HIT INDIANA...
Welcome to
Indiana
We're flat, but hey, Larry Bird lived here!
...WHICH CONTINUED WHEN THE BUS STARTED MAKING A HORRIBLE NOISE, WHICH CAUSED THE DRIVER TO PULL OVER...
...AND WHICH WAS STILL GOING STRONG...
...WHEN THE DRIVER GAVE THE ALL-CLEAR SIGNAL, AND EVERYONE GOT BACK ON BOARD AND...

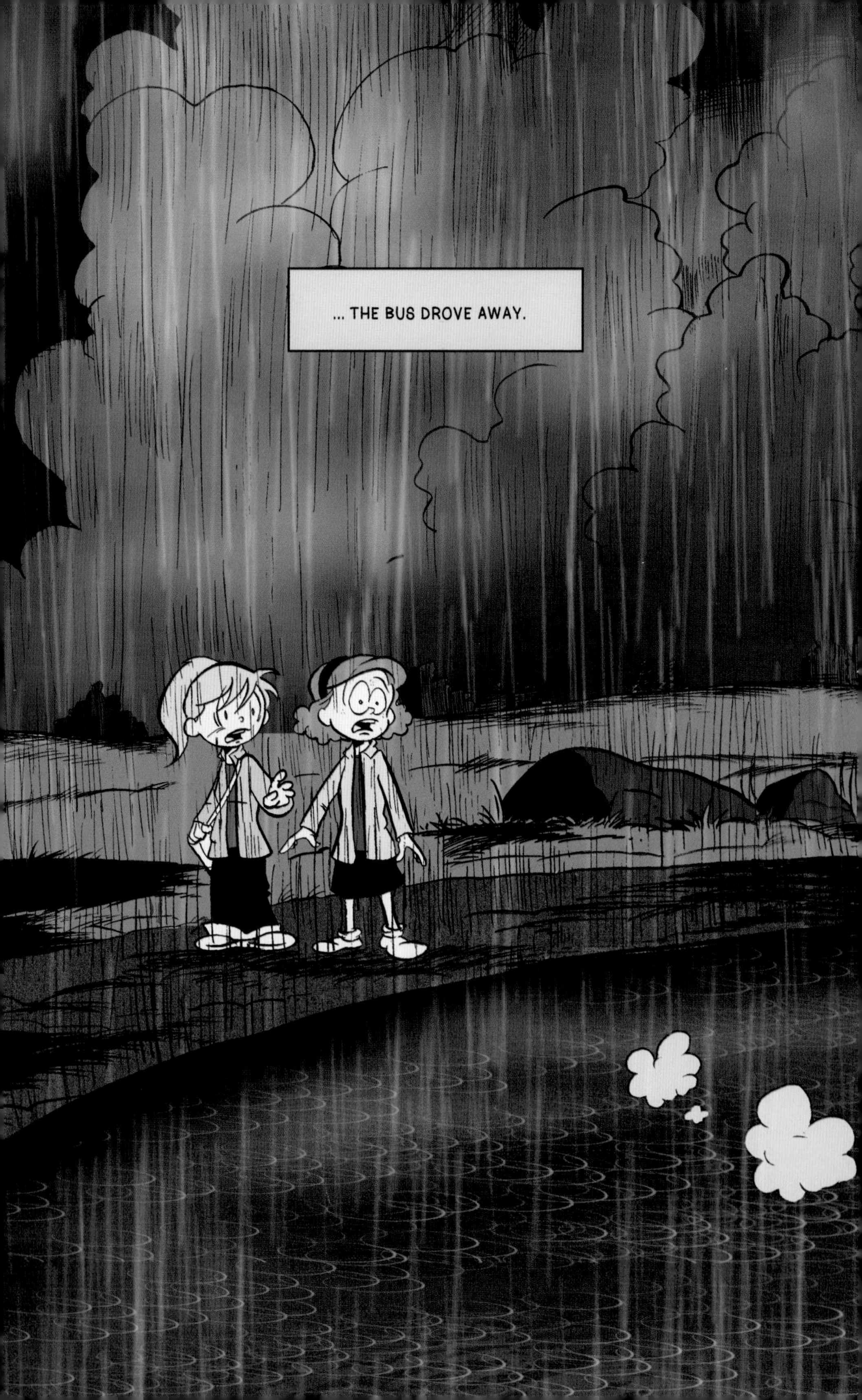
... THE BUS DROVE AWAY.

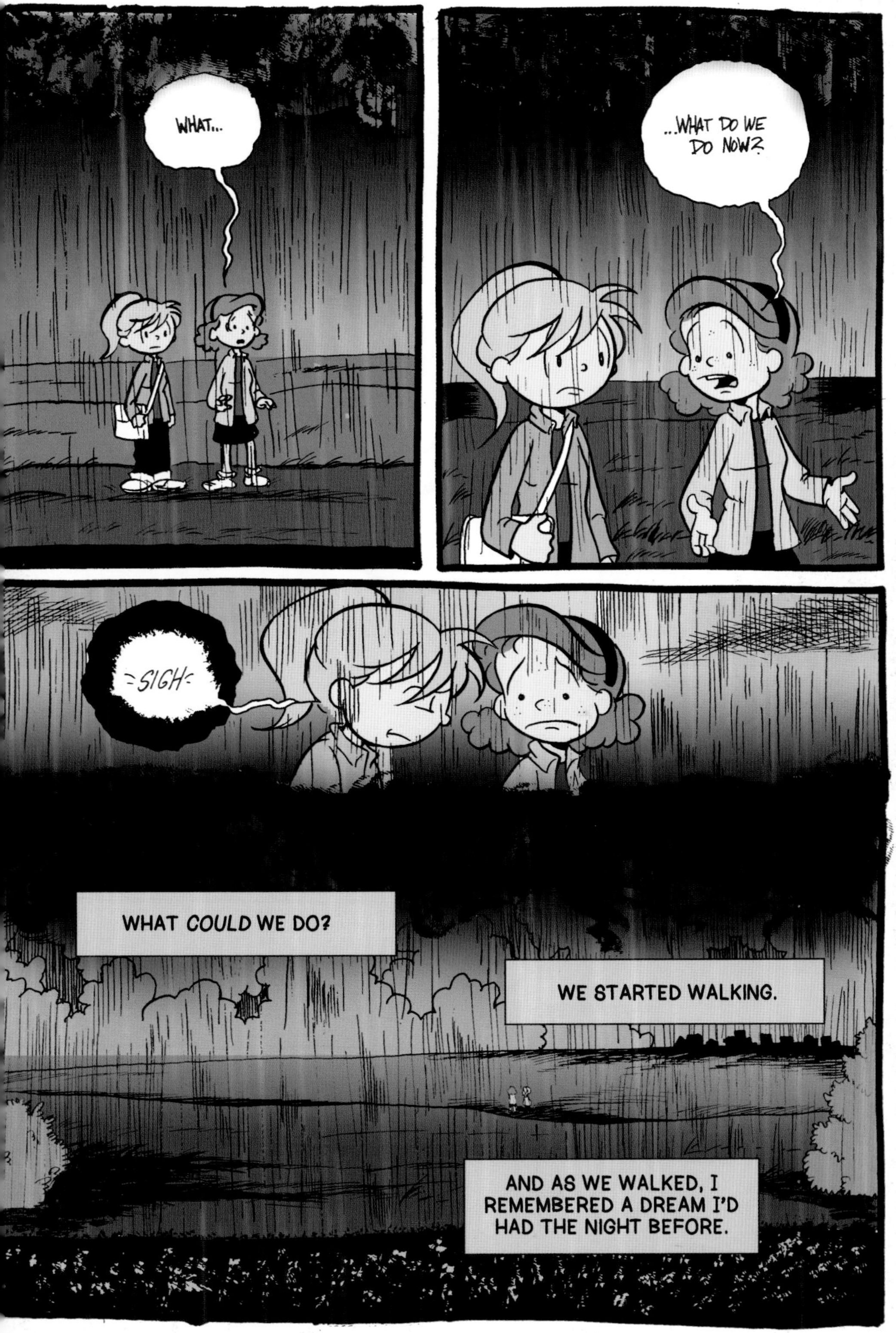
WHAT...
...WHAT DO WE DO NOW?
SIGH
WHAT COULD WE DO?
WE STARTED WALKING.
AND AS WE WALKED, I REMEMBERED A DREAM I'D HAD THE NIGHT BEFORE.

I WAS LOST IN THE WOODS, AND I WAS TRYING TO MAKE MY WAY TO A LIGHT THAT I COULD SEE IN THE DISTANCE.

BUT NO MATTER HOW LONG I WALKED, I NEVER SEEMED TO BE GETTING ANY CLOSER.

THEN SUDDENLY, RIGHT IN FRONT OF ME, WAS A BEAUTIFUL FAIRY PRINCESS.

SHE KIND OF LOOKED FAMILIAR, BUT I COULDN'T REMEMBER WHERE I SAW HER BEFORE.

SHE WAS BEAUTIFUL, BUT SHE ALSO LOOKED VERY TIRED. LIKE SHE HAD BEEN WORKING REALLY HARD.

I WAS TIRED TOO, I'D BEEN WALKING FOREVER, AND I JUST DIDN'T WANT TO GO ON.

I STARTED CRYING, SAYING, "I CAN'T DO IT ANYMORE. I CAN'T!"

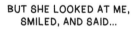

BUT SHE LOOKED AT ME, SMILED, AND SAID...

"...YOU CAN..."

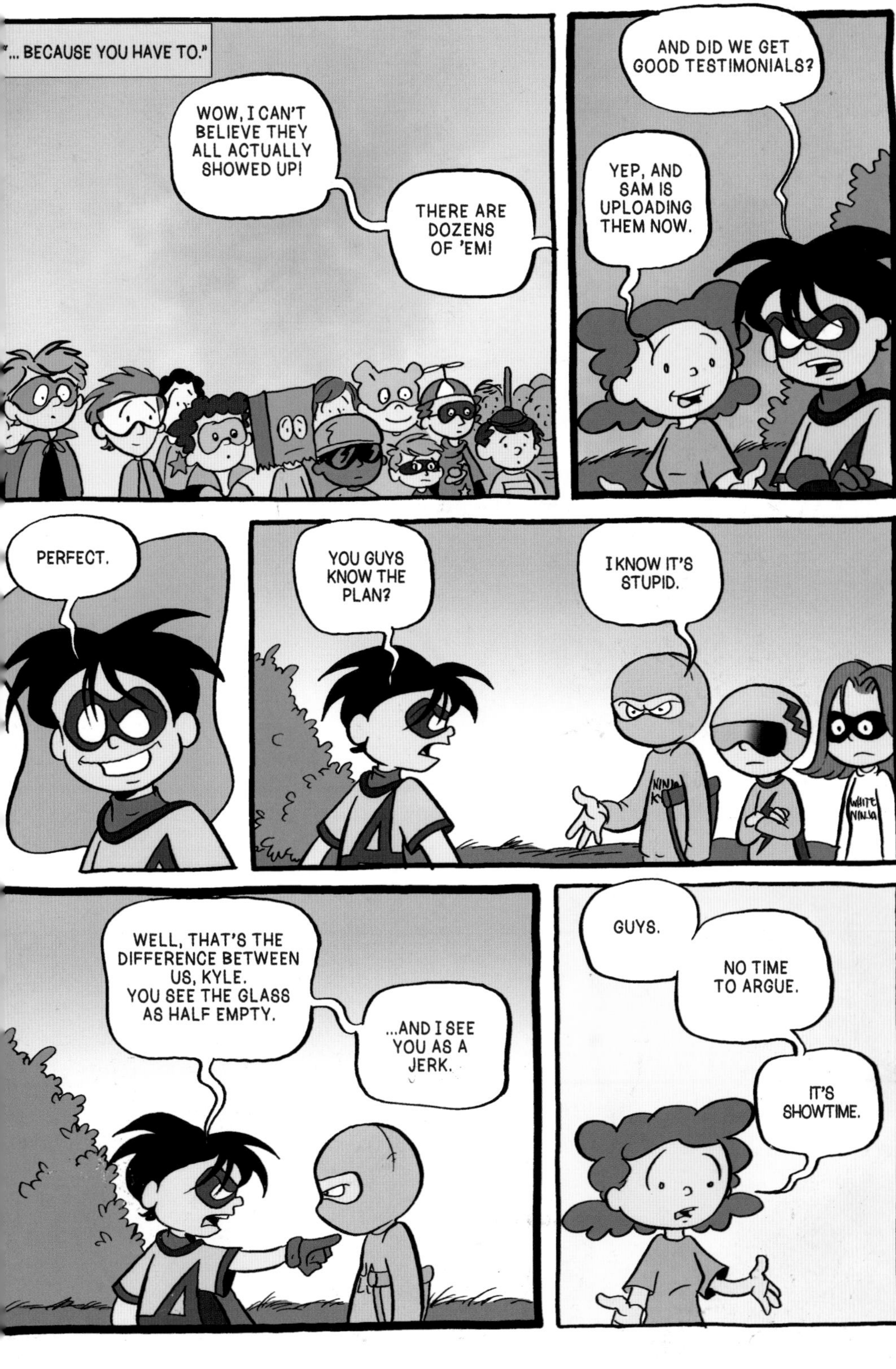
"... BECAUSE YOU HAVE TO."
WOW, I CAN'T BELIEVE THEY ALL ACTUALLY SHOWED UP!
THERE ARE DOZENS OF 'EM!
AND DID WE GET GOOD TESTIMONIALS?
YEP, AND SAM IS UPLOADING THEM NOW.
PERFECT.
YOU GUYS KNOW THE PLAN?
I KNOW IT'S STUPID.
NINJA K
WHITE NINJA
WELL, THAT'S THE DIFFERENCE BETWEEN US, KYLE. YOU SEE THE GLASS AS HALF EMPTY.
...AND I SEE YOU AS A JERK.
GUYS.
NO TIME TO ARGUE.
IT'S SHOWTIME.

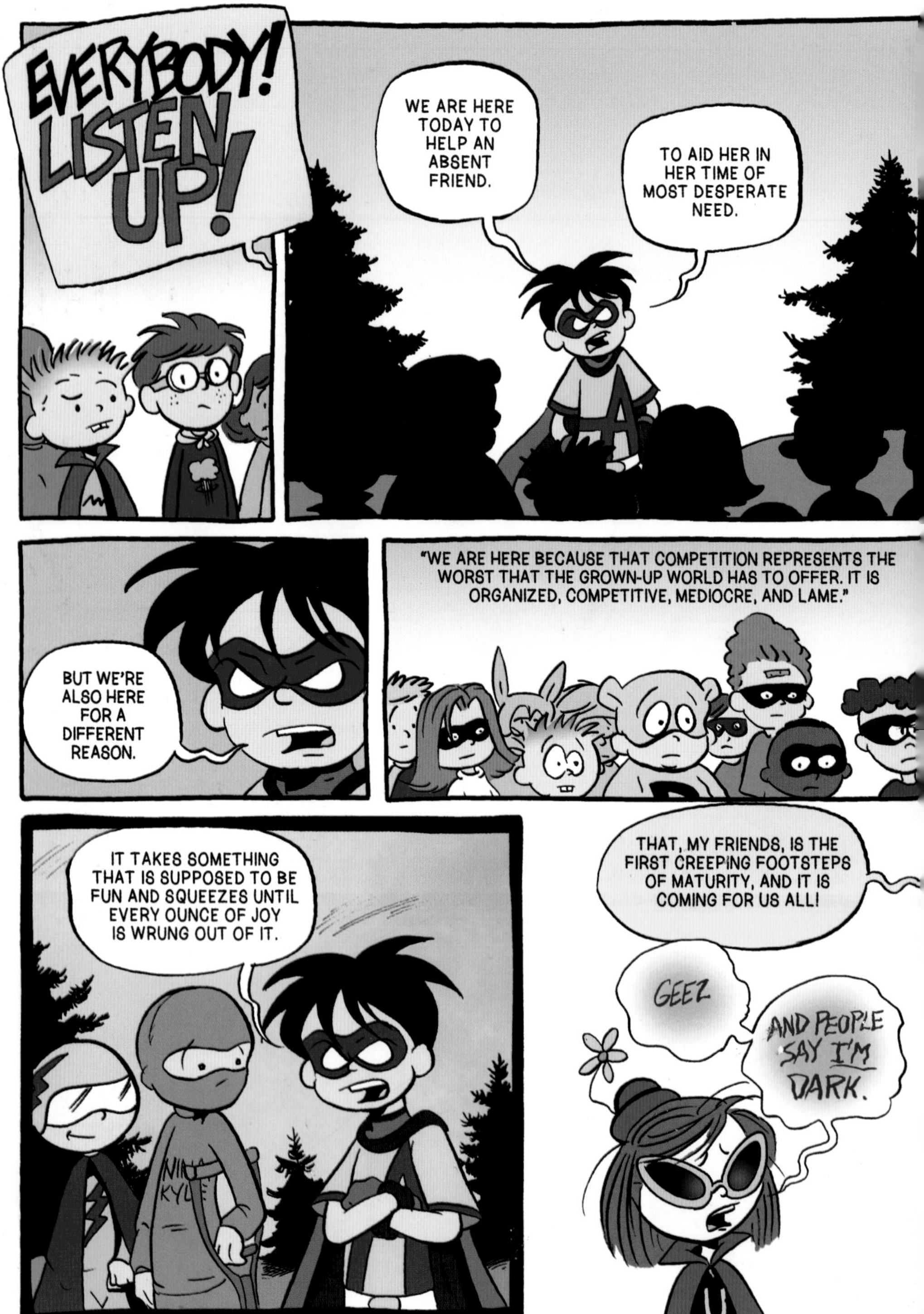
EVERYBODY! LISTEN UP!
WE ARE HERE TODAY TO HELP AN ABSENT FRIEND.
TO AID HER IN HER TIME OF MOST DESPERATE NEED.
BUT WE'RE ALSO HERE FOR A DIFFERENT REASON.
"WE ARE HERE BECAUSE THAT COMPETITION REPRESENTS THE WORST THAT THE GROWN-UP WORLD HAS TO OFFER. IT IS ORGANIZED, COMPETITIVE, MEDIOCRE, AND LAME."
IT TAKES SOMETHING THAT IS SUPPOSED TO BE FUN AND SQUEEZES UNTIL EVERY OUNCE OF JOY IS WRUNG OUT OF IT.
THAT, MY FRIENDS, IS THE FIRST CREEPING FOOTSTEPS OF MATURITY, AND IT IS COMING FOR US ALL!
GEEZ
AND PEOPLE SAY I'M DARK.

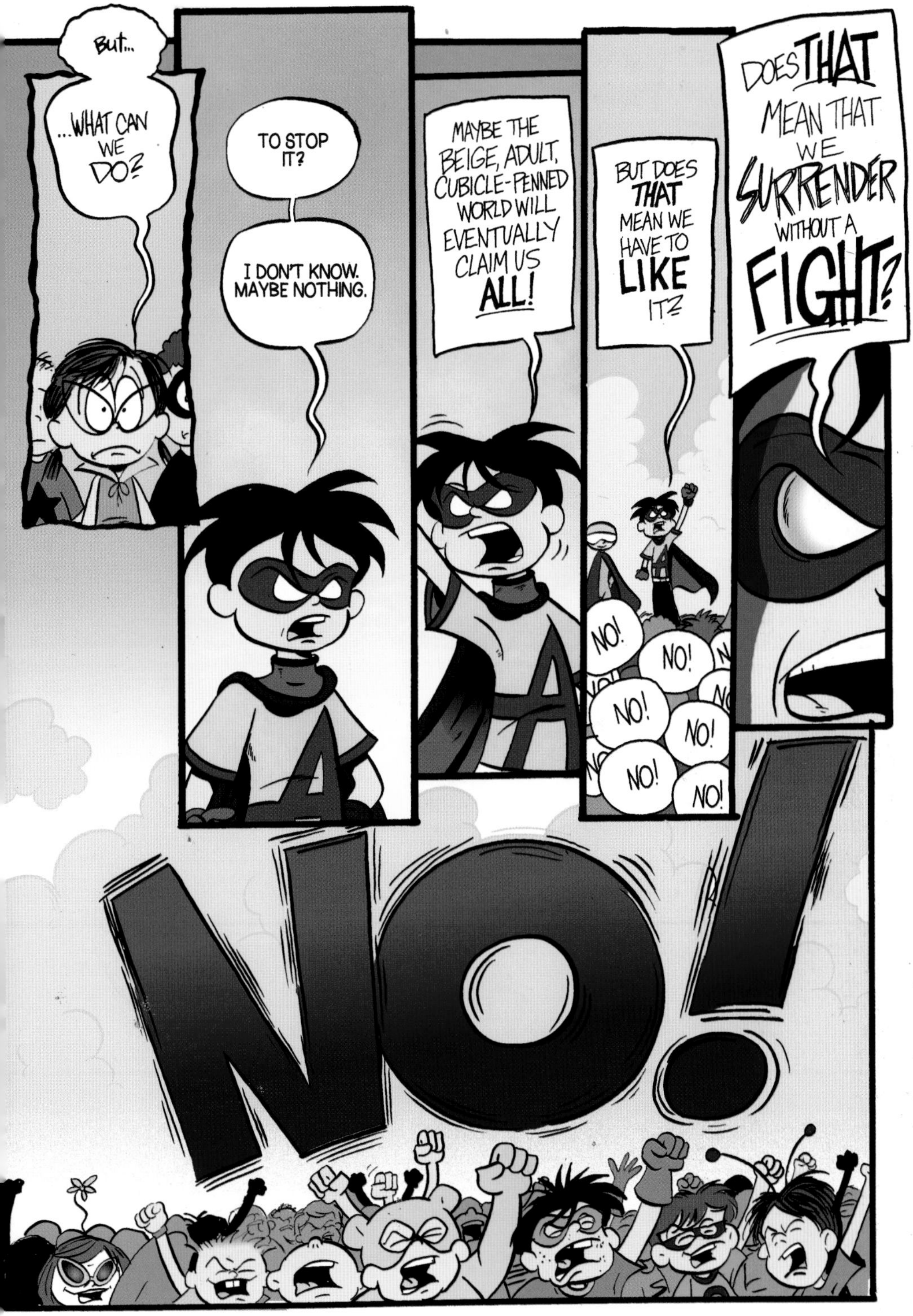
But...
...WHAT CAN WE DO?
TO STOP IT?
I DON'T KNOW. MAYBE NOTHING.
MAYBE THE BEIGE, ADULT, CUBICLE-PENNED WORLD WILL EVENTUALLY CLAIM US ALL!
BUT DOES THAT MEAN WE HAVE TO LIKE IT?
DOES THAT MEAN THAT WE SURRENDER WITHOUT A FIGHT?
NO!
NO!
NO!
NO!
NO!
NO!
NO!
NO!

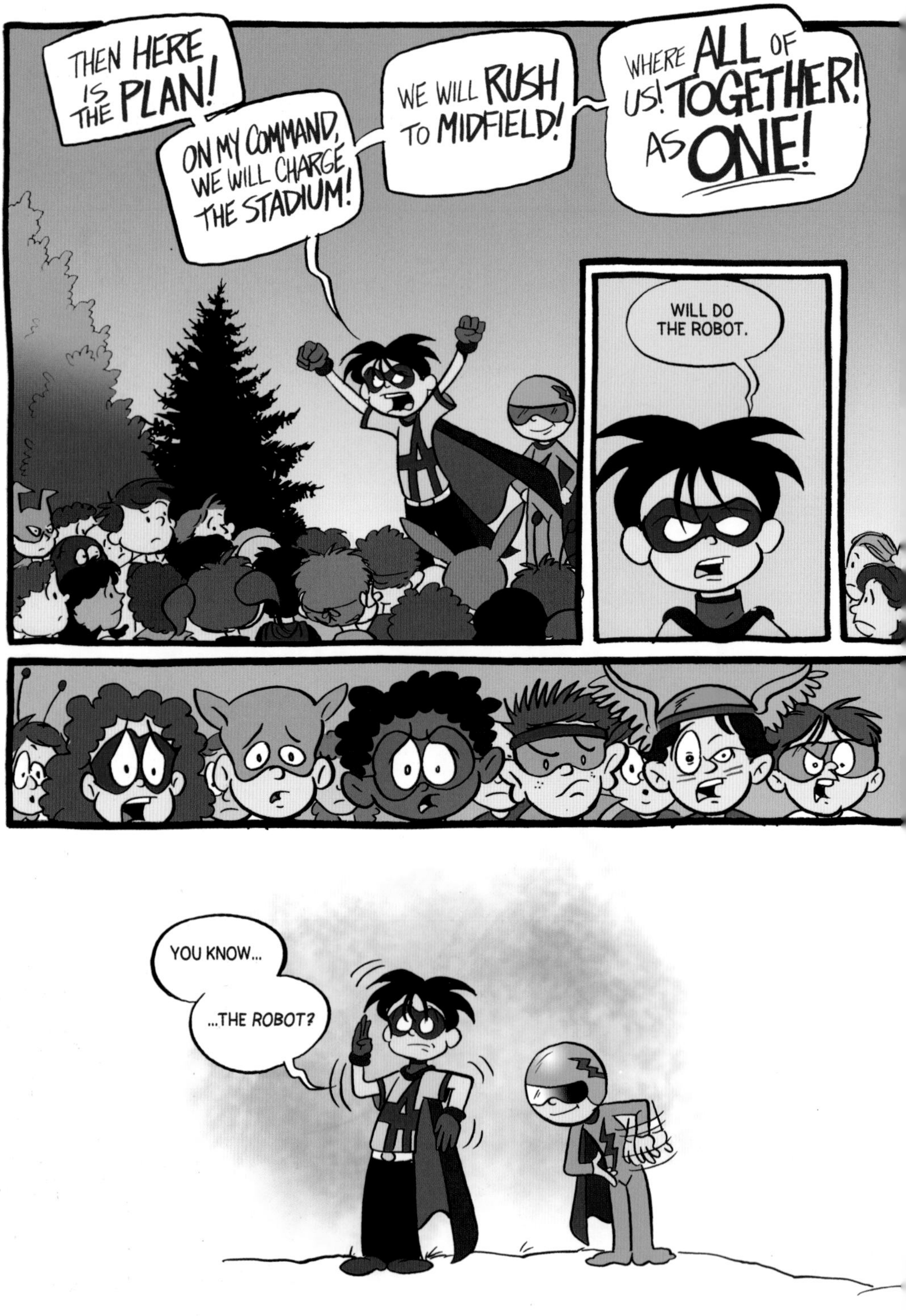
THEN HERE IS THE PLAN!
ON MY COMMAND, WE WILL CHARGE THE STADIUM!
WE WILL RUSH TO MIDFIELD!
WHERE ALL OF US! TOGETHER! AS ONE!
WILL DO THE ROBOT.
YOU KNOW...
...THE ROBOT?

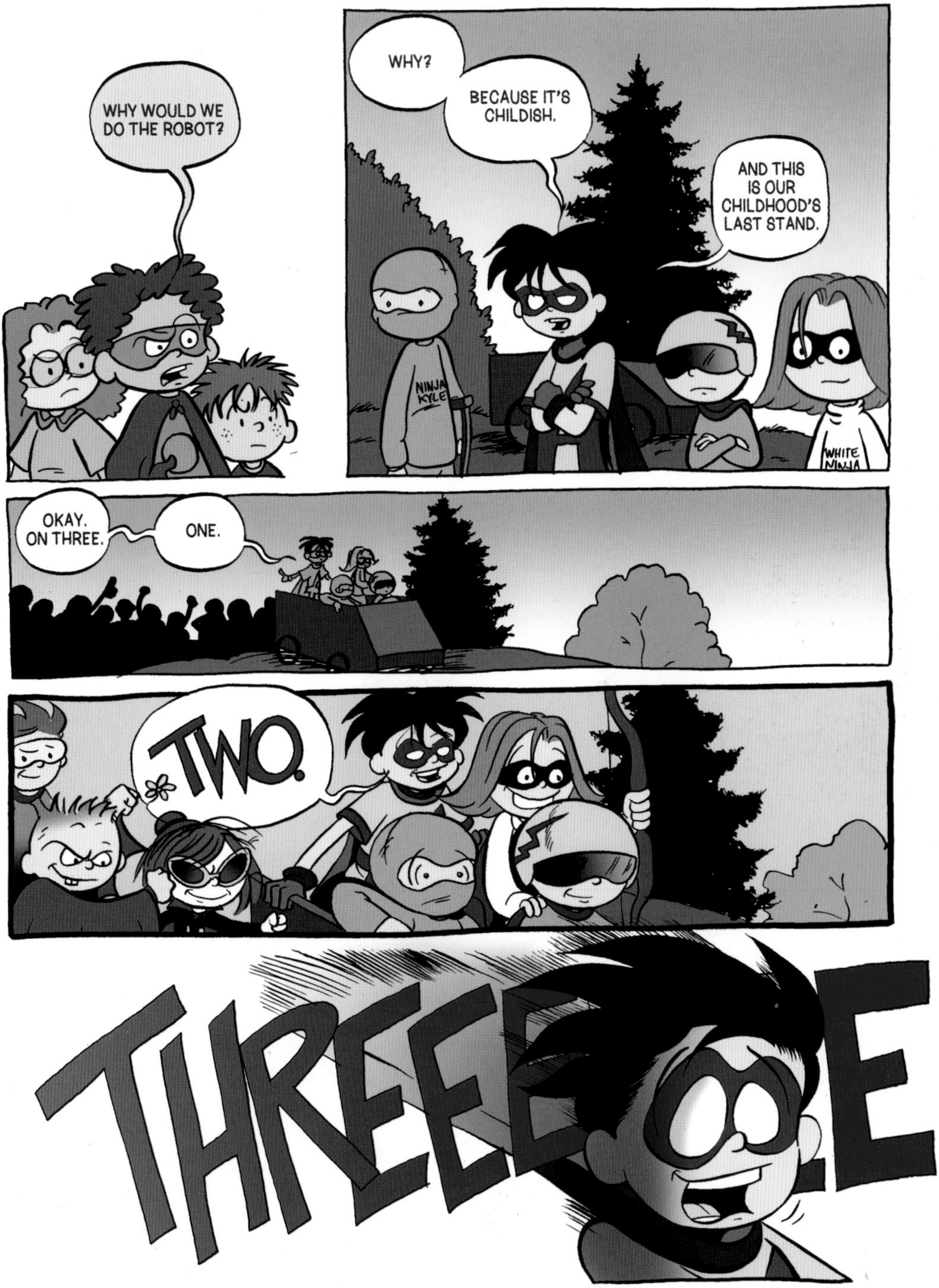
WHY WOULD WE DO THE ROBOT?
WHY?
BECAUSE IT'S CHILDISH.
AND THIS IS OUR CHILDHOOD'S LAST STAND.
NINJA KYLE
OKAY. ON THREE.
ONE.
TWO.
THREEEE

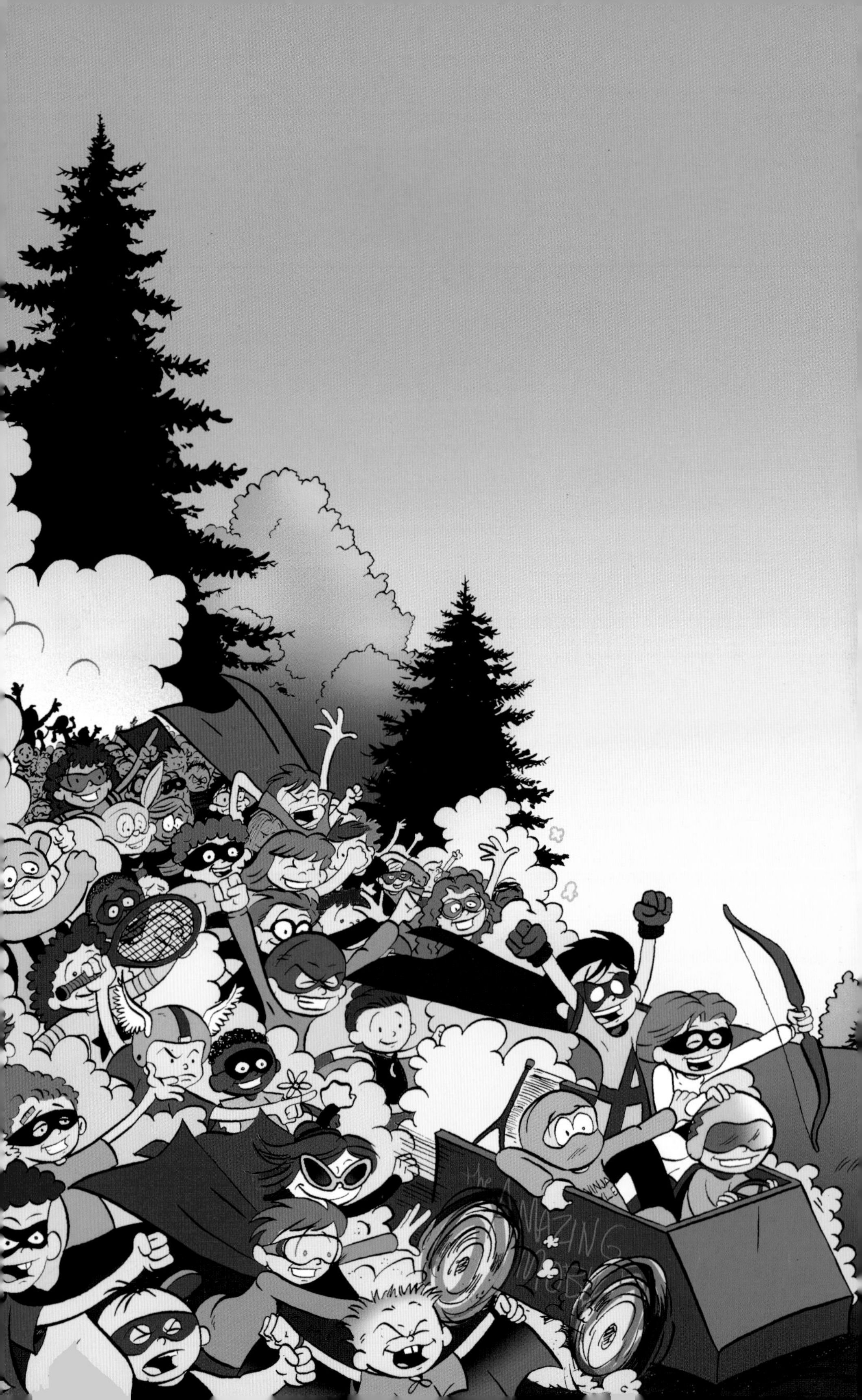
The AMAZING
NINJA

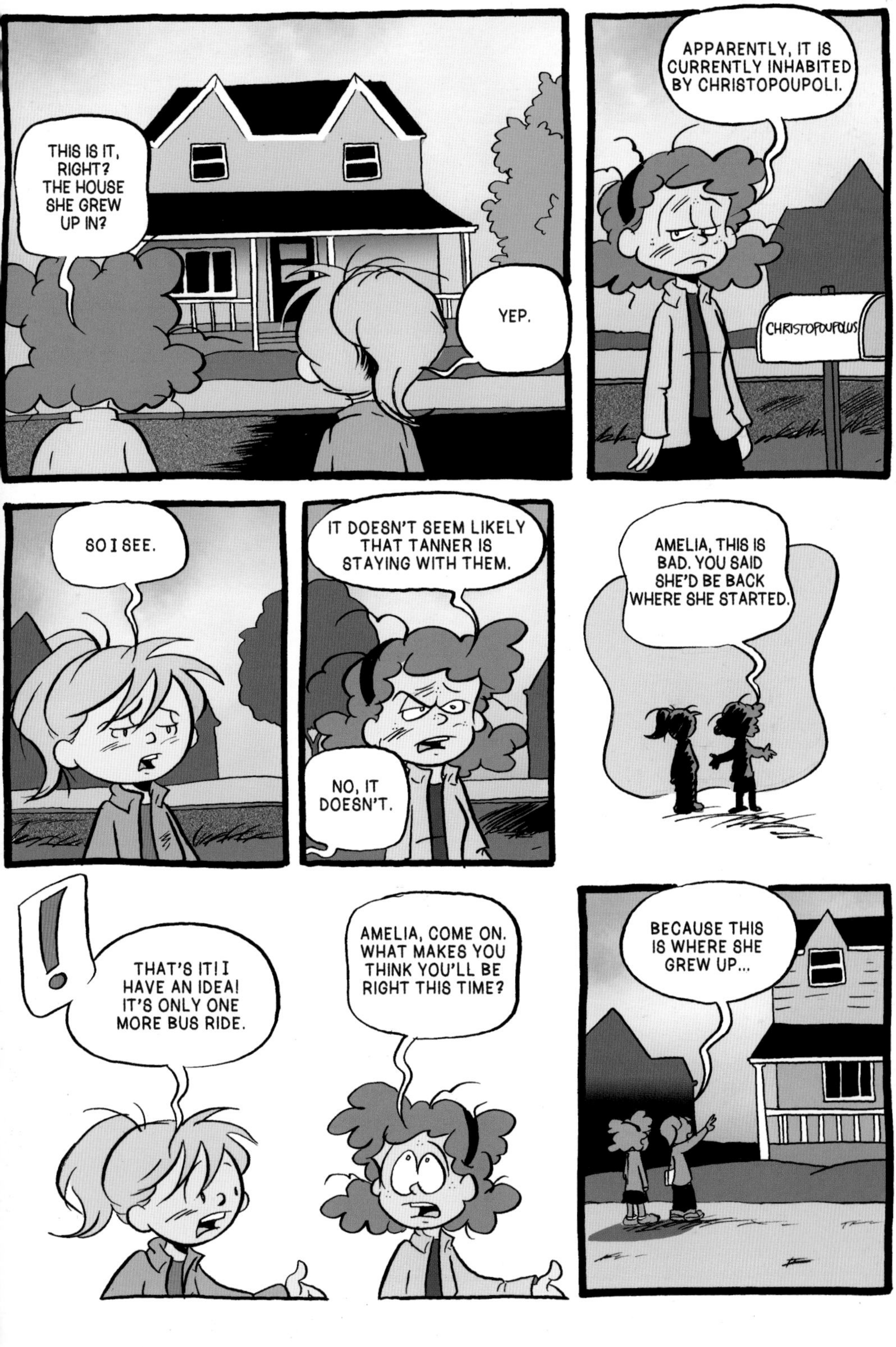
THIS IS IT, RIGHT? THE HOUSE SHE GREW UP IN?
YEP.
APPARENTLY, IT IS CURRENTLY INHABITED BY CHRISTOPOUPOLI.
CHRISTOPOUPOLUS
SO I SEE.
IT DOESN'T SEEM LIKELY THAT TANNER IS STAYING WITH THEM.
NO, IT DOESN'T.
AMELIA, THIS IS BAD. YOU SAID SHE'D BE BACK WHERE SHE STARTED.
!
THAT'S IT! I HAVE AN IDEA! IT'S ONLY ONE MORE BUS RIDE.
AMELIA, COME ON. WHAT MAKES YOU THINK YOU'LL BE RIGHT THIS TIME?
BECAUSE THIS IS WHERE SHE GREW UP...

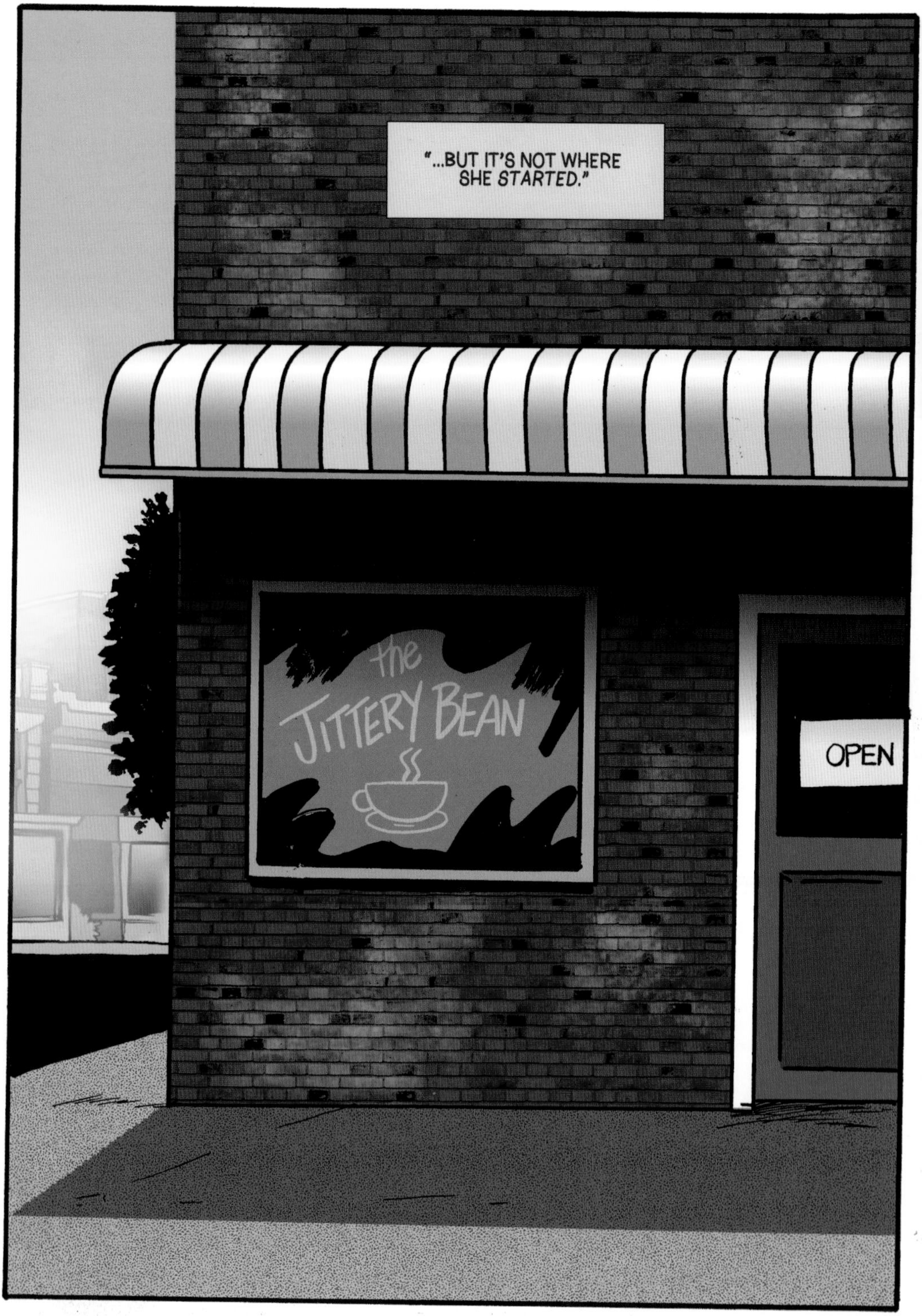
"...BUT IT'S NOT WHERE SHE STARTED."
the JITTERY BEAN
OPEN

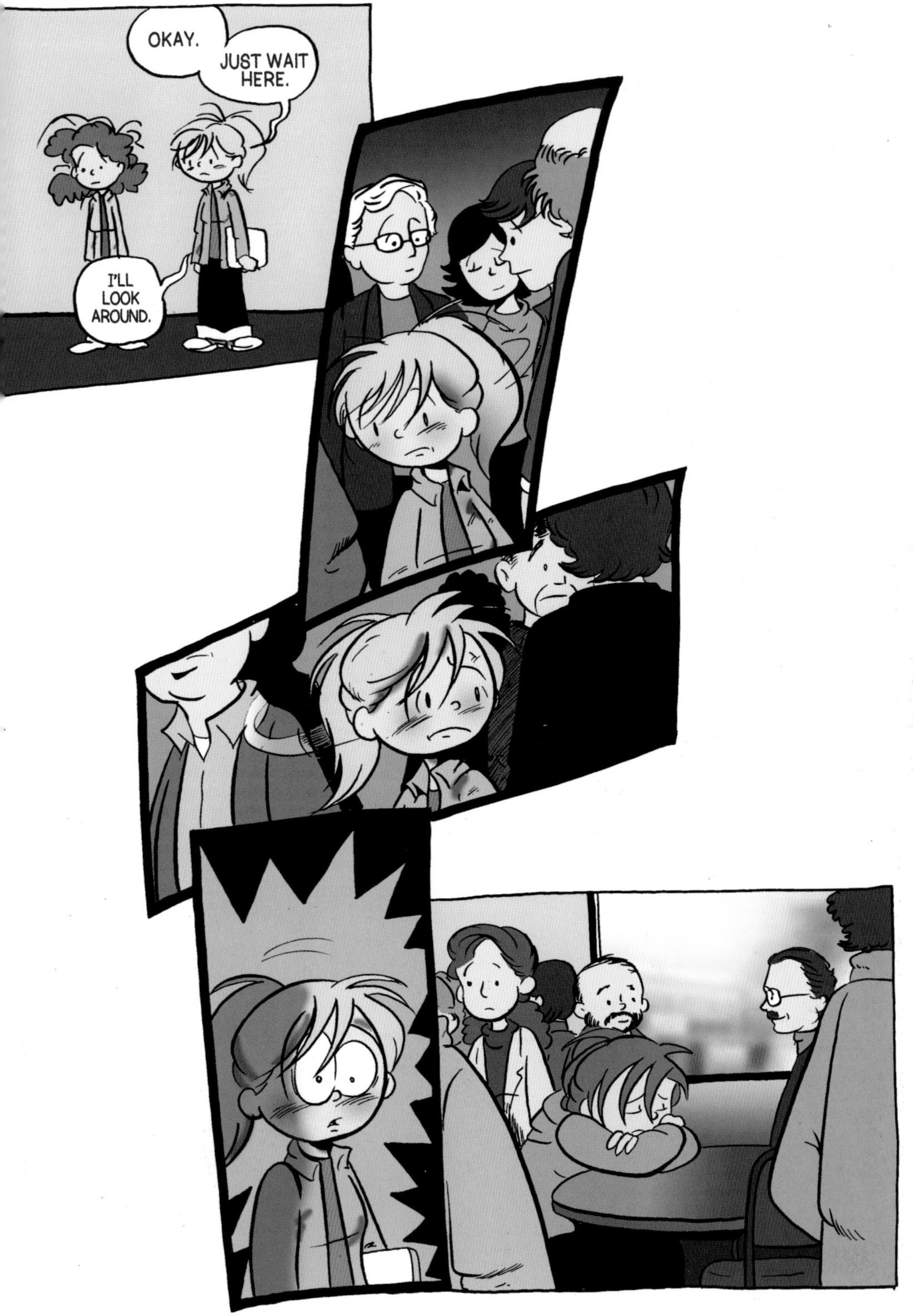
OKAY.
JUST WAIT HERE.
I'LL LOOK AROUND.

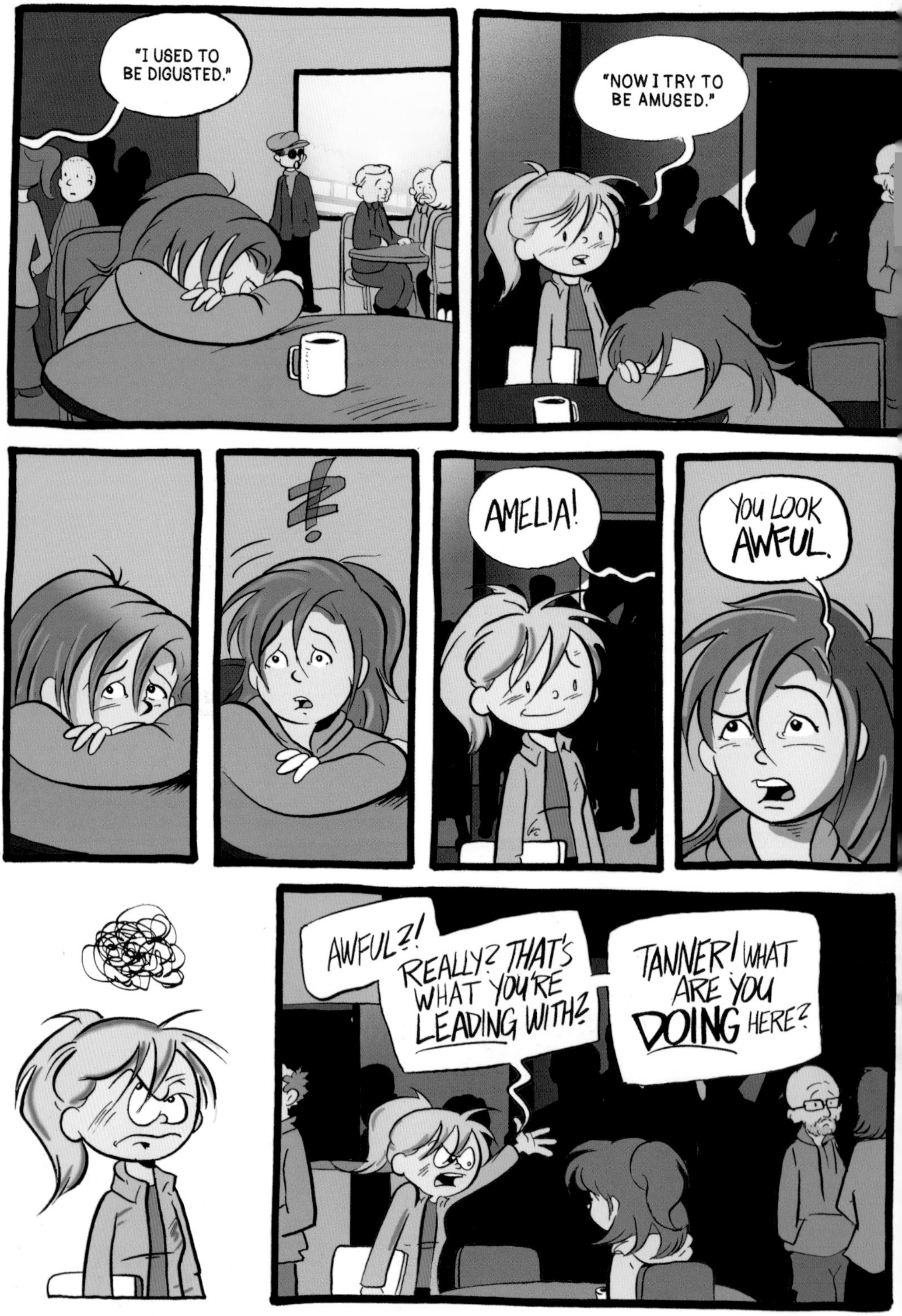
"I USED TO BE DIGUSTED."
"NOW I TRY TO BE AMUSED."
AMELIA!
YOU LOOK AWFUL.
AWFUL?! REALLY? THAT'S WHAT YOU'RE LEADING WITH?
TANNER! WHAT ARE YOU DOING HERE?

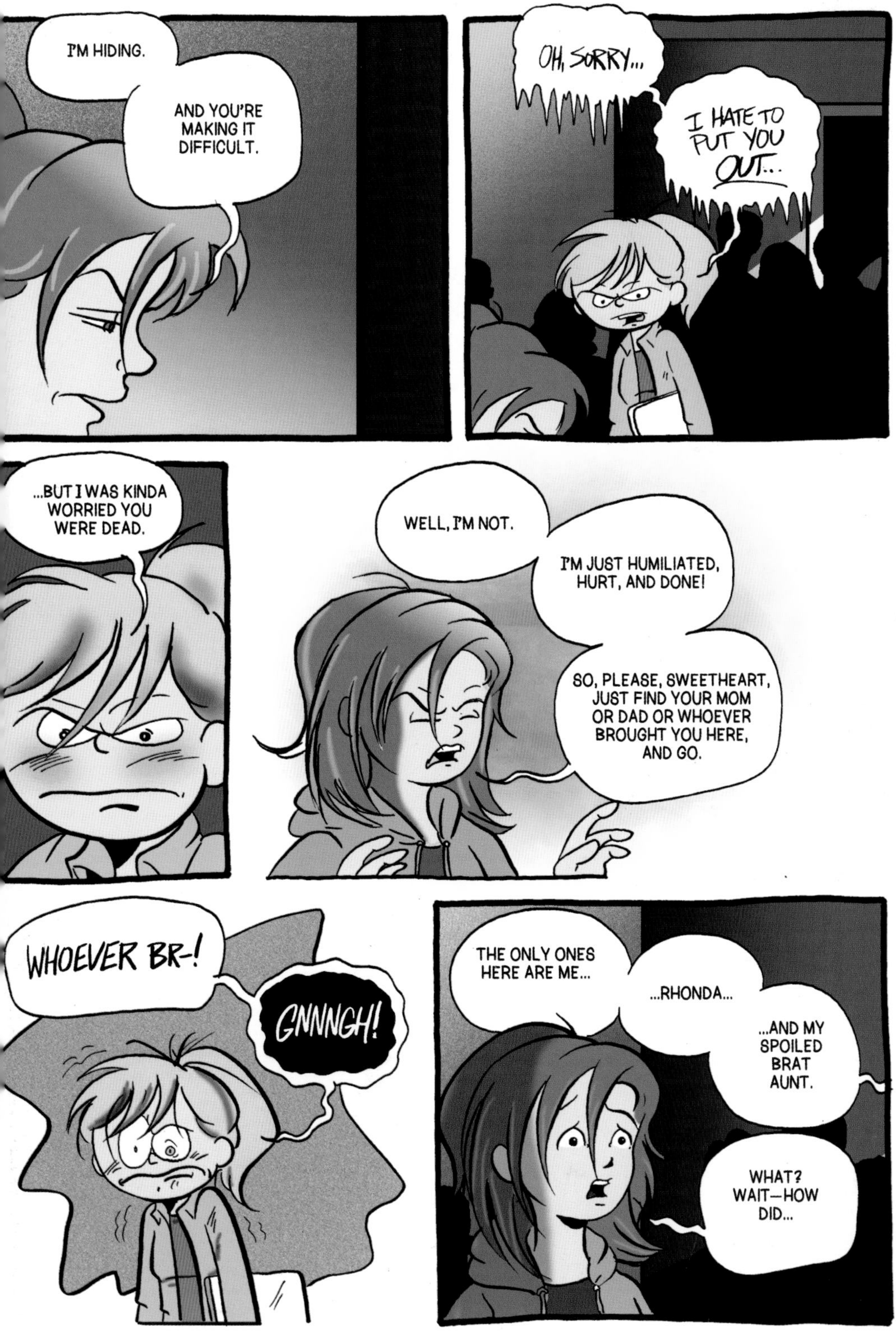
I'M HIDING.
AND YOU'RE MAKING IT DIFFICULT.
OH, SORRY...
I HATE TO PUT YOU OUT...
...BUT I WAS KINDA WORRIED YOU WERE DEAD.
WELL, I'M NOT.
I'M JUST HUMILIATED, HURT, AND DONE!
SO, PLEASE, SWEETHEART, JUST FIND YOUR MOM OR DAD OR WHOEVER BROUGHT YOU HERE, AND GO.
WHOEVER BR-!
GNNNGH!
THE ONLY ONES HERE ARE ME...
...RHONDA...
...AND MY SPOILED BRAT AUNT.
WHAT? WAIT—HOW DID...

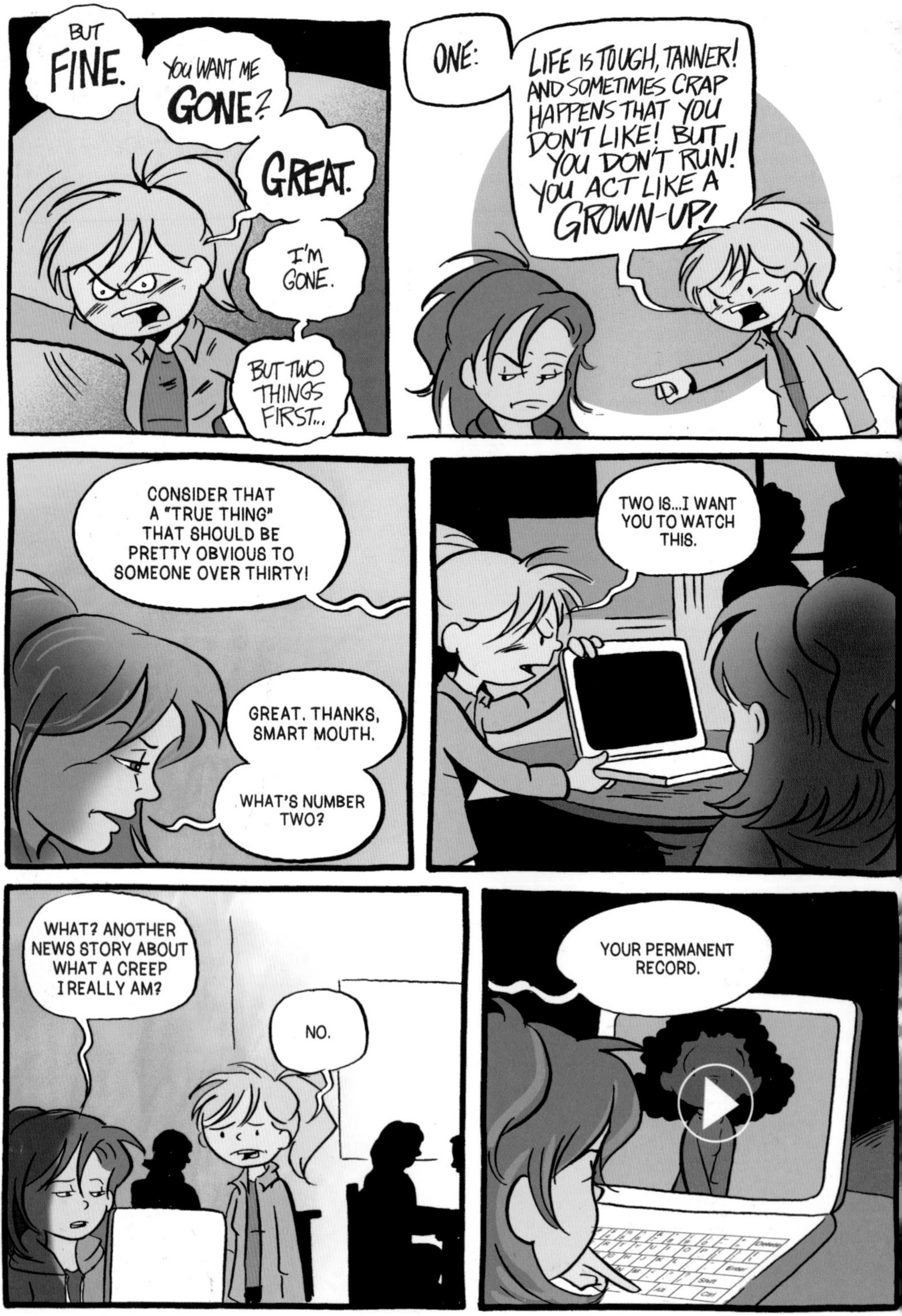
BUT FINE.
YOU WANT ME GONE?
GREAT.
I'M GONE.
BUT TWO THINGS FIRST...
ONE:
LIFE IS TOUGH, TANNER! AND SOMETIMES CRAP HAPPENS THAT YOU DON'T LIKE! BUT YOU DON'T RUN! YOU ACT LIKE A GROWN-UP!
CONSIDER THAT A "TRUE THING" THAT SHOULD BE PRETTY OBVIOUS TO SOMEONE OVER THIRTY!
GREAT. THANKS, SMART MOUTH.
WHAT'S NUMBER TWO?
TWO IS...I WANT YOU TO WATCH THIS.
WHAT? ANOTHER NEWS STORY ABOUT WHAT A CREEP I REALLY AM?
NO.
YOUR PERMANENT RECORD.

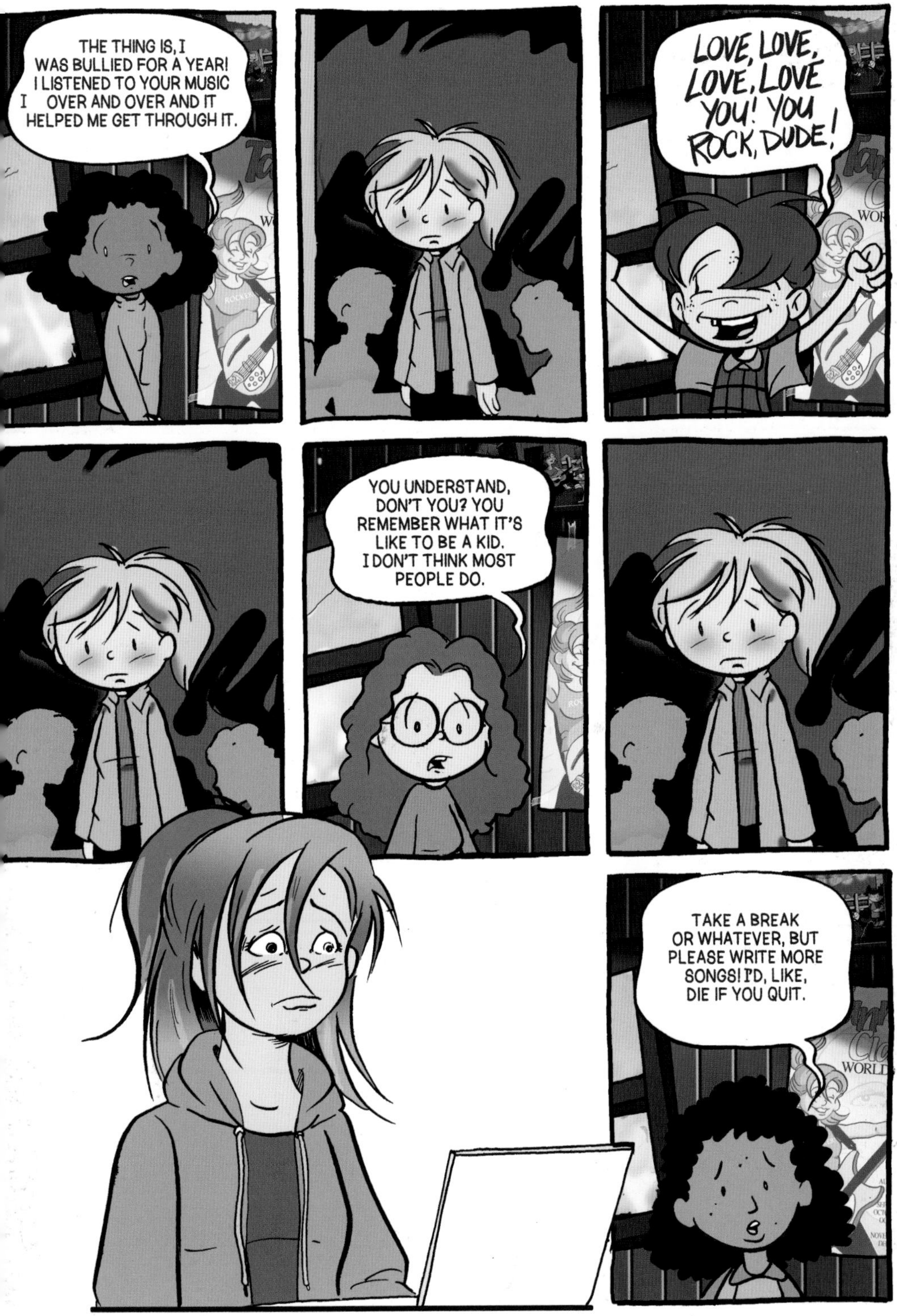
THE THING IS, I WAS BULLIED FOR A YEAR! I LISTENED TO YOUR MUSIC I OVER AND OVER AND IT HELPED ME GET THROUGH IT.
LOVE, LOVE, LOVE, LOVE YOU! YOU ROCK, DUDE!
YOU UNDERSTAND, DON'T YOU? YOU REMEMBER WHAT IT'S LIKE TO BE A KID. I DON'T THINK MOST PEOPLE DO.
TAKE A BREAK OR WHATEVER, BUT PLEASE WRITE MORE SONGS! I'D, LIKE, DIE IF YOU QUIT.

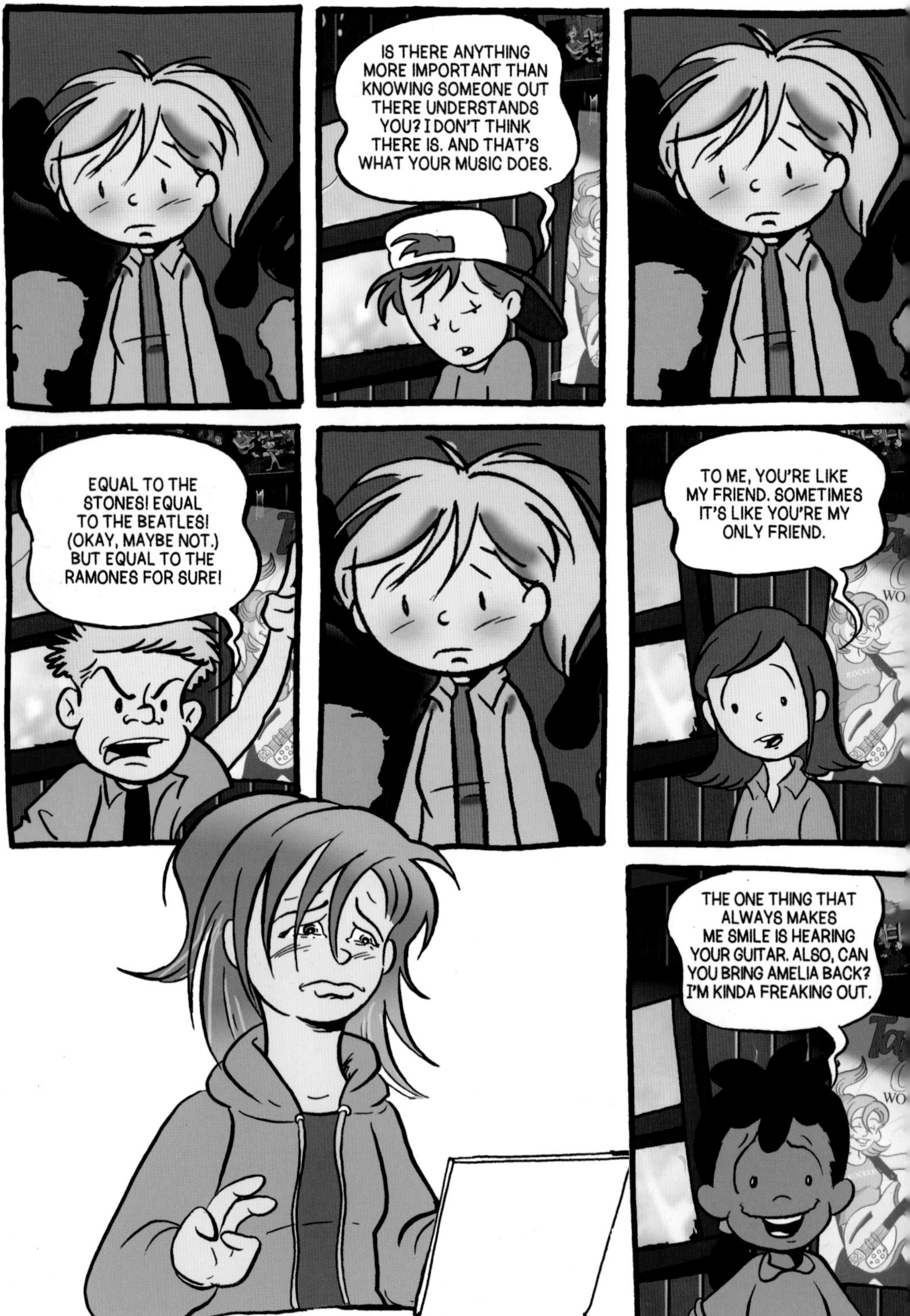
IS THERE ANYTHING MORE IMPORTANT THAN KNOWING SOMEONE OUT THERE UNDERSTANDS YOU? I DON'T THINK THERE IS. AND THAT'S WHAT YOUR MUSIC DOES.
EQUAL TO THE STONES! EQUAL TO THE BEATLES! (OKAY, MAYBE NOT.) BUT EQUAL TO THE RAMONES FOR SURE!
TO ME, YOU'RE LIKE MY FRIEND. SOMETIMES IT'S LIKE YOU'RE MY ONLY FRIEND.
THE ONE THING THAT ALWAYS MAKES ME SMILE IS HEARING YOUR GUITAR. ALSO, CAN YOU BRING AMELIA BACK? I'M KINDA FREAKING OUT.

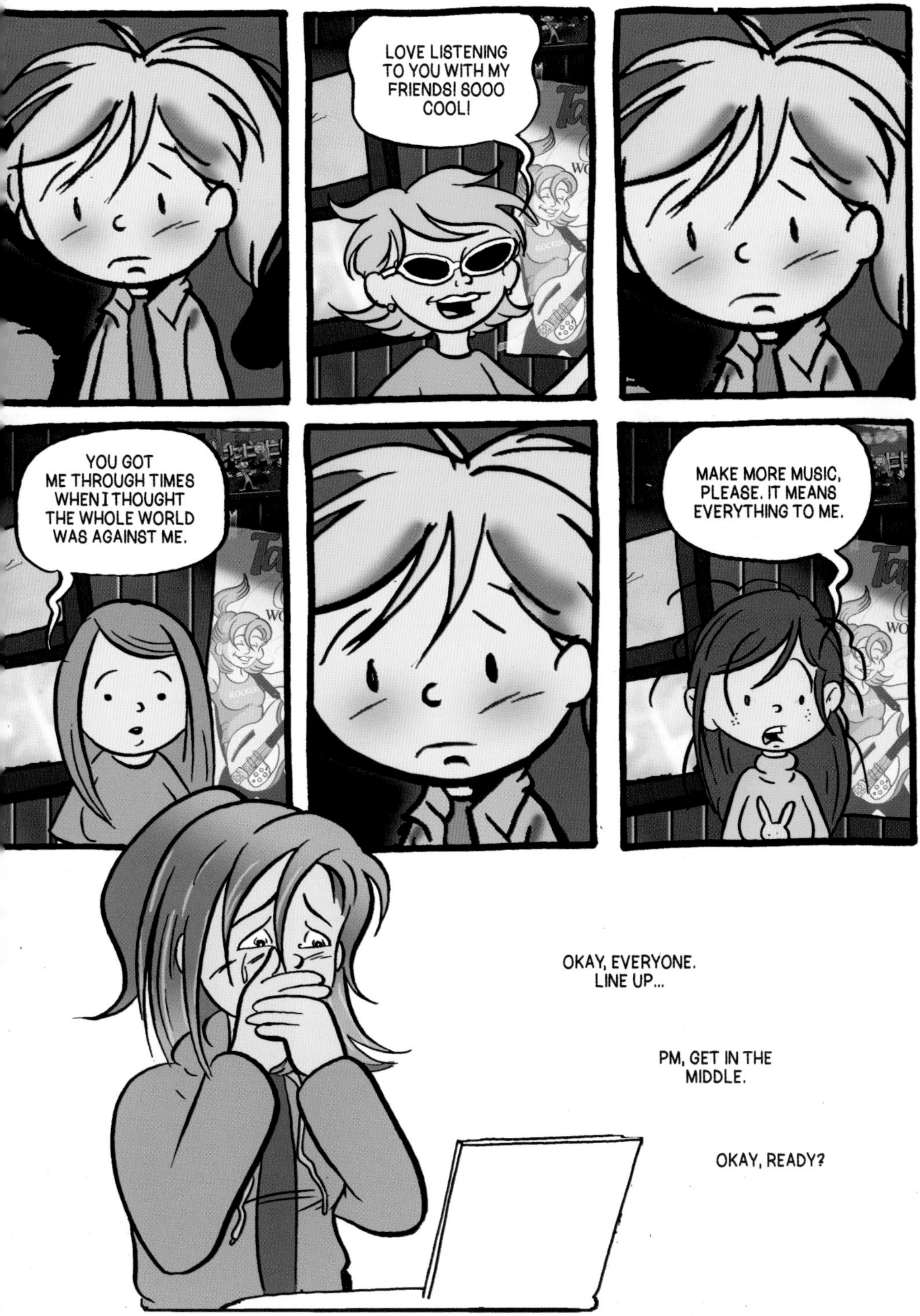
LOVE LISTENING TO YOU WITH MY FRIENDS! SOOO COOL!
YOU GOT ME THROUGH TIMES WHEN I THOUGHT THE WHOLE WORLD WAS AGAINST ME.
MAKE MORE MUSIC, PLEASE. IT MEANS EVERYTHING TO ME.
OKAY, EVERYONE. LINE UP...
PM, GET IN THE MIDDLE.
OKAY, READY?

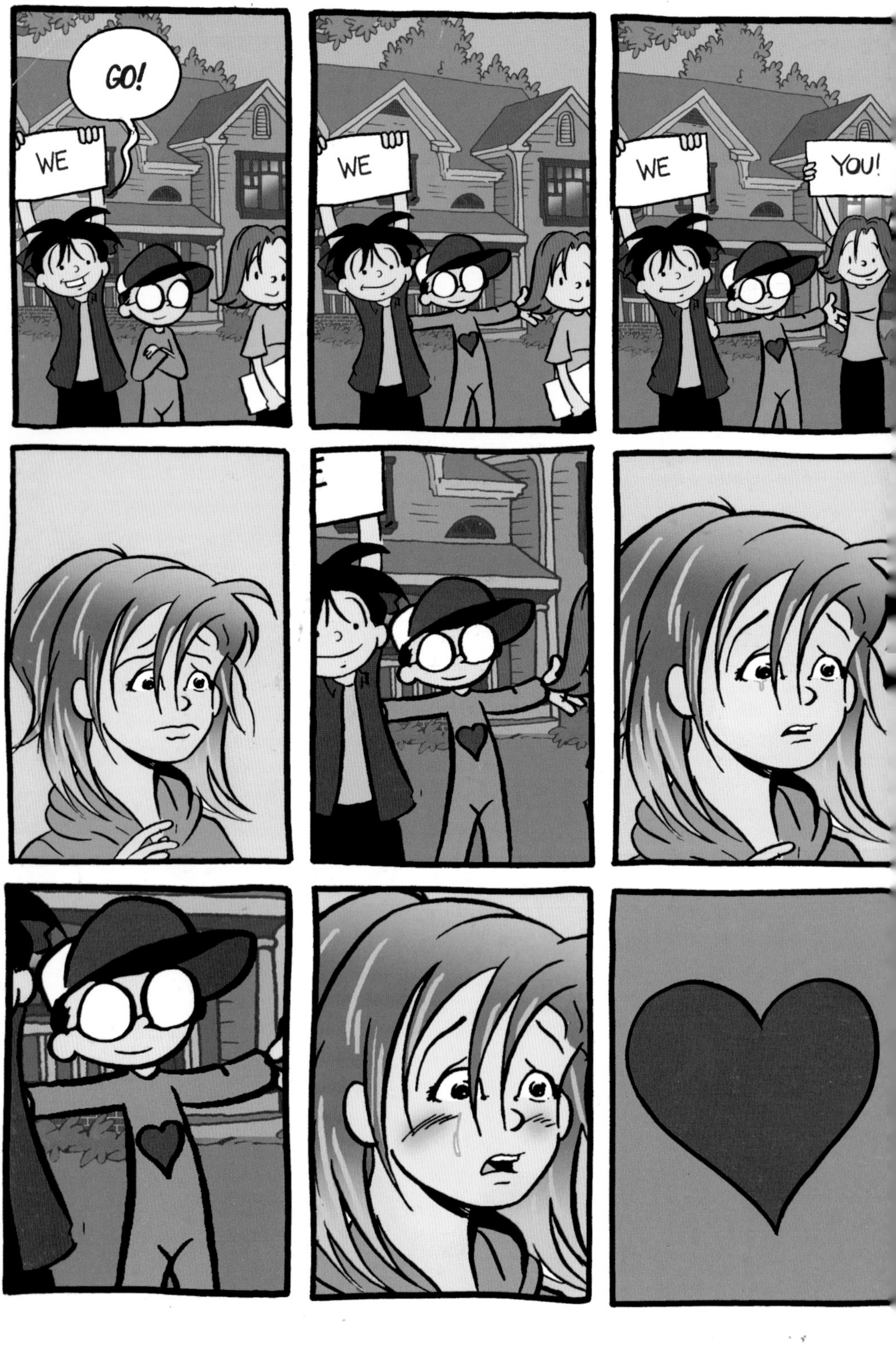
GO!
WE
WE
WE
YOU!

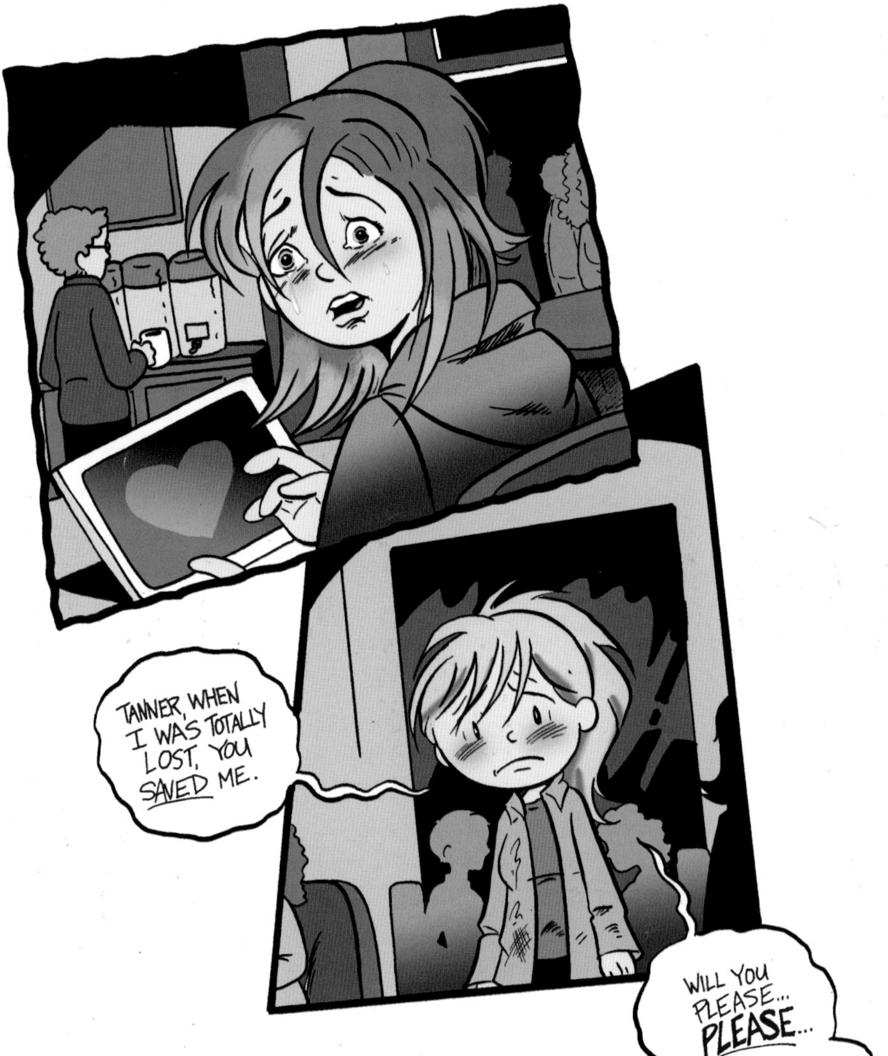
TANNER, WHEN I WAS TOTALLY LOST, YOU SAVED ME.
WILL YOU PLEASE... PLEASE...
..LET ME SAVE YOU BACK?

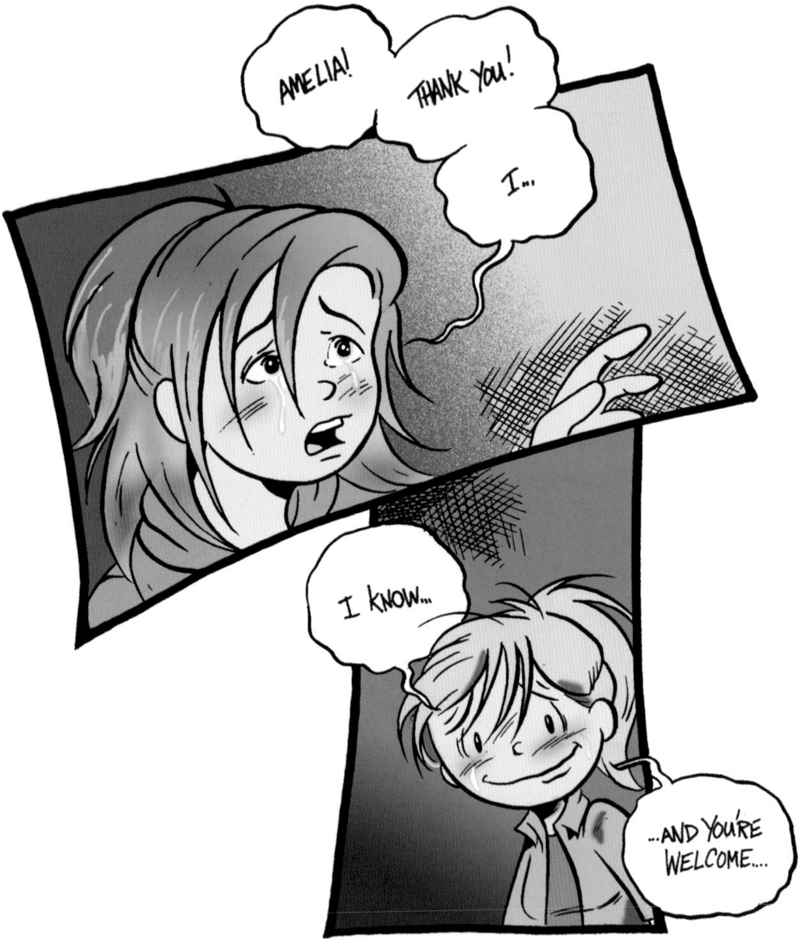
AMELIA!
THANK YOU!
I...
I KNOW...
...AND YOU'RE WELCOME...

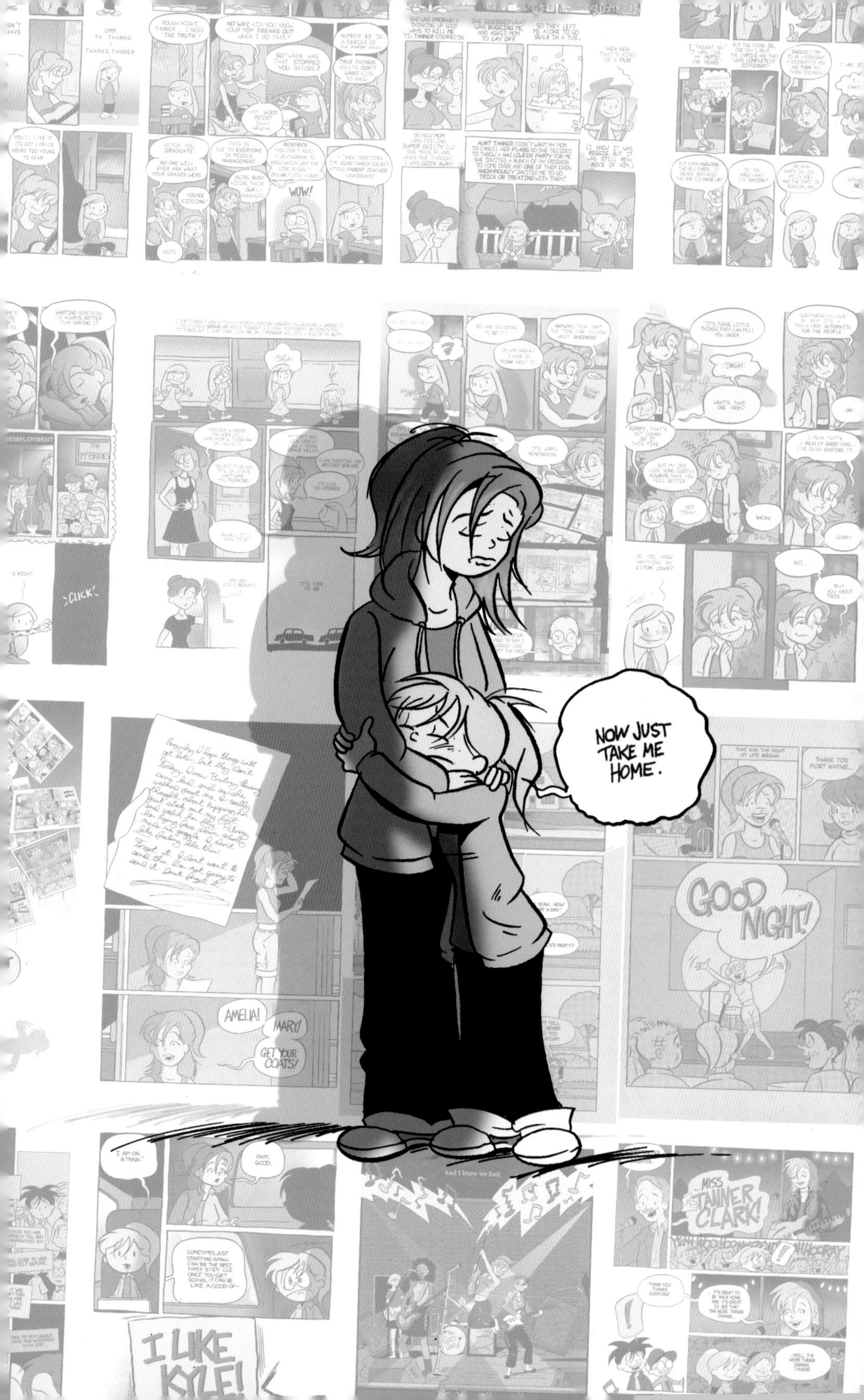
UMM TH... THANKS. THANKS, TANNER.
ROUGH NIGHT, TANNER... I NEED "THE TRUTH".
NO WAY, KID. YOU KNOW YOUR MOM FREAKS OUT WHEN I DO THAT.
SO! WHEN HAS THAT STOPPED YOU BEFORE?
NUMBER 45 IN A SERIES OF
TRUE THINGS ADULTS DON'T WANT KIDS TO KNOW:
AFTER YOU GRADUATE...
NO ONE WILL EVER ASK WHAT YOUR GRADES WERE.
YOU'RE KIDDING!
NOPE.
THIS IS DUE TO EVERYONE IN MIDDLE MANAGEMENT
BEING BUSY HIDING THEIR OWN C-AVERAGES.
WOW!
SHE GUESSED WHAT WAS BUGGING ME, AND ASKED MOM TO LAY OFF.
SO THEY LEFT ME ALONE TO GO SULK IN A TUB.
SO NOW MOM WAS FEELING SUPER GUILTY 'CUZ SHE MADE PLANS WHEN SHE THOUGHT I WAS GOIN AWAY.
AUNT TANNER DIDN'T WANT MY MOM TO CANCEL HER PLANS SO SHE DECIDED TO THROW A HALLOWEEN PARTY FOR ME. SHE INVITED A BUNCH OF MY FRIENDS TO COME OVER AND ONE OF THEM EVEN ANONYMOUSLY INVITED ME TO GO TRICK OR TREATING WITH THEM!
(I KNOW IT WAS REGGIE, BUT IT WAS STILL REAL NICE OF HIM.)
SIGH!
CLICK!
THE MCBRIDES
SIGH!
WHAT'S THAT ONE FROM?
SORRY, THAT'S NOT GONNA DO IT THIS TIME.
NOT TODAY.
WOW.
NO...
NOW JUST TAKE ME HOME.
THANK YOU FORT WAYNE...
GOOD NIGHT!
AMELIA!
MARY!
GET YOUR COATS!
I AM ON A TRAIN.
OKAY. GOOD.
SOMETIMES JUST STARTING SMALL CAN BE THE BEST FIRST STEP 'CUZ ONCE YOU GET GOING, IT CAN BE LIKE A FLOOD OF—
And I knew we had.
MISS TANNER CLARK!
I LIKE KYLE!

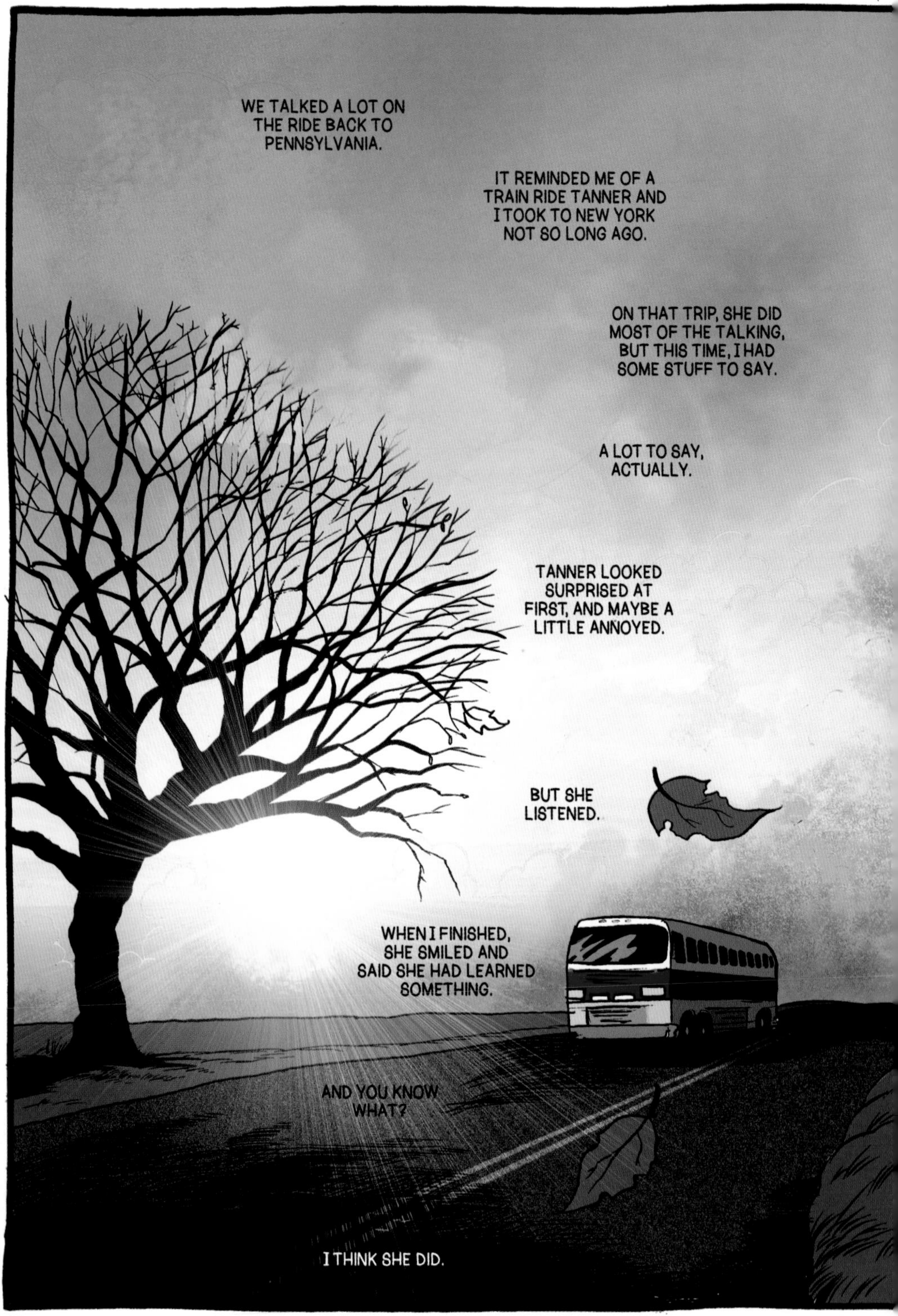
WE TALKED A LOT ON THE RIDE BACK TO PENNSYLVANIA.
IT REMINDED ME OF A TRAIN RIDE TANNER AND I TOOK TO NEW YORK NOT SO LONG AGO.
ON THAT TRIP, SHE DID MOST OF THE TALKING, BUT THIS TIME, I HAD SOME STUFF TO SAY.
A LOT TO SAY, ACTUALLY.
TANNER LOOKED SURPRISED AT FIRST, AND MAYBE A LITTLE ANNOYED.
BUT SHE LISTENED.
WHEN I FINISHED, SHE SMILED AND SAID SHE HAD LEARNED SOMETHING.
AND YOU KNOW WHAT?
I THINK SHE DID.

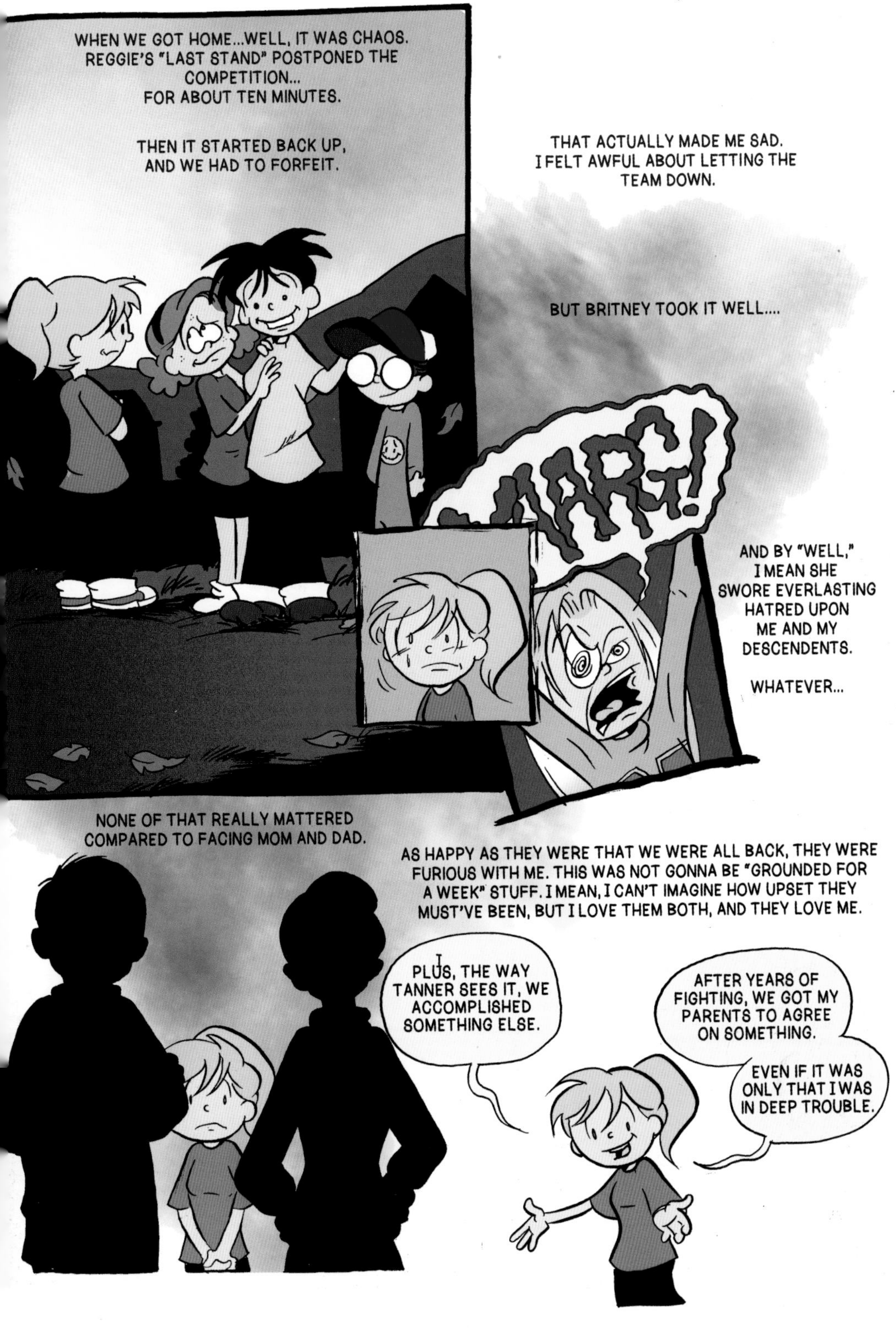
WHEN WE GOT HOME...WELL, IT WAS CHAOS. REGGIE'S "LAST STAND" POSTPONED THE COMPETITION... FOR ABOUT TEN MINUTES.
THEN IT STARTED BACK UP, AND WE HAD TO FORFEIT.
THAT ACTUALLY MADE ME SAD. I FELT AWFUL ABOUT LETTING THE TEAM DOWN.
BUT BRITNEY TOOK IT WELL....
ARG!
AND BY "WELL," I MEAN SHE SWORE EVERLASTING HATRED UPON ME AND MY DESCENDENTS.
WHATEVER...
NONE OF THAT REALLY MATTERED COMPARED TO FACING MOM AND DAD.
AS HAPPY AS THEY WERE THAT WE WERE ALL BACK, THEY WERE FURIOUS WITH ME. THIS WAS NOT GONNA BE "GROUNDED FOR A WEEK" STUFF. I MEAN, I CAN'T IMAGINE HOW UPSET THEY MUST'VE BEEN, BUT I LOVE THEM BOTH, AND THEY LOVE ME.
PLUS, THE WAY TANNER SEES IT, WE ACCOMPLISHED SOMETHING ELSE.
AFTER YEARS OF FIGHTING, WE GOT MY PARENTS TO AGREE ON SOMETHING.
EVEN IF IT WAS ONLY THAT I WAS IN DEEP TROUBLE.

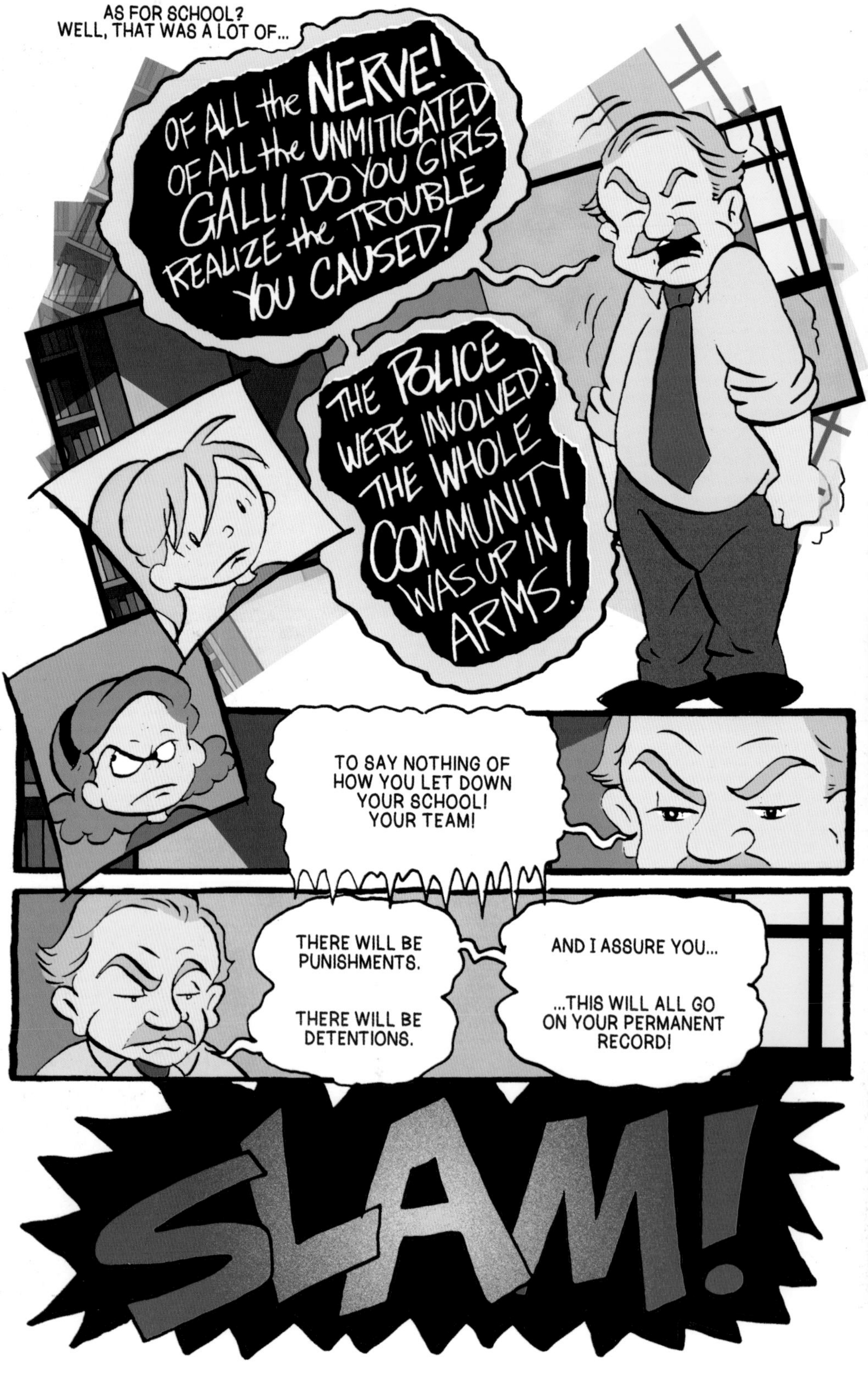
AS FOR SCHOOL? WELL, THAT WAS A LOT OF...
OF ALL the NERVE! OF ALL the UNMITIGATED GALL! DO YOU GIRLS REALIZE the TROUBLE YOU CAUSED!
THE POLICE WERE INVOLVED! THE WHOLE COMMUNITY WAS UP IN ARMS!
TO SAY NOTHING OF HOW YOU LET DOWN YOUR SCHOOL! YOUR TEAM!
THERE WILL BE PUNISHMENTS.
THERE WILL BE DETENTIONS.
AND I ASSURE YOU...
...THIS WILL ALL GO ON YOUR PERMANENT RECORD!
SLAM!

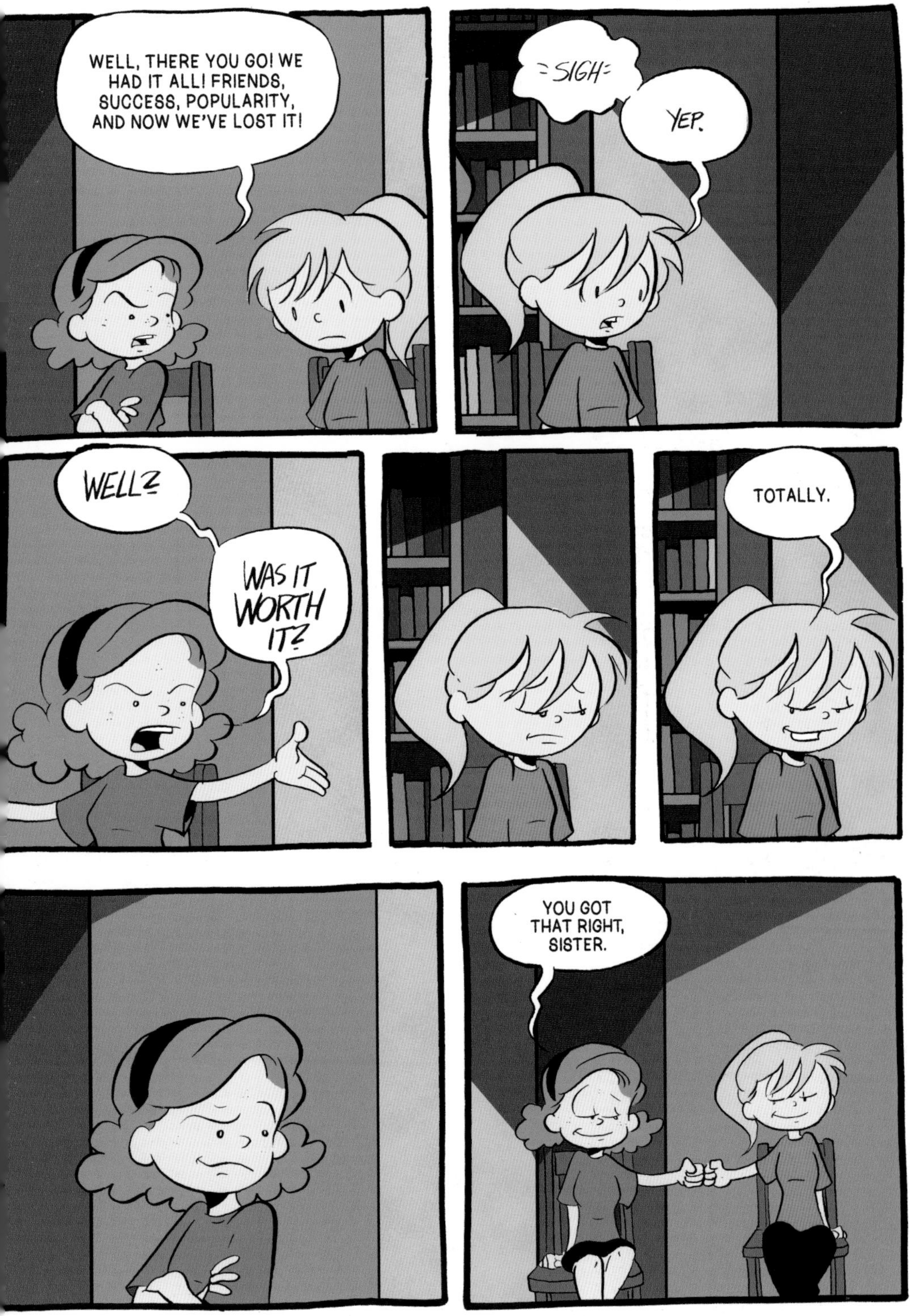
WELL, THERE YOU GO! WE HAD IT ALL! FRIENDS, SUCCESS, POPULARITY, AND NOW WE'VE LOST IT!
=SIGH=
YEP.
WELL?
WAS IT WORTH IT?
TOTALLY.
YOU GOT THAT RIGHT, SISTER.

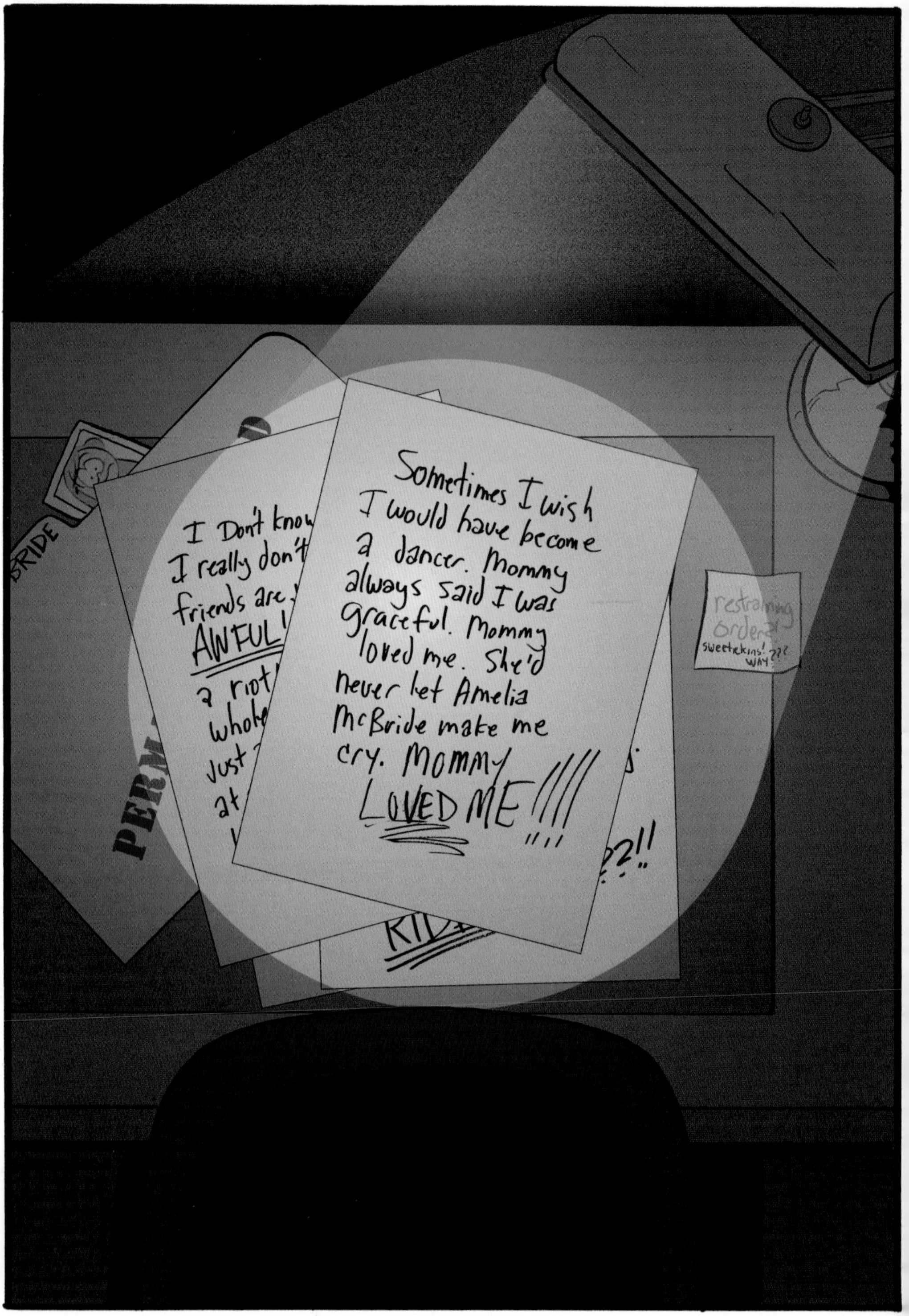
Sometimes I wish I would have become a dancer. Mommy always said I was graceful. Mommy loved me. She'd never let Amelia McBride make me cry. MOMMY LOVED ME!!!!
restraining order?!
sweetiekins! WAY???

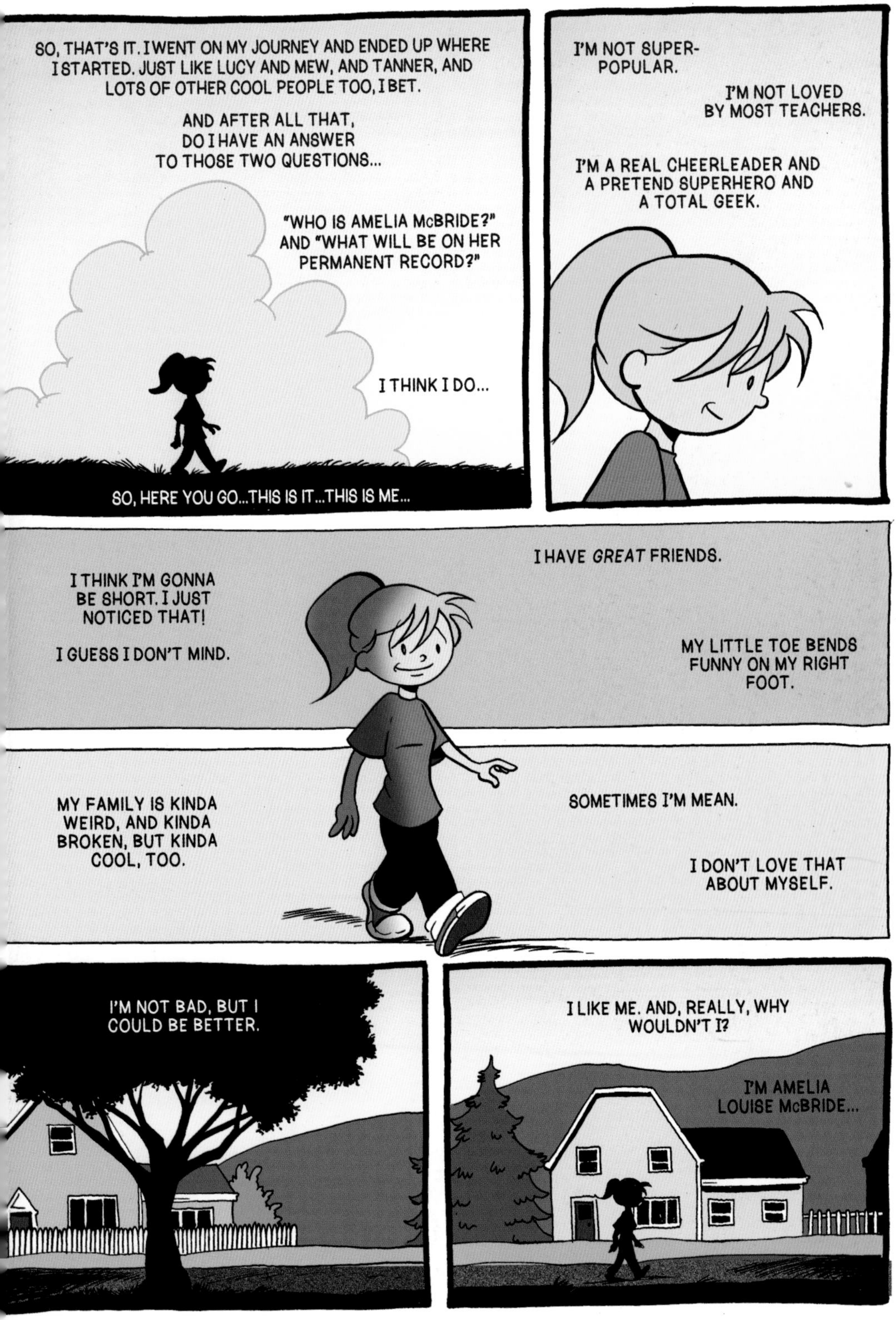
SO, THAT'S IT. I WENT ON MY JOURNEY AND ENDED UP WHERE I STARTED. JUST LIKE LUCY AND MEW, AND TANNER, AND LOTS OF OTHER COOL PEOPLE TOO, I BET.
AND AFTER ALL THAT, DO I HAVE AN ANSWER TO THOSE TWO QUESTIONS...
"WHO IS AMELIA McBRIDE?" AND "WHAT WILL BE ON HER PERMANENT RECORD?"
I THINK I DO...
SO, HERE YOU GO...THIS IS IT...THIS IS ME...
I'M NOT SUPER-POPULAR.
I'M NOT LOVED BY MOST TEACHERS.
I'M A REAL CHEERLEADER AND A PRETEND SUPERHERO AND A TOTAL GEEK.
I THINK I'M GONNA BE SHORT. I JUST NOTICED THAT!
I GUESS I DON'T MIND.
I HAVE *GREAT* FRIENDS.
MY LITTLE TOE BENDS FUNNY ON MY RIGHT FOOT.
MY FAMILY IS KINDA WEIRD, AND KINDA BROKEN, BUT KINDA COOL, TOO.
SOMETIMES I'M MEAN.
I DON'T LOVE THAT ABOUT MYSELF.
I'M NOT BAD, BUT I COULD BE BETTER.
I LIKE ME. AND, REALLY, WHY WOULDN'T I?
I'M AMELIA LOUISE McBRIDE...

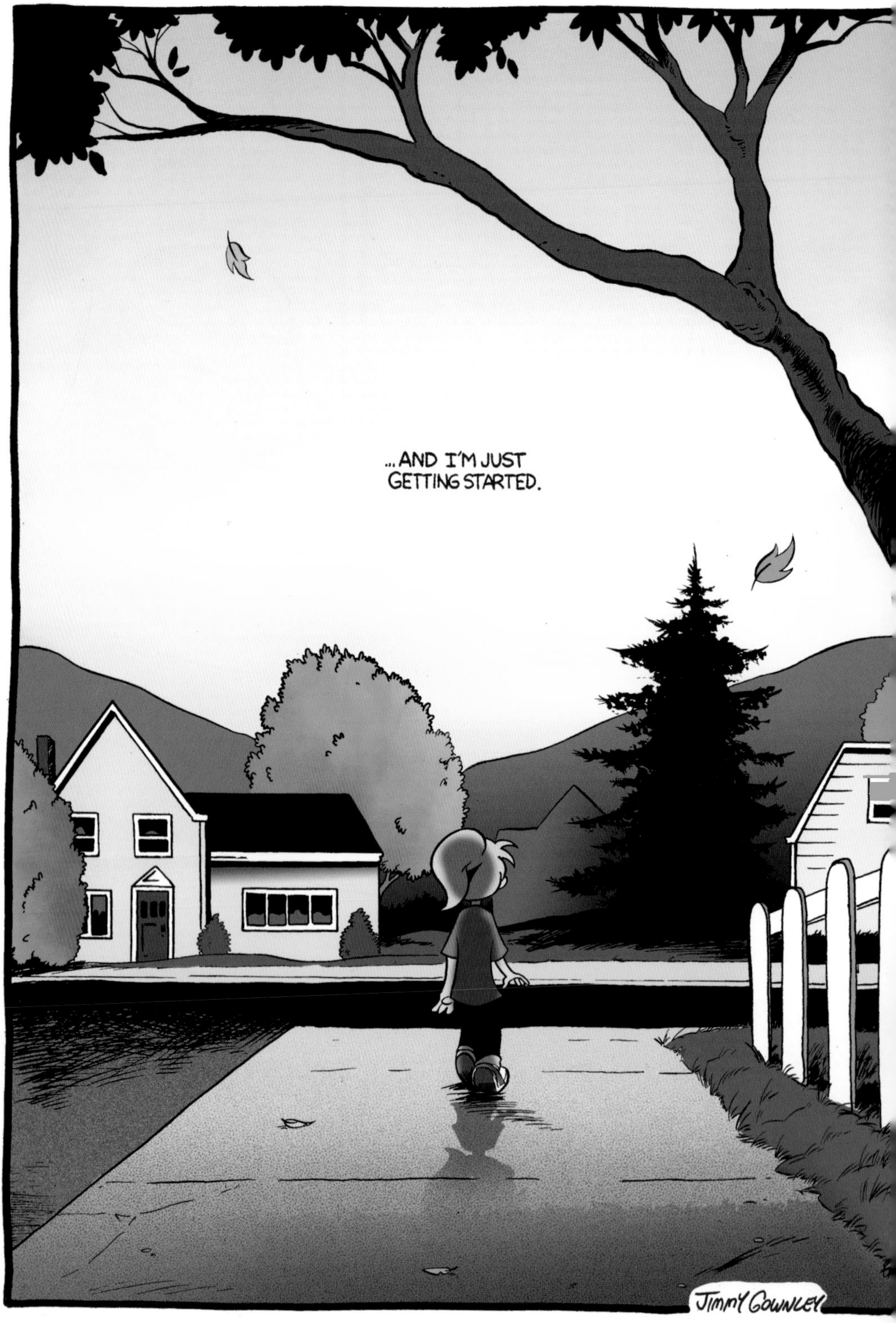
...AND I'M JUST GETTING STARTED.
JIMMY GOWNLEY

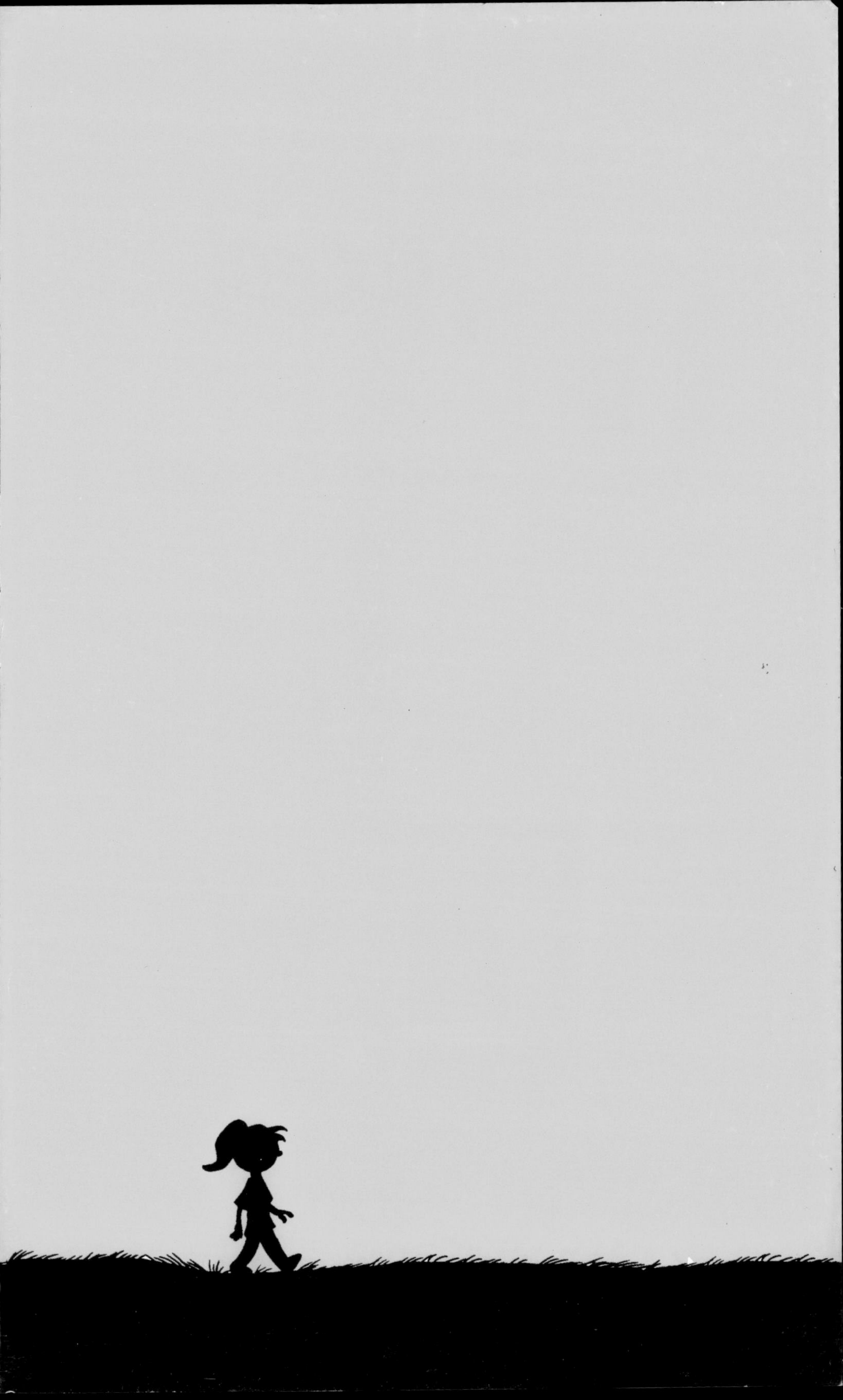

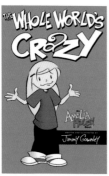
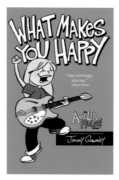
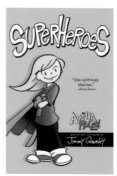

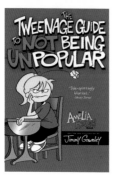